"Audacious and imaginative. You might not believe any of this thirty seconds after you close the covers, but while it's going on you're going to be dazzled by Garcia's energy and chutzpah." —*Publishers Weekly*

"Garcia plays it almost completely straight, respecting all noir traditions, and comes up with lovely touches." —*Chicago Tribune*

"A 'noir-asaurus' of a novel, bellowing for attention, the first and only of its breed in the dinosaur detective genre. Garcia has written something so strange, so bizarre, that he's to be admired just for the attempt. And he not only pulls it off, he also actually makes you wonder why someone hasn't thought of it before. Garcia's tough-guy deadpan is perfect for navigating his outrageous lost world, and the easy, familiar tone is probably what makes the premise so simple to swallow. Garcia talks the talk, and more importantly, he smirks in all the right places." —*The Miami Herald*

"Vincent Rubio, the protagonist of this first-person—er, first-dino— narrative is so likeable, the story handled with such deftness, that it actually, incredibly works. Spider Robinson meets Sam Spade. The writing is sardonic and strong in the hard-boiled tradition, and laced with jokes about the history humans think they know: Oliver Cromwell was a brontosaur, and 'Capone and Eliot Ness were just two diplodoci with a grudge to settle.'" —*The Richmond Times Dispatch*

"*Anonymous Rex* leaps out of its gumshoe formula fast enough to break the genre barrier. Imagine a hard-boiled detective novel crossed with magical realism. Think film noir with great special effects. Think fabulous read. Well-paced, well-plotted, and charming . . . a gem of modern detective fiction." —*Austin Chronicle*

"Great." —*Orlando Sentinel*

continued . . .

PRAISE FOR THE "DINOMITE"* SERIES WITH "ALL THE ELEMENTS OF A CULT CLASSIC."
—*Entertainment Weekly*

Casual Rex

"May be the most entertaining book out this year. It's so hard to resist stomping around in dinosaur metaphors in reviewing *Casual Rex*. But the book . . . is too good, too funny, and too inventive to get bogged down in Jurassic jargon . . . dripping with tongue-in-jaw wit, snappy action, funny lines, and plot twists. A genre-bending, species-bending, gender-bending romp of a mystery . . . What's really intriguing is Garcia's commentary about society and historical events as seen through dinosaur eyes . . . It's obvious Garcia had fun with *Casual Rex*. Readers will, too."

—*The Columbus Dispatch*

"*X-Files* meets Sam Spade . . . hip, knowing, and often very funny. Great fun."
—*Library Journal*

"Every bit as delightfully strange, richly imagined, and just plain funny [as his debut]."
—*The Seattle Times*

"A prequel that's as daringly, darkly loopy as *Anonymous Rex*."
—*Kirkus Reviews*

"You could call *Casual Rex* 'dinomite.'"
—**Gotham Magazine*

"A funny book. I can't remember an author pulling off a more difficult premise, unless it's T. Jefferson Parker."
—*Los Angeles Times*

"[Eric Garcia's] *X-Files* take on the classic detective tale will appeal to both mystery and SF readers. Here's a series with dino-sized legs."
—*Publishers Weekly*

"Hugely entertaining . . . Seamless, wonderfully clever world-building, a little dino-depravity, and an abundance of tongue-in-cheek humor to keep things rolling along."
—*Booklist*

continued . . .

"NEW, RARE, AND STRANGE . . . HILARIOUS AND CHILLING."*

Anonymous Rex

A *People* Beach Book of the Week

"First-time novelist Eric Garcia pulls it off, keeping the laughs frequent and the plot intriguing. After a few chapters, it seems downright logical to believe we're surrounded by a cast out of *Jurassic Park*. Apart from showing off a splendidly warped imagination, Garcia provides a solid mystery."
                                                                            —*People*

"Awesomely funny. Witty, fast-paced detective work makes for a good mystery, but the story's sly, seamlessly conceived dinosaur underworld contains all the elements of a cult classic. A."   —*Entertainment Weekly*

"Debut novelist Eric Garcia pulls off this parallel dino world to a T (rex). [His] descriptions are delicious . . . inventive and imaginative. He cleverly avoids what could have been a one-joke book with charm, sly humor, and a terrific narrative pace."   —*USA Today*

"What would the world be like if the dinosaurs hadn't gone extinct? As this very funny book shows, for one thing, L.A. would be even weirder than it is now."   —Dave Barry

"Garcia has come up with an imaginative twist to the detective fiction genre."   —*Daily Variety*

"If a novel, by definition, is new, rare, and strange, then Eric Garcia's *Anonymous Rex* is the most novel novel I've ever read. The central conceit is so startling and clever and the prose so fluid and assured, the reader doesn't even have time to blink. By turns hilarious and chilling, this is a terrific joyful read."   —*T. C. Boyle

Hot
and Sweaty
Rex

ERIC GARCIA

ACE BOOKS, NEW YORK

THE BERKLEY PUBLISHING GROUP
Published by the Penguin Group
Penguin Group (USA) Inc.
375 Hudson Street, New York, New York 10014, USA
Penguin Group (Canada), 10 Alcorn Avenue, Toronto, Ontario M4V 3B2, Canada
(a division of Pearson Penguin Canada Inc.)
Penguin Books Ltd., 80 Strand, London WC2R 0RL, England
Penguin Group Ireland, 25 St. Stephen's Green, Dublin 2, Ireland (a division of Penguin Books Ltd.)
Penguin Group (Australia), 250 Camberwell Road, Camberwell, Victoria 3124, Australia
(a division of Pearson Australia Group Pty. Ltd.)
Penguin Books India Pvt. Ltd., 11 Community Centre, Panchsheel Park, New Delhi—110 017, India
Penguin Group (NZ), Cnr. Airborne and Rosedale Roads, Albany, Auckland 1310, New Zealand
(a division of Pearson New Zealand Ltd.)
Penguin Books (South Africa) (Pty.) Ltd., 24 Sturdee Avenue, Rosebank, Johannesburg 2196,
South Africa

Penguin Books Ltd., Registered Offices: 80 Strand, London WC2R 0RL, England

This is a work of fiction. Names, characters, places, and incidents either are the product of the author's imagination or are used fictitiously, and any resemblance to actual persons, living or dead, business establishments, events, or locales is entirely coincidental.

Published by arrangement with Random House, Inc.

PRINTING HISTORY
Villard Books hardcover edition / March 2004
Ace trade paperback edition / March 2005

Library of Congress Cataloging-in-Publication Data

Garcia, Eric.
    Hot and sweaty Rex / Eric Garcia.
        p. cm.
    ISBN 0-441-01273-6 (trade pbk.)
    1. Rubio, Vincent (Fictitious character)—Fiction. 2. Private
investigators—Florida—Miami—Fiction. 3. Organized crime—Fiction. 4. Miami
(Fla.)—Fiction. 5. Dinosaurs—Fiction. I. Title.

PS3557 A665H68 2005
813'.54—dc22

                                                                    2004057418

PRINTED IN THE UNITED STATES OF AMERICA

10   9   8   7   6   5   4   3   2   1

Hot and Sweaty Rex

For the old Miami crew:

Alan, Brett, Gary, Julie, Mindy, Scott, and Steven.

Because in the end, for us dinosaurs,

it's all about loyalty.

I believe in America. It's where I keep my stuff.

Hot and Sweaty Rex

1

My name is Vincent, and I'm an herbaholic.

Recovering, that is. And this means, among other things, that I am honor-bound to the principles of sobriety and propriety, both of which are well-established stumbling blocks in the life of a private investigator. I have always believed that the truth shall set you free, but that a good lie, properly told, shall handcuff you to the bedposts, spread whipped cream about your body, and lick your nipples until they're red and raw, humming with vibrant ecstasy.

Not that that's my bag, mind you. I don't even have real nipples, and Vincent Rubio has never grooved on dairy. But I can fling out fibs with the best of them, especially if it gets me what I want, when I want it. Or, more precisely, if it *doesn't* get me what I *don't* what, when I *don't* want it. The problem is that I never know when to turn on the juice; I lie when I should be telling the truth, and I let loose with a burst of honesty just when a shotgun blast of bullshit would be best.

That's why I end up in the messes I end up in. That's why I regularly fulfill my monthly quota of flops, flubs, and falls. That's why

I remain on a first-name basis with all of my friendly neighborhood bail bondsmen.

And it's probably why I'm driving down to a South Florida race-track accompanied by two goons from the infamous Tallarico family, one of the less savory branches of the Cosa Lucertola, familiarly known as the dinosaur mafia.

Chaz is a skinny little thing, mop of blond hair up top, and I'd peg him for a skateboarder or surfer wannabe long before I'd ever place him in the mob biz. He smells of sweat—the human kind, bitter and acrid, but not so much that it makes your eyes water. Like a gym locker room after a heavy workout, only without the refreshing whip of soap to mellow it out.

His partner, Sherman, is one of those dinos who was never taught either good grooming habits or proper guise care, and, as a result, looks twenty years older than he should. Nearly all of the false hair follicles on his head have long ago relocated to some forgotten corner of the bathtub, and if the light hits his skin just right, I can see that the special latex has become worn across the elbows, daring the green scales beneath to poke through when he flexes the joint. I am well aware that Sherman has already killed at least one person I know; it would not surprise me to see him try and take out another. Sherman smells like cheese gone bad, jalapeños on the side. This is wholly because his entire diet consists of na-chos, pickles, and cola, which have somehow wormed their way into his system and overpowered what should have been a more natural, less curd-intensive scent.

These are my new colleagues. That's what I get for skipping out on a college education.

I've been instructed by Eddie Tallarico, my new boss—don't worry, we'll get there—to listen to everything Chaz and Sherman tell me. To hang back, do what they say. Don't get involved unless I'm instructed to do so. Fine by me—it's ninety-five degrees, with 80 percent humidity. The last thing I want to do is exert myself.

The Lexus we're riding in has seen better days. The seats are ripped in a number of places, foam poking through a series of parallel slashes. Dark stains splotch the inside roof.

Chaz catches my look. "Kinda messy, huh? These things happen, you know?"

"Of course," I say. "Messes happen."

"That's right. Messes happen, that's what they say."

"Looks like . . . bloodstains," I say, running my fingers over the dark blotches. They're dry, at least.

Chaz and Sherman shrug at each other as the car shoots across a wide causeway, heading for the mainland and the racetrack beyond. Perhaps in order to stem future conversation down this path, he flicks on the radio, and a static-drowned voice fills the air.

"—standing on the shores of Haiti"—crackle crackle—"waiting for the winds to strike, but we've seen no indication that the hurricane will be moving—"

Sherman flips the radio off again just as quickly. "That's all they ever got on," he grumbles. "Wind this, hurricane that."

We drive in silence for a few more miles as Chaz riffles through a small leather bag by his feet. I can't get a good look inside, but I do manage to catch a glimpse of some white plastic. This helps me zero. "Like the boss man said, you just sit back and look intimidating."

"So I'm muscle."

"Uh-uh," Sherman corrects me, "you're *pretend* muscle."

The climate in South Florida, abhorrent though it may be to those raised to know better, is nevertheless perfect for horse racing, and, as a result, they've got four well-known and respected tracks located within a thirty-mile drive of one another. Calder Race Course, down in Miami proper, has been given the dubious honor of running the horses during the hottest months of the year. If you want to sweat and lose your bread at the same time, there's no better place on earth, except for maybe one of those Vietcong Russian roulette matches.

The clubhouse itself is a beautiful homage to the days when horse racing was a sport for celebrities and diplomats, when *lunching on the green* was something other than a dirty late-night-television punch line. I close my eyes for a second as I walk through the wooden portico, and I can almost see the ladies in their white hoop skirts and bonnets, the men in full suits and cravats, the genteel manners and good nature of a day at the races.

And then I open them again to find a miasma of flesh and cash, tan and green waving at me from all directions, the press of human skin bearing down, nearly incapacitating in the crush. Mammals breathing down my neck, their breath fetid and rotten from the omnipresent beer and potato chips, their bodies thick with sweat and dirt. Their eyes, leering across the ground, harried, anxious, hoping to find a ticket, any ticket, maybe a winner dropped to the concrete in a fit of excitement. The depression when they realize that they'll never get their money back, and there's no magic fairy to wave her wand and make it better. Tinkerbell is dead for these folks, and clapping ain't gonna help.

"C'mon," Sherman says, "let's go on up."

We walk the stairs into the main grandstand, the peanut shells and beer-slicks underfoot reminding me of Dodger Stadium. I wonder if anyone goes to sporting events these days in order to actually watch the games, or if they've just become a new venue in which to ingest massive quantities of junk food. Miraculously, they've come up with new ways to pack more and more cholesterol into the same space. Beef on a stick. Hot dogs on a stick. Cheese on a stick. Chocolate-coated double-fried sticks on a stick. The mind reels; the heart attacks.

Up here, folks are shoving past one another in the rush to get to the edge of the grandstands where a metal bar keeps the fans from actually falling out onto the racetrack itself in prime soccer-hooligan style. I have no doubt that some of these folks would gladly leap the railing and push their horse on themselves in the hope of salvaging the three-dollar Trifecta bet on which all their earthly dreams depend. But there are security guards posted at thirty-foot intervals around the track, and although I see no telltale weapon bulges, I have no doubt they've got their methods of stopping intruders.

"Down here," Chaz calls, muscling through the crowd, clearing a space for me and Sherm at the bar. "Watch your step."

I wedge myself between Sherman and a man in a wrinkled brown suit, an older fellow who thinks it's still hip to wear fedoras. Hey, there was a time in my life when I donned a cap or two, but I draw the line at the 1950s and leave it at that. He's clutching a ticket in his hand, the knuckles nearly white as he grips it with a fervor.

"Do it do it do it," he's muttering, the steady stream of syllables spilling from his lips. "Do it do it do it . . ."

"You got a winner there?" I ask.

He jumps back; I must have startled him. His eyes cross, uncross, and focus, and now he's got me in his sights. "Lassie Liberty in the fifth."

"Oh, yeah?"

"Lassie Liberty," he repeats. "The fifth."

I look up at the board on the far side of the grandstand. The results for the fourth race have already been posted, and the fifth is about to start. "This time around, huh? Maybe I should place a bet—"

"My bet!" he practically yells, drawing a little attention. "My bet! Lassie Liberty is mine!"

I back off as Sherman pulls me closer, away from the guy in the brown suit. "Best not to aggravate the civilians," he says. "They get a little jumpy."

"Like a Mexican bean," I say. "Hope he doesn't lose."

"Oh, he'll lose," Chaz mutters. "Lassie Liberty's a nag."

"I dunno," Sherm counters. "She ran nice last Tuesday."

Obviously, these two have done this before. I wonder if they've got any other jobs in the organization, or if they're permanently assigned to the ponies, placing and collecting bets for Eddie Tallarico, cutting the odds when they need to be cut, spreading out the action when the off-site wagers warrant it. Not such a bad job, I guess, if you don't mind the heat, the humidity, the manure, or the smell of beer, sweat, and desperation.

A sudden jolt runs through the crowd, everyone surging forward at once, pressing into those of us up against the railing. What do they know that I don't? I take a look around, wondering if there's a fight somewhere, usually the most interesting part of any sporting event I've attended—

"There he is," Sherman says, pointing down at the track. "Lookin' pretty bad today."

Down below, the horses have been released from the paddock and are slowly being led toward the gates. Eight in all, each one a proud member of its species, walking tall, walking strong, those flowing manes waving in the light breeze, their hooves kicking up the dirt. *I am a Thoroughbred,* these horses exude. *Ride me, whip me, throw roses around my neck, but never forget that I am born to run.*

And then there's number 6. Poor, pitiful number 6.

"Jesus," the old man next to me coughs. "What the hell's wrong with that one?"

His gait is slow, almost limping, as if his front two legs have been broken, and then reset by a correspondence-school veterinarian. The hooves themselves are a dirty, mottled brown, cracks visible even at this distance. Those legs that do seem to work are shaky at best, trembling along like seismographs in earthquake country. Patchy fur covers the smallish beast, clumps of hair clinging to the skin with desperation, strands dropping off to the track below with every passing moment. The torso, at least, looks strong, firm, and tight, but there's a hint of a swayback forming in the middle, as if he'd been ridden too hard and too long by someone much too heavy for the task. He lopes along in a depressed, addled stagger. Think Eeyore on sedatives.

But it's the head—held low, staring down at his wrecked hooves—and the shamed cast to the eyes that tell the whole story. This horse knows he is finished. Don't ask me how, but the creature understands his shortcomings, and, I believe, secretly longs for the glue factory. A ridiculous notion, of course. Everyone knows that Compies make the best glue.

"Here," Sherm chuckles, "hold on to these."

He hands me a sheaf of wager tickets, the wad thick in my hand. I look down to see which horse Tallarico has placed his hard-earned money on, and a giant number 6 looks back up at me.

"That's him?" I say incredulously. "*That's* our horse?"

"That's the one," Sherman affirms. "Love My Money."

"Hold on, hold on." This can't be right. "We're betting on number six? The one with the—the one that's barely a horse?"

Chaz laughs. "You don't know the half of it."

"Look," Sherm says, drawing me closer, dropping the volume. "Don't make bones, okay? You'll understand it after. For now, hold the goddamned tickets and keep your mouth shut."

I shrug and check the big board. Love My Money is running at 35-to-1, which, should the completely impossible happen and he actually win the race, would pay off these tickets to the tune of somewhere over fifty thousand dollars. Of course, were that to occur, I would immediately duck and cover for fear that I'd be crapped on by all the pigs flying through the air.

The undersized jockeys—predominantly Compies, I am sure, though the great Willie Shoemaker is supposedly an undersized Coelophysis, which would explain the predilection for jodhpurs— ride their horses up to the gate and lead them in. The number 4 horse is particularly antsy, refusing to go anywhere near the metal cages.

"See that?" the guy in the brown suit belts out. "See that? Lassie Liberty. She's a feisty one! Do it do it do it! Feisty girl!"

Lassie Liberty is indeed feisty, enough so to take a sizable dump just before her handlers are able to squeeze her into the cage. Perhaps this will increase her odds of winning. At the very least, she'll be pushing along a lighter load.

As for Love My Money—well, he just glides right into the gate as if it's the most natural and depressing thing in the world. Somewhere in that little suicidal horse brain of his, I'm guessing, he hopes it's the entrance to a slaughterhouse.

"We're all in place?" Sherman asks Chaz.

"So far's I know."

I don't have time to ask them exactly what they're talking about, because a hushed silence falls over the crowd, a giant hiccough of sound as we all anticipate the break. The track announcer holds it for another second, teasing us, drawing out our excitement, our anxiety—

The buzzer sounds, the gates clang open, and they're off. The number 2 horse is the first out, running hard, fast, her legs tearing up the course, her flanks rippling in great waves of muscle movement. But number 5 is close behind, and Lassie Liberty herself darts out in third.

And—surprise, surprise—Love My Money is dead last, eating dirt, his pitiful legs clawing at the track surface, already five full lengths behind the leaders with barely an eighth of the course run.

"Nice choice," I mutter to Sherman. "Remind me to bet against you guys next time you run a Super Bowl office pool."

"Shut up and watch."

On TV, horse races seem to go by so quickly. Maybe it's the constant motion of the camera, or the infectious drone of the announcer—*she's-moving-up-running-along-and-it's-Touch-Me-Gently-on-the-outside-neck-and-neck-with-Are-We-There-Yet*—but it's always quick and more often than not uninteresting. Three hours of prattle about the Kentucky Derby, good Saturday-morning television time wasted on statistics and conjecture, and it's over in a matter of sixty seconds.

But the ponies take on a whole new meaning when they're live, in the flesh. For one thing, there's no close-up of the race, so the only view you can get is a panoramic shot, enabling you to check out the entire field at once. That's when you get a real sense of the distances involved, and the speeds at which they're covered. That's when you can really understand the glory of a come-from-behind finish.

"There," Chaz says, pointing to our nag way in the back. "Watch."

Love My Money is still dragging along, his legs in a sluggish shamble as opposed to the furious gallop set by the rest of the group, and I can sense other long-shot bettors tearing up their tickets all over the grandstand. That's what you get for playing the fool with your cash: 35-to-1 shots are, by their very nature, risky ventures. It's like eating sushi in Wyoming—little good can come of it.

A collective gasp—the crowd is buzzing. Between blinks of an eye, Love My Money has shot forward, his legs suddenly spinning wildly, slamming up and down like pistons in a V-8 muscle car and within two seconds he's past the number 5 horse, I'm No Fool, and no longer last in the race.

"See?" says Chaz. "What'd I tell ya? He's comin' on."

The horses round the halfway mark and the jockeys pilot their steeds into a straight line, each trying to keep the inside track for himself. There's some motion on the outside, a few of the nags attempting to pass the others, but for the most part there's only one big story in this fifth race, and it's all about the number 6 horse.

Love My Money keeps turning on the juice and is suddenly sixth in the pack, then fifth, the other jockeys glancing up as he passes them by, their incredulous looks visible even at a hundred yards. *How the hell is he running that fast?* their surprised faces seem to say. *How the hell is he even running?*

Now there's some serious energy in the crowd, and I get the feeling that even those gamblers who have their cash placed on other horses are rooting for Love My Money to take it all. This kind of victory—Rocky beating Apollo Creed, for example; or Rocky beating Mr. T; or Rocky beating that Russian guy; or . . . well, the *Rocky* movies in general, I guess—is what America is about. And even if a win by Love My Money won't prove anything about the American Dream, it will prove that a Joe Blow shlub can come to the track on any given day and walk home thirty-five times richer than when he got there.

Three-quarters of the race gone and the roar of the crowd has become deafening as Love My Money pulls into fourth place, then third, his flanks no longer pitiful and sad but somehow meaty, pulsing, powerful. That head, once drooping down low, is held high, bobbing back and forth as if already reaching for the invisible finish line. His tail whips through the wind, a clear barometer of his newfound winning spirit.

And as they round the final turn, Love My Money does the unexpected: he runs *even faster.* Maybe it's the adrenaline from the crowd, maybe it's the skill of the jockey, but that broken-down nag finds some hidden reserve of energy and turns the volume up to eleven. He shoots down the track as if on rails, a high-speed Disneyland thrill ride ready to break records.

Second place. A hundred yards left to go. I'm holding my breath, and it doesn't bother me a bit. Chaz and Sherm are doing the same. The crowd is going insane.

Neck and neck, nose and nose—it's Try Me On For Size and Love My Money blurring toward the finish line, stride for stride, their legs working in unison, both incredibly fast, incredibly strong, bodies heaving forward as one, as if they understand that the goal is so close, that it's going to take one final push, and that there can be only one winner in the end. One behind the other, one in front of the other, a millimeter on either side, the race changing hands with every stride, every surge, the jockeys floating just inches above their mounts, whipping with all their might, the horses not even feeling the sting, running on their own will to win, infusing the crowd with their own desire—

Thirty yards—Love My Money suddenly in front, a full nose, holding it—the grandstand pumping with energy—

Twenty yards—the lead growing—a full head now—no way the other horse will catch up—it's all happening so quickly and yet slow enough to analyze and comprehend, everyone in the grandstand storing it in their memories as a tale to tell their grandchildren, a story about how the most broken-down nag of them all came back to win it all, to take the big race, to—

Love My Money trips.

That's all it takes—a single misstep, a burp in the motion, and Try Me On For Size races the last ten yards in a vicious blur, regaining the lead and sealing it up, crossing the finish line two-hundredths of a second before Love My Money places in the race of his lifetime.

And suddenly it's finished, like a bout of bad sex—over and done and no one much wants to talk about it.

"Photo!" some loner in the crowd shouts out. "Photo!"

No. No way. It was close, but there's no need for a photograph to determine the winner. The collected energy seeps from the grandstands, sinking out between the bleachers, dissipating into the air. Everyone knows what happened. Everyone resolves to forget it as quickly as possible and get on with their lives. The boards pop up with the preliminary winners—Try Me On For Size, Love My Money, and good old Lassie Liberty popping in for a show.

"Holy crap," Sherm mutters. His earlier bravado is gone. "Eddie ain't gonna like this."

"Whaddaya wanna do?" Chaz asks him.

"Something's fishy," says Sherman. "You see the way he ran?"

I'm still dazzled by the whole thing, win or no. And the fact that Love My Money is still standing is doubly impressive, though I imagine the scene would have been more poignant had the horse won the race and then collapsed ten feet after the finish line, his jockey whispering sweet nothings in his ear as he passed into the Great Pasture in the Sky. "I thought he wasn't even going to make it out of the gate. Pretty nice run if you ask me."

Sherman shakes his head. "Pretty nice run?"

"I thought so."

"Look at those tickets," he instructs me. "Go on, check 'em out."

I do so. Number 6 horse in the fifth race. Love My Money. To win. Every one of them.

"Yeah," he says. "Now you got it. We got bupkis with those tickets. Use 'em to wipe your ass, all the good they'll do ya."

Chaz is shaking his head, as if he's come to a decision he's not entirely thrilled with. "We gotta go talk to him."

"I know," says Sherman.

"Right now."

"Yeah. Yeah, I guess we do."

They move away from the railing, back toward the staircase, and I follow along. I guess they want to have a word with the jockey; maybe they blame him for the horse's misstep at the end. I don't know much about the profession, but it seems to me that's like blaming a NASCAR driver if his engine blows a gasket. Or a piston. Hell, I don't know much about cars, either.

We move through the throng of gamblers, making our way from the grandstand to the clubhouse. Everyone's already lined up to place bets on the next race, the near-amazing finish of the fifth already fading from their memories. It's not about the past; it's all about the future, and the ninety seconds of adrenaline to come. There's no time for nostalgia at the ponies.

Sherman leads us through the clubhouse and down the front stairs, where we take a left and edge our way along the trailers set up a hundred yards away. These must be how they transport the horses from venue to venue, the owners and handlers and jockeys always on the move, always looking for the next place to take a shot at the winner's circle. It's no different from any other profession, I guess, businessman or CPA or attorney; it's all about jockeying for position, trying to keep yourself in the thick of things without getting busted down or making your move too early—though there's probably less manure in, say, a downtown law firm. Not a *lot* less manure, mind you . . .

The smell does become overwhelming after a few moments, and Sherman passes me a small plastic tube. Looks like toothpaste.

"Mint extract," he explains. "Coroners use it when they're working an autopsy. Rub it between your nose and upper lip."

I squeeze a small blob of the goop onto my finger and massage it into my fake skin. Instantly a sharp whiff of mint lashes my sinuses and a sudden craving for the real thing takes hold. This herb in particular has never had a great effect on me, except for one night back in the eighties when I drank enough mint juleps at an Atlanta bar to wind up naked on Emory University's football field, naked and singing Poison songs for two hours—don't ask, don't ask—but my prior lack of herbal intake has got me reeling at this sudden intrusion, and I can feel the warm glow of drunkenness come on despite the fact that all I'm getting is olfactory input. *No matter,* my body says. *An herb is an herb is an herb, and thank you, Vincent!*

But it has blocked out the smell of shit, and for the moment I'd rather be tipsy than nauseous. I can call my sponsor later and confess my olfactory sins; for now, we move past the trailers and into the stables, where the grooms from prior and future races brush down their steeds.

Chaz and Sherman are working the place like it's a nightclub, shaking hands and laughing with the owners and handlers, patting them on the back, wishing them well. They know the joint, and the joint knows them, and, by association, I'm now in the upper echelon, as well. I'm greeted with grins and open arms, and I don't say a single word when I'm introduced as Vinnie, a friend of theirs.

"We got stable four to ourselves," Chaz says after speaking with a mustachioed gentleman. "Says Stu's in there."

"All right," Sherm replies, then turns to me. "Like Eddie told you: sit back, don't do nothing unless we tell you to."

I know my place. Twenty grand to look pretty. "Pretend muscle, right?"

"Spot on."

The stable is relatively dark, the only light thin rays of sunshine streaming in through the slats between the wooden boards that make up the ceiling. It's a good thirty feet on either side, more than enough space for a horse, his food, and whatever accoutrements one needs to get a Thoroughbred up and running. Saddles and bridles and a host of other appliances hang on the walls, everything clean and fresh. I can no longer smell the manure through the mint, and for that I'm grateful. I'll have to remember to take along a tube of the stuff next time I've got a job down in Long Beach; if it can keep out horse dung, it should work wonders on the rotting fish down by the piers.

As we enter the stable, I expect to see the jockey waiting for Chaz and Sherm's arrival. A little fidgety, I'd guess, worried at what his fellow dinos are going to do to him. Maybe preparing a speech in his head about how it wasn't his fault, how the horse slipped beneath him, how they should blame the beast if they're looking for a scapegoat.

But there's no jockey in sight. It's just the horse—tired, no doubt, chest still heaving from the exertion, coat still mottled and patchy, thinning mane matted with sweat—standing in the middle of the barn, staring up at us as we enter.

"Afternoon, Stu," says Sherman, staring right at the nag.

"Nice race you ran there," Chaz chimes in, and I rub my eyes. Maybe the jockey is hiding behind the horse's flank.

"Hey, guys." It's a defeated whine, a sad little drawl. It's a pathetic voice. A loser's voice.

It's the horse's voice.

"Don't start all chummy on us," says Sherman, approaching Love My Money and giving him a slap on the rear end. "You're holding out."

"I'm not," the horse insists, and for a moment I wonder if it was really mint they gave me to rub beneath my nose or if there was something more mischievous inside that tube. Some of the stronger habanero extracts have been known to cause hallucinations—a buddy of mine once dropped some pepper and convinced himself that the Energizer Bunny had finally run out of batteries, which sent him into a full-blown panic—but this doesn't seem like a mirage. This horse is talking up a storm. Petrified, but chatty.

"Look," he says, his mouth moving with the proper cadence but his lips pretty much staying in place, "I did what I was supposed to do. You guys give the orders and we do our thing, right? I can only do what I can do, and—"

"Shhh," Chaz whispers, running his hand across the scraggly mane. "Shhhh." He grabs at the hair and gives a firm yank, and the horse yelps in pain.

"Hey," he squeaks. "The glue's tight—that hurts."

"Oh, it does, does it? I'm sorry." And Chaz yanks again.

I take a step forward but Sherman shoots me a look and I stop in my tracks. My animal-rights activism extends only to the point where my own potential for bodily injury begins. This will get figured out whether I'm front and center or in the back, and there's no reason to piss these fellas off.

"C'mon," the horse whines, "help me outta this thing and we'll talk, okay?"

"Where's the little guy?"

"I don't know," says Love My Money. "If I knew, you think I'd still be down like this?"

Chaz and Sherman shoot each other a look—I'm clearly not part of this decision—and, as one, approach the horse from either end.

"We're gonna help you out," Sherman says, "but then you're gonna tell us what we want to know. Something funny happened out there—"

"I was just doing—"

"Your job," Chaz finishes. "We know. Shut up so we can get started."

"Vinnie," Sherm calls out to me. "Come help me with this ass."

I shuffle toward the horse, moving around to the front end, just a few feet in front of his sad eyes and quivering lips. "Hey," says the nag. "How ya doin'?"

"Can it," Chaz instructs him before I can respond. "Don't talk till we say so."

The horse's wide rear is in front of me a moment later, and Sherman shoots me a toothy grin. "First time with a talking horse, huh?"

"You could say that."

"Yeah, I can see you got the Mr. Ed jeebies goin' on ya. Happens to everyone." He slaps the rump for good measure and leaves his hand resting alongside Love My Money's wide flank.

"Okay," Chaz says. "I got this end braced. Go for it."

Sherman moves aside and gestures toward the horse's rear as if he were a game-show assistant displaying the consolation prize. "All yours, Vinnie."

"All my . . . what?"

"Reach on in," he says. "Do your thing."

"My thing."

Sherman sighs. "It's like an R-series clamp and button, just an extra hook on the end, that's all. Go ahead, it don't bite." He lifts the horse's tail for me, and a puckered anus stares back.

"Where?"

"In there."

I still don't get it; rather, I don't *want* to get it. "In . . . where?"

Sherm shakes his head. "Jesus, Vinnie, you look like you never stuck your hand up a horse's ass before."

"Funny you should say that—"

Love My Money shakes his rump. "Can we get this over with?" he asks.

Chaz and Sherman yell as one: "Shaddap!"

I know what's expected of me, and at least now I think I understand what's going on. For my own sake—and for the sake of this poor horse—I hope I'm right.

I roll up my sleeve, throw my left arm up and over the Thoroughbred's rear end, and unceremoniously shove my right arm into the horse's rump. There's a little squeak from up at the front end of the creature, but otherwise he accepts the intrusion quite well. A hell of a lot better than I would, that's for sure. I went to a physician once who brought out some tool called an anuscope; that doc left the office needing more medical work than I did.

There it is—just like Sherm said, quite similar to an R-series clamp. I work the buttons in a familiar manner, and can feel the release of tension as the strap gives way.

"Ahhh," Love My Money sighs, "that's better."

Chaz manipulates the horse's skin up near the midsection of the animal, and soon the entire rear half of the creature is sliding to the left, loose and flapping through the air.

"Can I take my hand out?" I ask.

"Yeah, yeah," says Sherman, who has begun to manipulate yet another set of clamps down by the horse's feet.

Soon the whole rear section slides off, and a patchwork of brown and green scales slides into view, followed by a familiar set of legs and midsection. A thick sloping tail flops to the ground and traces small patterns in the dust, as if the appendage itself is happy to be free of its confines.

The half-horse/half-Raptor takes a few steps to the left, working out the kinks in its legs. "That's the stuff," he says. "Get the rest of it, get the rest of—"

Chaz clamps the horse's mouth shut with his fist. "You keep quiet or we'll put the first part back on again and staple it there."

It takes a while to remove the rest of this obviously custom-fit guise from the dinosaur within, but once we release the proper series of belts and girdles and pull hard on the latex covering, we're sharing the stable not with the near-winner of the fifth race at Calder, but with a hulking Velociraptor named Stuart who seems unable to keep his mouth shut for more than twelve seconds at a time.

"Thank you, guys," he keeps babbling, "thank you so much. So hot in there—you know how hot it gets? One time, I had to run a race with both guises on, you know that? No time to change out of the human suit, so I ran it in two . . ."

Chaz and Sherman wait him out, apparently deciding that Stu will talk himself to death long before they have to do the job for him.

He turns his attention to me. "Don't know you, do I?"

"That's Vinnie," Sherman says. "He ain't your concern."

"Hey, any friend of Eddie's . . ." says Stu. "You're a Raptor?"

"Yeah," I say, "and you're a . . . horse?"

Stu laughs. "Gotta pay the bills, right?" He chuckles a bit, but Chaz and Sherman don't join in. "Great costume, huh? Cost Eddie a fortune to have it made, best black-market specialty dealer in the country, but . . . Hey, it's worth it, right, guys?"

Sherman shakes his head. "Not when you place, Stu. Only when you win."

"Yeah, but—"

"We had you losing twenty straight races in a row just to get the odds up to thirty-five to one. Twenty straight. And the one time you're supposed to turn on the juice—"

"I did!" Stu protests. "You saw me—I was killing out there—"

"Until the end. Funny how that happens."

Stu is a hulk of a dinosaur. I've been in NFL locker rooms before, I've seen the size of some of these guys. Three-fifty, four hundred pounds. But they don't have the sheer muscle mass that Stu has packed on. And the fact that he's a Raptor makes it all the more impressive; he could hold his own with two T-Rexes, and probably come out on top. But his voice is high, fluffy, whiny, a timbre soufflé, and it doesn't endear him to the crew.

"Listen," Stu says, "I was running the race, just like we always played it. Wait at the beginning, then hit it with a burst of speed. I can take these horses—four legs, two legs—it don't matter—so I know I've got time. But I can't see for crap outta that horse's head, you *know* that. I gotta go with what Pepe's telling me to do, and if Pepe says run then I run. Two whips per second for run, one for backing off, three to take a hitch, right? I figure he's got a method, he can see what's going on, and I can't.

"So I'm churning along, doing my hangdog thing, and suddenly he's telling me to go, so I go. I kick it in, like during my track days, right? Like the time I did hurdles in the Olympics—"

"If I remember right, you got yourself a silver medal, didn't ya?" Chaz asks.

"Sounds like second place to me," Sherm agrees. "You got a habit of this."

"Yeah, yeah," says Stu, trying to blow it off. "Anyway, I'm eating up the turf, and though I got the damn mask over most of my eyes and can't see for shit outta my peripheral vision, I still know I'm passing these other nags like they're snails. And then I hear the crowd gettin' into it, and I know I'm good. So I really start laying it on, and Pepe's up top whipping the crap outta me so I know he wants me to keep up with the speed—must be someone else out in front. Now the legs are burning but I'm still going, right, because I don't wanna disappoint Mr. Tallarico—"

"You're a saint," I say, the words spilling out of their own accord, and Chaz looks at me approvingly. Guess I'm getting the patter down.

"—and I can feel that bitch next to me, pushing herself to the line. So I'm doing the same thing, and the crowd is so damn loud, but I don't got a good a sense of the finish, right? I know how long I been running, but not exactly. Still, I get the idea maybe we're almost done, here I go, finish line is mine—and suddenly Pepe's pulling me back."

"He drop off the whip?" Sherm asks.

"Nah," says Stu. "He's still laying it in, but he's pulling back on the reins. Like a warning signal, like a big stop sign. I got no other choice—this thing's attached to my neck from the inside, and the jerk's practically choking me. I figure we already passed the finish line and he's trying to get me under control, so I take a hitch step, just like we always planned, and start to slow.

"Wasn't till after when I realized what happened. Pepe led me back here, put me in the stable, and the whole time I'm asking him what went down, and he's not answering me. Next thing I know, I'm locked in here, stuck in that damned horse suit, munching hay till you all came in and got me out." He shrugs, the scaled shoulders thick and rippling with strength. No wonder he can run these races; most athletic dinosaurs could match an average horse in a footrace, but Stu's body was built for high-endurance speed and strength. "That's my story."

"And you're stickin' to it, huh?" Chaz shakes his head. "Sherm?"

"I dunno," he says. "Lemme think."

Sherman squats on the sawdust-covered floor, hands wrapped

around his thick head. I take a moment and sidle up to Chaz, jerking a thumb at Stu. "So this guy works for Eddie?"

"Just down at the tracks. Back in the day, he was part of the group, but he fucked up. Ain't that right, Stu?"

"Yeah," he sighs. "Frank kept me around, liked the way I did business."

"Real high-level," Chaz tells me. "Captain, right, Stu?"

He exhales again, unable to put into words how far he's fallen. "Sure. Sure. But Eddie . . ." His lips quiver; I can tell he's holding back a torrent of words detailing his exact hatred for the new boss in town. "Eddie says I talk too much."

"That's right," Chaz agrees. "But we found a new use for ya."

Stu's nodding along madly. "Oh, but I don't mind. I mean, it was great when I was in at the house, you know, with the guys. Frank always treated me real nice. Eddie . . . me and Eddie, we've had our differences. But they treat me pretty good down here. When I got on the horse suit, everyone talks real nice to me, and they brush my hair every day." He pauses, as if to think of the other pleasures of his newfound job. "And I get all the barley I want."

"That's . . . swell," I say.

"And when I win—I mean, it's not supposed to happen that often, you know, 'cause of the odds and tryin' to beef 'em up and all—but when I win, then I get to wear the necklace and . . . well, everyone's just great. Just great, 'cause—"

"Enough," Sherm interrupts. "I figured it out."

"Oh, good," says Stu. "I was wondering if we could go out for lunch—"

"Sit."

"What?"

"Sit. Vinnie, get a chair for our boy."

The only thing I find in the stable area are low grooming stools, and I bring one over to the center of the room. "How's this?" I ask.

"Crappy," says Sherm, "but it'll do. Stewie, siddown."

Stewie takes his seat, looking up at us like a lost pup glad to have found his master. Sherman nods to Chaz, who delves into his burlap sack and comes up with a length of rope. Before I have time to ask what's going on, Stu's thick arms are bound behind him, his powerful thighs strapped to the stool. This wasn't what I was expecting, and before I know it, my hackles are up. This is the point where most mobsters would send me out of the room. For some reason, Chaz and Sherman seem to be omitting this crucial step.

"Guys?" Stu says hopefully, the negative energy in the air finally penetrating his thick skull. "Guys, what's—"

"Vinnie," Sherm says, "this guy look like a dimwit to you?"

I nod noncommitally. "Are you sure you wanna do this?"

"I asked you if he looks like a dimwit."

No need to lie. "A bit."

"Yeah. Yeah, he does, doesn't he? Lemme tell you—that's his act."

Stu is shaking his head, sweat pouring off that shiny scaled brow. "No, Sherm, there's no act—"

"Uh-huh. Before you ran in the Olympics, where'd you go to school, Stewie?"

He mutters something under his breath. Sherman moves closer. "Sorry, pal, couldn't hear ya. Wanna speak up?"

"Princeton," Stu admits. "But . . . but I was a jock. I ran track."

"Right. And All-American," says Sherman, pacing a wide circle around the massive Raptor tied to the stool. As he walks, the light strobes on and off his body, flashing the sun in and out of Stewie's eyes.

"But the thing about Princeton," Sherman continues, "the thing about the Ivy League in general, is that they don't give scholarships for athletes. The Ivy League ain't nothing but a sports coalition, like the Big East or the Pac Ten. And their thing is that they only give out academic scholarships—basic financial-aid packages. That's why they suck at pretty much everything, 'cause most kids who are good at sports go where the cash is. So they got these sporting teams with mediocre players, but they do got one thing—brains.

"So anyone who graduates from Princeton—and I take it you did graduate, Stewie—"

"Yeah," he whimpers, sounding as depressed about graduating from Princeton as if he'd admitted to flunking out of L.A. City College.

"—has got to have more than two brain cells to rub together. So this tired old Stewie's-a-fuckup act ain't gonna cut it anymore. I think you been playing us—"

"No," Stu says firmly, his body shaking beneath the restraints. "No, that's not it!"

"—and I think you and Pepe are in on it together."

Stu's started to shake now as the gravity of his situation comes into focus. The ropes, tight about his arms, his legs, begin to rub hard against his scales, leaving indentations as he struggles against the restraints.

"Listen," Stu pleads, "that's not how it is. If Pepe's playing something with Try Me On For Size, then it's his deal, and—"

"Wait, wait," says Sherman. "I didn't say anything about Try Me On For Size. What makes you think I was going in that direction?"

A shake to Stu's voice, a slight hitch that gives him away. "Jesus, Sherm—don't do this to me—"

"I ain't doing a damn thing, Stewie. I'd just like to know why you brought up the winning horse when I didn't mention a damn thing about it."

Stu does the smart thing and clams up. Maybe he really is a Princeton boy. Then again, that ninny Sutherland, one of the detectives at TruTel, went to Princeton, which doesn't say much for the overall intellectual caliber of the school. Of course, Sutherland got in through his connections, while it seems poor Stu is about to lose his.

A few more minutes of Sherm pacing and trying to frighten in-formation out of Stu, but it's no use. The part-time horse is keep-ing his trap shut. Chaz tries to play good cop for a while—"Let's get this over with quickly, huh? Then we can all go out for a bite to eat, whaddaya say, pal?"—but his true nature takes over after a few softball questions and he starts slapping Stewie around.

"Knock it off," Sherman barks. He approaches Stu and squats down in front of him so that the two are face-to-face. They're ex-actly opposite in body type—the ectomorph and the mesomorph, one chubby, one strong—but today the power roles are reversed. It's the pale little fat kid who'll be ruling the schoolyard this after-noon. Power to the pudgy!

"Last time," Sherman says. "You got anything for me, Stewie?"

"I—I don't know what you want—"

"Didn't want to do this." Sherman sighs, and nods over to Chaz.

It takes a few seconds of rummaging through that sack of his, but Chaz lays a host of implements down by his feet, each one more frightening than the last. Surgical thread. Scalpel. Razor blade. Ax.

And six plastic dissolution packets. That's when Stewie starts shrieking.

Dissolution packets are nothing more than four-inch-square sacks of white plastic with a small black X in the upper-right- and upper-left-hand corners. Quite the odd thing to start screaming over, but of course it's not the packets themselves that started him on his hissy fit. It's what's inside:

Bacteria. To be more specific, bacteria that thrive on dinosaur flesh. In fact, they've been bred and engineered over the years so that it's the only thing they'll eat. Dump it on a human, a leopard, a Burmese python, it won't matter. Probably piss off the python, but that's your problem, not the python's. These microscopic gour-mands will eat one thing, and one thing only, and that's dino.

And they eat it voraciously.

The distribution of packets is firmly controlled by the Councils in order to prevent mishaps like the mess down in West Africa. Ebola, shmebola—it was dissolution bacteria run wild, and they couldn't trace the source. As such, all dinosaurs in public-oriented professions are given packets—to be kept on them at all times—for the sole purpose of disposing of dino remains should the need arise, and each one is registered with the proper authorities. I can recall a time not so long ago, in fact, when I had to use one on a dino-amalgam in a Bronx alleyway, wiping out the evidence of our battle, and my eventual victory, before the human police arrived.

That's the stated purpose of the packets: to be used on the deceased, only on the deceased, and only when absolutely necessary.

Looks like Chaz and Sherman haven't read the instruction manual.

"Stop squirming," Sherman grunts as he wrestles with the tip of Stu's tail. Chaz has already shoved a wadded-up towel into the big Raptor's mouth, drowning out much of his shrieks and moans. They haven't even started yet and already he's worked himself into a tizzy. "Knock it off. Chaz, a little help?"

I can see what's coming, but I'm powerless to stop it. Even though I'm here as pretend muscle, I can't help but feel a bit involved, though I swore to myself I wouldn't get mixed up in mob business. Still, I agreed to come along, and I'm in it until they really go over the line. My stomach is doing flips; for now, I can pretend it's the mint.

Chaz and Sherman manage to secure Stu's tail, Sherm planting his rump a foot above the tip and pinning it to the stable floor. "You got the ax?" he asks, and Chaz grabs the sharp implement in his hand, ready to put it to use.

"Go," says Chaz.

Sherman rips open the small plastic packet in his hands and pours the fine powder over the tip of Stu's wriggling tail.

The towel is barely able to muffle the piercing scream that

rocks the otherwise quiet stable. Flesh instantly begins to dissolve beneath the furious assault, the tip of Stu's tail disappearing before my eyes, a light-green goo pooling about the floor below. But that's just the waste products from the bacteria—they're eating every bit of dino meat they can find, skin and all, and pooping it out on the other side.

I'm stuck in the no-man's-land between revulsion and attraction—like watching an L.A. Clippers game—and can't tear my eyes away from the terrible sight in front of me. A full inch of Stewie's tail has vanished in under thirty seconds, and I can see a bit of bone now where the flesh has been eaten away, marrow and enamel the two things these bacteria refuse to nibble upon. The poor guy's eyes are bulging out of his head from the pain, his scales tight against the ropes, digging into his arms, his legs, drawing out huge welts—

"Do it," Sherm says calmly. "Now."

Chaz raises the ax high and whacks the blade through Stu's tail, an inch above the area where the bacteria continue their feast. A solid hunk of meat flops to the ground, and within seconds, the microscopic gourmands have consumed the rest of the flesh, leaving only a small bit of tailbone lying amid a puddle of green goo on the stable floor.

But the cut has saved Stu from further attack by the dissolution bacteria, and though his tail is bleeding profusely, he'll live to trot another day. Sherman reaches up and pulls the towel from the Raptor's mouth. He's blubbering, barely comprehensible, his eyes red and watery, his lips flapping in and out with every breath.

"Shhh," soothes Sherman. "Shhh. Tell us where the tickets are, and we'll end all this. Fix you up right nice, get you all sewn up."

Stu is beyond reason. The pain must be tremendous; the nerves in the tail are not quite as sensitive as those in the groin area, but it's no treat to get a whack down there.

Chaz reaches into that bag of tricks and comes up with a small brown bottle. He pours a bit of liquid onto a cloth and presses it to the bloody stump of Stu's tail. The big guy jumps at first—that raw contact with the naked flesh—but then eases up, and I can see his muscles relax.

"Topical anesthetic," Sherman explains to Stewie. "Feel better?"

"Yeah," he wheezes. "Yeah."

"Okay, so we can do this two ways. Chaz has the sutures to fix you up or another packet to start it all over again."

"Sherm—"

"Whoa, Stewie, lemme explain. We got . . . how many packets left, Chaz?"

"Five."

"Five. Yeah, that makes sense. One more to finish off the tail—and this time, I won't let him ax it off—one for each leg, that's three. Then I'll probably get bored and go right for the head. Ever wonder what it feels like to have your eyeballs eaten away?" I wonder how much Sherman is enjoying this; he's certainly good at it.

"I don't know where Pepe is," Stu insists.

"So you admit you two were gonna screw over Eddie Tallarico."

Stu looks away, but Sherman turns his head back, stares him down. There's no question who's got the power in this room, dissolution packet or no.

"Yes," Stu eventually admits.

Chaz gives a little laugh. "Son of a bitch . . ."

"He doesn't pay us anything," Stu blurts out. "I have to live on tuna and dog food. Hell, I dress up in the horse costume just to get some oats outta the deal—"

"Shut up," Sherman informs him. "Shut up this instant, you back-stabbing bastard. Then I want you to take a deep breath and tell me where the tickets are."

Stu practically gasps in a lungful of air. "They're with Pepe—"

"And where is that dead prick?"

"I don't know. I swear it—he's probably trying to keep the money all to himself—"

Sherm nods to Chaz, who readies another packet. Stu starts crying again; he knows where this is going. "Jesus," he blubbers, "I would tell you if I knew—"

"That may be," Sherman says. "But sometimes we don't know what we know until we're up against the wall and the firing squad is ready to shoot."

Chaz rips open the packet and approaches Stu's tail. They don't even bother shoving the towel in his mouth this time—they probably figure he'll pass out from the pain. Chaz holds the packet by one corner, dangling it over the Raptor's wiggling frame.

This is where I should step in. Say something. Do something. But I find myself rooted to the spot. This isn't my business. This is one mob idiot ripping off other mob idiots, only he got caught and now he has to pay the price. Getting involved is not the wise move.

But it's the only move I know how to make. I take a step forward. "Chaz—"

At that very moment, as the dissolution crystals are perched on the edge of the packet, preparing to drop onto Stu's already mangled tail, the All-American athlete from Princeton University wises up.

"Stable six, stall H," he yelps. "He's holed up in there for the rest of the night."

Chaz pulls back the packet, and I take a big mother-may-I step backwards. Hopefully, neither Chaz nor Sherm noticed my attempt to intervene.

"You ain't fucking with us?" Sherman asks.

"No," Stu insists. "He's there. He's there and he's got the cash."

"How much?"

"I don't know," Stu says. "We—I borrowed money from my family, Pepe borrowed from his family. Everything they had, ten grand. And we put it all down to place."

"So you came in second on purpose?"

Stu nods his head rapidly; the snot and tears streaming down his face dribble off his bottom lip. "It was Pepe's plan all along. I swear it."

Sherm turns to Chaz. "What'd he place at?"

"Twelve to one, I think."

"Hundred and twenty, give or take. Not a bad haul."

"Wait a second," I blurt out. "Why didn't you place your bets to *win*, come in first, and make everybody happy?"

Stu opens his mouth to answer, but his comeback catches halfway up his throat as the big lug realizes that my plan was a hell of a lot better than his. "Oh," he says. "I didn't . . . think of that."

"Princeton," laughs Sherman. "Forty grand a year and they don't even teach you the right way to screw over your boss." He checks his watch and turns back to Stu. "So you're telling me Pepe's got the cash on him right now?"

"Or the tickets—please, the Novocain's starting to wear off . . ."

Sherman and Chaz don't particularly care about Stu's level of pain tolerance. They're much more interested in the potential windfall that will erase Eddie Tallarico's loss at the track, and then some. They pop up and head for the door of the stable.

"Vinnie," says Sherm, "clean up the mess."

"What mess?" I ask. "Looks pretty clean to me."

Chaz grins and throws the new dissolution packet on Stu's tail. The screams are instant, piercing—"GET IT OFF! GET IT OFF!"—and I'm by the Raptor's side in a heartbeat, down on my knees as his tail is once more dissolving before my eyes. Sherman and Chaz are gone, and it's just me, Stu, and the amazing vanishing appendage.

"I can't—"

"Please!" he shrieks. "Oh, God—get it off me!"

"There's no way—" Another inch has disappeared, and now, without Sherman or Chaz to hold it down, the tail is flapping away, whipping around the stable, nearly slamming into me. I can't take that chance—if it touches me, even for a second, those bacteria could hop onto my body and open a new restaurant.

"Stay still—stop moving—"

But he's beyond words, his muscles suddenly bulging again, pulling at the ropes, straining to get free—the metal stool actually twisting under the pressure, the seat buckling beneath his weight.

I dump out the remaining contents of Chaz's sack, but there's not much left. The topical anesthetic, some gauze—everything you'd need to cauterize a wound—but nothing that looks like it could neutralize dissolution bacteria.

Convulsions have begun to wrack Stewie's body, the bacteria creeping another two inches up his tail. It won't be long now before an entire twelve inches is gone, and I can only imagine what will happen once those nibblers make it up to his torso.

My first thought is to use the scalpel to release him from his bindings, but I realize that he's not about to sit tight and take his treatment like a grown Raptor. He'll be flailing about the second I cut him free, and I'll most likely be the first thing he bowls over in his insane dash around the stable. So I leave him good and tied up for the moment; what I have to do will not be pretty.

The ax blade is still sharp, the weapon heavy in my hand. I've never swung one of these before—growing up in the wilds of L.A. there's not a lot of call for chopping firewood—and I'm surprised to find that the heft is comfortable, almost reassuring. I'm sure it's not so reassuring to Stu, but we make our decisions and we live with them.

My first shot misses wildly. I'm totally off the mark, and the blade barely catches the edge of his tail, drawing a spurt of blood three inches above the demarcation line.

"Whoops," I say. "Lemme try that again—"

Stu's beyond words. Beyond sounds, even—his throat clogged with pain, limbs twitching with intensity, tail dissolving away—

Another upswing, another strike—and this time, the ax would have hit home, only his tail whipped out of the way at the last moment and I buried the blade in the floor of the stable instead.

"Will you stay still already?"

But he's in too much pain to listen and follow directions. Fortunately, I can rectify that. Reaching into the pile on the ground, I grab at the brown bottle of Novocain and pry off the cap with my teeth.

I wait for the tail to whip around in my direction—that slab of meat flipping back and forth like an out-of-control windshield wiper—and stick out a hand, hoping I get the placement just right—

My hands thunk into the tail barely half an inch above the bacteria, the little boogers still chomping away, and I grab on tight. Without a second to lose, I pour the topical anesthetic over the wound and drop the tail back to the floor, backing away from the deadly germs.

Relief floods Stu's face, but I know it's short-lived. "Thank you," he says, big eyes blinking. "Thank you so much—"

"Don't thank me yet," I say. "Listen up. As soon as the bacteria eat their way past the Novocain, it's gonna hurt like hell again. So I'm gonna . . ." I take a breath, partially to steady myself, partially to steady him. "I'm gonna chop another six inches off your tail."

"Six—six inches?"

"It's the only way I can be sure to get it all. Okay?"

He gulps and nods slowly. There's no argument. There's no choice.

"Lay your tail down," I instruct him. "Right there, on the ground."

He does so, following directions like a straight-A schoolboy. "It's starting to hurt again."

"I know," I say. "Just another second."

There it is, in front of me. I have to train my mind not to think of it as a living appendage, as a useful part of a Raptor body, but as a hunk of meat at the butcher stand, ready to be carved and served to the masses. That's all it is. Lifeless. Dead. No problem. Lift and chop, lift and chop, lift—

And chop. I swing the ax down, the blade whistling through the air, and the squish of metal meeting flesh sends shivers through my arms. It takes me a moment to realize that my eyes are closed; when I open them, the dissected section of Stu's tail lies lifeless on the ground, the bacteria quickly reducing it to that thin green goo.

And Stu is howling. A new wave of pain washes over the poor fellow, and I dump whatever anesthetic is left onto his stump of a tail. There's some gauze in the pile on the ground, and I quickly wrap it around the wound as tightly as possible, forming a makeshift tourniquet. With surgical string I tie it up tightly, and soon I've stanched most of the blood flow. He's going to get an infection—no doubt about it—but at least his life has been spared.

"Thank you thank you thank you," he repeats over and over again as I use the scalpel to free him from the stool. The ropes fall to the ground beside the severed tailbone, now picked clean of all remaining flesh.

"You want that?" I ask, pointing down to the nubbin on the floor.

He nods and picks up the small bit of bone that was once a part of his body, and I help him locate his human guise, getting him dressed as quickly as possible. It's a crappy job—his navel is two inches off center, and without the extra heft to his tail, there's a definite sag where his butt should be—but it will do for the time being. He needs to get to a hospital, and quickly.

"I can't thank you enough," he says as I help him to the back door of the stable. There's no one out there of concern—just some handlers and their steeds—and the coast is clear. "You saved my life."

"Not yet," I say. "They come back and find you, it's all over.

Now you gotta promise me you'll disappear." I can't have him popping up alive at Tallarico's place if I'm planning on saying he's dead. That sort of thing might go on my permanent record. And with the Tallaricos, permanent means *permanent*.

"Where should I go?"

"Nebraska. Europe. Jupiter. It's not my problem—you just go away, and stay away, got it?"

He agrees, thanks me a hundred more times, tells me he'll be indebted to me for life, and takes off into the back alleys of Calder, hoping to flag a cab for the nearest hospital with a reptilian wing.

I'm on my knees in the middle of the stable three minutes later, gathering the remaining gear into the burlap sack, when there's a sudden commotion at the door. I realize that Chaz and Sherman locked it before they took off out the back entrance, and I cautiously approach.

"Stu!" an accented voice is calling in a hushed yell. "Stu! Lemme in!"

This ain't a hard one. Must be Pepe.

"Stu!" he repeats. "They're out here—the muscle from Tallarico's! They're onto us, man. Lemme in—"

I open the door and step out of the stable just as Pepe is about to knock again. He's just like I remember seeing him on the track—small, swarthy, jittery. Definitely a Compy.

"Hey there," I say. "Stu's not available right now."

Pepe knows the jig is up. His eyes widen comically as I take a step toward him, his legs backpedaling like a cartoon dog trying to build up steam before zooming off after a cat. But his heel sticks in an open gap in the wooden flooring and he falls backwards, whacking his head on the wall behind him. He's out cold by the time he sinks to the ground, his jockey's outfit bunched up tight around his waist and torso. I kneel down to check his pulse—

"Hot damn, Vinnie—you didn't have to kill him!"

I look up to find Sherm and Chaz—the older one out of breath, the young kid flush with the excitement of the chase—hopping around the corner. They approach and with their toes probe Pepe's prone body.

"He's not dead," I explain. "Unconscious."

"No shit," says Chaz. "You do this?"

No need to lie, no need to tell the truth. I just grin and let my teeth do the talking for me.

"Nice job," says Sherm. "Maybe you ain't so useless after all." I assume this is akin to a compliment, so I just grin once again. "You take care of the other thing?"

"Yeah," I say. "All taken care of."

"The bones?"

"All taken care of," I repeat. Technically, I haven't fibbed once. Don't know why that's so important to me right now, given that I've just been complicit in torture, extortion, and the chopping off of a perfectly good tail, but a guy's got to hold on to *something* when he finds himself in quicksand.

Chaz and Sherman share a satisfied look. They're one step closer to getting what they came for, and now the money is within their grasp.

"Look, Vinnie," Sherm says, taking me by the arm as he leads me away from the stable, back toward the trailers. "This next situation could get . . . delicate."

"More delicate than that last one?"

Sherman nods. "I think you did more than enough for your first trip. You did good."

"Gee, thanks," I say, and, dear God, I think I mean it.

Sherman throws an arm around my shoulder as he walks me back to the front of the racetrack. He hails a taxi and bundles me in the back. "Take him wherever he wants," he tells the driver and drops a hundred-dollar bill in my lap.

Sherman buckles me in tight and pats me on the head. "Chaz and I . . . well . . . hell, kid, we're proud of you."

And as the door closes and the cab pulls onto the road, I find myself smiling. Almost . . . happy. Am I so desperate for companionship and approval that I actually value the opinion of a monster like Sherm? Have I sunk so low that a few kind words from a mafia goon can erase an hour of gut-churning violence? And why has that whole scene lifted me to a warm, comfortable place that used to take three bushels of cilantro and a sidecar of basil?

What the hell is happening to Vincent Rubio?

2

Of course, it doesn't start out that way. It never starts out that way. If, at the beginning of each case, someone would give me a crystal ball so I could see the rivers of shit I'd be wading through as a result of saying *Sure, I'll do some work for you,* then I'd be out of the snoop game and living it up as a dairy farmer in Kansas. No PI worth his salt ever thinks he's going to get in over his head; no PI worth his salt ever does any less.

It all begins at a party, two weeks or so before the racetrack fiasco. It all begins with a mouthful of tuna and tarragon, hold the tarragon. Dry, flavorless tuna is at its best when it's not being ingested; certain manufacturing uses come to mind. But I can't throw back the spices like I used to. I've got sobriety to maintain. I've got a nine-month chip in one of these pockets. I've got friends and I've got a sponsor and I've got a lot of frustration these days, because one leaf is too much, and a thousand is not enough.

It doesn't help that the centerpiece at my table is a veritable rain forest of delights, ranging from the ferns ringing the bottom to the scrumptious calla lilies up on top, the delicate petals dangling down to within a few inches of my tongue. It's all I can do to keep my eyes averted, my nose clogged up tight, and my attention firmly fixed away from the shrubbery and toward the stage set up at the far end of this backyard garden.

Tommy Troubadour, an old client from my halcyon Ernie days, is wailing away up there, belting out standards like there's a William Morris agent in the crowd and he's got one last shot at the big time. I don't recognize half the tunes, but it's not due to any musical ignorance on my part. Tommy's a slacker when it comes to memorizing lyrics, so he tends to make up the words as he goes along, and it doesn't faze him when the lines don't rhyme. This one is either "Memories Are Made of This" or "An Evening in Roma," neither of which seems especially appropriate for a thirteen-year-old's birthday party. But Tommy's never been appropriate. He doesn't have to; he's got connections. Wink, wink.

"He's fantastic." This from the gal to my left, some elderly aunt of the birthday boy, a relative eighteen times removed but still rich enough to make the guest list. Slathered across her body is a floral print dress that might have fit her ten years and thirty pounds ago; a thatched hat with a wide, sloping brim covers half of her face. And for some reason, she feels the need to get my opinion of Tommy's antics. "Don't you think he's just fantastic?"

"He's certainly giving it his all," I reply.

"That warm baritone, those deep notes . . . Invigorating."

"I could introduce you to him, if you like," I offer. "He's a friend from way back."

The aunt's eyes widen in shock and delight. "You *couldn't*—"

"I could."

"You *wouldn't*—"

"I would. Please," I say, "it would be a pleasure." I figure it's the least I can do for my singing pal, who roped me into this shindig in the first place. All I'd wanted to do after a long day of snooping was cut back to my pad and get in a little shut-eye before a stakeout case down in Inglewood, but suddenly Tommy was on the line, begging me to come watch him perform.

"It'll be like the old days," he pleaded.

"I never saw you in the old days."

"Then it'll be like the new days. C'mon, it's my first big gig in a while, I want somebody there who I know or I'm gonna get all nervous."

"This a mob thing?" I asked, point-blank and all. "'Cause I've been strip-searched enough this week."

"No, no," he said, "it's just a guy I know, his son is turning thirteen—"

"So his claws came in."

"Yeah," Tommy said, relieved that I understood. "The kid's claws came in. Big bash, out in the Palisades. Beautiful house, great view of the ocean, lotsa food, you'll love it."

"Who is it?"

"Who?"

"The guy," I said. "Who's got the kid and the house and all that?"

"Buddy of mine."

He's evading. "Named . . . ?"

"Frank."

"Frank who?"

Tommy caves, tries to make it sound casual. "Frank Tallarico."

The laugh escapes my lips before I can sew it up. "The mob boss?"

I can almost hear Tommy's shrug over the phone, the slight toss of his shoulders. "Hey, whatever. He's a businessman. He sells blue jeans to immigrants. Look, it ain't important what he does. I'm looking to have someone there so I know I'm singing good, okay?"

"You sing great," I lied. That's where I should have told him the truth, should have let him know straight up that he'll never be more than a wedding singer at best, but my nature got the better of me and out flew the fib.

"You really think so?"

"Yeah," I said. "You got something special."

"So you'll go?"

I sighed, I hemmed, I hawed, and then I gave in, mostly because going to this gig would get me out of the next one. Plus, he's a client from way back who always paid his bills on time, and I make it a point never to alienate anyone with ready cash.

And then there's those connections. Wink, double wink.

Lunch is served during a break between sets, and Tommy saunters over while I'm halfway between bites of duck, the skin peppered with small bits of fennel. I manage to scrape most of the herb off the poultry and onto my plate, then decide to scrap the skin entirely and go for the herb-free meat. Most likely, these minor seasonings would do nothing to chemically alter my mood, but I'm holding fast these days, clinging onto the wagon with all claws. The twelve-steppers down on Wilshire, well-meaning party poopers to the core, would be proud.

"You having fun, Vinnie?" asks Tommy, throwing an arm around my shoulder as he pulls up a chair.

"Swell time," I lie. "And you . . . Parading around up there . . ."

"You like it, huh?"

"It's something," I tell him. "It's something, all right."

Tommy accepts this as a compliment and beams those Nanjutsu-knockoff Osmond dentures at me. "Maybe I'll do a little Buddy Greco for you later."

He knows I'm a bit of a lounge lizard. "Don't strain yourself."

Smiling again, wider this time, Tommy leans in closer and drops his volume a notch. "Listen, Vincent, I was hoping later, after the next set, you could come back to the house with me."

"You're leaving?"

"No, no—*this* house. Here. Inside."

I have no idea what Tommy Troubadour wants from me, but the hushed tones are enough to throw up big neon warning signs. "Party's outside, Tommy. No reason to go slumping around indoors."

"We been invited."

"'We' as in . . . ?"

"You and me, pally." Raising his eyes, focusing them across the wide, expansive lawn to a table set up closer to the stage. "Mr. Tallarico wants to have a word with us."

Mr. Tallarico. Great. "I'm sure he's got enough to do today, what with his son's claws coming in and all—"

"He asked for us," Tommy cuts in. "For you, specifically."

"He did, huh?"

"He did."

"Before the party?" I ask.

Tommy doesn't answer right away. He's trying to flash those teeth at me again, blinking his eyes like he's got a speck of dirt caught under the lid. "That might work on the dames," I tell him, "but it ain't getting you outta this. Answer my question: You call me and make me come to this shindig so your mafia friend could 'talk' to me?"

"Vincent—"

"Straight up, Tommy."

He lowers his head. "Yes."

And now it's too late for me to do anything about it. I'm at the man's party, I've eaten the man's food. I've sat on his chairs. I've listened to his mediocre choice of a band. And now, to avoid looking disrespectful—and, as anyone who's been around the block as many times as I have knows, disrespect for these folks is worse than squatting on the prize azaleas—I have to hear the guy out.

"Thanks, Tommy," I say. "You know it was my life's dream to get tangled up in mob business."

But Tommy's already out of his seat, the band kicking up a little intro music, waiting for him to retake the stage. "Don't worry," he assures me, patting my back like I'm a preschooler he can console with a kind word and a lollipop. "I'm sure it's nothing like that. We'll talk, we'll laugh. It'll be swell."

And then he's back onstage, bowing to imaginary applause, his feet kicking in time with the rhythm the drummer's laying down, thrusting the mike stand into the air like it's a lance, and launching into the Buddy Greco version of "Around the World."

As if that makes up for it.

I focus my attention away from the floor show and over toward Mr. Tallarico, seated across the way. Legs crossed, hands folded across his lap. Staring up at the band, half-interested, half-asleep, as if Tommy's giving a lecture on astrophysics. His expression hasn't changed much throughout the day's festivities, though I may have caught a crack of a smile at the corners of his sculpted lips when his kid thanked the crowd for coming. The rest of his face is grade-A generic goods, though it's pretty clear he's had some black-market work done on his guise; none of the major manufacturers make cheekbones that high for males. I should run a check with Jules down at the Wax Museum and find out who's got the mafia contract. Should be good business. Mostly cash, I'd assume.

I don't know much about the dinosaur mob here in Los Angeles. I don't want to know. Never have. Ernie always said that the best PIs were the ones who knew what they had to know exactly when they had to know it, and then promptly forgot it all the next day. *Selective amnesia,* he called it, and it's a code I've tried to live by. It doesn't always work. It sure didn't for Ernie.

But what I do know about the dinosaur mafia is enough to make me hope this afternoon's meeting is a quick one: they make all the human mob coalitions—the Italians, the Asians, the Latinos—look like suburban book clubs. The bloodshed is constant; cyclical revenge is the standing order.

And the last item I remember hearing about Frank Tallarico isn't exactly the kind of thing that winds up in a college alumni newsletter. The government, after years of hard, grueling work, had finally stuck him on seven counts of conspiracy under the RICO statutes and two more on a capital murder beef. Tack on another thirty-nine for good old tax evasion—their bread and butter, the way they finally nailed Al Capone—and that's one thick file down at the Department of Justice.

Seems the Feds had a snitch in the Tallarico organization by the name of Henry Tropp, a low-level soldier who was ready to sell out Frank and his gang for immunity and a trip through the witness protection program. Henry, it was well known, had something of a temper and wasn't good at keeping his head on straight. And when the local police found his body, dumped on the edge of the dry creek that masquerades as the L.A. River, it turned out Henry wasn't good at keeping his head on at all. Legs, body, neck, and that was the end of Henry Tropp.

They found the nose—both the guise Erickson model and the real green snout—buried in a ditch two miles away, wrapped in a brown paper bag, tucked inside an old shoe box. No one outside of the organization understood the significance, but everyone knew enough about Tallarico and his associates to know it meant *something*.

The charges, all forty-eight of them brought by both the government and the National Council, were dropped the next day. No witness, no crime.

So, yes, it's true: I'm hoping for a quick, how's-your-life, nice-to-meetcha, gotta-run meeting this afternoon. I have no urge to get wrapped up in mafia affairs. I am particularly attached to my head.

"You got an envelope for me?"

Behind me, a high-pitched voice, delivering the question with a tone natural to those born to privilege. He knows the answer. At least, he thinks he knows the answer.

"Congratulations," I tell Tallarico's son. "You must be very happy today."

"Sure," he says dully. "So, you got an envelope?"

I can see the lump of wadded paper inside his breast pocket, the mass of checks and cash balled up there, and understand the kid's expectations. But I don't have any money for him; this was a last-minute invite, and I didn't have time to hit the bank. Probably wouldn't have fronted the cash even if I'd run through an ATM on the way over, but now I'm on the spot, and the last thing I want to do is piss off Tallarico's kid on his special day.

"Can I see your claws?" I ask, stalling for time.

He sighs and pulls off the glove on his right arm, working the buttons quickly, expertly, the green hide beneath sliding into view. "I've been doing this all day," he whines. "Everyone wants to see them."

A slight strain on his face as he works the muscles inside his hand, the tips of his black claws poking out of their slits, holding there, trembling, before sliding back inside, the scales sliding over one another like shingles to cover up the holes. I can't remember exactly what my claws looked like when I was thirteen, but I'm pretty sure they were bigger than that. Then again, I developed early. Rubio boys always do.

"Nice claws," I say. "You'll get the chicks, no problem."

"So . . . the envelope?" he asks, rebuttoning his glove.

"You get right to the point."

"Look," he says, "if you don't have it, just tell me so I can get on with this. I got ten more tables and a lotta rich relatives."

The kid is straightforward. I admire that. He's also something of a little prick.

"You take credit cards?"

Young Mr. Tallarico looks me up and down. There's something of his father in that face; they obviously order their guises from the same manufacturer. "Do I even know you?"

"I'm a friend of the bandleader's," I say. "Vincent Rubio, I'm a detective."

"Oh," he says, then repeats himself: "Ohhh." He smiles, and it helps his looks immeasurably. "Then I should probably be giving *you* money."

Must not strike the child. Must maintain composure.

Twenty minutes later, Tommy finishes off his set with a swing medley and leaps off the risers, a sheen of sweat soaking his brow. He's got the PoreRight skin installed on that guise, and, according to the brochure, it's the patent-pending osmosis system that allows the moisture to seep through to the open air. Never felt the need for it; I broke down a long time ago and gave in to the human antiperspirant ads. It takes four times the normal dosage to get through the scales and work its magic, but as far as I'm concerned, mammal antiperspirant is strong enough for a dino, even if it is made for a woman.

"Let's head inside," Tommy suggests.

"This can't take long," I tell him. "I got a job tonight."

"It won't," he promises. "Mr. Tallarico is very to-the-point."

I think of Henry Tropp, of his nonexistent head, of his snout rotting inside a brown paper sack. "I bet he is."

I'd hesitate to call the main house a mansion, but here in the nice part of the Pacific Palisades, where the homes of movie stars and executives cling to the hills like barnacles to a ship, anything under five thousand square feet is practically a shack. It's your basic gargantuan Tudor, a staple of modern Southern California design, the main tenet of which seems to be Just Make It Big, Taste Be Damned.

Tommy seems to know his way around the place, and he leads me through a series of hallways and staircases until we reach the end of a long corridor. There, a pair of French doors, the glass etched in an abstract pattern, open onto a solarium. Walls of windows allow in the considerable July sun. Plants and trees line a stepping-stone walkway, their branches leaning down, leaves scraping the top of my head as we pass.

Frank Tallarico sits in a rattan chair near the far wall of the solarium, his legs crossed in that easy, no-nonsense fashion, a fitted suit contoured to his long, slender frame. He tosses oranges into his wide, thick-lipped mouth, one after another, their rinds still intact as he chews and swallows.

As I pass by a pair of palms on either end of the path, I sense the presence of others in the area; indeed, two of Tallarico's men stand nearby, their husky bodies barely obscured by the tree trunks.

"Mr. Rubio," Tallarico says, his voice smooth, easier than I'd imagined. I was expecting Brando; once again, my cinematic education has failed me.

"Mr. Tallarico," I begin, unsure of how to conduct myself. Am I supposed to kiss his ring? Hell, he's not even wearing a ring. Show deference? Act tough? And why isn't he stroking a cat? They never cover this sort of stuff when you go in to get your PI license. "Quite a little shindig you have going on here."

Tallarico smiles, and it looks genuine. Good start. "My wife," he says, waving a hand through the air as if to dismiss the matter. "She becomes involved in these things. One of the boys in my son's class, his claws came in a year ago, and his family held a party at the Four Seasons. They rented the entire hotel for a night, ballrooms, restaurants, all of it. Every room had a different band, every floor a different theme."

"How . . . excessive."

"We men have our competitions, Mr. Rubio—our businesses, our sporting events—but women . . . They burn so bright."

"Sure. Yeah, I guess." This is going nowhere fast. Tallarico's scent is strong, thick, a deep fusion of tar and molasses. I could get stuck inside that smell. "You wanted to see me?"

"Please," he says, snapping his fingers at his men, one of whom scurries over with a rattan chair identical to Tallarico's, only smaller. "Have a seat."

I plant my rump and cast around to find a second chair for Tommy. Tallarico sees my look. "Tommy isn't sitting," he tells me curtly. "Tommy can stand. Can't you, Tommy?"

"Yes, sir, Mr. Tallarico," comes the speedy response. "I'm great, I'm fine. I love standing. Good for the legs."

Another snap of the fingers, and the second of the two men is at my side, a black lacquered box in his hands. He pulls the lid back, and even before I get a peek, I can smell it, wafting out from inside, the scent racing up my nose and crashing hard against some forgotten part of my brain.

"Basil," I choke, trying to keep myself in check, my hands by my sides, my teeth and tongue firmly inside my mouth. It's there, right in front of me, the lovely, lovely green leaves nestled against soft ebony felt, only a foot from my face, my teeth, my lips, my stomach—

"Please, help yourself," Tallarico says. "We grow it on the grounds, out behind the house."

"Thank you," I manage to say, "but no."

Tallarico gives me a raise of the eyebrows, a decidedly human expression so many of us have picked up over the years. "No?"

I take a breath, close my eyes, and admit what I've been admitting for the last year or so at group meetings and seminars, in basements and coffeehouses and town halls and rotary clubs:

"I'm an herbaholic."

Tallarico nods, and suddenly the box is closed, suddenly the box is gone, and I can't for the life of me remember why I told him to take it away.

To his credit, Tallarico doesn't try to apologize or explain himself or pry into my personal life with insincere questions about my sobriety. He simply nods and waves that hand again, dismissing the matter as unimportant to our conversation. I like that gesture; I resolve to introduce it into my own body-language repertoire.

"There is still much left of this party," he says, tossing another juicy orange down his gullet, barely stopping to chew before he swallows it whole, "and my wife and son have been kind enough to allow me to do business on this day. So, in the interests of time, I'll be brief.

"Tommy tells me you are a detective of some note, a licensed private investigator here in Los Angeles."

"That's true." My license, revoked for a short period during my inactivity after Ernie's death, was reinstated some time back; I've got the papers to prove it, should the matter arise.

"And he also tells me that you are good at what you do, that you know the right people and the right places, and know how to make connections."

I shrug, attempt the hand wave. It comes across more like a stunted effort at shadow puppetry, but gets the point across. "It's part of the job."

"Indeed." Tallarico folds his hands beneath his chin, pressing his index fingers against the sides of his sunken cheeks. "He also tells me that you are loyal."

"To my friends, yes."

"And to your clients?"

"So long as they pay the bill, they deserve my allegiance."

Tallarico allows himself a touch of a grin, just that right cheek stretching up to the eyeball, but enough to tell me he's satisfied. "Mr. Rubio," he says, "you are a bright fellow, I can see that. And it would be foolish of both of us to pretend that you are ignorant of my business dealings."

I craft my response carefully and keep it short; sitting across from Frank Tallarico is not a good time to try out new verbiage from your word-a-day calendar. "I believe I know what you do for a living."

"In case you're not positive, then," he says, leaning in to me, "let's clear this up right now: I run a crime syndicate here in Los Angeles, an organization of considerable scope comprised solely of Velociraptors and working toward the common goal of amassing wealth and power for our family.

"I can tell you this without fear of reprisal for a number of reasons. First, my security experts, who have been tracking you all afternoon, tell me that you're not wearing a wire. Second, I understand that you've got something of an iniquitous past of your own, so you appreciate the value of discretion. And, most importantly, third, you are an intelligent man who knows how to connect the dots. You have heard stories about me, and you can separate the truth from the fiction. And, no doubt, you can extrapolate what would happen to you were you to tell anyone about our conversation this afternoon.

"I imagine, Mr. Rubio, that I've made myself abundantly clear."

"Sparkling."

"Excellent. Now, to my proposal: I want you to follow someone."

"That's it?"

Tallarico shifts in his chair, leaning back against the rattan. Yet another ripe orange disappears down his gullet, and now I'm getting hungry for citrus. "It sounds simple on the face of it, doesn't it? And it is, in a way. You must be discreet, but I imagine this is par for the course in your profession.

"My younger brother, Eddie, runs the Velociraptor family down in Miami. For some time now, in fact, and he's been doing a good job of it. Kind of a screwup when we were kids, but he's got his head on straight these days and I'm glad to see him doing well." He pauses, licking his lips. "Have you been down there?"

"Miami?" I ask.

"Miami, Fort Lauderdale—South Florida."

"Once," I admit. "For about three hours, in the Tampa airport."

Tallarico shakes his head. "Tampa's a different story. Tampa is a kiddie pool. The scene down there, deep in Miami . . . It's the Third World. A developing nation. The boys . . . they believe their actions go unnoticed. So for Eddie to flourish in that kind of environment . . .

"We help each other out, Eddie and me, not only because we're brothers, but because we work for the same family, despite the distance. A Raptor organization is a Raptor organization, and I'm sure you can understand that.

"Though our family holds dominance over the area, we are, unfortunately, not the only game in town. Other crews have begun to encroach on our territory. The Trike contingent has been on our backs as of late, along with a transplanted crew of Stegosaurs from Chicago. These are minor annoyances, dealt with in their own place and time.

"But we have been receiving a fair amount of trouble from a team of Hadrosaurs muscling into our space. A strong family. A growing family. Most of the time, we would say live and let live, and I'll tell you, that's how I'd like to handle this. It's a big pie, everyone gets a piece. To that end, I've organized a number of ventures with the Hadrosaur crew, in the hopes that we could work together, rather than butt heads, as has been the case."

"I'm still not sure why you're telling me this, Mr. Tallarico." I see Tommy, standing behind the mob boss, gesturing for me to hold on, to stay seated, to hear him out.

"Background, Mr. Rubio. I like my employees to go into a situation forewarned and forearmed. Now, this Hadrosaur group has sent a representative out to Los Angeles to do some business with our family. The fellow they've chosen goes by the name of Nelly Hagstrom. Does that ring a bell?"

I shake my head. "Should it?"

Tallarico shrugs. "He owns some nightclubs down on South Beach, likes to style himself a player. Gossip columns, that sort of thing. It doesn't look good for the organization, all that attention, but that's their family, and if that's how they want to play it, I couldn't care less.

"That said, I still have business to conduct with them, and with this Nelly in particular. He'll be out here for a couple of weeks, and what I suspect is that on his visit to the West Coast, my house will not be his only stop. I need to know where he goes, who he sees, and, if possible, what he says. That's why you're here today. That's why I asked to see you."

May as well make this plain, just to make sure I'm on the right track. "You want me to tail a ranking officer of a rival mob family."

"Did I say rival? Who's rivals? This is business, plain and simple. All I want is knowledge. I'm sure this is the kind of job you take on all the time."

I admit that it is. "But usually it's husbands going after their wives or insurance companies checking out suspicious claims."

"So you'll expand your horizons."

"Why don't you get one of your men to do it?" I suggest. "They seem capable."

"No doubt. But I can't have the risk of Hagstrom spotting one of them. It would not induce a sense of confidence in our business dealings if he knew I had planted a tail. No, I need someone from outside, but someone I can trust. You, Mr. Rubio, appear to be that someone."

I'm trying to find a way out of this, but my options are dwindling. "I'm very expensive."

"And I'm very rich."

"I've got a lot of cases—"

"Which you can farm out to others." With the grace of a ballet dancer, Tallarico lifts himself from the deep rattan chair and stands over me, his sunken eyes staring into mine, holding my gaze. "For the small trouble of following this Hagstrom for the next two weeks, I will gladly pay you twenty thousand dollars in cash."

"Twenty thousand," I repeat, my mouth filling with invisible wads of green paper, making it difficult to speak. "Cash."

"Or, if you wish, the equivalent in goods. You'd prefer a car? Or jewelry?"

"No, no—" I stammer, that beautiful string of zeros catching in my throat. "Cash is good."

"What you must understand is that Hagstrom and his associates are not to pick up on you, and if they do, you are never to divulge your connection to me. Is that clear?"

"Mr. Tallarico," I begin, in one last, feeble attempt to extricate myself, "I can't—"

"Please, Vincent," he insists, "call me Frank."

And that does it. I am now on a first-name basis with the Velociraptor mob boss of Los Angeles. I doubt this violates any of the actual twelve steps in my rehabilitation program, but I can't imagine it's the kind of thing that would be looked upon kindly at the next punch-and-cookies meeting.

I'm given the information on where to find Nelly Hagstrom once he reaches Los Angeles—the time and number of his flight into LAX, the hotel where he'll be staying—and instructions to report back to Mr. Tallarico—Frank—at least once every two days. And before I know it, Tommy and I are shaking Frank's hand and walking out of the solarium, one of the bodyguards right behind us. As soon as the doors are closed, the husky fellow approaches me, holding out a thick velvet bag.

"And this would be . . . ?"

"Payment."

Twenty thousand dollars, twenty bundles of ten hundreds, each neat bundle tied up with green banker's tape. Part of me wants to throw it on the ground and run; part of me wants to go buy a new stereo system. And one teensy, eensy section of my brain screams *Screw it all—it's time to hit the produce aisle!*

Tommy leads me back out of the house, and only a few yards

outside the massive oak doors, the full weight of what just happened settles upon me.

"So now I'm working for the mob," I announce, testing out the words as they hit the open air. "That's swell, Tommy. That's just swell."

"Oh, lighten up," he says. "Everybody does it."

3

The offices of Vincent Rubio Investigations, formerly the offices of Watson and Rubio Investigations, have undergone a dramatic change of late. Minsky, the squeaky little landlord who rents me the space in this Westwood office building, got hit by some Council inquiries into his cross-species dalliances, and as I was good enough to defend the little weasel in front of the Southern California chapter, Minsky cut me some slack on the monthly bill. As a result, I've had the extra wherewithal to update the furnishings. Of course, when you start out with nothing more than a table and chair, even the smallest improvement is worthy of a featured spot on *This Old House.*

So now I've got a sofa and an oak desk and some art and a coffee table and all those things I had back when it was just me and Ernie—all those things that I lost back when it was just me and the basil. A lamp, for example. With shade.

My friends down at Herbaholics Anonymous convinced me to attend a few Debtors Anonymous meetings as well, even though I was adamant that I knew how to live within my means. They brought up my bankruptcy, my repossessions, my continually vacuous bank account. I explained that I'd had some business problems recently, but that the situation had been resolved. They brought up my massive credit card bills, floating along at 21 percent interest. I blamed the lax California usury laws. They brought up my complete lack of a spending plan or anything resembling good sense regarding purchasing habits, along with my propensity to throw myself headlong into the nearest upscale department store for a quick pillage-and-loot. I had little response, other than to curl into a fetal position on the sofa and mew softly. That's what the bastards do—break you down until your natural defenses call a time-out and limp off the field. That's the first step.

Actually, the first step was to admit that I was powerless against the herb, that my life had become unmanageable. That's a slam dunk right there. My daily existence had reached the stage where any efficiency manager worth his salt would take one look around and instantly shut down the operation. So it was easy to move on to numbers two and three, which were to admit that there's a power greater than myself, and then turn my life over to His will. This was a bit of a tickler for a month or so; for any dino, even the most gung ho HA member, admitting a higher power is a toughie. You don't find many holy rollers in reptilian company. But my sponsor—a pitcher for the Los Angeles Dodgers who's good enough to score me free tickets every other week—helped me get past this by suggesting I take a look at the actual wording of the document. In its entirety, Step Three reads: "We choose to turn our will and our lives over to the care of God *as we understand him.*" This meant that as long as I understood God to mean the smile of a child and the kind word of a stranger and all that other rubbish, I was good to go, so hurrah hurrah for fine print.

Step Number Four: Make a searching and fearless moral inventory of myself.

I've been stalled there for a bit. Fearless is no problem. I'm ready to face up to whatever demons are lurking in the pits of my subconscious, and beat them back via those methods deemed necessary. It's the *searching* part I'm having trouble with. I just don't know if I have that kind of energy. A searching inventory sounds like an awful amount of work, and I don't want to go into it half-assed.

Taking a break at Step Four also keeps me from moving on to Five and the rest, even though my sponsor tells me I don't have to do them in strict order. Still, I'm a stickler for the rules when it fits me, and now I'm choosing to bring out the Felix Unger part of my personality. I will finish Step Four, and not move on until then. I'll get to it sometime after this Tallarico mess is finished; I'm sure it can wait.

Despite my reservations about taking on a case for an L.A. mob boss, the twenty grand he fronted me sure comes in handy. As part of my agreement with Debtors Anonymous, I've constructed a spending plan for myself, putting my needs first, my solvency second, and am attempting to conduct my life within those numbers. This has proven a massive failure. Unexpected purchases have arisen, and there was little I could do about it. Nordstrom's had a surprise sale in the men's department, for example, with their Armani suits going at 25 percent off, and I'm sure that everyone down at DA would agree that such an event qualifies as a valid exemption.

I have, on the other hand, tried to stay current with all my creditors and pay off as much of my considerable debt as I can whenever the cash flows my way. So it's with great relief that I call the credit card companies, the furniture dealers, the department stores, and promptly deliver a hunk of that $20,000 to its new rightful owners, leaving me with a good four grand in operating and living expenses.

Tallarico was right—I'm easily able to pawn off the other cases in my workload to the hacks down at TruTel, the PI clearinghouse owned by Mr. Teitelbaum that sends me a lot of my business. The

cks down there are more than happy to take the jobs and
wont me a 10 percent finder's fee. Sutherland, in particular, is
overjoyed with the prospect of taking on the stakeout in Inglewood; since he's been married to Teitelbaum's sister, he's shown a
sudden desire to get out of the house for extended periods of time.

So it's down to LAX, an easy twenty-minute drive from my offices during light traffic, a good fifty minutes or so the other
twenty-three hours a day. Nelly Hagstrom, according to the information given to me by Tallarico, is coming in on Delta's flight 782
out of Fort Lauderdale. I've got a blurry photograph that makes the
guy look like a Yeti, a very basic description, and instructions to tail
the Hadrosaur back to his hotel and beyond.

I arrive at the gate a few minutes before the plane touches
down and promptly busy myself, sitting on one of the uncomfortable semicushioned chairs, pretending to read this morning's
Times. I've got on a baseball cap and dark clothes, nothing to dis-
tinguish me from the thousands of other travelers in the airport
today. Baseball caps and dark clothing are to Los Angeles what
togas were to the ancient Greeks. You don't *have* to wear them, but
you stick out like a narc at a Grateful Dead concert if you don't.
Hopefully Nelly Hagstrom won't make me—that is, if I can even
make him.

But the second I see that tall, muscular body filling the space
in the jetway, that self-assured scowl as he brushes past the slower
passengers, the fine clothing draped across his broad frame, I
know I won't need to double-check the photograph. I follow him
down to the luggage carousel, where a limo driver pops up to assist
him with his bags. Prada, the new collection. The driver hauls the
heavy valises onto a cart and quickly wheels them from the termi-
nal. Hagstrom follows right behind, moving easily, fluidly; he's
been here before and knows exactly where he's going.

Fortunately, so do I. Hagstrom is staying at the Regent Beverly
Wilshire, better known to pretty much everyone outside of town as

the hotel where Julia Roberts and Richard Gere got it on in *Pretty Woman*. My agent friend Brian told me Julia's a Stegosaur, but with that lithe body, it's hard to believe. According to him, *everyone* in Hollywood is a dinosaur, only their publicists keep it well hidden with well-placed stories about their mammalian beards. Still, Julia's jaw's a dead giveaway, so I'll give Brian the benefit of the doubt on this one.

Hagstrom disappears into the hotel, and I wait outside, keeping my car idling on the small side street flanking the valet lot. I picked up another Lincoln after settling my debts with the folks down at the dealership, and though it's a used model, a few years older than I'm used to driving, it still rides like a dream. I've had the windows tinted out, 2 percent past the legal limit—that's right, I live on the edge—and it's enough to keep me safely hidden when I need to be.

Ten minutes after he enters the hotel, Nelly Hagstrom strolls back out of the Regent Beverly Wilshire's revolving doors and into the limousine. I gun the engine of the Lincoln and pull into traffic behind them, making sure to keep a few cars back. It's not hard; every ten feet, some idiot or another cuts me off. Since when did they remove the turn-signal feature from the modern automobile? Must have been the same time they decided to license the blind.

Speaking of licensing, limousines in Los Angeles are all awarded their permits via a highly technical and complicated process known as Paying A Lot Of Money. And as a result, each limo is given a TCP number, which basically designates them as an entity that may legally chauffeur others around the city and serve them as much alcohol as they choose. But as I drive behind Hagstrom's car, I notice that there's no TCP designation on it. This means one of three things—

One: the number fell off. This is nearly impossible, as the glue used is of the bumper-sticker variety, the kind of adhesive that will be around long after the twenty-megaton nuclear blasts vaporize the rest of the world. When that dark day comes and the radiation is finally falling, the freeways of L.A. will be littered with nothing but cockroaches and small rectangles proudly proclaiming MY CHILD IS AN HONOR STUDENT.

Two: the limo company is unlicensed. This is a possibility, but unlikely. The fines are stiff, the penalties greater than the benefits. Most just swallow their medicine and pay the fees and pass the costs on to their customers.

And, three, the choice I'm banking on: this is a private limo. That would mean that Hagstrom's already in touch with his other connections here in Los Angeles, as Tallarico didn't mention anything about sending a car for the guy.

I'm on the cell phone a few minutes later, dialing up the TruTel number and, after some frustration with the automated voicemail system, speaking to Cathy, Teitelbaum's secretary.

"Hey, it's Vincent."

Cathy's a mousy little mammal, plain and cool toward pretty much everyone who walks through the door. But when she hears my voice on the other end of the line, she manages to freeze up another degree or two.

"He's not in."

"I'm not calling for Mr. Teitelbaum," I tell her. "Sutherland around?"

"I'm not the receptionist—"

"I know, but she's away from her desk, and—"

"Hold."

I flip around for a radio station while waiting to be connected. Most of the stations I hit are in Spanish, and though I dig my share of salsa music, there's only so long I can listen to Latin talk radio. It's not just that I don't understand the words; I worry that they're talking about me.

"Go." The voice on the other line. It's Sutherland, the ninny.

"Go? Who says 'go'?"

"Oh, hey, Vincent. I dunno, I'm trying it out. You don't like it?"

"Look." I sigh. "I need you to run a license plate for me." I rattle off the numbers and letters, laying out exactly what I need him to do for me, down to the last detail, because Sutherland can't be trusted to think on his own. Last time that happened, I wound up with pumpernickel instead of rye and my entire sandwich was ruined. I can't believe he's a vice-president of TruTel, and all because he married the boss's sister. Seems I've been screwing the wrong people all these years.

"No problem. Thanks again for that Inglewood job, by the way—"

"Sutherland," I interrupt. "The license plate. Now."

I can hear him sulking away, the shuffle of his shoddy shoes on the TruTel linoleum floor. The clack of a keyboard; I'm glad he knows how to operate the computer, at least at a superficial level. A few moments go by, and he's back on the line.

"I couldn't find it."

"You typed it in right?"

"No, I mean I couldn't find the program. You know, we got this new computer system in here."

They got it three years ago. Sutherland's big accomplishment during that time was that he learned how to "boot up," as he put it. So I hold his cyber-hand, instructing him step-by-step on how to run a plate through the DMV registry, and soon he's got the information I'm looking for.

"It's registered to a business," he says, reading the data off the screen. "Lucky Palace Resorts, Inc. I could try to get an address for you—"

"No need," I say. "I know where it is." And before he can get in another inane word edgewise, I click off the cell and shut down the power.

Lucky Palace is a serious misnomer for the card-club gambling house down in the Norwalk region of Los Angeles. No slot machines, no roulette wheels—no "games of chance," as the legislature likes to call them—but poker and 21 and other representative "games of skill" are fully allowed. The few dinos I know who've gone there haven't gotten very lucky, and none would dare to describe it as a palace.

Which is not to say the owners don't try. The Lucky Palace has a showroom, just like the big Vegas casinos, where they spotlight aging lounge acts, just like the big Vegas casinos. And they offer a buffet for an ungodly pittance of money, just like the big Vegas casinos, where, depending on your overall digestive health, you may or may not contract food poisoning. And they've got cocktail waitresses whose combined clothing barely equals a single yard of fabric, and carpets that practically scream at you to stare away or go blind, and obscured exit signs, and ubiquitous ATM machines, and . . .

But it's missing that aura of glamour, of ostentation. When you're in Vegas, all your worldly cares drop away, replaced by a delicious haze of excess and consumption. When you're at the Lucky Palace, you're mostly worried about your car getting stolen.

Inside, the Lucky Palace is everything I expected, and less. The gaming tables are nowhere near as plentiful as they should be, the carpet nowhere near as thick. The paint on the walls is cracked in places, the ceiling tiles pocked with holes.

"You gonna play or you gonna loiter?" asks a casino guard, muscling his way up to me in a dull gray uniform.

"Does it matter?"

The guy nods. Human, no doubt. His cologne is both powerful and cheap; I wonder if he thought he'd be picking up any dates this afternoon. Chicks really dig a man with a walkie-talkie and name badge. "You can't loiter. State gaming rules. Play or move along."

"State gaming rules or Lucky Palace rules?" I ask.

He gives me a glance and reaches for his walkie-talkie, as if I'm the kind of guy on whose account you gotta call for backup. "I'm walking, I'm walking," I say, and continue my stroll down the gaudy carpet. I can't create a scene yet; Tallarico would probably look unfavorably upon having to bail my tail out of casino prison.

It takes me a while to locate Hagstrom again, but eventually I catch a whiff of his scent and follow my snout. There are a number of dinosaurs in the joint this afternoon, their smells intertwining with one another, but like a weaver at his loom, I'm able to pick up a single thread from the skein and follow it to the source.

Behind the poker room, past the bar with the free maraschino cherries and stale peanuts, is a small, sunken pit, surrounded by faux marble columns. The red velvet walls and thick umber carpet contrast with the otherwise bargain-basement decor of the Lucky Palace, and it only takes me a moment to realize I've stumbled upon the one game about which I know absolutely nothing: baccarat.

Hagstrom's inside the pit, sitting across from the house dealer at a small table. Next to him is the only other player in the room, an older gentleman with a mane of fine gray hair cascading across his shoulders. I can tease out the pine riding the air that's coming from his direction; the old guy is a reptile, no bones about it.

And now that I'm getting a good look at Hagstrom, I've got time to focus in on his face. The mask is familiar, in a way—perhaps, as Tallarico suggested, I've seen it in the gossip columns. But there's an odd scar in the center of his forehead that throws the thing out of alignment, a small patch of twisted skin that's decidedly out of place. Most of the time, cosmetic additions like these are strictly aftermarket, added in at extra expense; whatever happened to this guy's head must have been drastic enough to warrant extra guise manipulation. Then again, some dinos just get tired of walking around all day in the same old costume and dig a little body modification. I remember a few years back, all the young kids were going around getting extra moles and birthmarks sewn into their guises until the Councils cracked down on the accessories shops. Now the teens just pierce themselves silly, and no one complains.

Hagstrom looks at his partner as I enter the room and gives a little shake of his head. He doesn't seem especially thrilled that I've chosen to enter his territory.

"Afternoon, fellas," I say cordially, taking a seat next to Hagstrom.

Curt nods all around; I can't be sure that Hagstrom does anything other than grunt. But the older fellow gives me a quick once-over. "Afternoon. I haven't seen you here before."

"Usually I play up a ways."

"Up a ways? And where would that be?"

Think, Vincent, think. You've seen billboards off the 101 Freeway. "The Chumash Casino. On the Indian reservation."

"Didn't know they had baccarat," the older man says.

"Oh, they've got quite the operation."

He nods, and I can't figure out whether he's decided I'm for real or a world-class jerk. "You enjoy baccarat?" he asks.

"Of course," I say. "Sport of kings."

"Polo," Hagstrom growls. I can smell his scent now, a sharp stick of cinnamon and burnt soy.

"Excuse me?"

"Polo is the sport of kings."

"Oh," I say. "I thought it was the sport of rich assholes."

This one gets another snort of derision from Hagstrom, but a good laugh from the old guy. "Lighten up, Nelly," he says. "The fellow is here to play."

"And play I shall." I fish around for my wallet in my back pocket and pull out a couple of twenty-dollar bills. "Could I get some chips?"

Hagstrom and the dealer share a look of undisguised contempt.

Clearly I've made a boo-boo. "We use cash in the baccarat pit," the dealer informs me. "Perhaps you wish to play elsewhere."

"No, no," I insist. "Cash will do." I toss a twenty on the table. "You got change?"

Another condescending blast from the dealer's eyes. "We have a fifty-dollar minimum bet per hand."

Fifty dollars per hand? I'd better get a damned receipt for this. "Of course. Let's fire it up."

The dealer sighs and pushes a shoe of cards toward Hagstrom. "Bets?" he says.

Hagstrom snaps his fingers, and a younger fellow materializes from the darkness of the pits with a thick billfold in his hands. From his quick response and respectful mannerisms, I'd guess he's a soldier in training. Does the mafia have internships?

He hands the wad of cash to Hagstrom, who pulls four bills off the top and slides them to the dealer. "Four hundred on house."

Now all eyes are on me. It seems I've got at least two options— player or house—and it's probably best that I don't color outside the lines right now. "Player," I instruct the dealer. "Fifty. Start out light."

No response from the dealer; he turns to Hagstrom and nods. Nelly scratches the table in front of the shoe, his long fingernail dragging across the felt. Back and forth, left to right, he draws a lazy circle, keeping his eyes glued on the deck of cards.

"You really think that helps?" the old man says.

"Quiet, Douglas."

"I tell you, Nelly, I see folks come into this pit with all sorts of superstitions, and the odds play out the same every time."

Hagstrom doesn't stop scratching. "Don't get me going, old man."

We're all prisoner to Hagstrom's pre-deal ritual, waiting for our sentence to be commuted. Eventually, he lifts his hand from the table, raises it two inches above the felt, and slowly peels the top card from the shoe, caressing the plastic as if he were undressing a lover. I'm a little surprised that they're letting the players handle the cards; most casinos like to have a firm hold on that sort of thing. Maybe this is how they settle delinquent debts—working it off in the casino; the really bad gamblers have to park cars.

Hagstrom flips the card over. Eight of hearts. "Eight," the dealer announces, as if we'd all suddenly gone blind. He then draws his own card from the deck without all the pomp and circumstance, and sets it across from Hagstrom's card. Four of clubs.

"So player wins?" I ask.

Hagstrom sighs, but the older guy—Douglas, it seems—smiles as he instructs me that we're not yet done with the hand. "Closest to nine wins," he says, "after two or three cards."

"Of course." I pause, hoping he'll fill me in more, but no luck. I try for a little clarification. "Two *or* three?"

He proceeds to run through a list of arcane rules involving adding numbers to other numbers, checking them against some chart, and figuring out whether or not your moon is in Virgo, but when the cards are dealt and the game is over, I hear the sweetest words ever uttered on a gaming floor:

"Player wins."

A hundred dollars slides back into my lap. I could learn to like this game, especially if there's no need to waste my time actually understanding it.

Thirty minutes later, I'm more confused than ever, but up by nearly two thousand bucks. Nelly Hagstrom's grinding his teeth in what I can only assume is rage, because he's lost something on the order of a shitload, and doesn't seem amused that I, a complete novice, have bested the house 90 percent of the time.

"I'm done," Hagstrom growls, ripping the discarded cards in half and tossing them to the felt. "Fucking casino cheats . . ."

Douglas tries to soothe him. "Nelly, don't be that way. Last time you took us for forty thousand."

"And this time I lost it back."

Douglas shrugs. "And thus is the nature of the beast."

But the old man's platitudes do little to calm Hagstrom, as the Hadrosaur paces back and forth across the carpet of the baccarat pit, hands smoothing out his fine black wig over and over again. The young soldier stands, flanking Nelly, doing his best to stay near his boss without falling into a Rockettes-style kick line with the guy.

"I understand," Douglas says, keeping his tone soft, even. "Come, let's go on back, check out the new shipment of talent. Maybe after, you can come back, play again. On the house."

Hagstrom doesn't say a word as he and his foot soldier storm out of the baccarat pit and onto the main casino floor. Douglas turns to shake my hand. "You take care," he says to me. "And good luck."

"You too," I call back.

He gives a little laugh, shakes his head, and walks after Hagstrom and his partner. I watch as the three of them disappear into a small, unmarked door near the poker room, then turn back to the dealer.

"He wasn't making any bets," I say.

"Who?"

"The older one."

The dealer nods as he breaks open a brand-new deck of cards and runs them through an automatic shuffler. "Doesn't have to. He owns the joint."

"That Douglas guy?"

"Doug Triconi," the dealer tells me. "Bought it from the original owners a few years ago. Pretty swell boss, as bosses go."

I should process this information. I should get out of here fast and prepare to tail Hagstrom again and, in my free time, check out all I can about Douglas Triconi so I'm better informed when I give my update to Tallarico. But as I rise from the table, my hand grasping the green, green bills on the felt, the dealer's shadow falls over me.

"Play again, sir?"

I look down at the cards, at the new deck shining inside that shoe. At the reflective plastic, never before touched by skin or guise. And I think about the feeling of flipping them over, the terrible and wonderful anticipation of those bright-red and deep-black numbers.

"Just one more," I agree, falling back into that comfortable chair and pushing my money into the center of the table. "For the road."

4

hree thousand dollars later, I'm out of the Lucky Palace with half my bank account and a small shred of dignity intact. My operating expenses have now dwindled to about twenty-five hundred dollars, and I dread the prospect of having to ask Frank Tallarico for more cash. It's not in good taste, and, physically speaking, it's not in my own self-interest.

Hagstrom eschewed the limo on his way out of the Lucky Palace, opting for a cab to take him back to the Regent Beverly Wilshire for a quick change of clothes, then another one up into the Palisades, where he disappeared behind the Tallarico gates. I'm sure Frank doesn't need me to tail the guy when he's in his own abode, so I figure I've got a short bit of time to knock off and get in a rest back at the office.

As I pull into the small underground parking lot in the Westwood office building where Vincent Rubio Investigations resides, I notice with dismay that someone has parked in my space. This despite the large sign with my photograph on it plastered to the wall, the words below reading: IF THIS IS NOT YOU, DO NOT PARK HERE. So either I've got a doppleganger waiting for me upstairs or I'll be calling the towing company.

I pull into a spot on the street and trot up the stairs to my office, grumbling all the way about the little Ford crapmobile whose owner is either illiterate or rude, when I hear a familiar voice rocketing down the stairwell.

"Don't even start. Don't even fucking *start* on me. The guest spots were all taken, and you can deal with it for once and not give me a world of grief."

Glenda Wetzel is standing at my door. Five-foot-four, foul mouth eight feet wide, smelling of carnations and old baseball gloves, this gal has saved my butt twenty times in the last few years. Five or six on the McBride investigation alone. I drop my valise and envelop her in a hug; she pulls me in tight, her strong arms catching my midsection. "Jesus, it's good to see you," I say.

"You getting sleep?"

"Yeah," I reply. "Why?"

"You're dragging, that's all. Looking about one step up from dog crap."

I nod. "Lost a few bucks at baccarat."

"Bacca-*what*?"

"Don't ask. What the hell are you doing here?"

Glenda puts out a hand and checks my brow for a fever. Not that this would work anyway, what with her glove and my mask blocking the actual scale-to-scale contact, not to mention the fact that my relatively cold blood almost always matches itself to the ambient temperature. But this is yet another of the mammalian habits we've picked up for ourselves over the years; it gets so we hardly even notice it anymore.

"Don't tell me you forgot," she says.

Of course I forgot. "Of course I didn't forget."

Almost laughing now, shaking her head, surprised and yet not. "Rubio . . . you're a friggin' piece of work. Two months ago I said I was coming out to L.A., you said I could crash at the office, I said don't put yourself out, you said don't worry about it . . ."

"Right . . . right . . ." I have no clue as to what she's talking about.

Glenda gives me a look—one of *those* looks. The one that's wondering if I fucked up again. "You're not . . . You been going to meetings, right?"

"Every few days. Almost ten months clean and sober."

Glenda nods. It's a fair question—this certainly seems like a blackout situation if ever there was one. But I've been off the herb and amnesia-free for months now. Still, if she says we had the conversation, then we had the conversation. "Come on in," I tell her, unlocking the door and throwing it wide. "Mi casa es su casa."

Glenda pats me on the back and strolls into my office. "*Casa* means house, Rubio."

"House, office, whatever. I got a sofa, and it's all yours."

She's got a few bags by her feet, and I heft them off the ground, nearly straining my back in the process. I can't believe they allowed this much weight on the plane from New York. "Planning on bartering some of this molten metal while you're here?"

Glenda reaches for a suitcase and helps drag it into the office foyer. "Gal's gotta have a choice of clothes," she says.

"How long were you planning on staying again?"

A long, slow stare, like I'm in the zoo and she's wondering whether or not to toss me a peanut. "You really don't remember our conversation, do you?"

I'm trying—really, I am—but nothing emerges from the muddy depths.

"They said this would happen. Post-chew blackouts, they call 'em. My brain got used to forgetting things when I was on the herb, so now that I'm clean, sometimes it picks up the slack and drops out for a few hours." I strain to recall anything about our last conversation, over a month ago. "I remember . . . we were talk-ing . . . you were having some money problems. It was getting pretty bad, you told me."

Glenda shakes her head. "That's all done now. I'm good again."

Before I can admit to my complete lack of brain power regard-ing our supposed chat, the phone rings. I drop her suitcase to the floor—the resultant shock waves will probably set off seismo-graphs up at Cal Tech—and lift the receiver.

"Vincent Rubio Investigations."

"Come up to the house." It's Tallarico. Not entirely thrilled.

"Mr. Tall—Frank. I actually just left your place. Isn't Hagstrom still—"

"I'll expect you in a half hour."

Before I can get in another word, he's off the line and I'm hold-ing a dead phone.

"Client?" Glenda asks.

"Unfortunately." I check my watch; it's nearing five o'clock, which means I'll be lucky to make it out to the Palisades in less than forty minutes. "Can you wait here for me? We can head out for a quick dinner when I get back."

Glenda shrugs and hoists one of her massive suitcases onto the black leather sofa.

"It's gonna take me a while to get unpacked anyway," she says. "You got a closet I can use?"

"Broom closet," I tell her. "Kinda musty, kinda small."

"Remember my apartment back in the Village?" She grins.

"You'll feel right at home."

"Douglas Triconi is the second-in-command of the Los Angeles Brontosaur contingent," Tallarico informs me. We're back in the solarium, sitting on those rattan chairs. I wonder if he ever leaves this place. "He used to live out in South Florida—Boca, I think—

and came out west a few years back to increase the family stock. Got his claws in a lotta different pies."

I nod. It's all information I gleaned from some calls I placed on the way to Tallarico's estate. It's always easy to get the skinny on mobsters if you know folks at the local newspapers; mafia-watching is like a hobby to them. There's probably a field guide out there somewhere.

"And he owns the Lucky Palace."

"Technically," Tallarico corrects me. "The family owns it, but it's in Triconi's name. He's no concern of mine."

"At least," I say, "he hasn't been. He and Hagstrom disappeared for a while. It was a private room. I couldn't follow."

Tallarico understands. "They mention business?"

"Triconi did. Said something about a 'talent pool'—I didn't really understand it. But it was clearly more than a social engagement."

Frank absorbs this information, his long fingers gripping the sides of the chair. He stares up at the trees surrounding us, as if the leaves will have the answer he's searching for. Maybe they do; he could have crib notes on those things.

"We move on," he says finally, rubbing his palms together.

"I should follow him again?"

"You should," says Frank. With a grunt, he pops out his human dentures, the glue sucking against the roof of his mouth as he pulls them free. His pointed Raptor teeth glint in the fading light, and his tongue licks the razor-sharp tips. "But there's a bit of a twist."

This is how it always starts. One little variation, a teensy bit of snow teetering on the edge of a hill, and by the time it's all over I'm digging my way out from under an avalanche. "A twist?"

"Hagstrom's going home."

"To Miami?"

"Our business meeting did not go as expected."

I don't press for details; I don't want to know. "So . . . you want me to tail him to the airport, make sure he gets on the plane, that sort of thing?" I've been run out of enough cities in my time to know the protocol.

Tallarico shakes his head. "Not quite."

I'm afraid I can see where this is going, but I don't want to put ideas into anyone's head. Better to sit back and force him to come up with it on his own.

"I've paid you a fair amount of money to do a job," he continues, "and I expect that job to be done."

"As it was," I say, "I followed him from LAX, as requested. I kept a tail on him back to the hotel, out to the casino, returning to the hotel, out to your place . . ."

Frank nods, takes my hand in his, pats the back of it, softly, slowly. Oh, this is not good at all. "And you have done a wonderful job. I couldn't ask for more."

"But . . . ?"

"But I'm asking for more."

"Frank—"

"You will follow Nelly Hagstrom back to South Florida," Tallarico tells me curtly, turning in his chair to bring the full weight of his stare upon me. I can feel it, crushing against my sternum, like the time I tried to bench press twice my weight to impress a cute little Ornithomimus I'd been intent on dating and instead ended up in the emergency room with chest pains. "You will be my eyes and ears down there, and we'll remain in contact through my brother."

"Wait, wait," I say, trying to give myself a little space, some time to think. "Before, you were worried about your guys getting spotted, and you wanted to use me 'cause I'm an L.A. boy. But down in Miami . . . I don't know the area. I don't know the people I know here."

"And that's a benefit to me," he responds. "You can go in fresh, give me your observations unclouded."

I know, deep down, that I'm powerless to stop what's about to happen, but it doesn't mean I can't put up a fight. Even a drowning man claws at the water a few times before going under for good. Three is supposedly the magic number, but I doubt I'll get more than one shot at this.

"I've got a cat," I say lamely. The tabby cat in question is really just a mongrel who begs for food near my office. Every day or so I put out a platter of tuna and milk, so the little critter's gotten a bit attached. "Who's going to feed him?"

Tallarico doesn't even bother with that excuse.

"I've got house guests," I try. "A friend from New York, she came down just this morning—"

"And she can join you, if she wants. You'll stay with my brother, and I'll even front you for expenses. Think of it as a vacation. Everyone goes to Miami eventually, yes? The fun, the surf, the parties till dawn."

"I guess, but—"

"Vincent," Tallarico says, "let me make this decision easy for you."

"I wish you would."

"Your answer is yes."

"It is?" I ask.

"And I'll tell you why: the number twenty, followed by three zeroes."

The cash. His cash. His cash that became my cash that quickly became other people's cash.

"It was a fee."

"It was a fee to follow Nelly Hagstrom for two weeks."

"He was supposed to be in Los Angeles," I protest.

"And now he is not," Tallarico says plainly. He plucks a leaf from a nearby plant and sticks it in the corner of his mouth, chewing hard, sucking the sap from the useless fiber. "Things happen. Plans change. And I would venture to say that twenty thousand dollars for one day of surveillance is an awfully high price, even for the upscale market here in the City of Angels."

"I can pay you back."

A bit of interest on his part. He leans in. "Today?"

"Not exactly," I stammer. "But I'm sure we can work out a payment plan."

This gets him going. For a moment, I think I can see the yellow in those eyes shining through the dark-brown contact lenses.

"You listen to me," he growls, grasping the front of my shirt with one surprisingly strong hand, pulling me close, nearly ripping the fabric. "Payment plans are for banks. Do I look like a bank?"

It's an incredibly stupid question, but this is not the time to point that out. "Of course not."

"Which means that you have two options. Return my twenty thousand dollars, in cash, right now, or get your ass down to Miami on the next flight out."

He leans back in the chair, suddenly calm once again. A lackey brings him a new set of flat, mammalian dentures, and he pops them into his mouth, covering up the last traces of his true reptilian nature.

"Tell me, Mr. Rubio," he says, a single drool of saliva dripping down his lower lip, "do you have the cash?"

My lack of an answer is answer enough. Frank Tallarico smiles and offers me a final bit of advice: "Pack sunscreen."

On the drive from the Palisades back toward Westwood, I try to rationalize the situation. Sure, I'm working for a mobster known to make little distinction between his friends and enemies when the time for killin' comes. Sure, I'm heading into a pit of similar vipers, any of whom might off me on the slightest provocation. And, sure, there's no telling how deep I'll get in this thing before I'm finally cut loose to float away on my own.

But, hey, a free trip to Miami is a free trip to Miami. I feel like I've picked door number three and found out I won both the dream vacation *and* the booby prize.

I could go on the run, I guess, play it on the lam and keep an eye on my back. But Frank Tallarico doesn't strike me as the kind of guy who takes a forgive-and-forget approach when his money's involved. And though it would be easy enough to purchase a black-market guise, have my scent glands removed, and relocate to North Dakota, I don't relish a lifestyle of paranoia. I don't want to be worried that the guy playing Willy Loman in a Fargo dinner-theater production of *Death of a Salesman* is going to jump off the stage, grab a butter knife, and make me the main attraction for the evening.

I suppose I could appeal to Tallarico's better nature, but I think I've seen that side of him already. *Better* is a relative term.

By the time I make it back to my office in Westwood, I've re-signed myself to my fate. Glenda is waiting inside, stretched out on the sofa, dressed in a long skirt and cotton blouse.

"You have your meeting?" she asks me.

"Uh-huh."

"Go okay?"

"Sure."

I move past her, toward the closet. There's a shirt in there that I like for the hot days. It's linen, and though I can't feel it against my natural skin, it falls nicely over the guise. I pull off my white button-down shirt and toss it across a nearby chair, mindlessly fastening the new one across my chest, Glenda staring me down, hard.

"You doing all right?" she asks.

"I'm fine," I tell her flatly. "Decisions had to be made. They were made."

"Such as?"

"Such as where to go to dinner," I say.

"And?"

I tuck my shirt into my pants, smoothing out the few wrinkles I can see as I set aside a few bowls of Whiskas for the tabby cat that lives outside. "How do you feel about something . . . tropical?"

5

feel it as soon as they open the airplane doors. There's the slight whoosh of pressurized air being released, the sudden venturi effect as a vortex of wind whips through my hair, and then there it is, all around me, pressing in from every direction.

"Do you feel that?" I ask Glenda. We're standing in the aisle of the airplane, waiting for the geniuses in front of us to figure out how to open the overhead baggage compartment.

"Feel what?" she asks, looking around.

"No, no. That. This. In the air."

She stops for a moment, eyes cast before her, and then I see the change wash over her face, the curl at the corners of her lips, the squinch of the eyes. "Ew," she says simply.

"Ew," I repeat. It's the only word we can use.

Velociraptors are not great swimmers. Our arms are too underdeveloped, our bodies nowhere near buoyant enough to make the action either simple or entertaining. But, like all good human impersonators, we learn to paddle around a pool so we can fit in at little Timmy's birthday party. No one wants to sit alone by the punch bowl all afternoon.

So, when we're children, we take swimming lessons, which mostly consist of the instructors—former SS officers, I have no doubt—tossing us into a pool and yelling at us not to drown. I can still remember the first time I hit the deep end, feeling all that liquid surrounding my body for the first time, believing for a moment that I was surrounded not by water, but by impossibly heavy air.

Almost as if I could breathe it in, if I really gave it my all. Like I could walk around on the bottom of the pool for hours, my limbs moving slowly but steadily ahead, my hair perpetually damp, my chest slowly moving in and out as my lungs transformed into gills, sucking in the water and processing it into pure oxygen.

Welcome to Miami.

"Is that . . . humidity?" I ask Glenda.

"That's what they call it."

I shake my head. This can't be right. "Maybe there's a problem with the airport heater or something."

"It's August in South Florida, Vincent," Glenda chides, pulling her small carry-on bag out from under the seat. "What did you expect?"

"To breathe."

By the time I make it off the plane and through the jetway, I'm already feeling a bit sticky inside my guise. I wonder if there's an attachment I can buy that will help dissipate the moisture forming beneath my latex; perhaps there's a whole catalogue. If not, I should start up a business down here; I could make a killing.

The Miami Airport is wonderfully air-conditioned, though, and within moments I'm chilly and happy all over again. There's still that feeling that the air around me has weight, a tactile presence, but it's not cloying anymore. Not yet, at least—we still have to go back outside to hail a cab. If I'm lucky, they've domed and air-cooled the entire city. I can't think of a better use of taxpayer money.

But as we step off the escalator into the baggage-claim area, I realize that a cab won't be necessary. Tallarico, true to his word, has called ahead and made arrangements.

VINCENT RUBINO reads the sign in the limo driver's hand, and it's close enough for me. "Good evening," I say, heaving my carry-on atop the driver's cart.

"Hey, hey," he yelps, yanking the bag back onto the floor, "I'm waiting for someone." His accent is clipped but clearly Latino, the shortened syllables quite different from the drawled Mexican accents I'm used to back in L.A.

"Yeah, that's me. That's us."

"You're Rubino?"

"Rubio."

"My sign says Rubino."

"Yeah, and your sign is wrong. If you're here from Eddie Tallarico, then you're here for me. Vincent *Rubio*." I stick out my hand, trying to remain polite. No need to get into an argument here and now; I've already got a record with the airport police back in Memphis—don't ask, don't ask—and I don't need a rap sheet in South Florida, too.

"You don't look like a Rubio."

I shrug. It's not the first time I've heard that. "Sorry to burst your bubble."

He doesn't give. "You look more like a Lerner. Or a Carter. I picked up a Carter last week."

"That's fascinating." I can feel my temperature rising, and it's not the humidity getting to me.

Ten minutes and a few narrowly averted arguments later, Glenda, the driver—his name, I have learned, is Raoul—and I stroll through the automatic doors and into the lower level of Miami International Airport, where I nearly choke on the exhaust fumes hugging the air. My vacation has begun.

The limousine I expected turns out to be a beat-up Dodge Caravan without air conditioning, but beggars can't be choosers, and at least I don't have to wait around for a taxi. As we drive away from the airport, I stare out the windows at what passes for the local scenery. They never put airports in particularly nice areas; there aren't a lot of flight patterns zooming over Beverly Hills, for example. But we seem to be shooting past some particularly skeevy streets; I'm glad the speed limit is somewhere around sixty, and that the driver's added a good twenty miles per hour for good measure.

"What are the sunbursts for?" Glenda asks. She's pointing to the large signs hung above the freeway, upon which cheery cartoon suns have been painted in a bright orange glow.

"For the tourists," our driver tells us.

"What, they're gonna confuse it for the actual sun?"

The driver shakes his head. "You follow the sunbursts. Takes you to the beach. Takes you to the resorts."

"And if you don't follow the sun?" I ask.

He jerks a thumb out the window, toward another decrepit area, the small homes and buildings rife with crumbling plaster, the lawns thick with weeds and rusted-out cars. Graffiti everywhere, streetlights busted. "You end up in there."

Soon we're past the slums and merging onto another freeway, and the driver is telling us about his childhood in Cuba, about the freedom they had there until Fidel swept in and ruined it all. "So you came over . . . when?" asks Glenda.

"Seventy-nine," he says. "The boatlifts."

I remember reading about it at the time. Castro, in an attempt to cleanse his country of what he considered undesirables, shipped Cuba's prisoners off to Miami, where they were promptly detained and, eventually, released into the South Florida ecosystem. Sort of like a wildlife preserve, only the INS officials didn't get to wear any cool zookeeper outfits.

"You were in prison?" I ask.

The driver clucks his tongue. "That what you think? That the Mariel lifts were for convicts?"

"That's what everybody thinks."

He turns in the seat, his body twisted, his eyes clearly no longer on the road. It doesn't seem to affect his driving, but it sure as hell affects my ability to remain calm.

"That's what they *wanted* you to think—"

"Hey, you wanna look at the road?"

"The media," he continues, paying no attention to my protests, "they worked it so we all looked like convicts, right? Uh-uh. It was a racial thing, that's what it was."

"Great—can you watch the—"

"A *racial* thing, my friend—"

"Fine, it was racial, it was racial. Turn the fuck around—"

He casually spins back in his seat and retakes control of the wheel, unconcerned that we were moments away from imminent death. Glenda doesn't seem to have cared much, either; she's more interested in his story. "Racial?" she asks. "You were all Cuban."

"No, no," he says. "*Racial.* Castro . . . he never like the Raptors, you know? That's who he kicked out. Now, no more Raptors in Cuba."

"He's one of us?" I ask. I'd always assumed the guy to be human. The beard, the cigar—his entire look is too comical for any guise manufacturer to take seriously.

"No," my driver says somberly. I can see his jaw grinding, the teeth clenched down hard. "He is not a Raptor. He is not one of *us.*"

Glenda shoots me a quick look, preparing to open her mouth and give this guy a taste of her Hadrosaur charm, but I give a head-shake to cut her off at the pass. We encounter a fair amount of racial prejudice in our job; it's part and parcel when you deal with lowlifes, mammal or reptile. But in L.A., I've got the equilibrium worked out. I generally know when it's coming, and from who, and Glenda's got her own thing going in New York. But down here, we're both babes in the woods. Better to tread carefully and keep our mouths shut, at least for the time being.

Ten minutes later we're flying over a wide causeway, the water beneath us shining in the strong August moonlight. Sticking out from the causeway like twigs off a branch are two-lane roads, each leading to its own small island. I can make out a few houses in the distance, their yards butting up against the lapping surf. There are swimming pools out there. Gazebos. Tennis courts.

"This a good area?" I ask.

"Celebrities, politicians," the driver tells me. "It's nice. If you like that sort of thing."

I like, I like. Despite my aforementioned aversion to swimming and the fact that the only time I ever played tennis I ended up with a tail bruise and a bucketful of humiliation, the concept of a home with these amenities is still something to which I'm attracted. Perhaps it's the materialistic side of my nature. Then again, if there's a nonmaterialistic side, I'm currently unaware of it. I should probably try to locate that facet of my personality; it might be able to help out with the credit card bills.

One of these small clumps of land, I soon learn, is named Star Island, and it is onto this small bridge that our Caravan veers. We pass by a guardhouse and a set of gates, and make a few short turns down perfectly manicured roads. The homes are difficult to see from the street; most are set back behind their own private fences, with ample foliage to block the view.

We arrive at Eddie Tallarico's place a few moments later, and while I'm impressed with the overall magnitude of the joint, it's clear that maintenance hasn't been an issue around here recently. Tall weeds choke off the landscaping; paint peels from the house's facade. It's a Mediterranean-style home, rolled tile roof, white stucco walls, spots of bright color accenting the window and door frames, but whatever money was put into the house must have busted the bank. Either that, or they just don't care about the place anymore.

Raoul takes our bags and hustles us inside, where the theme of neglect continues. The carpets are worn, lightbulbs are blown, and the air smells of smoke and mildew. Raoul leads us to our rooms, two small spaces off a main hallway, a single bed in each one.

"You want the one with the faded wallpaper or the smell of cat pee?" I ask Glenda.

"Considering I already flew from New York to L.A.—in coach—and now you've dragged my ass down to South Florida—in coach—"

"Right, right," I say. "I'll take the cat pee."

Raoul throws our bags on our respective beds and asks, "You would like to see Mr. Tallarico?"

"We've got a choice in this?"

Raoul shrugs and leads us back down the hall and through a wide living room. The television is tuned to some cop show, the speaker blaring out with guns blasting. Five men huddle around the set, sitting cross-legged on the floor, the single sofa behind them unused. They're in jackets and slacks, their clothing rumpled, worn. A perfect living match to the decor.

"Hey," one says, a fellow with a tight monobrow and gruff voice.

"Hey," I say back, unsure whether or not I'm supposed to know the guy. Another one is giving Glenda the once-over, and she pointedly turns away. Good gal. This isn't the time or place to pick a fight.

As we head through the living room, a petite Asian girl—no more than sixteen, seventeen—enters through another door, carrying a tray of food. Her skin is a dark chestnut brown, her features delicate, innocent, untouched by time. But she doesn't move like a teenager; her gait is slow, paced, her back stooped, as if a heavy weight has been placed upon her shoulders. I watch as she sets the tray down in the middle of the men and receives, for her efforts, a few slaps on the rump. She disappears through the same door she entered.

"C'mon," Raoul says. "Boss is waiting."

We move up a set of narrow stairs, the walls feeling as if they're pressing in, rubbing against my shoulders. It's not an illusion; the plaster is cracking, splintering out where the walls have begun to bend inward, and our combined weight on the staircase can't be helping things. I'm relieved when we reach the top without causing any more damage.

Raoul raps lightly on the wooden door. "Mr. Tallarico?" he calls out. "It's Raoul. I come back from the airport."

There's no answer. Raoul presses his ear to the door, wiggling his lanky body, pressing it against the frame. "Sometimes, the boss . . . he does not like to be disturbed."

Great, another moody Tallarico. Just what the world needs. Raoul knocks again, and this time, a high, nasal voice calls back, "What is it already?"

"It is Raoul."

"Go away, Raoul."

"I have come back from the airport. With the guests from Los Angeles."

Silence. Glenda and I share a look. Raoul shrugs. He presses his ear against the door again, his body weight firm against the wood, and suddenly it swings wide, dropping the driver to the floor.

Eddie Tallarico looks nothing like his brother. The facial structure, the features themselves . . . night and day. Most guise manufacturers will try to include certain familial traits when a fraternal set is ordered. Not here—the two might as well be from different species, let alone families. And the substructure, as far as I can tell, differs even more. Whereas Frank Tallarico is thin, almost to the point where he could strut the fashion runways of Paris, Eddie has a paunch on him, a serious gut that I don't think is part of the guise. Sure, there are places where you can order body-modification attachments like the Bill Shatner Love Handles or the Orson Welles Insta-Belly—how do you think De Niro gained and lost all that weight for *Raging Bull?*—but to my untrained eye, that's not just garb. That's gobble.

But if you put me in a room with Frank Tallarico, his younger brother, Eddie, and a thousand other dinosaurs, then blindfolded me and spun me in a circle until I was ready to lose my lunch, I could still pick these two out from the crowd in an instant. Their scents are nearly identical.

Smells are visceral for me, almost hypnagogic. I can't speak for all dinos, but I imagine it's the same way for them, as well. I get mental pictures with every whiff I manage to catch. The cleaning lady who comes in to scrub down the office floors, for example, has a buttery-maple-syrup smell, and damn it all if I don't get an image of Aunt Jemima rocking on her porch every time she comes in with her mop and broom. I can be looking right at her, wishing her a good morning, suggesting places that need to be scrubbed extra carefully, but some part of my brain sees that old black woman laugh and rock and laugh and rock.

So it's the same image that pops into my mind when I smell Eddie Tallarico as it was when I sniffed down on his brother, Frank: a construction crew, eating lunch. Something about that tar, about that molasses, and I can't escape it. There they are, a couple of burly guys up on the scaffolding, opening up their metal lunch boxes to reveal the sandwiches their old ladies packed that morning.

"In," says Eddie, barely clearing a path for me to scoot by his belly and into the room. Glenda follows, and Eddie nudges Raoul back out into the stairwell before slamming the door in his face. After a moment, I hear the Cuban stomping back down the crumbling stairway, muttering under his breath.

This small study is packed with papers piled three feet high, barely a spare inch of floor on which to stand. Glenda and I shuffle around each other, trying to find a space to make ourselves comfortable. It's simply not possible.

"He drive okay?" Eddie asks us.

"Who?"

"Raoul. He drive you here okay?"

I nod. The guy was a little heavy on the gas pedal, but I see no reason to make a federal case out of it. "Yeah, peachy." I thrust out my hand; the guy's providing room and board, and I'm trying to remember my manners. "Thanks for having us here. I'm Vincent."

"I know who you are," he says, ignoring my proffered handshake. "My brother gave me the scoop." He looks toward Glenda. "Her I don't know."

"And vice versa," she says. I shoot her a look, and she backs off. "Glenda Wetzel."

Eddie doesn't look entirely satisfied. He shuffles across the room, keeping his eye on us as he moves. "Okay, do your thing."

"Our . . . *thing*?" I ask.

"Strip, strip, go."

Glenda takes the reins. "Strip?"

Eddie sits behind his desk, his belly coming to rest on the wooden top. The chair squeaks something awful, and I resist the urge to whip out some lip balm and grease the thing down. "You think I'm gonna take you on your word who you are? I got twenty security systems in here ready to take you out if you make one move, ten guys downstairs who'll be up here in a heartbeat, and you think I'm just gonna accept you on your *word*?"

"That's what we were hoping," I say. "We didn't make Raoul show us ID at the airport."

"Your ass, your call. This is my ass, my house, and my call, so shut up and strip."

"You want us all the way down?" Glenda asks.

"All the way, sister."

I've never had a problem with nudity; I just like it better when it's someone else doing the stripping. But, as a rule, most dinosaurs don't have the same hang-ups about baring their behinds as do our mammalian counterparts.

So I get the ball rolling by whipping off my clothes, pants and shirt first, undergarments last, and, almost instantly, I feel better about the overall climate. South Florida could be a grand place to live if only it weren't for clothing. Bring on the humidity—I'm naked and free.

But not totally naked, which is how Tallarico wants me. I quickly set to work on my guise, pulling at the hidden buckles and buttons, unfastening the straps and loosening the clamps. It takes a while to release the G-series—I need to have that looked at by a professional tailor when I get a chance—but soon enough my human costume lies limp on the ground, splayed out over the assorted papers, and I'm au naturel in the middle of the room.

I'm not quite sure what he's looking for—my only weapons are my claws and tail, the implements of any proper dino. But if I pass muster, I pass muster, and I'm not going to argue it.

"Yeah, all right," Tallarico barks at me. "Now her."

"You gonna stare at me the whole time?" Glenda asks as she removes her clothes, gently laying them on a nearby chair.

"That was the plan, sweetheart."

Glenda's guise comes with all the right curves in all the right places, and, revealed piece-by-piece as it is, I'm struck by the workmanship. The seams are impossible to detect, the skin smooth and flawless. Nipples perked right to perfection, everything flawlessly symmetrical.

But I've seen Glenda in her bare human skivvies before, come to think of it, and I don't recall the design or craftsmanship as being particularly outstanding. Did she swap guises sometime in the last six months?

"What is that?" asks Eddie, also clearly impressed. "Taihitsu?"

Glenda shakes her head as she continues removing her garments. "DuBochet," she says with a wink. The panties come down.

"Couture?" I ask, surprised.

"Only the best."

"Thought you were a ready-to-wear kinda gal."

"Tastes change," she tells me. Never figured her for the fashionable blushing type, but maybe she's tired of the tomboy-with-an-attitude shtick. Maybe she's ready to move along. Still, I'm surprised that she could come up with the scratch to buy a DuBochet, especially after our late-night phone calls wherein we both bemoaned our lack of funds. A DuBochet isn't your everyday catalogue or boutique wear. That's the kind of guise you see strutting down the red carpet come Oscar night.

"Nice gams," Eddie says, "but off with 'em, and fast. I got a business to run here."

Glenda starts with her G-clamps, and doesn't have her tail halfway out of the straps before Tallarico is on his feet, pushing back from his desk with an excited grunt.

"Out!" he shouts, waving his arm through the air. "I knew it! I shoulda smelled it on ya—"

"Whoa, whoa," I say, stepping in front of Glenda, shielding her from the stocky man's wild gestures. "Let's take a breath, here."

"You take a breath. She can take her goddamned Hadrosaur ass outta here."

"Now, wait a second," I start.

"No discussion," Tallarico yells. He's worked himself into a miniature tornado of activity, limbs flailing about as he butts up against me, against Glenda, bouncing her around the room like a sumo wrestler gone batty. "She's outta my house, outta my goddamned sight—"

"What the fuck?" Glenda shouts back. "You wanted me to undress, so I undressed."

"And you thought you were gonna sneak in here—"

"What?"

"—under the radar, just slide in and stay as a guest in my house, with my family." Tallarico edges forward another step, and it's getting hard to keep him at bay. "Wait until we got all cozy with ya, real friendly-like, then creep outta bed in the middle of the night and slit our throats. That the way it was planned out?"

Glenda throws her hands in the air and restraps her tail in place. I can see it quivering a bit, the tip shaking back and forth with anger. "I don't know what the fuck you're talking about," she says, "but you got a lot to learn about being a host."

As an outsider to this little argument, I feel honor-bound to make some sense of it. "I'm sure we can solve the problem," I say. "Let's talk this out rationally."

"Ain't nothing to talk about," Tallarico says. "Raptors stay. Everyone else—goddamned Hadros, especially—can make themselves scarce."

"So this . . . this is a racial problem?"

"Fuck racial," Tallarico spits. "This is smarts. You think I lived this long trusting one of *them*?"

I'm about to protest again, to put up a fight for Glenda, but she waves it off. She's got her bra and underwear on, hurriedly redressing, and I can see that she's already donned a mask of nonchalance. It's a brave front. "Forget it," she says. "I know where this prick's coming from."

"I bet you do," Eddie grunts.

"I'll find a hotel," Glenda tells me, her voice shaking a bit at the edges.

"Glen—"

"No, it's fine. Hey, business is business, right?"

I look at Tallarico, at that satisfied smirk spreading across his wide face. The kind of grin you just want to introduce to the business end of a shovel. "I'll come with you," I say, reaching down for my own straps and buckles. "We'll find a nice place on South Beach to hole up."

"Uh-uh," Eddie says, yanking my P-clamp from my hands and tossing it over his shoulder. It lands with a clang upon his desk and disappears into a mountain of papers.

"What the—that's my only one—"

"My brother said I gotta keep a watch on you."

"Yeah, and he also said you'd put up my friend."

Eddie shrugs. "Frank know she was a Hadrosaur?"

"He didn't ask."

"Then it don't matter what he said. You're down here to work for the family, you stay where I can see you."

The money. He knows about it, of course. Frank's not shy about such matters.

"Oh yeah," he continues, picking up where my thoughts left off. "I know what you're in for, pal. Twenty large, and I don't see you forking it over any time soon. So till your two weeks are up, you'll be staying right under my thumb. As for her . . ." Eddie reaches into his back pocket and pulls out a fat black wallet, the leather bursting with old receipts and useless business cards. Plucking a few twenty-dollar bills from within, he crumples them into a ball and tosses them at Glenda's feet. "That's for the striptease." He chuckles, and turns back to his desk.

This time it's Glenda who restrains me from attacking the corpulent son of a bitch, firmly grabbing my upper arm and delivering a slow, meaningful head shake.

"He's not worth it," she says quietly. "Not now."

It only takes her a few more moments to completely dress and gather her wits, Tallarico no longer paying us any attention, his head bent over the desk, shuffling papers back and forth.

"Thank you for your graciousness," she says without a hint of sarcasm. "You have a lovely house."

Eddie mumbles, "They'll call you a cab downstairs," and waves his hand in that dismissive gesture mastered by the Tallarico family. I get a quick hug, a peck on the cheek.

"I'll call you when I find a place," Glenda tells me. "Keep your cell on."

I want to fix this, to tell her to stay, to piggyback along on her ride across the causeway, but I'm in a bind. The same forces that sent me down here to Miami are keeping me inside this house, and there's nothing I can do about it. Before I can even mutter any salutations, Glenda is out the door and down the stairs, and I'm alone in the study with Eddie Tallarico.

"So . . ." I say, unsure of where to begin or end. "That's it? We done?"

He stops messing with the papers on his desk, raises his thick eyebrows at me. "You think that was wrong, what I did?"

"I think that was chickenshit," I tell him. He might own my ass, but not my mouth.

Instead of the rage I expect, Tallarico just shrugs. "You ain't from here, you don't get it. Can't trust no one but your own kind. 'Specially Hadros."

"Sounds a little paranoid to me."

Tallarico shrugs. "I'm alive. And I'm tired. You gonna stand here and bug me all night or you gonna do your job?"

I'm not in any particular mood to do my so-called job—whether or not impersonating a Lo-Jack is an actual job is something I don't need to argue right now—but I certainly have no urge to spend any more time with Tallarico than necessary. "You want me to find Hagstrom?" I ask.

"We're paying you to keep your eyes and ears open."

"They're open."

"Not here," he sighs. "Go, yes. Out. Talk to the boys downstairs, they'll tell you where to get started."

And with that, he's working again, that feverish look to his eyes, hands flipping pages back and forth. It barely looks likes he's giv-

ing the papers a good glance. I wonder if there are words on them.
I wonder if he can actually read.

Downstairs, the motley group of fellows still surrounds the
television set, only now the show is some raunchy sitcom that
forces a few laughs out of the group every ten seconds or so. I approach the one who gave me the nod earlier, hoping he'll be
amenable to dispensing a few directions. I can't tell if the smell of
cheese and feet is coming from him or from the bowl of nachos on
his lap.

"Hey," I say, shuffling into view. "I'm Vincent."

"Sherman," he says, and as he moves to shake my hand, the
stench of Limburger past its prime grows stronger. Maybe he's got
an infection in the scent glands. Happens to the best of us; word
is, that's why they sent Lewis and Clark west—no one back east
could stand the smell anymore. "Siddown, take a chip."

"Maybe later. Eddie said you could tell me where to find Nelly
Hagstrom."

A new punch line pops out over the TV audio and Sherman
bursts into a series of chortles, slapping his pal on the back a few
times to complete the effect. He leans back, his body nearly tip-
ping over and onto the carpet before he rights himself again.

"Look, I'm just trying to find out where they hang out—"

"The Sea Shack," he grunts. "Restaurant up on Biscayne
Boulevard. Get Raoul to take you."

"Raoul took off," another one of them interrupts. "Like, ten
minutes ago."

"That's okay," I say. "I'll take a cab."

"Suit yourself," says my new pal. "Phone's in the kitchen." He
jerks a thumb over his shoulder, and I turn to make my way out of
the living room.

But I stop as he calls out, "Hey, wait a sec," and I dutifully turn
and step back onto the dirty carpet. "Come back, come back—"

"Something else?" I ask.

"Yeah," he says, nodding his head at a small rectangular device no more than five feet away. "You wanna pass me the remote? I hate this freaking show."

The Sea Shack. We have places like this back in L.A. Only there, we *know* it's supposed to be a joke.

Stuffed sharks hang from the walls, their glassy eyes practically pleading with the patrons to put an end to their misery. *Put me in a box, a landfill, even a moderately tasteful living room,* they say. *Anywhere but here.* Nothing doing; this is kitsch korner, and right where Jaws Jr. belongs. Empty conch shells strung along strands of fishing line hang like streamers from the ceiling, dangling down to annoy the taller customers and frustrate small children. The requisite seashell-bead curtain adorns the front entrance, a throwback to some sad seafarer's concept of seventies style.

But the first thing I notice upon venturing into the Sea Shack is the smell. This fish is funky. They've got the Atlantic Ocean less than a mile away; you'd think they could afford to run down to the beach and do some spearfishing when the last catch started to ripen up the place. Alas, it's probably a human-owned joint; they can't sense the stink until it's way past salmon and into salmonella.

The other river of scent riding past my nostrils is more familiar: the pine, the autumn morning. Here there be dinos. I step past the bronze sculpture of a tortoise and make my way into the restaurant, toward the back bar, where a good number of patrons have gathered, hunkered over the wooden countertop. A series of television sets, hung above the bar, are tuned to a Marlins game, but no one's watching the tube. It'll be nice to have some conversation for a change.

"Evening," I say to the bartender. "Think I could get a—"

"Shhhh."

"Shhhh?"

"Shhhh."

So it's a quiet bar. I can dig that. I'm running through my repertoire of sign language, trying to figure out how to order up a soda,
when I realize that not everyone in the bar is here to rest their
vocal cords. There is one voice riding above the silence, a strong,
commanding lilt that's both familiar and new.

". . . and I'm called in to have a word with him. Now, this is the
phrase that was used. A *word* with him. And when Francesco
wanted a *word* with someone, more often than not, that individual
was well advised to prepurchase a headstone and plot."

The sound is coming from within the center of a massed group,
some storyteller plying his trade on the bar patrons. I can't see him
from here; the crowd is thick, evidently entertained. Maybe this is
the South Florida version of a lounge singer. Some dope gets up
and starts prattling on about his life, and every once in a while
someone throws a dollar into his jar. I edge closer.

"So I enter Francesco's office," the guy is saying, "the one he
had down by Vizcaya. And everything's dark in there. I'm thinking,
first things first, I gotta make out a will, I gotta get my affairs in
order, right?" A little laughter from the crowd, but he doesn't let it
go on too long.

"Francesco tells me to sit, and I tell him I prefer to stand. He
tells me to sit again, and this time I listen, 'cause I figure I'm already in trouble with the guy, I don't wanna stoke those fires any
more. Maybe I'm dead already, but if I'm nice, he could let me go
quick.

"So I sit down, and before I can apologize—me not knowing
what I did, right, just ready to apologize for every damn thing out
there—Francesco says to me, 'I need you to do a job.' Just like that,
from the man himself.

"And I say, 'A job?' And he nods and repeats it. *A job*.

"So now I'm getting all nervous, but in a good way. 'Cause now
I know he's gonna put me up for my button after this thing, some-

thing big, something that's gonna make waves, get me known. 'Whatever you need,' I tell him. 'I'm here for you.'

"And he stands up, puts an arm around my shoulder, and leads me up to this door in the back of his office, this little tiny thing I never even noticed before. I'm starting to shake, but keeping it together, keeping it tight, knowing this is where I learn the secrets, here is where he's gonna tell me what he knows about the life.

"Francesco looks me in the eye, and nods. I nod back, and he turns around on me, facing away. 'This is a job I cannot do myself,' he says. 'I hope you can handle it.' And I take a breath and look up—

"And there's Francesco, a sponge in one hand, a bar of soap in the other, and he's popping out the spikes on his back, one by one. Francesco says, 'My nurse went out of town and I need someone to wash my spikes. Make sure you scrub the third one good. It's so hard to get it clean without help.'

"And that was my entrance into the Francesco family."

Applause and laughter from the circle—it's a tale they've heard before, I can tell, but enjoyed all over again. There's something dastardly familiar about that voice, though, and I muscle closer, trying to pick up on a scent. It's tough—the overriding smell of fish is clogging up my nostrils, making detection difficult.

So I sit and wait for the crowd to clear out, to move away from the center of attention so I can get a visual make. The bartender has gone back to fetching drinks, and I take this moment to grab myself a diet soda.

I'm just a few sips into my drink when I feel a firm hand clamp down on my shoulder, and a very familiar whiff of cinnamon and soy climbs up my nose. "Don't I know you?"

Hagstrom. I keep my body toward the bar, hoping he wasn't interested in smelling me that day at the casino and won't recall my face. "Don't think so," I mutter, and take another sip of my pop.

"Yeah, yeah, I know you. You're the one who smells like cigars."

"Lots of us do."

"And lots of you play baccarat in Norwalk?"

Whoops. I can sense a crowd building around us. Hagstrom's friends, no doubt, backing him up. I turn around, trying to keep my eyes steely, my glare constant. I can't bluff my way out, but I might be able to keep them at bay with a few well-placed sneers.

"There a problem with that?" I ask. "You lost, I won. Luck of the cards."

I can't take my eyes off Hagstrom's forehead, off that puckered scar twisting the skin between his eyebrows.

"You following me?"

"Yeah," I snort. "That's what I'm doing, I'm following you." With a grunt, I turn back on my stool and down another sip of soda.

He's not giving up. "You turning your back on me?"

"That's what it looks like, pal."

Before I even realize what's going on, my arms are caught up by two of Hagstrom's associates and I'm yanked from my stool and thrown to the sawdust-covered floor of the Sea Shack, joining a mash of peanut shells and dried beer. Breath escapes me for a moment as I thud to the ground, my field of vision twisting, the world turning itself upside down.

Hagstrom's shoe—dark leather, polished to a shine—is on my throat a second later, pressing down not on the human-guise larynx but right below it, where the dino soft spot is located. He's got his anatomy down tight.

Pressure. Lack of breath. Intriguing.

I wonder if the bartender or the waitstaff or anyone will come to my rescue, but soon realize that this is the kind of place mobsters patronize for the very reason that the bartender and the waitstaff are blind, dumb, and deaf exactly when they need to be.

"Now," says Hagstrom, standing over me, lauding his little conquest. "You gonna turn your back on me again?"

He starts pressing down harder with that shoe, and suddenly I can feel my air starting to go, the breath catching in my throat. I flail my arms to get up, but the same two goons who threw me to the floor are suddenly on their knees, holding me in place. I've got no leverage, so I've got no chance.

"Wait—" I try to say, the words coming out in a choke, a gurgle. "Wait—"

But Hagstrom isn't listening. His body swims in my suddenly blurring vision, that scar on his forehead pulsing in and out, his lips twisted in a sick combination of joy and rage. My legs are feeling weaker, my arms wet linguini against the firm grip of Hagstrom's friends.

And just as I think it's all going away—the sights, the sounds, the smells—just as Hagstrom's shoe comes pressing down harder, just as it feels my life is finishing up, wiping its hands on the napkin of existence and leaving the restaurant for good, just as I realize I'm making absolutely no sense whatsoever—

The pressure disappears. For a moment, I think I might be dead, then figure out that heaven probably doesn't smell like day-old tuna.

"Let him up, let him up." It's the voice from before, the one that was telling the story about sponging the big guy's spikes. Presumably, the buccaneer in charge of this ship. "Help him, for chrissakes . . ."

I feel arms, lifting me back onto the stool, patting me on the back, keeping my body balanced. It takes a few moments, but I'm able to come back to myself, regain control of my limbs. They're buzzing, tingly.

"You okay?"

"Yeah."

"You sure?"

"Yeah," I repeat, looking up into the wide face of the man who saved my life, if not my dignity—and catching nothing but air. I let my gaze fall a few feet to find a well-groomed chap strapped into a powered wheelchair. His voice is still familiar, but not the look. Never seen the guy before. "Your boy got a little carried away, but I'm cool."

"Nelly's high-strung," he says to me, placing a hand on my shoulder, keeping me steady. But my head is coming back to me, my nostrils are beginning to gear up again, working past the fish, trying to get a bead on my momentary savior. "But if you're feeling better—"

"I'm good."

A push of the joystick on his chair and he spins away, preparing to leave. As he turns, though, I see a flash of thought slide across his face, lighting his eyes, furrowing his brow. He turns back to me, nostrils flaring, chest heaving deeply. Even as I'm smelling him, he's smelling me, and suddenly the picture-in-picture inside my head pops up with an image, a series of stills that's been stuck in the craw of my brain for years and years.

Lemongrass and copper. A small Asian boy walking through a field, flipping a penny into the air.

"Jack?" I say involuntarily, the word escaping my lips before I can stop it.

And the man—this fellow, whose face I have never seen before, yet once knew as intimately as I know anyone on the whole damn planet—just grins and spreads his arms to envelop me in an all-out, no-holds-barred bear hug.

"Vincent Rubio," he croons, pulling my face down into the fabric of his suit, his hand running over the back of my head, caressing my hair as if I were a lost child suddenly found. "I don't know whether I should kiss you or kill you."

"Jack—"

"Shhh, stay still. Let me think this over."

6

Los Angeles isn't the place to make friends. Not anymore. You ask an Angeleno about his neighbors, six times out of ten he won't know their last names; when he does, it's because of the little signs on the mailboxes. Eight times out of ten, he won't know their first names; if he does, it's because the mailman screwed up a delivery and sent a piece of junk mail to the wrong address. Nine times out of ten, he won't particularly care.

But back when I was growing up, when L.A. was still choked with cloying smog, when you were as likely to find a businessman catching a wave as in his office, when people still thought it was possible to come west and find your dream in sunny Southern California, Los Angeles was a place like any other, a place where you could meet your best pal right next door. I did. Then again, I was a kid, and that's what kids do; we can't drive, so we make nice-nice with the local folks and hope they turn out to like us back.

Still, I like to think that even if I'd first met Jack Dugan when we were eighty-year-old codgers sitting on the porch of a rest home, trying to keep our tails from sliding under our rocking chairs and talking about the grand old days while a steady stream of drool dribbled down our double chins, we would have hit it off just as swell as we did when we were ten-year-old tykes with hell to raise.

Jack's dad ran a grocery store on Vermont Avenue, in a section of the city that's now considered Koreatown. Drive down that street today and you're lucky if you see two signs in English for twenty straight blocks; even then, it's usually just to appease the few Caucasians who drive out there for the food. But back when Jackie and I were growing up, it was a mixed neighborhood, both in ethnicity and species. Asian, Hispanic, black—it didn't matter, so long as you had a tail and didn't mind flaunting it at the right place and time.

Dugan's Produce was a busy little joint, with all the locals coming in for their herb fixes two, three times a week. And Harold Dugan—Hank to his wife, Pop to Jack and, by association, me— ran a tight ship. He knew everyone's name, their jobs, their hobbies, and, of course, their personal vices. If Mrs. Dategglio hobbled in on a Wednesday, he had her grated parsnips ready to go; if it was Saturday, he doled out the cilantro. The main store wasn't more than six hundred square feet, but the room in back— the special room—had shelves stocked to the ceiling with spices of every taste and effect, an herbaholic's wet dream and nightmare rolled into one, and it all got replenished every two days. Ten-wheeled trucks would pull up to the loading docks and unload crate after crate of the stuff. Jack and I would help haul the pallets into the store, box by box, where Hank's people would pat us on the heads, throw a few bucks in our direction, and take over from there.

Jack was a pretty big kid, his mop of hair hanging down low, the bangs nearly covering his eyes. I learned later that his pop had gotten into an argument with the wig manufacturer down at the chop shop where he bought his family's guises, and he didn't want to have the hair cut until he was sure it could be replaced, but at the time, I just remember thinking *cool bangs*. It was the seventies; sue me.

Now Jack was a Hadrosaur and I was a Velociraptor, and by all rights we should have hung out with different crowds. But it wasn't like that where we lived; you mixed with the folks you got along with, and that was that. I knew a bunch of Raptor kids who went to my school, and most of 'em would sooner spit at you than say a friendly word. Don't know why it is, but my species doesn't have the best track record when it comes to preparing welcome wagons. Maybe if Custer had been an Ornithomimus instead, things would have gone better at Little Bighorn.

Most of the time, we biked around Los Angeles with the full blessing of our parents, who were either comfortable with the safety of the neighborhood at large or unconcerned about our well-being. Despite the cavalcade of adventures awaiting tourists and businessmen alike in the Greater Los Angeles Metroplex these days, there weren't a hell of a lot of things for kids to do back then. The parks were overrun by vagrants, the museums dry and dull, and the movie theaters were filled with overlong epics or barely comprehensible psychodramas; even the cartoons flew over our heads. So it was the bikes, and endless riding.

Which is not to say we didn't hop off for the occasional round of mischief. Between the two of us, we knew practically every prank in the book, and the rest we made up on the fly. Jack was the creative one; I was the problem-solver. Together, we could embarrass even the most self-confident of the neighborhood adults.

Most of it was little things, pranks designed to annoy and frustrate, maybe get a laugh or two out of our peers. One time, we covertly followed around the local dog catcher—the tax base was wide and strong enough in those days to allow for such frivolities—and waited until his truck was full of squirming canines, yelping and pawing for a way out of captivity. The next time he stopped to snare a pooch in an alleyway, we snuck into the back of the truck and unlatched every cage, keeping the outer doors closed

but letting the animals roam free inside, their thick tongues lapping at our faces in premature gratitude. Jack and I worked hard to
get 'em all riled up, scratching their ears, playing tug-of-war with a
length of rope we'd brought along, until the small six-by-twelve
cargo area was rocking with canine adrenaline.

When the dog catcher returned with his latest conquest and
opened the outer doors to make his deposit, a manic mass of fur
and bad breath flew out of the truck, knocking him to the ground,
trampling his squirming body beneath a hundred filthy paws. Jack
and I managed to claw our way out during the confusion, woofing
at the top of our lungs, hoping that even if the guy managed to get
a glimpse of us, he'd be so shell-shocked he wouldn't put two and
two together.

Most of our pranks were of the garden-variety call-a-pizzeria-
and-order-ten-pies type, the punishments, if it ever came to that,
no more than a few days without television or the like. But there
was one time when we laid it on a bit too thick, when our collective minds came up with a plan that outran our concept of the potential consequences. And it was only then, as we faced the
heaviest of penalties, that we truly knew each other for what we
were.

Jack's mom, like a lot of mothers back then, was a housewife,
but at the same time, she was a housewife who wanted to feel that
she was doing her part to support the family financially. Dugan's
Produce was a popular spot, but the real cash cow of the business—the herbs—was somewhat dependent on the economy.
During a dip, some folks could do without their basil and rosemary. If they were heavy into the stuff, real junkies, they could always go bulk or dried, the low-quality stuff that Pop Dugan
disdained to carry. So during the down times, Jack's mom found a
way to help pay the bills.

Guises and their attachments are, for the most part, governed
by the Councils at the local and regional levels, and, in a broader

sense, by the National and World Councils as well. They're the ones who license the manufacturers and distribute new permits to those wishing to enter the human costume business. Few are accepted; most don't even have the money to apply for the permits in the first place, and those who do are often bankrupted by the staggering amount of bribery it takes to get any paperwork pushed through the Council offices.

But back in the day, one company was poised to make a splash in the guise community, and they had the wherewithal to do so, the salesforce to make it happen, and a smashing brand name already known and loved in households, dinosaur and otherwise, across America:

Tupperware.

Their business proposal to the Councils, as I understand it, was simple. They already had the manufacturing plants, the workers in place. Eight percent of their factory-floor workforce—every dinosaur member of the Tupperware organization—would be given a small raise and transferred to a new guise plant down in Chile, where, twenty-four hours a day, they would produce beautiful costumes of quality and style that—and here was the twist— were interchangable. No longer would you need to replace your entire guise if something went wrong on a leg or two; now you could simply reorder a section of the costume from the Tupperware corporation, and they would seamlessly attach it to the rest of your fake body and have it back at your home with a three-day turnaround.

Two years and, rumor has it, over fourteen million dollars in back-pocket exchanges later, the World Council approved the Tupperware business model and Chile had themselves a growth industry. Word came from South America that the local reptilian population, many of whom had been recruited to work at the factory once it was evident that the original workforce was too small to handle the immediate orders, had begun spending money like it was going out of style, buying themselves the lavish items they were never before able to afford, such as food and, in some cases, shelter. Life was good.

Back in the States, the Tupperware salesforce went into action. And, true to their word, the Tupperware folk did, indeed, have a ready and willing group of women eager to hawk their product in living rooms across America. They'd been doing it for years with plastic containers, and when it came down to it, a guise wasn't much different, except that they didn't require quite as much burping.

Jack's mom was an arms dealer.

Oh, sure, she sold the other stuff too, they all did, but Jack's mom had an eye for arms that outstripped even the professional appraisers; she could pick out a mismatched pair of triceps at thirty feet. And her knowledge of hand structure was such that she was once called down to the Tupperware branch offices in San Diego to give the supervisors a lesson on the metacarpal bones, and how they might best be enhanced in their well-known Society Matron line of guises.

And she had parties. Oh, did she have parties. Daylong affairs starting at noon and lasting until well after sundown, during which time the ladies of the neighborhood would pile into her living room, dressed to the nines, the tens, pillbox hats perched atop their fancy coifs, gold buttons and polyester a-shining. All horribly overwrought outfits, especially considering that they were coming off as soon as Jack's mother—Tiffany—rang her little chime and announced that the festivities would begin. But they were there, they were giddy, and they were primed to buy.

Jack and I were usually banished from the house during these shindigs, and we weren't exactly despondent over it. The last thing we wanted to do was hang out with all the old ladies in the neighborhood, listening to stories about ripped seams and how to fix a tail snag with a bit of household cleanser and tape. Most of the time, we'd head down to Dugan's Produce and toss around the lettuce heads, or bike down to the reservoir and spy on the older kids making out.

But one afternoon, Jack had a better idea. It had come to him in a dream, he claimed, but I think he'd been cooking it up for a while, waiting for the right moment to strike. And on one hot August afternoon, the L.A. sun unforgiving in the sky above, we decided that the day of reckoning had finally come.

Thirteen ladies at the house that afternoon, thirteen purses ready to be snapped open at a moment's notice. Jack's mom had just gotten in a shipment of new gams from the Tupperware folks, and the gals were eager to test drive the new line of thighs (*now with SpringForm action!*). They gathered in the living room, false hips pressed against one another, the noise level growing with each successive arrival, like a menagerie of birds squawking at the introduction of a new playmate.

Tiffany called us over. "Jackie, Vincent," she said, holding out a five-dollar bill. "Go have a nice time, boys."

Jack took the bill and gave his mom a peck on the cheek, but he had no intention of spending the money that afternoon.

"Thanks, Mrs. Dugan," I said, and she tousled my hair playfully.

"Go on, run along."

The other ladies paid us no mind as we trotted out the front door, hopped on our bikes, and took off down the street. We rounded the corner and quickly circled back, running our bikes over the small backyard lawns of Jack's neighbors.

By the time we reached the back of Jack's house, the ladies were at full volume, laughing and shrieking and generally reverting to adolescence in their prepurchasing frenzy. We could hear Betty Deruda above the rest, her girlish, high-pitched squeal sounding out across the not-so-open plains of the city.

"She's gotta be first," I suggested. "Just to hear the scream."

"Oh yeah," Jack said. "She'll break windows."

We waited a few more moments, just to allow the full crescendo to build, then slipped in through the back door, sliding through the laundry room and into the far hallway. It was only a few more steps into the master bedroom and an exceptional hiding spot inside the closet. From here we could still get a good view of the living room through the slats in the door, without giving ourselves away. It was crucial that we watch this stage; the rest of our plan hinged on it.

Five minutes later, Jack's mom produced a small dinner chime, which she held aloft and struck soundly with a tiny ballpeen hammer. The *ding* was loud and clear, sending a strong, sharp note amid the assembled housewives.

"The Tupperware party," she announced, "has begun."

Jack and I stood slack-jawed as a whirlwind of activity enveloped the living room. Rather than the careful, orderly manner in which most of our kind remove their clothing—taking time to place every strap and tag of latex in a precise, logical arrangement—these ladies went at it like it was amateur night at the Go-Go-Club. First it was the dresses and hats, the undergarments, the shoes, piled atop each other in the mad rush to strip down to bare scales. They wanted at the new guises, and they wanted at them *now*.

Jack and I kept a close watch on each housewife—now naked as crocodiles, tails swishing across the shag carpet of the living room—as she gathered up her costume and brought it into the bedroom, placing it on the bed, the floor, the chaise. Both Jack and I had pretty good memories, and between the two of us, we kept a close tab on whose guise had been put where.

Soon enough, all of the ladies' guises were in the bedroom and they'd reassembled in the living room to start the fun and games. Jack and I weren't interested in this part of the festivities. We had our own fun and games in mind.

None of them heard us scamper out of the closet, and none of them noticed when the bedroom door swung closed. Now we were alone in the room: just two young boys, thirteen ladies' costumes, and the twisted, bored imagination of youth.

"Where do we start?" Jack asked.

"Betty," I said. "Betty and Mrs. Taylor."

For every Betty Deruda in the world, there is a Josephine Taylor. Josephine was an older woman, her half-Tupperware/half-Erickson guise tailored to match her sagging frame. A bit heavy around the middle, she carried much of her weight in the hips, giving her human look an overall pear shape; the thick tail didn't help matters, increasing the size of her mammalian rump. But it seemed that she was content in her guise, happy to live her life as part of the larger set.

Betty, on the other hand, was the youngest member of the Tupperware brigade; her son was only ten months old, and she'd moved to the neighborhood just a year before he was born. Betty was the girl all the other women talked about behind her back, the one the neighborhood boys—Jack and I included—would follow around town, offering to carry her bags, her baby, anything. She was the official Hot Mom of the bunch, and, as such, a natural target.

"You get Mrs. Taylor's," I told Jack. "I'll get Betty's."

"Why do you get Betty's?" he asked. "It was my idea."

"Fine, fine," I said, eager to get started. "Switch. Let's just do this."

It took only twelve minutes to go through the whole room, and once we were done, we didn't linger at the scene of the crime. Jack and I pried open the bedroom window—too risky to try slipping back out through the laundry room—and fell into the rose bushes, laughing even as we cursed the thorns.

Once out front, we hopped on our bikes and rode down to Dugan's Produce, where we fell in with the employees and helped them stack a new shipment of herbs in the back, grinning at each other all the while. It was the perfect alibi.

"What's so funny, you two?" Pop Dugan asked us. "You look like the T-Rex who ate the Compy."

"Inside joke," Jack told his dad, and the old man left it at that.

Six hours later, we figured the party would be ready to break up, so we pedaled back to the neighborhood and waited a block down, keeping our eyes trained on Jack's front window. As soon as we saw movement inside, we made a beeline for the house and strode up the front walk, just as the first ladies began scurrying out to their cars.

There was Jean Gordon, clutching a shopping bag full of accessories, only she was walking along inside Susie Fenster's lower body. And Susie Fenster, normally content inside her tall, lanky frame, had to make do as a short, rotund size twelve. Similar guise troubles had befallen Sue Klau and Cathy Vargas, JoEllen Zalaznick and Patti Goldstein, and every other lady who had the misfortune to attend Jack's mom's Tupperware party that afternoon.

We'd switched the guises. Heads to bodies, a great swaparound, mixing and matching, using our creative talents to decide whose mask went "best" with whose body, doing all we could to create the ultimate incongruities in size, shape, and color. And, just to make sure they wouldn't catch the error and swap back before Jack and I got an eyeful, we used Super Glue to hold the additions in place. A lot of it.

The last pair to emerge from the house, though, represented our crowning achievement, the real reason we'd concocted the scheme in the first place:

Betty Deruda and Josephine Taylor.

Josephine was walking tall, her wrinkled mask set in a wide, thin-lipped smile, the sparkle in her eyes belying the words coming out of her mouth. "I'm so sorry," she rasped, turning to face Tiffany in the doorway. "Tell Betty I'll get it back to her as soon as I can. I'm so, so sorry."

But beneath that sixty-year-old face was a curvy, sexy, twenty-four-year-old body, the hips sliding out from beneath that slim waist, the breasts shaped and angled in all the right places. It was a knockout guise for a knockout gal, but Josephine Taylor was its proud owner now, and she swiveled her rump with the best of them.

And then came Betty. At first, only her head appeared in the doorway, poking out and quickly back in again, like a tortoise deciding that the world was still too dangerous a place to enter. Jack and I exchanged a quick glance—this was odd.

A moment passed, and then Betty popped her head out again, her eyes downcast, dull. Her cheeks twitched in spastic, arrhythmic contractions, brow tight and furrowed, and it took me a second to realize what was going on.

"She's crying."

She stepped out like an outcast, like a leper, trying to maneuver that big body out the door and down the front walk, unable to control the oversized legs after so many years of piloting a much smaller ship. She tripped, stumbled, and righted herself, bracing Josephine Taylor's body against a nearby tree. A false layer of fat, designed to jiggle precisely so, crested up and down across her midsection.

"Let me help," Tiffany said, stepping forward to catch Betty/Josephine by the arm, but the neighborhood's Hot Mom shrugged Tiffany away and waddled toward her car, fumbling for the keys, fighting back a fresh round of tears.

Jack and I couldn't take our eyes away. This wasn't in the plan, this flood of tears, all this sadness. At the most, we expected a few indignant huffs, maybe a shriek or two. But the absolute defeat in Betty Deruda's eyes instantly told us all we ever needed to know about this lady. She'd lived her life inside her looks, and Jack and I had inadvertently shown her that it could all be taken away in an instant. Hard enough to accept after years of slow and steady decline; an impossible pill to swallow when it bats you over the head all at once.

I tried to hop back on my bike, to get out of there, flee the scene. Maybe if I wasn't present, it would all go away, and everyone could go back to their normal guises, no harm done. But I wasn't looking where I was stepping, and suddenly I was crashing down hard on the bike, the metal clattering to the ground, the scraping sound of pedal on asphalt echoing through the cul-de-sac.

Betty stopped cold, one hand on her door handle, one clutching the massive, drooping breasts hanging off her once-petite frame, as if struggling with heavy groceries. Her head swiveled around, and she looked straight at us, straight at me and Jack, standing there, dumbfounded, stupid grins plastered across our lips. From her point of view, it must have seemed that we were mocking her, that we were poking fun at this young broad turned old.

Her lips moved, and though I couldn't hear the words, I knew instantly what she was saying. *You did this.*

And before we could react, apologize, or somehow make it up to her, Betty was in her car and shooting down the street, off to the safety and shelter of her own home, where she could shut the blinds, seal the windows, and rip off the humiliating folds of human skin.

Jack's mom stood in the doorway, staring at us. Hers was the only guise we didn't mess with, and her arms hung loosely by her sides, her face slack with dismay. It would have been easier if she'd had her hands on her hips, her lips turned in a scowl, but this expression of profound disappointment was worse than any scolding we could imagine.

"Vincent," she said flatly as we stepped toward the house, "you'd better go home."

"Mom—" Jack started, but he didn't get far.

"Go home, Vincent," Tiffany repeated. "I'm not going to call your mother. You tell her what you feel is right."

I nodded—no clue what I was going to do, but I sure as hellfire wasn't going to let my parents in on the deal—and Tiffany took Jack by the shoulder and calmly led him inside. I got a last-second glance from him, a terrified look that said all that was needed, and then he was gone, inside the house, the door locked up tight.

I never saw him again.

Nah, I saw him two days later, after his mom had laid down the law and taken away his bike and his football and his television time and all the other things that made life worth living.

Tiffany also insisted that Jack help out at future Tupperware parties, and that he serve punch and treats to the attending ladies; she thought it was only fitting, especially considering he had damaged her credibility among the housewife set. So Jack was fully expecting to have his Saturdays booked up for many many weeks to come.

What he wasn't expecting—and neither was I—was how much more there was in store. Because while most of the women who had been at Jack's house that day went home, undressed, reguised themselves in a spare costume, and then swapped with their counterparts as soon as it was convenient, there was one who didn't take it so lightly. One who saw no humor in the matter, and who couldn't understand why the culprits should go unpunished.

Betty Deruda went to the Council.

At first it was just the local Southern California chapter, where she supposedly harangued them about declining moral values in the youth today—herself only a scant five or six years removed from that youth, but no matter—but eventually her complaint was remanded to a higher court.

By the time the Regional and Western councils got to it, a month and a half later, they barely needed to hear the facts before they realized it was not in their jurisdiction. Situations like these had to be handled on a higher level, and they promptly sent Betty and her claims further up the ladder.

This was a National case. Minor though it was, insignificant though it might have been, it nevertheless fell under their auspices. Because in the rigid, precise, yet always confusing code of the Councils, all manner of dinosaur misconduct can be categorized in one of three ways:

Indiscretions are those infractions of the rule book that are either accidental, minor, or both, and do little, if anything, to jeopardize our place in society. A businessman who wants to lose a little weight off his human guise, for example, will often decide to purchase his new stomach through a black-market guise dealer instead of through the proper channels, because they'll carve in an extra-nice six-pack of abs for him, or they'll give the guy a break on the price if he pays in cash. Or two friends will be chatting at work near the watercooler and some human or another will overhear them referring to the "filthy mammals" scurrying around the workplace. Such infractions do little to put the dinosaurs at risk, and the punishments are usually meted out in dollars and cents. There's nothing like a healthy budget surplus to mollify Council members.

Violations are more serious, and it's in this category where most of the major crimes are classified. Most of the dino-on-dino crimes are listed here, including murder, which you'd think would come in the most serious category, but the Councils don't exist in order to prevent actions that society would otherwise cover. Murderers can go to a normal death row just like anybody else; more care is simply taken within the penal system to make sure they're separated from the other inmates when need be. So under Council rules, dino-on-dino murder is considered a violation. This is also the category that covers all the infractions by which our security might be compromised, such as failure to properly dispose of a deceased dinosaur via a dissolution packet, or improperly buttoning one's costume so that a hint of scale pokes out for all the world to see. Most dino-human relationships are covered under the Violations rule, as well, including the most carnal of transgression. I remember seeing the rule book back when I was on the Southern California Council, and the list of violations went on and on; it was longer than the L.A. phone book, and only slightly more interesting. Punishments here can range from heavy fines to imprisonment, though usually not for an extended period of time. In the case of a greater societal crime, the Councils will often allow the criminal to get off with time served, as long as he's spent a few good months in a state-run lockup.

The third category is reserved only for those crimes that carry the most serious threat of exposing our existence to the humans, and the punishments, as a result, are proportional to the act. There have been moments throughout our history when certain crimes have been perceived to be so great, in fact, that the perpetrators have been put to death, to serve as a warning to future lawbreakers. The last time such a punishment was exacted was decades ago, but since that dark day back in 1953 when Julius and Ethel Rosenberg were sent off to meet the Great Ancestors, no one else has merited the ultimate penalty.

These are the *High Crimes* of dinosaur society.

And that's what Jack and I were charged with.

Yes, long before I was ever brought up on various indiscretions and ousted from the Southern California Council, years prior to getting myself run out of New York for investigating Dr. Emil Vallardo's experiments into human-dino crossbreeding and generally making a mess of things during the infamous McBride case, yours truly was a hardened criminal of the reptilian underground. Top of the world, Ma!

It seems that while unauthorized guise manipulation is a minor indiscretion when done to one's own costume, the infraction gets bumped up to a violation when it's performed on someone else's skin. And there are a host of special circumstances that can drive it up even further into the High Crimes category. Multiple victims, for example, or serious costume mutilation, two addenda of which Jack and I were most certainly guilty, sealed the deal.

The National Council headquarters are located in central Alabama; no one has ever properly explained to me the reason for this. I always assumed that Washington, D.C., would be the logical place to locate our seat of power, but it's been Alabama since long before the elders can remember, so Tuscaloosa it is, and Tuscaloosa it will remain.

We were allowed to stay with our parents until the trial—the *hearing*, they called it, but we knew what it was—yet were not allowed to see each other whatsoever. That had never stopped us before; it wouldn't then. One night, at 11:37 on the dot, we snuck out of our respective homes and met under an elm near Dugan's Produce.

"You're not gonna say anything, are you?" Jack asked me. "All they got is what Betty saw."

"Or thinks she saw."

"Right. And some of my glove prints on Mrs. Taylor's guise—"

"But she'd just come over the day before," I said.

"Exactly." Jack and I had gone through this once before; it was important to get the story straight.

We both knew that the consequences could be serious. High crimes were never dealt with lightly; the stories that dinosaur parents tell their children are fraught with villains plotting to expose the race, or of humans learning of our existence and threatening to do away with us, and the messy ends of these characters were meant to help guide our moral compass. And though some of the stories were probably apocryphal, the punishments were real. Death was a long shot in our case, but imprisonment—especially at one of those dino-juvie workcamps out in the Louisiana bayou,

where sweatshop labor produces the finest discount-quality clothing money can buy—was a very real possibility.

"We stick together," Jack reiterated, "and we're cool on this."

I nodded. I'd seen enough movies in which coconspirators
eventually cracked under pressure and gave up their friends; these
flicks weren't the feel-good films of the year. Watergate had just
passed us by, and though I'd barely followed the events (to a kid,
politics is like imagining your parents kissing—you know it happens, but it's easier not to think about it), I was nevertheless aware
of the fact that some bad folks had snitched on some other bad
folks, and that if they'd all just kept their damn mouths shut, no
one would have been the wiser.

"No matter what they do to us," I said, envisioning torture
chambers and cattle-prods, lie detectors and bare lightbulbs
swinging back and forth in a darkened room, "we keep it quiet."

Jack took my forearm in his and stared intently into my eyes.
"Scratch on it."

I solemnly unsnapped my glove and pulled off the index finger.
My claws had yet to come in fully, but I was able to slide a single
dark tip out from between the scales. Jack did the same with his,
and I used the tip of my claw to scratch a small white line into the
surface of his own black spur. Then Jack marked me similarly. It
was less painful than becoming blood brothers, comparatively hy-
gienic, and, to us, infinitely more meaningful.

They separated us for the plane flight and kept us in different
locations down in Tuscaloosa. I don't remember much about Alabama, except that the bugs were gigantic and fearless. In L.A.,
the roaches run when you turn on the light; in Alabama, they all
scurry out to sunbathe and demand that you fetch them daiquiris.

The National Council headquarters, like most of the Council
offices around the world, is located underground. Six stories
under, to be precise, and in a place like rural Alabama, that means

no elevators and a lot of stairs. That's the overriding memory of my journey down to the trial chambers—step after step of damp, mildewy staircase, the smell of fungus wrapping around my sinuses and daring me to run away, the fear starting deep in my belly and slowly crawling up into my chest. My father's hand on my shoulder, pressing down hard with every step. As if he knew something I didn't. As if he already knew how this was all going to play out, and that the audience wouldn't be leaving the theater humming any happy tunes.

"You will tell the truth," I heard my father say, his voice a low whisper.

"Sure," I responded.

His hand dug further into my shoulder, and he repeated himself, the words tight, clipped. "You will tell—the truth."

I didn't need to be told twice. I also didn't need to listen. Jack and I had sworn on our claws, and that was that.

The sixteen Elders—three of them female, even back in the seventies—sat in a circle, their seats ringing the walls, each atop its own alabaster pedestal. The lighting was dim, save for one brightly illuminated spot in the center of the room. There was a single chair in the middle, a simple wooden seat, and it was this area to which I was directed.

"Leave him," a voice called out, and my father, understanding the instructions, backed out of the room without question. This was the National Council, and the only dinosaur dumb enough to disobey them was a preteen dinosaur.

I'd like to say I was brave, but the little swagger I felt was overridden by the knowledge that these sixteen creatures held my life in their claws. They were Caesar in the Coliseum, and I was the unfortunate gladiator under the sword. One thumb down, and it would be curtains for young Vincent Rubio.

So when they told me to sit, I sat, and when the Brontosaur

representative stood and began to speak, I listened to every damn word he had to say.

"Vincent Rubio," he began, his deep, rich voice singsonging my name, "you have been charged with the High Crime of unwarranted guise alteration in a public setting, and despite your young age and lack of prior befoulments of the law, we have nevertheless decided to take this case quite seriously. Do you understand the charges brought against you?"

I nodded, and tried to say the words *I do.* But my throat was dry, my larynx vibrating too rapidly, and all they got was a squeak, a croak, and a head bob.

"And how do you plead?"

I took a breath, thanked my stars that my father had left the room, and muttered, "Not guilty."

From there, it was an hour of testimony, all depositions, none live, from the ladies at the Dugan house that afternoon, along with a little forensic evidence introduced by an associate member of the Council. It was hard to get past the sound of my own heartbeat, the flow of rushing water enveloping my head, but I was alert enough to realize that for all of their high talk and bluster, the Council had very little evidence by which to convict either Jack or myself. It was just a bunch of old folks blowing hot air, and as long as we stuck to the plan, we'd come out on top.

After all of their evidence had been presented, the Brontosaur rep—clearly the one in charge—stood again and asked if I wished to change my plea, or if there was any additional information I would like to provide at this time. I said that there wasn't, and a light murmur went through the Council members.

"You do know," the Brontosaur continued, "that your friend has confessed."

A shock ran through my body, a sudden jolt of electricity, and I concentrated hard to keep my legs stiff, my hands steady. It had to be a trick; that was why they were keeping us apart. I'd read *1984* in school—well, the last few pages, anyway, but I got the gist—and knew that this was a common tactic. Separate and destroy.

"Confessed to what?" I said, keeping the front.

"Come," said the head Council member. "It will be easier if you just tell us what happened, and we can all get on with this. Jack has done his part. It's your turn now."

But I held fast, and despite a fifteen-minute barrage of questioning, I stood fast, the whole time wondering if Jack really had cracked. They seemed to know an awful lot about what we'd done that afternoon; could they have picked that up from the testimony? From conjecture?

They were about to start in on me again when a shadow separated itself from the wall and stepped into the light. It was the Velociraptor representative, a small, thin fellow who moved with effortless grace, slipping to my side before I even noticed.

"Please," he said, his sibilants slightly occluded, just short of a lisp. This happens sometimes with both Raptors and Ornithomimi—our elongated snouts can get in the way of the tongue. "Let me speak with the boy."

The others shrugged and backed off as the Raptor led me from the chair, out of the Council chambers, and into a small, darkened room off to one side. There, we both sat on the floor, across from one another, the tone light, almost friendly, despite the chill that was creeping from the tile and up my spine.

"You understand why you're here?" he began, and I nodded. "Of course you do. You're an intelligent young Raptor, Vincent. I can tell that about you. And you've been put in a terrible situation."

He seemed to be waiting for me to speak, so I grunted lightly. "Yeah." Ever the chatterbox I was.

"These old dinosaurs—the lot of them—they're not out for revenge, though it can seem that way. They have constituents, they have rules, and they're just trying to do what's expected of them.

"But," he continued, "they often get caught up in their work. All crazy, like you saw them back there. Teeth gnashing, claws flying—wild things—"

This got a little laugh out of me, and he grinned back. "All I'm saying," the Raptor rep said, "is that we don't have to go through this. If they had their way, they'd have you down there all week. Asking questions, breaking you down, and in the end, I bet you'd tell them what they wanted to hear. I've seen it before, it's not pretty.

"But here it's just you and me. And I'm going to let you in on the truth, okay?"

I was ready for some straight talk. "Okay."

"They've got Jack. The prints, the bike tracks, someone catching a whiff of his scent all over their guise. They've got him dead to rights, and the Council isn't letting go of this one."

"He—he talked?" I asked.

"No," the Raptor said. "He's kept quiet, I won't lie to you about that. But he's in a big mess of trouble, and they're thinking about some serious punishment. It won't be juvenile workcamp for him. There's been too much frivolity with the guises lately—all that B-strap burning up in San Francisco threw them into a tizzy—and they're looking for a scapegoat. Looks like Jack's the one."

I swallowed hard. This was never part of the plan. "Will they . . . I mean . . . a high crime—"

"Will they kill him?"

"Yes," I said breathlessly.

"No. He's young, and word is that no mammals caught on to what was going down. But that doesn't mean they'll let him off easy. He'll be considered an adult during sentencing. That means one of the prisons up in Canada."

Canada. Three syllables, one terrifying word. No one knew exactly what happened in the reptilian lockups way up in the frigid northland, but the very thought that Jack might be force-fed a diet of bacon and snow was enough to throw me into panic mode.

"He can't go up there," I said, scooting forward, keeping my voice low, even as the words poured from my mouth. "He'll be—he can't!"

"I agree. Jack's tough . . . for his age. But they'll eat him alive. Quite literally, I'm afraid. You've heard the stories."

I had. Tales of cannibalism and rampant violence inside the prison system, aggression not only unchecked but encouraged by the guards who ran the place. Jack would be little more than an appetizer to those monsters from the Great White North, and suddenly it was up to me to save him.

"What do I do?"

"We'll go back in there," the Raptor said, his eyes soft and bright, his long snout curled at the corners in a simple, easy smile, "and I'll ask you what happened. You let it all out, explain how it was all just a simple boyhood prank, a nothing incident. No one was hurt, no one the wiser. They'll give you both a small fine, you can work it off at a Council rec center, and within six months we'll all forget it happened." He paused and caught my eye. "Does that sound like something we could do, Vincent? Together, you and me?"

Before I knew it, I was nodding and being led back into the Council chambers. The Raptor gave me a sly wink and took his seat among the other Council members. I kept my head down, staring at a mosaic of the Council seal—the Earth, covered in green scales—embedded into the floor.

"All right now, Vincent," said the Raptor, taking the lead as he'd promised. "Why don't you tell everyone what happened?"

Moment of truth. Fork in the road. Jack and I had discussed our options, but it had never come down to this. I had a chance to save my friend from certain doom, and all I had to do was tell the truth. It seemed like an easy choice. A few months of work detail, just like the nice Raptor said, and we'd be free. If half a year scrubbing floors and cleaning up toddler puke would keep Jack from the dregs of Canada, I was willing to do it. And despite our solemn vow never to speak about that afternoon, the oaths we had scratched upon each other's budding claws, I knew that in time, once he'd been told of the choices with which I'd been presented, Jack would understand.

I opened my mouth to speak, feeling every muscle in my jawbone creak wide. Tongue dry but ready, preparing to spill all the secrets of that summer afternoon. "It was like this," I began—

That's when I smelled the prunes.

Forget about the scent of fear as a stench of decay or the odor of sweat—no, fear is prunes, ripe and redolent, and this time the odor wasn't coming from me. It was streaming off the Council members. Fear that they were going to let me get away. Fear that they'd screwed up yet another national-level investigation. Instantly I knew that they had nothing on Jack, that the Raptor had made it all up, and that if I gave up the goods, Jack wouldn't be the only one rotting away in Ottawa.

"We were at the store all day," I said, repeating pretty much what I'd been saying for the past month straight. "We didn't have anything to do with it."

There was a moment of stunned silence as the elders realized that I wasn't going to fold under their pressure, and then the Raptor was out of his chair and lunging at me, roaring furiously, teeth bared and headed for my throat. But he was old and I was hopped up on adrenaline, and I easily dodged out of the way as he slammed into the wall behind me. Before he could rise to mount another attack, the other Council members rushed their comrade and restrained him; it's one thing to interrogate a child, another to dismember him in a legal forum. Claws flew; teeth gnashed.

A Compy squirmed his way out of the melee and hooked his beak toward the stairs. "Get outta here, kid." He sighed. "You're free to go."

I was still too scared to toss out any parting shots—for all I

knew, this was yet another trick designed to get me to confess further—so I scampered to my feet, dashed through the Council
chambers and up the six flights of stairs, falling into my father's
arms at the uppermost landing.

I slept well on the plane ride home.

After we got back to L.A., Jack and I were tighter than ever.
We'd made it through their interrogations, their Cheshire grins
and crocodile tears, and come out on top. Jack told me he didn't
say a word during the whole ordeal; he just sat back and shrugged
a lot. I told him I'd done pretty much the same. There was no need
to let him know about the Raptor rep, or our talk behind closed
doors, or the fact that we were five seconds away from a lifetime of
misery and that only my sensitive snout saved us from extreme
Canadian justice.

As far as I know, he still has no idea.

So that's not why he's hugging me to his breast, loving me and
hating me, contemplating whether he should buy me dinner or
take me out in the alley and put this PI out of his misery.

It's all because of what I did to his sister. Noreen, well . . . that's
another story.

7

"Vincent Rubio," he's crooning, my breath short as he squeezes me even closer, his strong arms clamping my sternum to his. "What's it been, kiddo? Fifteen, twenty years?"

"Something like that."

" 'Something like that' . . . listen to this guy, cool as ever." He pushes me back to arm's length and holds me there. There's strength in those hands, in that chest. Despite the lack of action below the waist, Jack Dugan grew up to be quite the musclehead. "A cucumber, you know that? That's what you were."

"A cucumber."

"Cool as. Remember the time we got spotted by Dolores Treacle, up on that hill over the ladies' spa, digging all those holes for the garter snakes to come out?"

"Vaguely."

And he's pulling me close again, the nose and mouth openings of my mask pressed hard against his muscular chest. A bit hard to breathe down here. I flail my right arm up and down in the hopes that he'll take it as a signal of surrender.

"Damn, I missed you," he says.

"Mmmm—"

"What?"

"Me too," I mumble. He's letting up, allowing me to get a breath in. "You look good. Strong."

"We ain't kids anymore, Vincent."

I nod, flexing my muscles as best I can. It's been a while since I've seen the inside of a gym—two years, and even then I was just tailing a former Mr. Universe who was cheating on his wife with Fritz, his workout partner—and my underworked body shows it. But Jack doesn't seem to notice or care; he's beaming left and right, one happy Hadrosaur.

"Nelly," he calls out, "Nelly, come over here. I want you to meet someone."

Hagstrom drags himself off a bar stool and approaches, keeping me under a heavy stare.

"We met already."

"Yeah, he met your *fist*," Dugan says, "but that ain't what I'm talking about."

"Hey," I say. "I'm Vincent."

"We met in Los Angeles," Hagstrom grumbles.

Jack's eyebrows raise a bit. "Oh yeah? Small world. You still living in the old neighborhood, Vincent?"

I shake my head. "Westwood. Wilshire area isn't what it used to be."

"Bound to happen," he says, nodding along. "Even when my family picked up and left, mid-city was turning south. Lotta mammals moving in." He pauses for a second, then turns back to Nelly. "So, you guys meet at a party?"

"At a casino," I say. "Down in Norwalk."

Hagstrom steps in closer. "And I find it kinda coincidental you're hanging around here, too."

I shrug. "Guy's allowed to roam the country, take in the sights. Right, Jack?"

My old pal pats me on the shoulder, either convinced by my lame explanation or too thrilled at our reunion to care. "That's right. Don't mind Nelly, he's a bit high-strung."

"So I've noticed."

"But now you two are all patched up."

I grin. "So says you, huh?"

"So says me. Go on, shake."

There will be a time and a place to exact any revenge I may wish upon Nelly Hagstrom, but this is neither. So I'm first to offer up my paw, and Nelly takes a second before accepting, grudgingly, and pumping my arm up and down. Below us, Jack grins, and the feud is officially on hiatus.

"Great," says Jack, clapping his meaty hands together. "We're all pals. First things first—what the heck brings you down to my neck of the woods?"

Before I can craft an answer—I can't very well tell him about Tallarico, not right out of the gate—there's a sudden shift of movement near Jack's arm, a blur of white cotton. I look down, then drop my eyes even further to find a petite older gal tugging on his sleeve, waiting for his attention.

She's got to be fifty-five, sixty, but she's kept her guise in tip-top shape over the years; probably uses that popular wrinkle cream that isn't much more than clear Elmer's glue in a twenty-dollar jar. Her coif of gray hair is styled short and neat, and large plastic glasses frame a thin oval face. A nice-looking older gal, somewhat out of place here at the Sea Shack.

Jack positions his ear near the woman's mouth as she begins whispering; as she speaks, Jack nods, grunting every few seconds. "Okay," he says finally, "we'll do it as soon as I get back." She slips back into the crowd.

"I need to be back at the house early tonight, but I've got a few things to do first," he tells me.

"Sure, sure. Great seeing you, Jack—"

"Hell," he laughs, "you ain't gettin' off that easy. Early means sometime before two A.M., and you and me got a lot of catching up to do. Hey, you remember my dad?"

"Pop Dugan? Not an easy man to forget."

Jack allows himself a smile and throws an arm around my waist. The weight is tremendous, and, for a moment, I wonder if he really bulked up since we were kids, or if he just had some La Lanne attachments sewn into his guise. "Pop's slowed down some, but I know he'd like to see you. Talk about old times. Wanna take a ride?"

It's one of my cardinal rules that whenever a suspected mob boss asks me if I want to *take a ride*, the answer is an automatic no. This is Jack, though, and this is the bonds of an old friendship. Still, I've got my standards.

"The car's got air conditioning, right?"

"We had to put him in a home three years ago," Jack tells me on the ride down to Villa Lucila, the nursing facility where Pop Dugan is living out his twilight years. "I offered to put him up in my place, or give him round-the-clock care at his own house, but he wouldn't hear of it."

"And your mom?" I ask.

"Passed on about ten years back."

"I'm sorry, Jack. She was a good lady."

Jack nods and shifts himself in the back of the limousine. He grabs his right leg with his hands and folds it over his left, almost as naturally as if they were crossing under their own power. "It was one of those middle-of-the-night things. The doctors say it's pain-less, the best way to go, but . . ." He shrugs. "Then it was just Pop. But he never wrote the checks or took care of the house or any of those things Mom always did, so once she was gone, it was pretty much a time bomb. Listen, though—when we get there, don't mention her. It tends to get him all worked up. If *he* wants to talk about her, that's fine, but—"

"I understand."

We sit in silence as the limo heads across town—me, Jack, and Nelly Hagstrom, all buddy-buddy in the wide backseat. I'm still getting some serious vibes off Hagstrom, little shock waves of hatred rolling off his body. It was bad enough in Norwalk; since he roughed me up in the bar and I started tagging along with his boss, the amplitude has increased tenfold.

"You like it down here?" I ask him, hoping to break a little ice off our relationship.

"The fuck you care?" he spits back—and I'm talking literally: my rayon jacket is splattered with small dots of expectorate.

"Nelly," chides Jack, "that's no way to treat a guest."

Hagstrom fixes his boss with a thinly veiled look of exasperation. "He ain't a guest in *my* house."

"Yeah, and he is in mine. Just as good, if not better."

As we fall silent again, Jack uncrosses and recrosses his legs once more; this time I guess I let my gaze linger too long, because he finally breaks the ice on the one subject I wasn't going to broach first.

"You wanna know 'bout the legs, huh?"

"Not especially."

Jack laughs and slaps Nelly on the back. "I love this guy. 'Not especially.' Don't you love him?"

Nelly's grunt indicates otherwise, but Jack keeps on keeping on: "It's no big deal anymore, it's just I gotta explain it every time I meet someone new. Or, in this case, someone old.

"'Bout five years ago, I was getting outta the bathtub and my tail gave out on me. Just like that, it felt a little weak, and boom, I was back in the tub, water splashing and I'm trying to figure out what the heck went wrong. Figured maybe I'd slipped on the soap or pinched a nerve or something, 'cause a minute later it was fine again.

"Only it kept happening, more and more often. I'd be getting ready in the morning, and poof, there'd go the tail, limp as a wilted stick of celery. Or I'd undress at the end of an evening out, take off the G-clamp, and it'd just lie there, drooping down to the ground between my legs. That's a fucking embarrassing situation when you're with a gal, lemme just say."

"You couldn't feel anything?" I ask.

"That was the weird part," says Jack. "I could feel pain, no problem. I just couldn't move it. Went in for tests, the whole jazz, and while they were trying to figure out what was going on, my legs started to go, too. By that point, they got the diagnosis. It's called spinal muscular atrophy—basically, the motor neurons down my spine are dying off, so I get progressively weaker as time goes on. The neurons die, so the muscles waste away and, just like that, I ain't gonna be winning any Olympic relays. Been a good two years since I could move my legs at all."

I don't have any good responses to this, other than "I'm sorry, Jack. That pretty much sucks."

"Nail on the head. But, hey, I got a power chair, I got a good guy to drive me around, it's not so bad."

I'm curious if there's a drug, a regimen of treatment, anything that might reverse the effects of the disease, but I get the feeling Jack doesn't want to talk about it much. Fortunately, we pass the wrought-iron gates of the nursing home, which provides a natural end to an otherwise uncomfortable conversation.

"We're here," Jack says as the limo pulls to a stop. "Everyone put on your smiley faces."

The chauffeur helps Jack into his power chair, and Nelly and I follow behind as Jack zips up the front walk. The grounds of Villa Lucila are well kept, the lobby clean and respectable. Back in the days when I'd take any case that came along, when a two-hundred-dollar fee meant a shopping spree down the produce aisle, a woman hired me to tail her mother-in-law, to find out where the old gal kept her jewlery. The old lady lived in a nursing home in southwest Los Angeles that was so dilapidated, the owners of the crack house across the street complained that it brought down their property value. Turned out she was keeping her jewelry inside her pillowcase; turned out, also, the so-called jewelry was all of the costume variety.

This joint, though, is first-class. As a nurse escorts us down the hallway toward Pop Dugan's room, we're greeted by the other residents, many of whom seem to know Jack. Even those who don't tend to smile in our direction, and we beam it right back. Even Hagstrom's up to the task, which is impressive, given his predilection for scowling.

"Jackie!" Pop Dugan calls out as we enter. "The Dolphins beat the spread. You owe me fifty bucks."

"Pop, it was a preseason game. That doesn't count."

"It always counts." He turns to Nelly for support. "Tell your boss it counts."

Nelly wisely holds his hands up and backs away. "This is family business," he says, "not *family* business."

"You're a smart one, you." He turns to me. "New guy. What do you think?"

I look to Jack, who nods for me to go ahead. "I think if you're betting on preseason football, you've been chewing some of your own product, Pop."

Maybe it's my voice, or the way I've laid it out for him, but suddenly Pop Dugan's got me in a bear hug of his own, and now I know where his son gets his strength. For the third time today, I'm momentarily unable to breathe.

"Vincent Rubio," says Pop, pressing my head into his chambray shirt, "you've grown into your smell. That chewed-up cigar . . . I always knew that would make a real fine scent one day."

"Thanks, Pop," I manage. "You smell good, too."

"Well, a little on the musty side, maybe, but, all in all, I'm okay." He holds me at arm's length, and I'm half-worried he's going to go for another hug. But he just stares at me for a few more seconds before releasing my shoulders and hopping into a standard wheel-chair in the corner.

"I stole this from Mrs. Greenbaum's room," he says, pulling the chair into an impressive wheelie as he scoots around the room. "Come on, Jackie, let's race down the hall before she wakes up."

"Jesus, Pop, you can't keep doing that—"

"Aha! You're scared I'll win this time."

Jack turns to me, his arms spread wide. "I command an em-pire," he sighs, "but I can't control a single eighty-year-old Hadrosaur."

"Seventy-nine, and no, you can't. If Jackie won't race me, Vin-cent will. Let's see . . . Murray's got an X ray later tonight, we can get his chair when he's on the table—"

"Pop, enough. We gotta get going."

I check my watch; it's nearly past ten. "I didn't know we were taking a field trip."

"What, you got someplace else to be?" asks Jack. "You're on va-cation, right?"

I don't think this is the time to tell him about the Tallarico brothers. I don't particularly know if *any* time will be the time, but I'm pretty damned sure this ain't it.

"Right. It's just . . . I'm down here with a friend."

"Say no more. I've got a cell phone in the limo, you can invite her along. Allow me to be your guide to Miami nightlife."

I don't have much of a choice; Pop Dugan's already got his arm around me as we all walk out of his room and into the wide Villa Lucila hallway.

"Your parents, Vincent—how are they?"

"Both gone. A while ago. Dad first, then Mom a few months later."

Pop shakes his head. "Shame. She died of a broken heart, huh?"

"Something like that." Not one of my favorite topics, so I cast about for a new one. "I didn't notice any security checkpoints on the way into the home. No smell test, nothing."

Pop Dugan shakes his head. "It's an integrated joint."

"What, the whole nursing home?"

"Kit and kaboodle. In fact, my old roommate was human. Good man, as apes go."

Most reptilian medical-care facilities guard against accidental discovery by instituting strict security measures. Everyone who comes in must be sniffed, inspected, and announced; if a human should manage to wander past the gates, everyone's on full-guise lockdown until he wanders back out again. "I'm surprised," I say. "What if someone doesn't properly clamp up, or misbuttons a glove, or—"

"Or any of the other million things us old farts forget?"

"Your words, not mine."

Pop stops in the hallway and I come to a halt alongside him. He pokes his head into an open door, and then drags me inside, leaving Jack and Nelly in the hallway.

A petite, jittery old man sits in a plush chair that overwhelms his small frame; it looks as if it might swallow him whole at any moment. He watches the news crawl by on CNN on a TV set into the wall.

"Howard?" says Pop, and then again, louder, "Howard!"

The smallish man cranes his neck to get a look at us and pulls on a pair of wire-rimmed glasses. "That you, Hank?" he crows.

"Harold's an ape," Pop tells me, then turns back to the old man. "Isn't that right, Harold? You're human?"

The octogenarian gives a confused grunt. "What the hell else am I gonna be?"

"Exactly." Pop shoots me a wink and, before I can stop him, shoves his left hand up his right armpit, working loose the hidden buttons beneath.

"What are you doing?" I ask, suddenly realizing where he's going with this. "Pop, wait—"

With a flourish, he rips the human guise flesh off his right arm and flashes his claws into the open, flailing a green scaled arm two feet in front of Harold's bespectacled peepers.

"Roar," Pop says softly, prancing in front of a suddenly petrified Harold. "Grrrr."

Harold doesn't scream so much as hoot maniacally, and by the time he's gotten back his breath, Pop is already reguised and looking innocent as a choirboy at rehearsal.

"Lizard!" shrieks Harold. "Man-sized lizard!"

I drag Pop Dugan out of the room as Harold continues to rant and rave; in the hallway, Jack and Nelly are laughing it up. They've seen this act before.

I'm still stunned. Careless violations of the guise are one thing; willfull overt violations are another. "Did you just do what I think you did?"

"Just proving a point," says Pop.

"And that would be?"

"That integration ain't so hard when you're dealing with old-timers. Look, next time Harold's family comes to visit, he's gonna scream bloody murder that there are dinosaurs in his nursing home, right? And what's gonna happen then?"

"They're going to pat him on the head and up his meds."

"And go home sighing about how Dad used to have it together, but it's been all downhill since the fall. No one listens to us, Vincent. And I'll tell you what: sometimes it's a real blessing."

I look to Jack, who shrugs and powers his chair down the hallway. Nelly follows behind, and Pop takes my arm in his.

"Now," he says, "let's go hit the night."

On the drive over, Jack's chauffeur doubles back six or seven times on every side road and changes direction at least twice on each major highways.

"He a bit lost?" I ask.

Jack shakes his head. "Protection. We're in a bit of a tiff these days with some other businessmen down the way. If they don't know where I am, so much the better."

Though it would be so easy to let Jack in on my involvement with the Tallarico brothers, I know it would pretty much kill whatever is left of our one-time friendship. The time will come eventually; for now, I keep my knowledge of the situation to myself.

"So you drive fifty miles to actually go ten—"

"To throw off anyone who might be tailing us. Best defense is a good defense."

Glenda meets us outside a nondescript building on the Fort Lauderdale beach; from the swagger of her hip and the tapping of her toe, I'd say she's been waiting a while. When I called her from Jack's cell phone, she wasn't entirely thrilled about the prospect of spending her first night in South Florida at a mob club, but she didn't have anything better planned for the evening. The hotel concierge had already hit on her twice, and she didn't want him making her any dinner reservations for fear she'd show up and there he'd be, waiting at the table with a bottle of Chablis, quivering lips, and bedroom eyes.

"First you forget I'm coming to visit, then you drag me across the country, then you dump me on the side of the road, and just when you call and bestow your mercy on me and allow me to join you, you show up half an hour late and leave me sweating out here in the middle of nowhere."

"Right," I say. "Glenda, this is Jack. Jack, Glenda."

Jack takes Glenda's hand—she jumps a bit, and for a moment, I think she's gonna sock him one—and kisses it lightly. Glenda then does a strange thing, completely counter to everything I know about this grown-up tomboy: she smiles. Jack closes his eyes and takes a deep breath, his fake nostrils moving in and out with the air.

"Your scent," he says to Glenda. "It's very deep. Most women I meet . . . their smell is fine but shallow. Yours is full, blossoming, like a young girl first growing into womanhood."

"That's me," says Glenda. "In the throes of puberty. We going inside anytime soon?"

Pop climbs out of the limo. "A girl who knows what she wants. I like that. She's coming with me." He extends his arm, and Glenda, with a shrug, takes it. "I'm Pop Dugan," he tells her. "But you can call me Hank."

Hagstrom leads us around back, where we follow him up a ramp and through a small metal door. Inside the club, the lights are on, the dance floor empty. There's no one else around.

Glenda takes a step onto the dance floor. "Real hoppin' place you've got here. Tax shelter?"

Jack nods to Hagstrom, who jogs off behind an unattended bar. The club, though small, is well appointed, all burnished woods and thick carpet, and I wonder for a moment how they keep the rug so clean, what with all the mixed drinks sloshing around. The sound and light systems are similarly high-end, and the dance floor, while nothing John Travolta would ooh and aah over, is perfect for the size of the room. There's an intricate wooden pattern laid into the dance floor itself, and I take a step forward to investigate—

"Watch it," Jack says, pulling me back. "Okay, Nelly, hit it."

I hear a low hum as the floor begins to vibrate, that inlaid wooden pattern suddenly separating from the rest of the boards around it, revealing a ramp leading down to the real party below.

Jack wheels himself to the top of the ramp and spreads his arms wide. "Welcome . . . to Dugan's."

We climb down through the dance floor, single file, Pop and Glenda pressing into my back as we navigate the steep descent. "A bit showy," Glenda mumbles.

"That's what I told him," Pop says. "In my day, we didn't have all this fancy gadgetry to hide our hangouts. A door, maybe a deadbolt or two, and that was that. If a human accidentally wandered in, that was his own damned fault, and he'd just have to learn how to deal with living his life as a dead man."

The club below—the real club, as I have begun to understand it—is nothing like the austere, upscale Dugan's on the surface. Up there is where the mammals go when they're tired from a long day of sunning themselves on the beach, or when they want to hear some French Canadian music tra-la-la-ing through thirty-inch tweeters. Personally, I can think of a million things I'd rather listen to than Quebecois rock—my own tortured screams among them—but mammals can be funny when it comes to their tunes.

But down here . . . Down here is where the lizards get it on. Where they come to shake a little tail and see a little scale. Twenty girls in various states of dress, undress, and redress, prancing away on raised stages, on tables, twirling around poles and various other large, immobile objects, some of which have been carved to represent the great phalluses of the world. The lights are on some sort of recognition system, allowing them to highlight only the most lascivious parts of each dancer's anatomy. And the music, rather than the garden-variety, hair-band, beer-commercial anthem or power ballad, is electronic, pulsing, and throbbingly erotic.

This is not your father's strip club. Unless, of course, your father was Godzilla.

Jack's men from the Sea Shack have already made themselves at home, surrounding the available tables, shoving bills into clamps and buckles, their libidos healthier than their wallets. Bellying up to the bars, getting their faces in as close as possible to the writhing bodies in front of them, the drool slipping out of their mouths and onto the carpet below.

"That's some good saliva action," Glenda clucks, staring at the crowd. "Didn't know the glands turned on that fast."

"Guys have no middle speed," I explain. "We've got stall and full-throttle, that's about it."

"Men," she sighs. "Freaking men . . ."

Jack pulls up to my side and gives my arm a slight tug. "Come on back, I wanna show you something."

Glenda is more than happy to accompany me and Jack to the rear of the club, where we enter a bustling kitchen area. The first thing I notice is the waitstaff: young, attractive, and Asian. In fact, they all have a similar look—and scent—to the girl who was serving drinks out at the Tallarico place.

"Where'd you get the waitresses?" I ask.

"Temp service," Jack says dismissively. "Now, here's the thing I want to show you. I'm pretty proud of it."

He pulls open a cabinet door to reveal a hearty stock of bottles, each filled with some clear liquid. Must be gin, or vodka.

Glenda grabs one of the bottles and holds it up to the light. "This liquor?"

Jack nods. "I'm an importer—I gotta import *something*. IRS don't like it when a taxidermist has a penthouse and a yacht."

He pulls a glass off a shelf and thunks it down on the counter, then fills it halfway with the crystal liquid. "Go on," he says, "have a taste."

"I don't really dig on mammal shots," I tell him. "Never did much for me."

"Me either," says Jack. "Trust me, this is different."

He pours another shot for Glenda and one for himself. I shrug and grab the glass. Very few of the human liquors have any effect on dinosaurs—our metabolisms don't react the same way. Sure, we can overdose on the stuff, but it's pretty much the same thing as overdosing on Diet Coke. You'll be squatting in the bathroom for hours on end, but you can still drive home afterwards with a clear head.

One quick throw, down the hatch, the liquid burning a bit as it hits the back of my throat, coating the inside of my mouth, but I know that the gin won't do a thing, that it won't alter my mood in the slightest, that it's perfectly A-okay as far as my nine-month chip down at HA goes, because liquor is a mammal's problem, not—

The room dips. A sudden lurch to the left, and I put out a hand to steady myself against the bar. Suddenly my taste buds are assailed by a familiar flavor, the smell reaching back through my sinuses and grabbing at some forgotten part of my brain—

"What—what the hell—" I manage to spit out.

"*Infusion*," says Jack. "That's what we're calling it, anyway." He turns the bottle of gin around, and through my suddenly swimming vision, I can see that the bottle of what I took to be Beefeaters is actually a brand I've never seen before. A pale-green label is affixed to the front, a classy design of alternating light and dark strokes against the background, the pattern forming what looks to be a long, curving leaf.

INFUSION it reads up top in bold green lettering, and beneath it, in script: *The Classic Blend*.

"Herb-based alcohol," Jack says proudly. "It's all the rage—at least, down here it is. Basil gin, cilantro vodka, even a cinnamon-stick rum. For dinos who want to get high socially when they mix with mammals. Bars, company retreats, that sorta thing. And if the humans drink it too, so much the better. That's the beauty of it—liquor and herbs. It gets *everyone* off."

"Oh Christ," I hear Glenda mumble. "Here we go . . ."

I'm getting over that initial burst of confusion, that too-familiar plunge into the senselessness of the senses, and now the hunger is coming on strong. It's been over three-quarters of a year since I've felt it like this, and in an instant those nine months have been erased. It's amazing to me that I was ever able to repress this desire. How did I do it for so long? *Why* did I do it for so long?

"We're setting up a distribution deal to bring it up north," he continues, oblivious to my conflict, "then we'll move it out west. Well, they'll test-market it first, but . . . hell, they got the name right."

"More," I say, slamming the shot glass onto the table. My hand is shaking, but another hit of this elixir will fix that.

But Jack's backing up, looking at me cross-eyed. "Vincent . . . you okay?"

"Yeah, yeah, sure," I say, and now I'm feeling it, the warmth running through my veins, the nice glow at the edges of the world. "I'm feeling great, Jack. I just dig your drink, that's all."

Glenda steps in front of me. "I don't think that's such a great idea, partner."

"Funny," I say, hearing the words coming out of my mouth but not under my own control, "I don't remember asking you."

Jack sits back in his chair, observing our exchange. Trying to get a handle on the situation as he gets a good look at my eyes, as if he knows there's something there, separate from what I'm telling him. I try to avert, to stare up at the ceiling, down at the floor, or, preferably, across at the bottle. "Something happening I should know about?"

"Nothing," I say, fixing Glenda with a look.

Glenda backs off. "Know what? I ain't your baby-sitter. Knock yourself out." She backs away from us and out of the kitchen, leaving just me, Jack, and that glorious bottle of liquid happiness.

I try to laugh it off, show Jack it's just a joke. "Don't mind her, she's . . . she's Glenda. Hey, why don't we try another shot of that stuff? Just one more. Consider me your own personal test-market group."

As Jack hoists the bottle, a single drop, balanced on the rim ever since he poured that first glass, drips down the side and falls off, splashing onto the floor. For a quick second, I consider dropping to all fours, shoving my face down into it, and sucking at the kitchen tile in the hopes of getting that milliliter of basil gin into my mouth and body and brain.

That's when it hits me: I'm willing to suck linoleum to get at this stuff.

"I'm an herbaholic," I squawk, twice as loud as necessary.

Jack recoils as if slapped. "Jesus, Vincent—you shoulda told me."

"Just—just take it away," I manage to say, an instant before my arm shoots out, grabbing at the bottle—

Jack yanks it back just in time. "Hey, hey, slow up—"

"Please," I repeat. "Put it away. Lock the cabinet, okay?"

He instantly does as I ask and hides the Infusion in the low cabinet. "There's no lock—"

"Then let's just get out of here."

We head out of the kitchen and back into the lounge—some part of me dying to run back in and start funneling bottle after bottle down my gullet—my feet coming back to me with every step. But I can still feel the herb running strong through me, and I wonder how long it will last. "How . . . how much is in there?" I ask.

"One shot? Probably about two leaves."

That'll keep me going for an hour or so, the way I figure it. It's amazing how quickly it came back, and with such force. Back in the day, two measly leaves of basil would barely have me ready for breakfast; now I'm ready to leap on the nearest table and start lap-dancing with a potted fern.

"You really shoulda told me," Jack says once again. "I never woulda had you try it out—"

"Don't worry about it," I say. "It's just . . . it's not the first thing you tell a guy after you haven't seen him for fifteen years. 'Hey, great to see you, how's your life? Me? I'm a fuckup of the first degree.'"

"Nah, Vincent, it ain't like that . . ."

But I know it is. He's already pitying me a bit—his eyes have softened, his head tipped to one side. It doesn't matter. It's no different with anyone else. This is what I live with, and this is what I accept.

Up on the center stage, another stripper makes her way out from behind the black gauzy curtain. She's fully clothed, which is to say completely naked except for her human guise. A tall redhead with pert breasts and wide hips, she'd do well in any human strip club she chose, but this isn't where her talents lie. As the music pulses above, she slowly goes to work on her skin, seductively releasing and removing one fake leg after the other, exposing a long, green gam with a set of lean, sharp claws to match. She's keeping the tail hidden until the end; it's an old stripper trick, but it sends the customers into a frenzy.

Jack's men eat it up. They're shoving twenty-dollar bills into the fold of skin where the scales meet her false hips, tucking the money way down so they can touch the raw flesh themselves. And the girl doesn't seem to mind a bit; in a place like this, you keep your feelings clamped up tight and your clamps on the floor. A gal's gotta make a living.

"Infusion?"

I look down to my side to find another of the small, Asiatic gals that swarm around both Jack's and Tallarico's empires. "No, thanks," I say. My left hand suddenly shoots out to snatch the glass, but my right one grabs the offending arm at the wrist and wrestles it back into place. The waitress gives me the kind of look she probably reserves for curiosities at the zoo.

"Could you put the drinks down for a second?" I ask her, motioning to a nearby table. "I'd like to ask you a few questions—"

"We can't date customers," she says automatically.

"No, it's not—I mean, you're very beautiful, but that's not . . ." Now she's giving me the look she probably reserves for horny curiosities at the zoo. "Haven't I seen you somewhere before?" Great, Vincent, start out with a pickup line.

"I don't think so."

"Maybe it was one of your coworkers. You've all got a similar scent, did you know that?"

She shakes her head and looks nervously around the room. "I have to work—"

"What about Eddie Tallarico?" I ask, keeping my voice low. "Do you work for him, too?"

For a moment, I think I smell those prunes—the anxiety, the fear—but it's gone a second later. "I'm not supposed to talk to the customers," she says. "I just serve drinks." And with that, she's off, swallowed up by the thirsty crowd.

"That's a Rubio for you. Always knows how to scare off the ladies." It's Glenda, at my side. "You through with your little slip?" She's not my HA counselor—not by a long shot—but I know I put Glenda through a lot of shit back in my chewing days, and I can understand why she'd want to keep a good friend seated firmly on his wagon.

"Momentary lapse. I'm walking the line, same as every day."

To a cavalcade of catcalls, one of Jack's men has leaped upon the stage, and now he's dirty-dancing with one of the half-dressed gals. He's got a pompadour hairdo and swarthy skin, and he spins his hips like he's twirling a hula hoop, arms high in the air, playing it up for his buddies down below. The girl on the table looks mildly pissed, but the steady stream of cash making its way into the fold of her armpit—the bills sticking out of a flesh-colored B-strap—chills everything down a notch.

"Antonio!" Jack calls out. "Get the hell off the stage."

The pompadoured underling pouts. "But Jack, I can make some good money up here. Ain't that right, fellas?"

The other guys in the bar laugh and pull Antonio away from the limelight as the girls get back to business. Glenda pulls a drink off the tray of a nearby waitress. She tosses it down in a single belt and places it back in its spot. "What?" she says when I raise my eyebrows at her. "Just 'cause you can't handle your herb means I can't have any fun? Your buddy Jack's hit on something here. This Infusion is some keen shit."

"Glenda Wetzel," I say. "Ever the lady."

"Fuck it, I'm in a strip club. Etiquette is out the window when the entertainers tear off their breasts."

"Another drink?" a new waitress asks, and as I look down to tell her I'm not interested, she winks at me.

Glenda helps herself to another glass, though, and it gives me an opportunity to assess the situation. Is the waitress coming on to me? Is she trying to tell me something? I look back at Glenda, tossing back that shot of cinnamon-based Infusion, then down to the waitress again—

Another wink, and this time there's no doubt about it. Unless she's got one massive speck of dirt in that right eye, the gal is trying to tell me something. There's a smell there that I just can't place, something that's tickling the back of my brain. Before I can place it, she takes her tray and vanishes into the growing throng of Jack's men, wending her way through the crowd.

The herbs have already begun to take their toll on Glenda. She's a happy chew, for the most part, never too out of control to draw attention to her inebriated state. At HA, she's what we'd call a social chewer, but, once upon a time, so were a lot of us. You approach the cliff's edge one foot at a time, but that last step can be a doozy.

". . . lucky for you," she's saying, "I'm used to squalor. Hell, this motel room I'm in doesn't even have a tub. Just a lousy shower stall, and I'll be damned if my tail doesn't hang out the curtain . . ."

"That's great, Glen," I say, my feet already in motion, following that smell across the club. "Stay here, I'll be back."

And I'm off, tracking the waitress through the crowd. Was she trying to get me to follow her? If so, I'm more than happy to see what's what. I leap into the air—not so easy with my Johnston & Murphys, their thick soles preventing me from getting the height I truly need—and catch only a momentary glimpse of that long, black hair.

I follow, and soon find myself back in the kitchen, industrial appliances shining in the glaring lights, everything clean and wiped down to proper health-inspection codes. It'd take very little in the way of bribe money for this place to pass muster, I would guess. Of course, the mammal health inspectors don't come down here, and the reptilian ones couldn't care less about a few code violations. The Council has bigger things to worry about than a few rats doing the backstroke in a pot of gazpacho.

Swarming all through the place, scurrying back and forth from station to station, are the waitresses, each of them similarly dressed and coifed, their guises so near to identical as to make them difficult to tell apart. Every one is young, female, and Asian, and I'm sure there's a porn site on the Internet devoted to this very experience.

"Did someone just offer me drinks?" I call aloud, and within seconds, three of them are at my side with glasses full of Infusion.

My mouth suddenly fills with saliva and my left hand begins to shake. Just the mere thought of the herbs—inches from my mouth, so close, so easy—sends me reeling.

"No," I manage to say, "I don't *want* a drink. I just want to know if one of you *offered* me a drink—"

"Would you like a drink?" asks one to my right.

This isn't working. I'm about to think of a new tactic when that smell hits me harder, and this time I can identify it. A hunk of cheese, three days past ripe. Familiar, but that single shot of herb liquor is still clouding my mind, making identification difficult.

I turn to find the waitress who winked at me sliding past, and I get a quick glimpse of the tray of drinks she's carrying, one of the glasses of Infusion frothing slightly up top.

"Wait a second," I call, but she's out through the double doors and into the crowd before I can get a bead on her.

Out in the club, where the music has dropped to cocktail-hour level, the girls have come down from their stages and the guests are now mingling with the lovely ladies. *Groping* is perhaps the better term. I'm twenty feet behind the waitress, but it's hard to make my way through the clutch of arms and hands and naked tails in my way.

There's something about this gal that's given me the willies, and it's not just the enigmatic wink. Pop Dugan grabs me as I pass by and begins a little rhumba to the music, tapping his feet and swinging his hips. I can smell the basil on his breath; a half-drunk shot of Infusion is in his hand.

"Tiffany used to dance a mean rhumba," he says. "That woman had a serious set of legs. She had a more cheerful set of legs, too, but most of the time those stayed in the closet."

I give in to the dancing for the moment. If you can't rhumba with an elderly Hadrosaurus at his son's mafia nightclub, when can you rhumba?

"Pop," I say, leading for a moment so that we're turned toward Jack and his crew. "Does that waitress seem weird at all to you?" I point across the room, where the server has just infiltrated Jack's inner cadre. She's passing out the Infusion, glass by glass, and they toss them back easily, casually. Hagstrom, Antonio, and a few other beefy soldiers surround Jack, keeping him protected even in this obviously safe haven.

"Who?" asks Pop. "The talent-pool girl?"

" 'Talent pool'?"

"Sure," he says. "Jackie and some business associates have a whole pool of girls they get to help with the chores. All come from someplace overseas. Jack puts 'em up in some house, free room and board. It's a good deal."

"Mail-order waitresses?"

A drunken Pop shrugs and returns to his rhumba and reminiscence. He launches into a speech about the saintliness of his late wife, and soon he's back in the past, reliving some marital event from their days together. He drains the rest of his Infusion and bangs the glass down on a nearby table.

The sight of the clean tumbler sets something off in my brain. Makes me flash back to thirty seconds ago, when the waitress passed by, her tray full of cups—one of them foaming.

Alcohol, herb-based or otherwise, doesn't foam. Beer foams. Champagne bubbles. But liquor stays put.

The rest of it falls into place instantly. The wink—not a signal to follow, but a knowing catch of the eye. A signal to say *Heya, pal, we're in on this together.* She knows me. And I know her. And *she* ain't a *she* at all.

Because that smell *was* cheese—cheese and jalapeños, and it's not just a natural dino odor, but one due to ingestion of massive quantities of nachos. And since there's no possible way that Marlon Brando has found his way down to the lower level of Dugan's nightclub, it can only mean one thing:

Tallarico's goon Sherman is in the club.

"Jack!" I scream, my legs already pushing me along as I stumble over thick tails, falling into the guests, but I don't care, it doesn't matter. "Jack!"

There he is, not hearing me yet, laughing it up with Hagstrom and Antonio and the others, a glass of Infusion in his hand, and even at this distance, I can see the thin layer of white up top, those small crystals floating along the surface.

Dissolution powder. In Jack's drink. The kind of hangover you don't wake up from.

"Jack!" I yell again, only halfway across the club but too far. Definitely too far. "Don't do it—don't drink it—"

He hears me this time—my voice, if not my words—and raises his glass in salute, holding it aloft—

"Put it down!" I shout, my throat raw, voice carrying over the music, everyone turning to look at me, to laugh at the Raptor in their midst, but I don't care—I'm focused on Jack's drink—heading toward his mouth, his lips parting wide—"Drop the drink!"

But I'm fifty feet away and Jack's all smiles as he lifts the tumbler to his lips. "Don't worry about *me*, Vincent," he calls out, laughing, grinning. "I know how to hold my herb."

It should crawl into slo-mo right now, my *no-o-o-o* falling into some unearthly scream as I futilely howl out my frustration and rage, but unfortunately, nothing of the sort happens. Jack's hand continues its unabated rise, the drink aiming for his lips, the dissolution crystals a split second away from hitting his unprotected flesh and washing it away forever.

And I'm leaping, throwing myself forward, my arm reaching out to bat away the glass, knock it to the ground, the ceiling, anywhere it can do no harm, extending my body as far as it can go, willing myself to grow an extra inch as I hurdle Hagstrom's body, locked on that deadly glass—

Coming up way too short, thudding to the ground three feet from Jack's entourage. I look up, already cringing as the glass tips back, liquid shifting toward Jack's open mouth—

An arm, sliding into my field of view, the hand knocking at the thick glass of the tumbler, whacking it up into the air, the liquid sloshing around, everyone watching it twist over and over in some warped recreation of the *2001: A Space Odyssey* opening sequence, before turning their attention to the woman who had the audacity to knock a drink out of the big boss man's hand.

"Vincent's pretty adamant about this not-drinking thing," says Glenda. "I think you should at least hear his reasons."

I open my mouth to explain, but suddenly find myself drowned out by a piercing scream no more than five feet away. A shriek of pain, loud and getting louder, and I'm on my feet, claws ready for action, glancing back and forth across the room as this wake-up call continues to slice through the crowd.

Antonio, the dino with the easy grin, loose hands, and wild pompadour, has already fallen to his knees, the howl of agony and terror breaking through the musical din, galvanizing the whole club. His hands cover his face, but the sound comes through un-muted, clear and perfect in its horror. Everyone is rapt, terrified, unable to turn away as a thick green goo pours from between Antonio's fingers, the flesh beneath rapidly dissolving away beneath the fury of the microscopic bacteria.

"It's dissolution powder!" I shout. "Get something—"

But there's no hope. Once the bacteria start working, they don't stop chowing down until there's nothing left to eat. Now there are new screams throughout the club as the dancers take off in a hundred different directions, scurrying around as if they're on the run from some exterior threat. Jack's men, at least, are keeping their wits about them, and though most seem quite horrified at what's occurring right before their eyes, they know there's nothing to be done.

Antonio's shrieks are beginning to lose their piercing quality as his lips dissolve beneath the attack, his face melting away as if he'd had the audacity to tie up Indiana Jones and open the Ark of the Covenant. Another one of Jack's people drops to a knee beside him, reaching out—

"Don't touch him!" Hagstrom barks, yanking the guy away from the writhing creature bleeding green muck onto the carpet.

"He's right," I say, though I hate to agree with Hagstrom. "Don't touch his skin. Stay back."

Antonio's body shakes in arrhythmic spasms, and now his hands are not enough to hide the devastation of his face and chest, especially now that the fingers, too, are dissolving away. Small choking noises kick out from his partially eaten throat, his legs jerking with every new mewl and chirp.

"Stand back," Jack instructs us. "Let me in."

"There's nothing you can do," I tell him. "You can't stop it—"

"Stand back," he repeats, his voice flat, steely. Not a voice I want to argue with right now. I take two big steps backwards and let Jack approach.

I hear the sharp report of the pistol before I see the piece itself, before I see the sudden hole blown open in Antonio's skull and smell the burning powder in the air. Antonio falls to the ground, and his body jerks one last time before settling into a final, peaceful rest as the dissolution bacteria continue their rampant feast. A third of his body is already gone, leaving only a bare skull and a thick puddle of emerald sludge.

"Goddamn," says Jack, softly, quietly.

"Goddamn," repeats Glenda.

And Hagstrom, kind, caring Hagstrom, straddles the body as it disintegrates into nothingness, his shoe brushing over the ruined carpet beneath. "Goddamn is right. I am never getting these stains out."

8

We search the club. More precisely, Jack's men search the club, while I kneel in the middle of the room, dazed, scraping green goo into a bucket, trying to figure out exactly what I should and should not tell my old friend at this precarious juncture in our relationship.

I know full well who placed the dissolution packet in Jack's drink, and even if I weren't a hundred percent sure based on the smell of nacho cheese and jalapeños alone, the wink is enough to seal it. Tallarico sent his goon Sherman into the club in order to carry out the hit, and only a last-second catch by my schnoz was enough to save Jack's life.

Of course, the big question is how Tallarico knew where Jack would be at that precise time. I wonder if they've got a tracer on me, but a quick self-patdown indicates I'm clean. Maybe they put a homing device in the toothpaste and my enamel is giving off signals. Good reason as any to neglect dental hygiene for a few days.

"One of my best men," Jack muses, and I can't tell whether his low tones indicate reasoned thought or imminent rage. "He had a kid. A little boy. He's a stupid little thing, but a kid. Jesus."

I've got nothing constructive to say; at least, nothing constructive that will keep me alive. If I tell them now that I've been staying with Tallarico, that I know who placed the spiked drink and wound up killing Antonio, there's no way Jack could let me remain among the living. I've been lying for too long to start telling the truth now.

I really need to call my sponsor.

On the other hand, if I feign complete ignorance, it's just going to be another tally in the negative column should they ever learn about my deal with the Tallaricos. It's an easy call, really: lie and save my ass for the time being but maybe get myself killed in the long run, or tell the truth and almost definitely blow it all right here, right now.

I'm a short-term kind of guy.

"Any ideas who it was?" I ask innocently.

Jack runs a hand through his hair, smoothing out the rangier strands. "Oh, I have some ideas."

"You do."

"I've got no illusions, Vincent. This is a dangerous business I'm in, and I accept that. I make friends and I make enemies, and that goes with the territory."

Hagstrom pulls up a chair and sits next to his boss. "We combed the place. No sign of anyone we don't control."

"What about the guise?" I ask.

Nelly starts to move away, ignoring me completely. Jack puts out an arm, stopping him.

"Vincent asked you a question, Nelly." Hagstrom grudgingly turns back and fixes me with a bored stare.

"What guise?"

"The one the assailant was wearing." It sounds good to use the word *assailant* where others would do just fine. Makes me sound like a cop, which throws Hagstrom off balance.

"Didn't find a guise."

"And all your staff are accounted for? All the . . . Asian gals, and their guises?"

"Yeah," says Hagstrom. "Anything else, Einstein?"

Trying to lead these guys in the right direction without giving myself away is no picnic. I feel like a guide dog for the blind whose master has decided to cross a four-lane intersection on his own.

"So what you're saying is that all of your waitresses and their guises are accounted for, and that the assailant who snuck in here did so because he or she was wearing a costume so similar to the rest of your staff that no one noticed anything odd about it. Doesn't that strike you as the least bit strange?"

Hagstrom gets it now; Jack got it before I even started talking.

"Talent pool," Hagstrom mutters, and Jack nods.

There it is again. "This 'talent pool,' " I ask, "what is it?"

"It's like an employment service. A lotta the girls . . . they're from elsewhere."

"So maybe someone else has access to this talent pool," I suggest. "Someone who isn't too happy with the way you're running your business."

Jack nods; he's right along with me, and probably a step ahead. "We got crews down here," he's saying, "and everyone needs support staff. So we all dip a little into the pool. Here and there. So, yeah, there are guys, might have the access." He turns to Hagstrom. "Get the girls out here. Undressed, unguised."

"But—"

"Do it."

Though things are quieting down now, an hour ago, the place was still in bedlam. As soon as Jack's gunshot cleared the air, Hagstrom took over the scene, barking out orders to the underlings as they sealed the doors, the windows, any possible chance of escape for the assassin. The older woman who's always at Jack's side had him off in a corner, whispering something in his ear. The more often she's around, the more nervous I get.

"I want everyone out here in the main room inside thirty seconds," Hagstrom announced, racing through the club, herding the guests and dancers into the center of the room like a prize sheep dog. Glenda and I found ourselves shuffling along with the rest of them, complicit cows in a willing herd, rapt by Hagstrom's commanding voice and presence.

"Guises off," he insisted, "all of you. Hold the straps and clamps in your left hand, the skins in your right. I want to see scales, people, and I want to see them now."

And we all complied, a mass disrobing, and Jack's soldiers were so stunned by the turn of events they forgot all about rubbing themselves up against the strippers, now in close nude proximity. Because despite all the naked flesh and scales rubbing up against one another, it's tough to be erotic when your friend and coworker has just melted into a pile of mint jelly.

Glenda's buzz was gone, the horrible scene sucking all the life from her semiherbaholic stupor. "It's freaking cold in here," she said, wrapping her arms around her body as she pulled off her skin and draped it carefully over her arm.

"You, too, Nelly," Jack said softly.

His jaw tightened; his shoulders fell. I loved it. "What?"

"Off with it. Come on."

"But, Jack—"

"Nelson," he said flatly, and I nearly lost a gasket at the use of his real name. No wonder he went by Nelly—Nelson Hagstrom is quite the mouthful, and a moniker destined to get your ass kicked on the playground. "Take it off. Now."

He bickered and fussed but in the end he disrobed, removing not only his legs and arms and torso, but also that mask, and for the first time I saw the wide, flat Hadrosaur face of Nelly Hagstrom. And aside from the blunt snout, the odd set to the teeth, the most interesting feature was a twisted, bent scale between his eyes, in the same location as the scar on the forehead of his human guise.

"See that?" I whispered to Glenda. "Something happened to his head."

Glenda chuckled. "You're one to talk."

I was one of the last to fully disrobe, not for any prudish reasons but simply because I was so intent on watching the others that I forgot to join in. "Let's do this, Vincent," Jack said as he wheeled up to me. "Get it over with."

I disrobed and deguised. For some reason, I wasn't concerned with the reaction of the other dinos in the room; I guess I should have been.

"Raptor!" growled Hagstrom, launching himself from across the room as I threw my arms into a cross of self-defense. Claws flashed out all around me, a hundred stilettos ready to make me into a scaled sieve.

Glenda hit Hagstrom low, throwing herself into his knees as I ducked out of the way and slid around to give him the old alley-oop over my partner's back. But Hagstrom was ready for it and leapt over Glenda's bent body, whipping around for another attack.

The rest of Jack's men drew into a tight circle as Glenda and I faced down Hagstrom's sudden wrath. I had no doubt they'd jump in if Glenda and I managed to get the upper hand, leaving me with two ugly choices: run, or die fighting. I spit out my bridge and bared my teeth, ready to go down gnashing—

"Enough!" The single word cut through the hum of rage and tension. "Enough with all of this!"

The crowd parted as Jack guided his chair over whatever flesh was in his way—you wanna hear a dino whimper, try running over the tip of his tail with a metal-rimmed wheelchair—zipping into the middle of the circle, placing himself amid me, Glenda, and Hagstrom.

Nelly was still worked up. "He's one of *them*," he barked. "A fucking Raptor, and we let him in this club. He's the one set the whole thing up—"

Hagstrom's voice cut off as Jack's hand shot up, just reaching the softer parts of Nelly's thick neck. He grabbed on tight, choking out the rest of Nelly's words before they could leave his mouth.

"From day one, this bullshit," he yelled, and suddenly his soldiers were beginning to inspect the floor, the walls, anything to avoid looking at their boss. "This is the kind of thing that got us in bad with every other crew in the first place. We let this bullshit get in the way."

Jack waved toward another one of his men, the one they call BB. He looks like Richard Greco, his hair thinning slightly on top. I wonder if they order from the same guise catalogue. "Get the other guys outta the back room, bring 'em all in here."

"Jack, really," I said, concerned with where this was heading. "I can just leave. You don't have to do this."

"Yes, I do, Vincent. Now stand back."

He released his single-hand choke hold on Hagstrom, and the big Hadrosaur stumbled backward, gasping for air.

Within a minute, everyone had joined the circle. Jack sat in the middle, wheeling around to make sure all of his employees got an eyeful from the boss man. "We are a family," he began, "of Hadrosaurs, that is true. If you look at us, if you smell us, if you feel us—we're Hadrosaurs, every one of us, and we should be proud of that.

"And I like to think we're a family when it comes to the best interests of our organization. We watch each other's tails, we sacrifice for the good of the whole. That's what makes us strong. That's what makes us stronger than the others.

"But we've become insular, and insularity begets weakness. We think we're sly and coy and have all the answers, and that—

precisely there—is where it all comes tumbling down. When you think you've got it all is when you've got the least of it. Am I making myself clear?"

A low rumble surfed through the crowd, though no one had the balls to actively disagree. Jack moved on. "So when I bring a trusted friend of mine into this family, when I ask him to be my guest in my home and at my place of business, there are certain things I expect in return."

"Okay, Jack," I said, sidling up and whispering in his ear. "Let's not piss off the locals."

"First," he continued, "I expect respect. If not for my guest, then at least for me. Respect that I have the right to bring in whoever I want, sight unseen. Second, I expect courtesy. If not for my guest, then the courtesy to smile to my face when he's in my company. And third, I expect compliance. If I ask you to befriend my guest, then you befriend him. If I ask you to stick a mushroom up your ass and dance a tango for him, then you'd better start looking for fungus and an Arthur Murray studio.

"But let's pretend that none of that existed. Let's pretend that I'm not Jack Dugan, that I'm not in charge here. Let's pretend that this is just an ordinary get-together, and I'm introducing you to a guy I once knew."

Jack extended his arm, inviting me into the center of the circle. And though I wanted to protest—the way you do to avoid seeming the teacher's pet—I couldn't derail his speech. I stepped next to him and gave a little wave to the crowd, which probably didn't do much to endear me to them any further.

"This is Vincent Rubio," he said, "and he is a Velociraptor. When we were kids, just twelve, thirteen years old, he faced a choice. He had to make the decision between Canadian prison"— and here, I could hear the murmur shooting through the room, the horrors of Ottawa well known to this crowd—"and ratting me out and skipping free. Him or me, that was his choice, back in the day. We were a couple of brats, thrown in front of the Council and forced to make a terrible decision.

"And this dinosaur before you—this Raptor—chose to subject himself to the tortures of the forty-sixth parallel rather than squeal on his Hadrosaur friend." Jack leaves it at that, staring at me with a glow of pride and friendship, and I'm feeling more like worm dung than ever before. I grin back meekly, and can only imagine the look on Jack's face were I to tell him of my employment with the Tallarico family, or how I was about to let it all fly back in that Council inquisition twenty years ago before the smell of prunes got me off the hook.

"Thanks," I muttered.

"And just an hour ago," he continued, turning back to the crowd, "Vincent—this Velociraptor you all revile—"

"Layin' it on a little thick, Jack."

"—saved my life yet again, noticing what I could not—or would not—seconds before the drink would have killed me where I sat. None of you Hadrosaurs came to my rescue. None of you Hadrosaurs were quick enough on the draw.

"So listen up, lizards, and hear me straight. Vincent Rubio is not to be harmed. He is not to be ostracized. You will treat him like a member of this family, and you will get to know him and love him like I have. He will become your brother.

"That is," he said, turning back toward me, extending a single ceremonial hand, "if he will have us."

Like I had a choice. I shook Jack's hand firmly, forcefully. "What the heck."

And just like that, it was over, the circle dispersed, Hagstrom slunk off into the shadows, and Jack's men were all over me, slapping me on the back, apologizing for their rudeness. And though I was happy to be part of the crew, happier still to be alive and not in a state of trauma, I couldn't help but wonder what percentage of their sudden change of heart was forced: Did Jack actually turn their minds around, or are they just following orders? Do I care?

BB and one of the older soldiers were put in charge of Antonio's bones, a single dinosaur skeleton lying on the carpet of Dugan's. Antonio was slim of stature, and his bones hinted at his petite frame—barely five feet high, most of his mammalian height must have been fitted into his guise, like the organic lifts Tom Cruise has sewn into his heels every few years. I know, I know, he's still pretty short, but there's only so far they can go without turning the things into stilts. Vanity, even for the rich and famous, has its limits.

BB grabbed a thigh bone in his hands and exerted pressure, bringing his knee up into the center. A sharp crack echoed through the air, like a rifle shot, and attention swung around to the center of the room.

"Hey, hey," said Jack, "guys, do that elsewhere."

"But you said we gotta—"

"Yeah, I know, but we don't wanna hear it."

BB nodded, and headed into the back room; when he returned, he was carrying a wide green sack, just about the perfect size for a dead body. I find it curious that they've got one of these handy, but thought it better not to ask. They loaded the clean white skeleton into the bag and carted it out a back door. Basic rules stipulate that you've got to break down any modern dino skeleton before dropping it off at one of the Cleanup Crew collection centers, but no one was interested in listening to Antonio's bones cracking like breadsticks.

Now, over an hour later, the cleanup job is done. Bones collected, goo all soaked into rags and burnt to a crisp back in the kitchen.

"Line up," Hagstrom calls out behind him as he walks out of the kitchen. "Go on, in front of Mr. Dugan. Put your guises by your feet."

The waitresses pour out single-file, stepping demurely as they head toward Jack. This is my first glimpse of them with their guises off, and I'm surprised to find that none of them are Hadrosaurs; each is an Ornithomimus, their rough skin a mottled green with marbled veins of brown running through it. The predictable curve to the neck, the slope down the spine, and the long, waving—

Their tails are missing.

Not entirely, but enough so that it's one of the first things I notice. A few of the girls have the typical long, counterbalancing tails typical of the Ornithomimus population, but most of them sport stubbier models, short little nubs of flesh where a flowing appendage should be. Some are more compact than others, some are nearly full-length, but it's clear that most of these girls are missing a crucial part of their anatomy. It's not a religious or cultural gesture; the ancient dinosaur practice of ritual tail circumcision went out with ancient dinosaur table manners.

I shoot Glenda a look; she shoots it right back at me. We're the only ones in the joint who seem to notice, or care, that these gals aren't quite all *there*.

Jack pulls between us. "Vincent, Glenda, where are you staying?"

"Hotel down south," I lie. Glenda gives a little smirk.

Jack accepts it. "You want to go back to the house, stay with us there?"

Tough situation. If I say no, I may look suspicious. If I say yes, I'll end up in hot water with Tallarico.

Hagstrom saves me. "Christ, Jack—there's a limit," he says, but his voice trails off as Jack fixes him with a glare I wouldn't want to be on the other side of.

"It's fine," I say, taking this chance to backpedal. "The hotel's all paid for, anyway. One of those package deals."

Jack isn't interested in hearing the minutiae of my vacation plans. He looks to Glenda. "What about you?"

I try to nod with my eyes, to give Glenda some impression that I'd like her to be my eyes and ears inside the Dugan compound, if only so that I can eventually help Jack figure out how the Tallaricos are gaining access to his family. She must pick up on the hint, because she accepts Jack's offer. "So long as I get my own bathroom," she adds. "A gal's gotta keep herself dainty."

Nodding, Jack waves a hand toward Hagstrom. "Nelly, get one of the guys to take her back to the house." He wheels past me, toward the line of waiting, tail-free waitresses. "Go on back to the hotel," he tells me. "Have a spa, get a massage. I might need you later."

As I head for the ramp and exit Dugan's, I can hear Jack start in on that odd group of Ornithomimi. "Okay, ladies, let's take it from the top," he says, and though I know he's going to interrogate them about the last few hours, part of me can still imagine that he's going to clap *five-six-seven-eight* and lead them into a kick-line.

But that part's growing smaller by the day.

I take a cab back to Eddie Tallarico's compound down on Star Island. The guards at the gate have to call back to the house and, once they let me through, the guards at the house have to call up to some unseen command center, but eventually I get in, and I head right for my room. The day's events have left me drained, and I kick off my shoes and fall onto the bed, half-asleep before my head hits the pillow. There's too much to think about between Eddie and Frank and Jack and Hagstrom and some unseen mole infiltrating the Dugan family, and the only way I'm going to make any sense of it is to turn off my thinker for a while and give it a rest. Tomorrow, if I'm very, very lucky, will indeed be another day.

I wake to the sound of a fifty-foot goose honking out a note of frustration, his elongated bill a foot from my ear. A single, squawking note, riding high and loud above any thoughts in my own head, all my dreams vanishing in a clarion call of brass and air.

Eddie Tallarico is playing the trumpet.

"Rise and freaking shine," he yells, one foot on either side of my body, his weight pressing into the mattress as he jumps up and down, up and down, like a five-year-old in the carnival Bounce House. "Up, Rubio, up!"

I clasp my hands over my ears, but it's not much use. He's torturing the instrument, positively mauling anything good and true about that beautiful horn, and I wouldn't be surprised if Miles Davis himself were to rise from the dead and drag Eddie Tallarico down to hell for his sins against brass.

"We got work to do—"

"We do, huh?"

"More precisely, *you* got work to do." Eddie sticks out a hand. I grab it, and he hoists me up and off the bed. "That's right," he says. "I heard about last night."

"What'd I do?" I really can't remember; the cobwebs of sleep have yet to clear. But something's coming into focus, something ugly, green, and gooey.

The club. The powder. The attack. Right.

Tallarico's mole must have told him I fouled up the attempted hit on Jack. I've got to come up with something to explain myself.

"Now, see, here's the thing," I begin, an instant before realizing that I haven't got a single word with which to follow up.

"I know everything," he laughs. "I got a guy on the inside, gives me the whole scoop. We had that Dugan fuck dead to rights till some broad popped up and played Wonder Woman, got some poor shlub instead. Hey, a hit's a hit, but I woulda liked to get the big job done sooner rather than later."

"Sure, sure," I say, trying to buy time while I make sense of the whole thing. The mole must have missed the fact that I was the one to warn Jack, that Glenda was only knocking away the drink on my suggestion. This is good; it only helps my situation with Tal-larico.

"Fucking broad," I mutter, trying to get a good sandpaper edge to my voice. "Dames."

Eddie blasts out another few notes and hops off the bed; the mattress springs back up, and I can almost hear it sigh happily as the load is removed. "Today, my new friend," he says, "you're gonna fill in."

This stops me cold, a tendril of dread muscling into my chest. "Fill in?"

Eddie reaches into my closet and starts rummaging through my clothes. He's touching my shirts. The bastard is actually *touching* them, his grubby hands creasing the linen and silk.

"Know what?" I say, leaping over to the closet, muscling him out of the way. "I been dressing myself since I was six. Think I can handle this one."

Eddie shrugs and shuffles away. Couldn't care less. "I got a number of business ventures," he says, "and I'm spread kinda thin. This can be a bit of a . . . problem some days."

"That's a shame."

"Usually," he says, "we can handle it."

"Great. Then handle it."

"See, I'd love to, only when I said I was spread thin, I mean like one scoop of peanut butter and a hundred slices of bread. So I got jobs I gotta devote guys to, and other jobs which go lacking. Some-times, all I need is presence. Guys don't have to do nothing on the job but show up and look pretty, but when one of my guys doesn't show up—"

"Then you need a fill-in. I got you," I say.

"Great. Then we're settled."

"But it doesn't mean I'm agreeing."

Tallarico takes a moment to think this over, then allows himself a deep burp. He doesn't excuse himself.

"You don't have a choice," he informs me. "I own you, Rubio, for eleven more days. What *I* say, *you* do—"

"That wasn't the deal."

Tallarico shakes his head. "You're some fucking piece of work, Rubio."

"Likewise."

"My brother gives you twenty grand—"

The little bit of herb left in me takes over. "Screw that angle," I yelp, standing up, standing over Eddie, looking down at his pudgy face and dirty feet sticking out from beneath the robe. "Twenty grand to tail a guy, okay? To tail him, that's all. And I'm doing a hell of a lot more than that. Frank wanted investigative work, he's getting investigative work. So if you're not happy with it, then take it up with your brother, but I'm doing what I was paid to do, and that's that, and you can go fuck a monitor lizard before you yell at me again for doing my job."

Eddie doesn't answer for some time. He holds my gaze, and it's me versus him, his stare versus my stare. A minute passes. Two. It's incredibly difficult to keep this up, and it's not just my contacts, which are rapidly drying out. There's a sense that he's looking into me, that he's reading what's in my head. That he knows it all already.

He breaks it off. Feels like an hour, might have been three minutes tops, but he breaks it off and allows himself a short chuckle. "Fuck a monitor lizard," he says. "I like that."

"Feel free to use it at parties."

Eddie nods; I fear he actually may.

"So, you'll do this thing?"

That's when I realize that there's no way to say no to a Tallarico. I could complain till I'm tan in the face, but what a Tallarico wants, a Tallarico gets. If I want to remain a general semblance of *intact,* it would probably be best to cooperate.

"Okay," I say. "I understand."

"I thought you might."

Though I'm sure this decision will come back to haunt me in one way or another, I can't see another way out. Unless . . .

"I wouldn't suppose there's a temp service you could call?"

This little job Eddie sends me on is the one in which I end up in a bloodstained Lexus sedan with nacho-cheese Sherman and surfer-dude Chaz. This is the job in which I spend an unexpected day at the races and quickly learn that not all Thoroughbreds are thoroughly bred. This is the one where Sherman pulls his second dissolution-packet trick of the last few days and unleashes a legion of starving bacteria on poor Stewie's flesh. And this is when I learn the fine art of tail-chopping in an intensive five-minute hands-on seminar.

But it's all over now. Pepe, the jockey, is somewhere back at Calder Racetrack being worked over by Sherman and Chaz, and dear old Stewie is hopefully at a local hospital, getting the help he needs in advance of the painful rehab process for his busted stump of a tail. For a moment, I wonder if this is the same thing that happened to the waitresses at Jack's club, but for some reason it doesn't ring true.

On the cab ride from the racetrack back to Tallarico's, my cell phone rings. I'm still dazed from the previous few hours, so it's a few moments before I recognize my own ring-tone.

"What *is* that?" the human cabbie asks me. "That song, I heard that before."

" 'Crocodile Rock,' " I tell him. "Sort of a personal favorite." I find the SEND button and press the phone to my ear. "Hello?"

"Hey, Vincent, how you holdin' up?" It's Jack, sounding casual as ever despite the fact that he's only hours removed from a gruesome attempt on his life. "Listen, I want you to drop by the house. Got someone here wants to see you."

"Sure, Jack," I say. "Lemme just get back to the hotel, freshen up."

"Better come by now. You need a limo?"

"I'm already in a cab."

"Good," he says. "Hand the phone to the driver, I'll give him directions."

Jack and the cabbie have a lovely chat, and some time between relaying directions and hanging up, they wind up in a whole conversation about the weather and the dangerous possibility of a hurricane hitting the coast. It's not like I resent their concern for the neighborhood, but . . . I do worry a bit that they're wasting my free minutes!

The cabbie heads north, into a posh, palm-tree-lined part of town. "They call this Aventura," the cabbie says.

"Aventura. What's that mean?"

"Means 'too rich for my blood.' "

We pull through a series of gates and the driver drops me off at a thirty-story apartment building ringed with huge bay windows. As I step into the lobby, I get a whiff of Hagstrom.

"This way," he grunts, leading me down a hall and into what looks like a private elevator. Indeed, there are no buttons—only a single keyhole. Hagstrom pulls a brass key out of his pocket, inserts it, and twists firmly. The elevator shakes once, and rises.

"Everything settled from yesterday?" I ask. "We good and all?"

No answer. Hagstrom stares straight ahead as the express elevator shoots us skyward.

"Oh, good."

When the doors open, I expect to see Jack, decked out in some fine suit or another, waiting for me with open arms, or, at the very least, Glenda sipping an Infusion martini.

What I don't expect—and precisely what I find—is a tall, thin gal in a stunning strapless dress, the wave of saltwater and mangoes washing over me even before the elevator doors part to reveal her presence.

There's no need to take a step forward—she's right there, not eighteen inches away—and I open my mouth to say hello, to say something witty, to surprise her with the ways in which my lexicon has grown and flowered in the fifteen years since we've seen each other—

She slaps me hard across the left cheek.

"Afternoon, Vincent," purrs Noreen. "It's good to see you again."

And she slaps me hard across the right. These Dugans sure know how to greet a guy.

9

oreen.

What can you say about a gal like Noreen? That she had a tail to rival that of the great seductresses of the ages? That her scent could carry me away on waves of olfactory bliss? That she understood me well enough to rip my heart to shreds and then fit it back together again, piece by piece, just in time to start the process all over again?

Sure, you could say all those things. You could also say that she was beautiful, smart, kind, giving, and all the other words folks use when at a loss for what to say. But when it comes to Noreen, there's one overriding way to describe her:

She confused the hell out of me.

Normally, I'm a loquacious kinda guy. I know how to turn on the verbal faucet, and when it comes to charming gals outta their unmentionables, I'm a Raptor who can rap with the best. But there's always been something about Noreen that's clammed me up tight and thrown me into a mental tailspin. You might say that's love. I say it's just radar-jamming; she's got my frequency and blurs out the signal.

Wasn't always that way, I guess. In the beginning, she was just Jack's younger sister, a little kid getting in the way of our fun and games. Only two years our junior, but it was enough to make her the pipsqueak and us the mature men trying to do man's work, such as depositing bags of flaming poop on neighbors' doorsteps.

"Gonna tell Mom," she'd say, as all little sisters would.

"Gonna chop your hair off," Jack would counter.

"Like to see you try," she'd taunt, and Jack, pressed into a corner, would begin to loosen the glove on his right hand, sliding his claws up and down their slots, purportedly in preparation for an amateur barber job. Noreen would break first, shrieking and scurrying back home, clutching her long blond wig as she ran. Sometimes he'd threaten to tie her legs together or pull out her claws, and though she almost always lost in the end, she never backed down from the battle.

She was a scrappy little thing, and I took to her, like a kid picking up a stray puppy on the street. "It's okay," I would tell Jack. "She can hang out, she's not bothering us."

"She ain't *your* sister," he'd tell me, and I had to give him that.

So that's how it was, and I didn't give it much thought. We'd play our games, and sometimes, when Jack was feeling particularly gracious, or if he just didn't have the energy to shoo her away, Noreen would join us, and I learned early on that she was tenacious and bright and quick and witty.

Jack and I had formed our friendship in a day, and cemented it in the fires of the Tupperware incident, and we were, for the most part, inseparable. We rode our bikes to school together—most days even going so far as to attend—and when it came to signing up for classes, we made sure that our submission forms looked exactly the same.

Each day, after the final bell had rung, we'd tear out of the building and over to the bike racks, where we eagerly waited for the daily fights to begin. It was like Cus D'Amato's gym out in back of the school, only without the protective headgear or any actual knowledge of boxing technique. *Meet you by the bike racks at three* was the code for requesting a battle. If the other combatant showed, the match was on; if not, there was usually torment and teasing in the halls for weeks. It was preferable to show and get beaten down than to skip out and receive wedgies and swirlies for an unspecified period of time.

Middle school is an awkward time for most teenagers; for dinosaurs, it's doubly agonizing. Along with the inevitable hormone changes and acne—one human ailment which fortunately has never affected our species, though certain local Councils will force their teenagers to add BlistaSkin zits to their otherwise flawless guises—come certain bodily changes, and in reptiles the transformation can be downright painful. Tails grow longer; more teeth press through the gums. And a certain percentage of the population matures early, their claws coming in fully before their hands or minds are ready to accept them, and the combination of pain and confusion often turns these otherwise placid dinosaurs into the biggest of bullies.

Case in point:

Garrett Miller was already the biggest kid in middle school, an easy six feet tall in the eighth grade, and no great brains to go behind it. Big ole steam engine but no engineer. Word was that he came from a family of Brontosaurs whose members had interbred with the Missing Link, and that he carried the strength of a dino combined with the stupidity and overall nastiness of a subhuman human. His father and uncles and great-uncles and so forth had a long and storied history with local law enforcement—and not on the right side of it, either.

Garrett Miller would storm through the halls like a tornado, kids leaping to either side in order to get out of his destructive path. He picked on the good students, mostly, the ones who knew the answers and had a future ahead of them; they were slow fish in a small barrel, the natural targets for middle school bullies the world over.

Jack and I watched Garrett Miller from afar, in awe of his power, never worried that the laser focus of his anger would come to bear on us. After all, we were in the second tier of students, neither geniuses nor doorknobs, causing a little mischief in our spare time but never really hurting—or helping—anyone of consequence. In other words, safe.

Then I bumped into Garrett Miller in the hallway, and that was the end of my innocence.

It was a mild little hit, really, a stupid shoulder-to-shoulder thing—though due to our difference in height, it was shoulder-to-waist—that should have gone unnoticed, or at least easily forgiven. I'd been walking along, gabbing to Jack about something, and didn't notice the other pack animals stampede away as Garrett came to bear down the center of the hallway. I just kept walking and talking and suddenly I had made contact with . . . *something,* and within the next few seconds I found myself jammed up against a locker, Garrett Miller twisting the front of my shirt into a tight knot.

"You shoved me," he growled. I believe this was the longest sentence anyone had heard him utter to date.

"No—no—" I stammered. "I was walking—I was walking along and I didn't—I mean I didn't mean to—"

"Three o'clock." I knew the rest; didn't want to hear it. "Bike racks."

There. It was done. And the crowd of twenty that had gathered in just those few seconds knew it, too. Within minutes, it would be all over school: Garrett Miller was going to beat up on that smart-ass kid at three o'clock. Everyone would be there, except for any adults who might care to stop it. The administration and staff had a knack for staying away from the bike racks after school, even though they knew full well what went on. Plausible deniability was a concept that had its inception in the American public school system.

"Three o'clock, huh?" Jack said as he helped straighten out my shirt.

"Guess so."

"Garrett Miller, huh?"

"Guess so."

There was no backing down from the fight; Jack didn't even suggest it. Fortunately, Garrett Miller had yet to actually kill or cause permanent injury to anyone out by the bike racks, and I was hoping to put up enough of a fight so that I wouldn't go down in the history books as the first.

The day slipped by faster than I ever thought possible, and during that time I went through all the endgame permutations in my mind, each of which ended up with me becoming great friends with an ice pack. But if that was how it was going to be, that was how it was going to be, and there was no use whimpering about it.

The school bell rang at 2:45, which gave me a quarter-hour to prep myself. Jack had already appointed himself my corner man, and Bernard, a friend of ours whose dad ran a local television station, said he could get a camera and film the event for posterity. I declined; if I was going to get my ass kicked, I didn't see any reason for future generations to pay-per-view themselves into hysterics over it.

"You sure you want to do this?" Jack asked, a perfunctory question to which we all knew the answer.

"No choice," I said. It's become something of a motto over the years.

So we set to talking strategy, much of which focused on the fact that I was relatively bright while Garrett had an intellect that rivaled cardboard. If I were to have even the slimmest hope of beating him, it would be through my smarts rather than my fists.

Now, this is the part where I give a blow-by-blow description of the events and explain exactly how my superior cunning brought down the Goliath of Arlington Middle School, how my brain power was the sling and stone that crushed his once-mighty reign.

Uh-uh. I got whupped.

But it started out on a positive note, and considering what followed, that was all that mattered. Jack and I showed up at the bike racks at 3:03, and the crowd was already growing restless. Garrett was there, in the middle of a ring of kids, scuffing at the dirt like a bull ready to maul the first matador stupid enough to get in his way. I wouldn't be surprised if he'd been angered by the red shirt I was wearing.

He saw me as I squirmed my way through the crowd, the other students patting me on the back, egging me on, whistling taps. Garrett gave a snort of derision, shooting a wad of mucus into the dirt, and shouted out, "Prepare to—"

That's when I kicked him in the groin.

If he'd been human, I'd have won, hands down. I'd seen enough of these fights by the bike rack to know that a groin hit, no matter how minor, usually brought about the end of the skirmish, unless it was the rare but coveted catfight, in which the girls would claw each other until red and raw and bleeding, or someone lost a nail.

But Garrett Miller, as stated, was a Brontosaur from a family of mean old Brontosaurs, and his tail, tucked between his legs and held firmly in place with the G-series of clamps—and hidden, of course, beneath his faux human costume—absorbed most of the blow.

Not all of it, though. He went down on one knee, his face twisting in a mask of dismay, and I could tell that I'd done enough damage to make him nauseous. There was a fleeting moment there—I can still remember it now, it filled my heart with elation—when I thought I had won, that my nightmarish after-school battle was over before it had begun, and that Jack and I could pedal home and celebrate our victory with Cheetos and Coke in front of the tube.

The crowd cheered; Jack whooped it up. I pranced around the bike racks with my hands held aloft in my best Muhammad Ali impression, juking and jiving, floating like a butterfly, stinging like a bee—

Garrett Miller stood up. He stood up and pulled back his fist and whacked me till next Tuesday, and I don't remember much after that. All I've got is a series of images to rival the best of basil blackouts—knuckles flying toward my face, feet kicking at my midsection, arms pulling me back up again, the whole cycle renewing itself again and again.

When it was all over, when the punching and the kicking and the inevitable spitting came to an end and it was just Vincent, the dirt, and the pain, I lay on the ground for a few moments, gathering my thoughts, taking inventory of my major body parts. I was pretty sure he'd split my guise in a few places, and the faux skin would have to be fixed up before the rest of it. I could taste blood, but my dentures were still in place, so most likely I'd bitten my tongue or lip, neither of which was a life-threatening injury. All in all, I had survived, and would continue to do so.

"That was pretty brave, what you did." A voice, above me. Soft. High. Either female or Brandon Carmichael, a seventh-grade pipsqueak who, I later found out, wound up as a powerful baritone with the Philharmonic. But at the time he was a Vienna Boy all the way.

I forced my eyes to open—*not Brandon, not Brandon*—and was treated to a view of dark brown hair, a button nose, and a pair of bright, shining eyes. There was no way that sucker-kicking a guy in the cojones could qualify as brave, but I wasn't about to contradict this beautiful creature staring down at me, helping me to my feet.

I knew who this was; it was impossible not to. This was a gal whose name, face, and body were already legendary at Arlington

Middle. She was the be-all, end-all of the gentler gender, the essence of femininity, the cat's pajamas and the bee's knees and—

Ah, hell, let's lay it on the line: she put out.

This was Rhonda Reichenberg. And she was standing over me, dabbing at my wounds. It was the perfect start to my first crappy relationship.

I was almost fifteen at the time, and expecting things to go slow. Little did I realize that nothing went slow with Rhonda. She was decades ahead of the rest of us, sexually mature to a point most women never reach before their thirties, if at all. She understood her body—both the fake human one and the real Ornithomimus underneath—like she'd read some user's guide the rest of us hadn't, and had no qualms about using this knowledge to the full extent of her abilities, schooling my fragile young mind and body in the ways of carnal pleasure.

Not that I minded the tutoring.

Neither of us was old enough to drive at that point, so we snuck in our sexual escapades wherever we could: in our homes when our parents were at work, behind warehouses, in deserted alleyways. Or I'd sit her on top of picnic tables and reach beneath her skirt, between her legs, moving aside the necessary garments and buckles to get at my target, and no one was the wiser. From a distance, it just looked like two kids snuggling and chatting on a tabletop; up close, it was a different matter entirely.

She wanted to be a flight attendant—stewardess, back in those days—and I would spend hours watching her, naked, run through the preflight ritual. Sometimes she did it with her guise on; sometimes, when she was feeling particularly outrageous, she did it with her guise off, using her tail to point toward the exit doors at the rear of the cabin. This would usually set me off, and we wound up in bed or on the floor, going at it like we were the newest inductees into the Mile High Club.

Rhonda also introduced me to a new group of kids, and

throughout that first year we dated, I made friends left and right. Couldn't tell you most of their names now, or where they are today, but they were friends in the sense that they had parties and I was invited.

Jack got dragged along for the ride, and he didn't complain one bit. Rhonda set him up with a few of her like-minded girlfriends, and soon he, too, was lost deep in the thick jungles of adolescent lust. Our time together dwindled down to weekend movies and dinners, usually with at least Rhonda and one other girl in tow, but this was always how we knew it would be. The days of Vincent and Jack, together against the world, were coming to an end; it was bittersweet in a way, but the constant sex pretty much made up for any hard feelings.

As a result, I didn't get over to Jack's house nearly as much as I used to, and by the time I entered high school, we were meeting up either at school or on double dates, and that was it. Jack's sister was no longer a feature in my life, and I assumed that she'd just gone on with her existence and found some other older brother and his friend to hang around and annoy.

Sometime in December of my sophomore year, Rhonda got us invited to a high-end party up on the other side of town, a swank affair over in West L.A. Today I know that West L.A. isn't much different from regular L.A.—some houses, a lot of condos, blocks of apartments, maybe a few more sushi joints than the rest of town—but back then, it seemed like the place to be. So we accepted the party invite, wangled one for Jack and his girlfriend Toni, dressed up in our finest duds, and drove the four and a half miles, preparing to impress and be impressed.

Eh. It was a party, like any other, only the house was a little bigger than most we'd been to, and I think they had a pool. The parents were away in Asia somewhere, and it was pretty much accepted that the place would be trashed before they returned from their trip, so there was much herbage on display.

Until this point, I'd only dabbled in the stuff. A leaf here, a sprig there, but only to get me in a good mood, and never to excess. I'd seen all the after-school plays about the dangers of drinking and driving, and the after-after-school plays that they put on for those of us in the reptilian camp, and was sufficiently warned away from the stuff, at least in theory.

But whoever had thrown this party had decided that this was their one chance to inebriate the dino youth of Los Angeles, and, as a result, had imported enough fresh produce—no small part of it from Dugan's, I would imagine—to keep an entire commune in good spirits for months. It was high-quality, too; a single snapdragon held Jack in a trance for a half hour, his gaze firmly fixed on a black spot someone had accidentally burned into the wall with an errant lighter.

"Have some," Rhonda cooed, dangling a bit of basil over my mouth, onto my tongue. The smell was strong, the taste overpowering.

"It's good," I mumbled, chewing as I spoke.

"'Course it's good," she said. "But I've got something better . . ."

The closet was dark. Her guise was tight. I had no problem getting rid of the outer garments; human clothing is a joke to unlatch in comparison to human skin. Bras are a simple matter of push, twist, and release, and sweater buttons are child's play. Try unhooking an R-series chest clamp from a G-series restrainer belt with one arm while spinning the firm latex disc beneath an Erickson heel attachment with the other, all the while fighting off hormones that are screaming *Forget about the damn polysuit, do it like the monkeys do!*

The caps were off our tongues, the two fleshy forks poking at each other, twisting into a single snake of excitement as we tore at each other's guises. This was a clear violation of Council laws; it would never fall under the umbrella of "emergency deguising." But we didn't care; as teenagers, we felt ourselves exempt from such laws, even though we were probably the ones who needed them the most.

There we were in the closet of some stranger's house in West L.A., high on basil and full of party dip, crazed with lust, fully naked and half unguised. I had Rhonda's tank top draped around my neck, and was quickly unfastening the latex breasts clinging to her naturally scaled hide, my hands firm around the cups, kneading the fake flesh solely in an attempt to remove them from their backing. Rhonda was tugging at my G-clamp, at the protection cup I'd taken to wearing since the fight by the bike racks, and we were nearing the crucial moment—

The closet door opened wide. Light poured in from the outside, a cascade of dance music thrumming along with it, and I shoved a hand in front of my face to ward off the intrusion. I wasn't even embarrassed at being caught with my guise half off and my human skin baring all—the basil was doing its job, settling in for a long, long stay in my bloodstream.

"God, already," Rhonda drawled, similarly unconcerned with our public display of nudity. "Close the door."

But it stayed open for another moment, and I heard a somewhat familiar voice break through the din. "Vincent?"

I squinted through the light and the noise and the basil and saw a pretty blond thing staring back, her long hair cascading down to a small waist, but it wasn't the guise that clued me in—it was the scent. The same one she'd had since she was just a little brat telling on her brother and me, but stronger, more powerful, the saltwater and mangoes taking a slice out of me and keeping it forever.

"Noreen?" I managed to croak, but suddenly the door was closed again, the music muted, and she was gone.

"Stupid freshmen," Rhonda mumbled. "Come on, baby, let's keep going . . ."

But I was no longer interested in Rhonda Reichenberg. Her

good looks and sultry smell of musk had no pull on me. I felt her in my arms—the weight of her body tugging at my back, as if expecting me to give up the fight, to fall on top of her and do as nature dictated—but when I looked down, there was just a stranger looking back.

"What?" she said, clearly annoyed with the pause in the proceedings. "Forget about it. She closed the door, no one's looking."

"No," I said. "It's—it's not that—"

"You're having problems?"

"What?" It took me a second, but I got her drift. "God, no—no, it's . . ." *It's just that I'm in love with my best friend's sister,* I wanted to say, realizing as soon as I thought it that it was cliché, ridiculous, and staggeringly true.

"Come on," she whined, tearing off her breasts with a practiced flip, then ripping off the rest of her guise, the verdant sheen of her skin barely visible in the low closet light.

"It's . . . it's my tail," I lied. "It's asleep—the clamp—" I mumbled and muttered and futzed my way through an excuse, the whole time throwing my guise back on, buckling up tight, hoping that Noreen hadn't left the party. Within two minutes I was back to looking like a monkey and out the closet door, Rhonda still fuming and naked.

Noreen was gone. I found Jack, making out in the corner with a gal we knew from gym, and tapped him on the shoulder.

"Busy," he said, and went back to smooching.

"I just saw your sister."

"And?"

Good point. I wasn't about to tell Jack I'd just fallen for his sister in a split second after years spent drowning her out. "And . . . I just thought she's a little young to be here, that's all."

Clearly, that was the right thing to say, because Jack broke off the kiss and took a look around the room—at the sex, the herbs, the general lasciviousness of it all. We were fifteen, sixteen—we were *adults*—while Noreen, at a youthful fourteen, was but a babe in the woods. "It is a pretty raunchy scene," he mused.

"That's what I was thinking. We should probably go find her."

"You think so?"

"Yeah," I said. "You know—to see if she's okay."

She was okay enough, hanging out in a corner, talking with some friends, until we got there, at which point she stood and gave me a look like Michael gave Fredo toward the end of *Godfather II*. *I know it was you, Vincent,* she seemed to be saying. Hopefully she won't shoot me in a rowboat out on the family lake, but I never put it past a Dugan to hold a grudge.

"Go home, Noreen," Jack told his younger sister. "Mom'll be really pissed if I tell her you were here—"

"Wait, wait," I said, picking my moment. "It's okay. I can take care of her—"

"Take care of yourself," Noreen spat. "Or is that Rhonda Reichenberg's job?"

I was alternately elated and mortified that Noreen knew of Rhonda. Mortified because if she knew the Legend of Rhonda, she knew exactly what we were doing in the closet, and elated because the anger infusing every word signified jealousy. And if Noreen was jealous, then it meant she was interested, and if she was interested . . .

But before I knew it, she was storming out of the party, two of her little friends in tow, Jack was back to his newfound gal and their furious game of tongue jousting, and I was alone and hopped up on basil for the rest of the evening.

As a newly single man, though, I had an excuse to visit Jack at his house, and the Dugans were delighted to see me for dinner, for dessert, on weekends. Rhonda disappeared from my life; she found some other young buck on the debate team who could handle the sexual workload and I was forgotten.

Noreen wasn't quite as thrilled as the rest of her family with my frequent social calls. She spoke little during meals when I was present, and refused to hang out with Jack and me afterwards. "Better off," he said one time after she declined an invitation to the movies. "She'll talk the whole way through."

Which would have been fine with me. Her reluctance to exchange even a word with me was maddening; I was sure that if I could just get fifteen minutes alone with her, a little bit of time to work the Rubio charm, she'd be mine and I'd be hers, and off into the dusty sunset we'd ride. But it was all business—pass the peas, pass the salt, go away.

After nearly half a year of rebuffs and resignation, I decided that my slavish devotion to Noreen was to no avail. I could follow her around like a lost puppy all I wanted—that smell taunting me from across the table, through the house, in the hallway at school—but if she wasn't going to bite, then it was pointless to keep dangling the line. My fishing days were over.

So when Wednesday night rolled around, I stayed home instead of heading out to Jack's for dinner. Same thing on Thursday, and that weekend I hung out with a different set of friends, trying to forget my troubles. The first day I must have thought about Noreen a thousand times; the second day, I was down to 999. It was a start.

Within two weeks, entire hours could pass by without that saltwater-and-mango scent popping up in my mind, and I knew I was on the way to a full recovery. If she wasn't to be, then she wasn't to be, and who really cared, anyway. Rhonda Reichenberg and her tantalizing sweets were just a phone call away should the urges build up once again.

It must have been a full month later when I was sneaking back into school after dropping a few classes, darting from niche to niche in the hallway like a commando trying to elude detection. I'd just spun around a corner, preparing to shoot down a side hall and into my classroom—

"What do you think you're doing?"

It was Noreen. Arms crossed, jaw clenched. Waiting for me. I don't know how she knew I'd be there—*I* didn't even know I'd be there—but it was clear that I was her intended target, and she'd staked me out.

"Going to class," I answered. Hell, at least it was true, if not suave.

"Not that. With this whole I'm-not-coming-over routine. It's stupid."

"It is?"

"Extremely." She uncrossed her arms and leaned into me, her hands against the wall on either side of my head. "Don't think I don't know what you're doing."

"I don't. You do." This was going swell. "What are we talking about, again?"

Suddenly I was up against the wall, her lips on mine, too stunned to do anything but kiss back. It wasn't supposed to happen that way—it was supposed to be my seduction of her, the older man, the younger woman, the butterflies in the stomach, the giggling to her girlfriends—but it went down just like that, and it was perfect. She sighed and she kissed me and I kissed her back and we stayed that way until Mr. Saponaro, the anatomy teacher, came out of his room and gave us both detention for loitering in the halls during class time. We took the detention slips, stuck them in our back pockets, and kept right on smooching.

Noreen and I dated all through high school. We weren't the *it* couple—that was reserved for the jocks and the cheerleaders—but people knew who we were, and regularly lumped us together. VincentandNoreen, NoreenandVincent, it was practically a single word. It was rare that one of us would be asked to a party or function without the other being invited along, and in those circumstances, we'd just crash the event anyway.

Jack played the older brother, making a big show of standing up for his little sister, berating me if I showed up late for a date or didn't get her back home on time. Threatening to mangle me if I broke her heart, that sort of thing. But it was the same between us as it had always been, and I knew that deep down, Jack was thrilled we were like family.

Two years went by, and the bond only grew tighter as my schooling came to a close. Graduation was a nothing affair, a chance to walk across a platform and grab a rolled-up sheet of paper that wasn't even an actual diploma; those would be mailed to us six weeks later. I wasn't the college-bound type, though my grades were okay, but technical school wasn't up my alley, either. Back then, there were no universities where you could spend four years majoring in sitting on your ass, making out with your girlfriend, and cracking jokes. Nowadays they call it a "communications degree."

Plus, Noreen was still in high school for another year, and though she'd discussed accelerating her course load so she could graduate early, I dissuaded her from doing so.

"Take your time," I told her. "Have fun, cut class. I'll stick around."

I needed a job, though, and in the tight economy, there was only one place I could go to get the bread I needed: Dugan's Produce. Yep, it was old Pop Dugan himself who came through, offering me an assistant manager's position at the store. At this point in my life, I had neither been anyone's assistant nor been particularly capable of managing anything, let alone an entire store, so I was shocked and elated and terrified and said yes instantly.

"Figure you been unloading herbs for five years now," he told me, rubbing his hands against that green-stained apron as he tallied up the day's receipts. "Jack ain't interested in the job, and you've seen how it works."

"I have." That was half statement, half question.

"And I gotta make sure you got a job so you can keep taking my girl to the right places." He gave me a little wink; I did not attempt to return the gesture. "If you get poor on account of me, I'll never hear the end of it."

And so I became the assistant manager of Dugan's Produce and promptly learned all there was to know about the business of running a neighborhood produce shop. Took about a week. You take the inventories, you place the orders, you mark up the food, you mark up the herbs even more, you make your money, you pay your suppliers, you take the inventories again, and around and around we go. I had the patter down within a month, and soon became expert at working the phones, locating special orders for special customers.

"Look, Harry," I remember saying to one of our suppliers, a cilantro dealer whose farm up in Oxnard produced some of the finest-grade herb we'd seen in central L.A., "I'm telling you, these folks want it yesterday." I was twirling a pen between my fingers, an affectation of Pop Dugan's that I'd picked up and cultivated for myself. "Yeah, yeah, the cilantro, the rosemary, that bundle you guys do so well—"

The door chime gave a tingle, and I didn't bother looking over at the entrance; perhaps if I had, it all would have turned out differently. If I'd seen them coming in, maybe I could have made a break for it, pretended the store was closed, and the whole nasty chain of events would have been halted right there. Probably not; the mob isn't easily rebuffed.

They were huge, both of them, big beefy guys with legs of lamb for arms and lemon-sucking scowls for lips. "Where's Dugan?" asked the first, who I later learned was named Mr. Tajecky.

I held up a finger—dumb, Vincent, dumb—and the second one grabbed it in midair and promptly bent it backwards, a millimeter away from breaking. He knew exactly how far to go before the telltale snap—guy had his anatomy down cold, though I doubt he did pre-med at an accredited college.

Hanging up the phone with my other hand, I shook my head through the pain. "I'm the assistant," I managed to blurt out. "Pop's not here—"

"I can tell Pop ain't here," Tajecky grunted. He was wearing a leather Huggie Bear coat, and to this day I can't figure out why he would want to affect that hipster fuzz look. It did not flatter his figure, I'll say no more than that. "Where is he?"

"I don't know," I said, truthfully. Pop had a habit of disappearing sometimes, middle of the day, seemingly at random. But he usually returned with armfuls of produce, so I never asked and always assumed he was on purchasing runs. "He left an hour ago."

Was this a shakedown? I'd heard the stories, but never been present to actually witness the act. Was it a protection racket? I had a feeling these guys weren't looking for a special price on saffron.

Tajecky and his cohort—Sal, we all later learned—conferred in private, ducking down behind the newspaper racks as I tended to my rapidly swelling finger. I could feel it pressing against my human glove, the thick flesh filling with blood.

"We'll be back," said Tajecky, swiping a bunch of scallions from the rack. "Tell Dugan that his new business partners dropped by."

And like that they were gone, and I was on the phone to Jack seconds later. He came rushing over to help, but there was nothing he could do, other than wait with me until Pop Dugan returned to the store.

Two tense hours later—Jack and I staring out the window of the store, worrying that those two huge silhouettes would appear over the horizon—Pop returned, pulling along behind him a wagon full of dandelion sprigs. These weeds, when properly grown and harvested, were a delicacy for certain customers—Compies in particular would spend their last few bucks to get in a chew or two—and it was a little unsettling to see so much at one time.

"You like it, boys?" Pop said as he entered. "Take a taste or two—go on, it's all right."

But Jack and I were too on edge to sample the wares. Jack looked to me; he might have been the son, but I was, after all, the assistant manager.

"Pop," I said, "two guys came by today—"

"You take care of 'em?"

"They weren't customers. They were . . . They said they were your new business partners . . . ?"

I was hoping Pop would deny it, that the look on his face would be one of confusion, or of mirth. That it would all turn out to be one huge misunderstanding, and we'd head out for pizza after closing up and laugh about the whole thing. But that's not what happened.

First, his lips fell. That perpetual grin—the one that always seemed to be hiding just beneath his current expression, waiting to explode at any moment into a full-on smile—disappeared. As far as I know, it never returned.

Then his cheeks sunk in, half an inch of flesh suddenly sucked into his face. I don't know if this was due to a faulty guise or whether his actual skin withered away, but there it was—that gaunt, hollow look, the look of the condemned, and all within five seconds.

"They leave their names?" he asked me, and I shook my head. It didn't matter; Pop Dugan knew who they were. He gave Jack and me a few bucks and told us to go find Noreen, hit a movie, go to dinner. He'd close up shop tonight. I tried to argue, but knew there was no hope. This was Pop's business, and he had the last word.

When I came back to the store the next morning, I found Tajecky and Sal behind the counter, aprons strapped around their massive waists, as Pop directed them in the mechanics of the cash register. I nearly backed out the door as I saw them there, but Tajecky caught sight of me and called me over.

"We got off on the wrong foot, you and me," he said, extending his hand. "If we're gonna be working together, we gotta get along."

He shook my hand, taking no mind that my pinky was nearly busted. I nodded politely in his direction.

"What are you guys . . . doing?" I asked.

"Like I said yesterday," Tajecky replied. "We're your boss's new business partners."

Now, I'd seen the movies. I knew that when the mafia says they're coming in as "new business partners," they don't actually intend to roll up their sleeves and get to work. They just want a cut of the profits—of the gross, more likely—and a comfy place to sit back as the dough comes rolling in.

Not these guys. They wanted to work. "Gonna run inventory," Tajecky would say, and then, by God, he would actually take a clipboard and walk the store, tallying up our needs and overruns for the week. Sal was a monster on the loading dock, and thought nothing of hauling five-hundred-pound crates from pallet to shelf, the weight evenly distributed across that wide, thick back. Truth be told, they were the best damn employees Pop Dugan ever had.

Within two months, there was nothing left for me to do. Tajecky was brilliant with the customers, soothing and plying, the consummate salesman who outshone even Pop Dugan when it came to knowing what the people wanted and how to give it to them. And Sal did all the back-room work, the heavy muscle, even going so far as to reorganize the herb storeroom every week to reflect the changing tastes and demographics of the neighborhood.

And suddenly, years before it became popular, I was downsized.

"I can't afford to pay you anymore," Pop told me one afternoon. "I'm sorry, Vincent, I am, but—"

"It's okay," I interrupted. There was no need for me to see him like this. It wasn't right. "I understand."

"I'm barely keeping above water. The guys—they run the place, but—I take a cut, you know?"

I knew. Somehow, the natural order of things had gotten reversed, and Pop Dugan had become a silent partner in his own business. And the meager stipend allowed him by Sal and Tajecky wasn't cutting it. He had expenses. He had a wife. He had a family. And though I didn't know how he'd originally made the acquaintance of Tajecky and Sal, I had a hunch he had a few bad habits up his sleeve, too.

Noreen was worried about it, too, and we spent a sizable portion of our time together fretting over how to save Pop's dignity, if not his business.

"I don't know what he'll do," she would say to me, cuddled up tight in my arms, her hands wrapped around my neck, pulling me close. "He's always worked."

"He could get another job," I suggested.

"He needs to have his own place. To own something. To be proud of it."

Two months later, it was done. Sal and Tajecky approached Pop Dugan one evening, flashed a wad of cash in his face, and informed him that he'd just been bought out. They liked the work, they liked the neighborhood, and Dugan's Produce was no longer his store. Not only that, he wasn't to open a competing market anywhere in the entire state of California. He could still shop there, of course, and they'd gladly sell him produce at a reasonable discount, but as far as they were concerned, Pop Dugan was just another shlub on the corner trying to score some turnips.

This was right about the time when Noreen was preparing to graduate from school, and the two of us were busily planning our future together. She wanted me to go to one of those technical schools they advertise on television—the kind where they train you and promise you a job with a steady paycheck and the ability to move up. Plus, the commercials had funky graphics—always a draw. Her plan was to go to work for her father, help him build a new business.

But Pop didn't have it in him. Most of the time, I'd find him sitting on the Dugan living room sofa, reading the paper, his eyes barely taking in the words. He was staring off somewhere else. At first, I thought he might have been hitting the basil, but Jack told me the old man didn't touch the stuff. Maybe he should have. Considering his prospects, it certainly couldn't have hurt.

Two months before Noreen's graduation day—which was itself just two days before her eighteenth birthday—Pop Dugan laid it down for the family. I was there for dinner, some pitiful concoction of second-rate meat and cheese, holding hands with Noreen under the table.

"We're moving," he said plainly, and suddenly Noreen's fingernails—a set of Nanjutsu special Eartha Kitty Klaws I'd bought her for Christmas—dug into the heel of my palm, nearly breaking through to the scales below.

"What part of town?" asked Noreen, voice trembling.

Pop Dugan shook his head. This would be harder on him than it would be on the rest of them, but he couldn't let them see that. "Different town," he said. "We're moving up near Grandpa. Back to Michigan."

Suddenly there was silverware flying and dishes crashing and Noreen was up and out of the room, tears streaming down her face as she ran out of the house, slamming the door behind her.

There were tears, and there were cries of protest, but Pop's plans were set. The day after Noreen's graduation, one day before she turned eighteen, the family would be packing up and heading out to Michigan, where he would join the furniture refurbishing business started by his father. It wasn't glamorous work, or even work that Pop particularly liked—the smell of wood stain and varnish was omnipresent through his childhood, and in later years he couldn't walk past the lumber section at Home Depot without some serious flashbacks—but it would allow him to earn a decent wage and keep the family together.

Noreen's future, on the other hand, was suddenly wide open, and I was willing to do anything to help her figure a way out of this. I suggested that she refuse to go, that she move in with me—that we find an apartment and live in sin, but her moral core was too set for that. If she was going to defy her father, there would have to be a stronger rationale.

Eventually, we found one. I don't remember if it was my idea or hers, but it didn't really matter once it was out there:

We would get married.

And Vincent, dear little Vincent, barely a year out of school and already fancying himself something of a Raptor of the world, prepared to become a husband, a family man. Had anybody known of our plans, there's no doubt they would have stepped in, shown us the foolishness of our ways, and been heartily scorned for trying to help. It was a secret, however, and that made it all the more delicious.

We went about the planning like a pair of four-star generals, mapping out each and every step, detailing the scheme moment by moment. The night of Noreen's graduation—the 18th of June—she would leave a note for her parents, sneak out of the house, and meet me at the bus station, where we would hop a seven-hour Greyhound out to Vegas. By the time her parents discovered her note and figured out what was what, Noreen would be eighteen and legally empowered to do whatever she wished. It would take only that single act of defiance, and then we'd be together, and her father would have to give us his blessing. We'd live together wherever we wished—Los Angeles, Seattle, maybe even settle down in Vegas. Hey, I knew how to play poker; how hard could it be to earn a living?

Our secret only brought us closer. As the weeks passed and the Dugans began to pack up their household in preparation for the move, I became more and more convinced that what we were doing was the right thing, that it would all work out in the end. We both knew there was no way Noreen and I could survive a long-distance relationship, and no chance that Pop would let us stay together without the sacrament of marriage. We'd already found the perfect venue: the Scales of Love Chapel, beneath the Golden Nugget in downtown Vegas, was a reptile-run joint that specialized in cross-breed marriages. No prejudiced eyes to shoot scornful looks at a Raptor and a Hadrosaur getting it on, no one to *tsk-tsk* as we walked down the aisle. Our life together was going to be perfect.

Unfortunately, and perhaps this is where it all began to unravel, I'm lousy at keeping secrets. Should the world ever turn topsy-turvy and I am somehow elected president, I'll be organizing a press conference the very next day to tell everyone exactly what's been going down in Area 51. So the fact that Noreen and I had agreed to keep this close to the vest only increased my desire to let it loose. And I had only one individual to entrust it to.

I told Jack.

The day before Noreen's graduation, two days before we were to flee off into the wilds of Nevada and the sanctity of a quickie marriage performed by a mail-order minister, I broke down and told him our plans. I guess in a way I wanted his blessing, because I couldn't get one in advance from Pop Dugan. If Jack approved, then I could clear that final hurdle with a clean conscience.

"Hot damn!" he said when I let it fly. "We got to have you a bachelor party!"

It wasn't exactly the reaction I expected, but in retrospect it made some sense. Jack was elated that I would truly become a part of the family, and I think a part of him was glad that the hubbub over Noreen's elopement would overshadow the sadness of their departure from Southern California.

Noreen wasn't thrilled about the party, but she trusted me

enough to believe that I'd be on my best behavior. Jack had a night of general debauchery planned, and we hit the town at nine o'clock on June 17th, which gave me more than enough time to have a blast, clear my senses, and pack up for our departure on the night of the 18th.

Not everyone blacks out when they chew. I do. It's not so much a complete loss of memory, but the strobe effect of recollections—images flashing on and off, sounds flickering back and forth—is almost worse. If I were completely ignorant of my actions, then it would be easier to deny complicity. What I wouldn't give for a good case of amnesia at the right times.

What I do remember is ingesting a fair amount of basil at an underground strip club, a little more on the ride to the next bar, and a heaping helping of sage at some late-night diner. There's a flash of a long, open highway after that, and a few seconds' reminiscence of an endless field of oregano, six of us down on all fours like cows, grazing away on some stranger's farm.

At some point, Jack left the festivities, and tried to get me to go with him. There was an argument, some shoving, maybe a scuffle, and he left, disgusted, as I returned to my bovine binge. I don't even know if the other guys were with me anymore; I didn't much care. After nineteen years of searching for a purpose in life, Vincent Rubio had found his calling, and its name was herb.

"Hey! Get up! Get up, boy!"

There was this voice, calling me, and for a moment, it worked its way into my dream: someone had installed a fifty-foot lemur above the 101 Freeway, its long ringed tail dangling across the four lanes of traffic. And for some reason, the lemur was telling me to get up.

"I'm not gonna tell you again, boy. Get your sorry ass up or I'm blowing it off right here, right now."

This last bit was followed by the distinctive sound of a shotgun's action being cocked, and I was suddenly on my feet before the rest of my body had time to react, the ground violently lurching away.

The world was spinning, but I got enough of a glimpse to know I was not in Westwood anymore. There I was, in the middle of a field, my clothes dirty and smelling of cow manure, and an old coot with a double-barreled shotgun was standing barely five feet away.

"Morning," I drawled, my lips not yet able to form all the consonants properly.

"You got ten seconds to tell me what you're doing here," said the farmer. Part of me was convinced that this was part of my dream, only I'd never been this nauseous before while asleep.

I took another look around. The mountains in the distance, the fields beyond. The smell of strawberries in the air. With a fair bit of luck, this would be Camarillo, a farming community only about forty-five minutes' drive outside of L.A.

"Think I was eating part of your field," I told the man. I was too hung over to lie properly.

"Yes, I think you were." He gave me the once-over, then lowered his gun, and I got a good whiff, past the manure and the strawberries beyond. He was human; no chance he'd understand.

"I must have had too much to drink," I said, slowly backing away. "Me and some friends, we tied on a few."

"Uh-huh," he said. Not a bad guy, just concerned that I was up to some chicanery.

"I had a bachelor party," I heard myself say. "I'm getting married—"

Married.

Right.

Oh, crap.

I cut myself off and started running even before I finished the sentence, suddenly unconcerned about the shotgun that was no doubt pointed at my back. I had to get back home. I had to pack. I had a million things to do before I could take Noreen and make her my blushing bride.

It took me three hours to hitch a ride back into L.A., and two more to pack up all my belongings. I called Noreen's house a hundred times but got no answer, eventually remembering they were all at the graduation ceremony. I should have been there, too, but Noreen would understand; as long as I was at the bus station, everything would be fine.

I made it to the Greyhound station by eight P.M.; our bus wasn't leaving until just after midnight. I settled into a bench and tried to read a paperback I'd brought along, but the jitters kept me from getting past the first page. I found myself rereading the same sentences over and over, and eventually chucked the book and stared at the doors of the station, waiting for Noreen to arrive.

And waiting.

And waiting.

Every time a silhouette appeared behind the frosted glass, my heart beat faster, my throat caught, and I prepared to leap from my seat and envelop her in my arms. But each time it was just another stranger, some other shnook like me too poor to afford private transportation.

Ten o'clock turned to eleven, which turned to midnight, and soon I was at the front counter trying to arrange for a later bus to Vegas. The last Greyhound left the station at one in the morning, and still Noreen wasn't there. I thought of calling her house, of trying to sneak some message to her via Jack, but knew it was pointless. Something must have been delaying her, I figured, and I only hoped it wasn't Pop Dugan. What if Jack had told him what was going on? What if he'd locked Noreen in her room? There was no way to know.

The next bus wouldn't be leaving for six more hours, and by then, it might be too late. But I figured I had to try and get us on that trip, somehow, so I approached the counter in order to exchange our tickets.

"We missed our bus," I told the disinterested clerk. "Can I change them for the next one out?"

"Sure, honey," she said. "Whatever you want."

She took the tickets, gave them a cursory glance, and tossed them into a small bin by her feet. "Okay," she said, "so you want the six A.M. bus to Vegas on the twentieth?"

"No," I corrected her. "On the nineteenth of June. This morning."

"Honey," she drawled, "*yesterday* was the nineteenth. You gotta get yourself a calendar."

The only sensation I can recollect is that my feet felt like they were being drawn up and through my nose—a compressed, choking feeling in my lungs, the tightening of my chest—and the next thing I remember I was at home, trying to call the number I'd been given for Pop's father up in Michigan. Some old man answering, and me yelling into the phone, pleading with him to tell Noreen that I loved her, that I screwed up, that I would make it up to her. Ranting about herbs and Greyhound buses and Las Vegas and lord knows what else, and not being in the least surprised when Grandpa Dugan summarily hung up on me and took his phone off the hook.

I tried calling for months, but Noreen refused to come to the phone. Pop Dugan said he didn't understand it, and would regularly apologize to me. "I'm sorry, Vincent," he'd say, his voice sounding older, weaker than it ever had. "She doesn't wanna talk to you. I'm sorry, son—you know I always thought you two would make it."

My letters came back unopened. My postcards ripped to shreds. Finally, six months after the move, I called once more, hoping that she would at least hear me out, if not forgive me.

"Hello?" It was Jack. He sounded older, wiser. Like he'd grown up, and I'd stayed a pipsqueak of a teenager.

"Hey, Jack," I said as casually as I could. "It's Vincent."

There was a long pause on the line; I could hear him breathing, but that was it. After a minute had passed, I decided to continue. "Look, I—"

"It's over," Jack said, a thin stream of rage shaking his voice.

"It was that night," I tried to explain. "The bachelor party—"

"It's over, Vincent. You broke her heart. Noreen won't forget what you did, and neither will I." Then, softer, as if coming from some personal inner pain, "Don't call here anymore. She'll never talk to you again."

And damn it all, the son of a bitch was right.

Until this afternoon.

10

"Afternoon, Noreen," I say as I step off the elevator, my cheeks stinging from the double slaps. "Love the nails."

Noreen smiles, and it's the same grin she had when I knew her in days past, a smile that plucks my heart from my chest and lodges it in my gullet. "Family heirlooms," she tells me, flashing the inch-long claws before my face. "Tupperware, of course."

Jack's penthouse is beautifully appointed, with massive bay windows on all sides looking out over the Intracoastal Waterway and the Atlantic Ocean beyond. The light streaming in illuminates Noreen from behind, casting her tall, lithe body in a stark silhouette.

"You look well," I say. "The years have treated you nicely."

"Likewise," says Noreen, and I can feel it now. We're doing the dance, a little fox trot around the past.

Noreen does look smashing, though, her body in top-notch shape, the skin flawless, the hair cut just so. She was always good at maintaining a guise; even back in high school, she did her own tailoring, and was quite adept at smoothing out the inevitable wrinkles that always bunched up around the genitals and buttocks. It was doubly fun when she did it to *my* guise; triply so when I was still wearing it.

"Jack's occupied right now," she says, turning on a three-inch heel and strutting into the main section of the penthouse. "He'll be out in a bit. Come inside."

Inside, a number of Jack's men mill about, sitting on sofas and pouring themselves drinks. A few nod or give me curt little waves; some actively ignore my presence.

"Drink?" asks Noreen, and suddenly a tumbler is in her hand.

"No," I say. "Thank you."

Noreen steps closer, that glass looming large in my vision, the liquid inside spilling and sloshing. It would be so easy to gulp it down. "It's a special blend," she says. "We call it Infusion—"

"I know what it is," I interrupt. "Jack gave me . . . I had some earlier."

Her eyelids close halfway; she's inspecting me. "You didn't like it?"

"I did. Very much. Please, take it away."

She's confused—that wrinkle in her nose hasn't changed a bit—but complies. When she returns, I find myself trying to explain. About the drink, about my presence, about everything.

"I'm an herbaholic," I blurt out, possibly a bit too loud. Not that I care; my sins are miracles of nature compared to the crimes most of these folks have probably committed in the last few hours alone.

"I'm sorry to hear that."

I shrug. It's a common response; there's nothing good to say after someone confesses that they're powerless to manage their own lives. *Hey, how's your golf game?* is the best rejoinder I've gotten so far, but that was Sutherland, and it was easily the most intelligent thing he'd said in months. "Recovering. It's actually . . ." Hell, might as well go for broke. "That night, back in Los Angeles, when we were supposed to meet at the bus station—"

Noreen extends a single finger and presses it against my lips. "Uh-uh," she whispers. "None of that."

"I just thought—"

"Uh-uh," she repeats, and walks away, over to a large sofa where some of Jack's men are staring intently at the television.

"Yeah, okay, and how 'bout this," says the one they call BB. "Why do they call 'em meteorologists? They don't tell ya when a meteor's gonna hit."

This gets a good chuckle out of a little guy with crooked teeth and a smell of baby powder, but an older guy nearby just shakes his head. "I heard that bit before."

"What bit?"

"The meteorologist bit. You stole it."

"Hell," says the first one, "I wasn't even doing a bit."

"Okay, boys," Noreen says, wedging her way next to BB, "make room for mama." They clear a spot for her on the sofa, and she pats the small empty spot next to her, hooking a finger in my direction. "Ever see a hurricane report before?"

"I've seen earthquake reports," I say as I wedge myself between Noreen and the armrest.

"World of difference. An earthquake report just tells you about the damage that's been done. A hurricane report . . . well, watch."

The weatherman—meteorologist—stands in front of a radar graphic, pointing to the swirling mass of white a few hundred miles east of the Dominican Republic. "Hurricane Alison could do a lot of damage if she decides to come ashore," he's saying, talking about this weather system as if it's an overweight gal trying to get out of a canoe. "She's sucking up a lot of the warm Atlantic water and really building up steam. Let's go in for a closer look—"

And suddenly the image is lurching up and over, pivoting in a way television images should never pivot, especially when the screen is over sixty inches, diagonally. I'm taken along for the ride as a computerized effect takes us viewers down through the heart of the hurricane and into the eye of the storm itself. Wholly useless, of course, except the TV station gets to justify its technology budget and some geek in the back room can congratulate himself for writing the code.

The figures are all there for us to see—89 mph winds, heading due west at 15 knots, landfall in the Dominican expected sometime within the next three to four days, all this according to thirteen out of the twenty-six possible computer models.

"Nine other models have it taking a more northerly direction," the weatherman continues, "and three have it going south. The last model has Alison turning back around, skirting the Cape of Good Hope and eventually petering out near India, but we think there may have been a computer error on that one."

Noreen smiles as her leg presses against mine, her fake but firm thigh contoured against the material of her skirt. "See? A hurricane report isn't about the damage that's been done; it's about the damage that *could* be done, if everything goes right. Or wrong. It's all about the possibilities."

She leans back against the sofa, a soft sigh escaping her lips, and for a split second, we're back in my childhood bedroom, *Star Wars* sheets on the bed and Rush posters on the walls, preparing to make out. Her back is arched just so, and my arm slides beneath her shoulderblades, my body coming around to hers, our faces pulling together—

Then I'm back on the sofa, and it's just me and Noreen and the TV weatherman droning on and on. The rest of Jack's men have disappeared for the moment.

"I don't seem to inspire much camaraderie," I confess.

"Why do you think that is?"

"Folks are distrustful of things they don't know," I say. "They fear the unknown."

A little laugh escapes her. "They fear you, is that it?"

"Perhaps."

"Is that what you've become since last I saw you, Vincent? Someone to be feared?"

I turn to her, swinging my right leg up and onto the sofa so that we're truly facing each other. "You know, this isn't the way I expected our conversation to go."

She feigns shock. "You were expecting a conversation?"

"You know what I mean."

"I'm sure I don't." Noreen's playing this to the hilt; I can see that now. She's older, of course, wiser, and I wonder if our ruined relationship had anything to do with the creation of this tougher but sadder gal. There's a restrained undertone of anger running through her words, but she's barely letting it trickle out. That pair of slaps out by the elevator—her handprints still burned into the more sensitive parts of my faux skin—were carefully planned releases, and nothing more.

"Look," I say, trying to figure a way out of this and into a more normal mode of conversation, "we could sit here all day and pussy-foot around—"

"Excellent," she interrupts. "Let's."

I'm not that easily swayed. "Or we could come right out and be done with it. You're pissed at me."

"I assure you, I'm not."

"Then you were. Back then, the day at the bus station, when—"

"Ah-ah-ah," she says once more, and the finger is back across my lips.

"It's hard to talk when you do that," I mumble.

"That's the idea."

I smell Hagstrom before I see him, and my shoulders tense instantly. He slides next to Noreen, and, with the ease of a world-class lech, throws an arm around her bare shoulder. A wave of chivalry washes over me, and I hop off the sofa to defend Noreen's honor—

Which is when she leans in and kisses him. This bears repeating: *she* kisses *him*. Leaving me standing in front of the sofa, frozen, my arm cocked back in a pre-punch, crouched for balance, looking for all the world like a Heisman Trophy statue after it's been crushed by a steamroller.

Noreen pulls her lips off Hagstrom's and stares me down. She looks nearly as confused at my posture as I am at her liplock. "Have you met Nelly?" she asks. "We're engaged."

"Engaged," I repeat mindlessly. The word bounces around my head without making any major impact. "Engaged."

"For about a year now." She pats Hagstrom's knee and leaves her hand there. The diamond on her finger is large, without being ostentatious. I want to rip it off. "At first, Jack wasn't too happy about it. Mixing business and pleasure, but now . . ."

She kisses Hagstrom again, and I do my best to regain control of my body and walk away. No good can come of staying and watching them snog like . . . well, like Noreen and I used to snog. I don't get more than ten feet away when I feel someone sliding up next to me.

"Man, look at those two go at it. Get a nest!"

Glenda's at my side, a tumbler of Infusion in her hand. She swirls the ice around the clear liquid. "That's Noreen," I tell her.

"Yeah, we met last night. Jack's sister. Swell gal."

"Noreen," I repeat. "*High school* Noreen." Glenda's heard the stories, sat through countless drunken recollections of my lost love.

It takes a moment to sink through her herb-addled brain, but the connection finally rings true. Glenda turns back and gives Noreen the once-over, in the way that only women can inspect other women. Half beauty show, half criminal lineup. "Ohhhh, *that* Noreen. The one you stood up."

"Thanks so much."

Glenda shrugs and tosses down the rest of her Infusion. "This place is amazing," she says. "The mattress I slept on must have been three feet thick. The pantry's stocked, the herb cabinet unlocked and climate-controlled . . . Shit, they even got a little private movie theater downstairs."

"Glad you're enjoying the accommodations. Did you find anything out for me?"

"Like what?"

"Those girls—the waitresses—"

"Oh yeah," she says, "they got 'em all over the place. Here at the house, back at the club."

"But you didn't notice anything else about them? Anything odd?"

"Nope. Why, was I supposed to?"

"Maybe. I'm not sure." At this point, I'd just like to find Jack, see if he needs me for anything, and then get back to Tallarico's place. I can still feel the grime from the racetrack coating my guise, and I worry that small particles of dissolution powder may be hiding out on my clothes, waiting for their chance to contact raw dino flesh.

"Where's Jack?" I ask.

Glenda nods toward the back of the penthouse. "Saw him disappear back that way with some little old chick."

"Gray hair, well kept?"

"That's the one. Who is she?"

"I don't really know. No one seems to."

Glenda and I move toward the back of the massive apartment, skirting antiques and art I should probably admire—but what the hell do I know about art and antiques? A long hallway is lined with doors, all closed.

"Jack?" I call out. "You back here?"

A muffled groan from the end of the hall. Glenda and I take a few more steps.

"Jack, that you?"

Another groan, and now I'm thinking this is the part in any good horror movie where the audience would be yelling at me to turn around and run, out the door, and perferably to the local police station. But like those oblivious scream queens, I keep walking forward.

A grunt, a moan, a clipped roar, all coming from behind that far door. I look to Glenda. "Should I?"

"It's your shoulder," she says.

I brace myself, prepare to take a running start—

The door opens, and Jack wheels out. He's neither a crazed beast, nor does he have a knife poking out of his back like a giant piece of rumaki, but he looks drained. Withered. A balloon animal three days old, loose and wrinkling.

"Vincent," he whispers, his chest rising slowly as he catches a deep breath. "I didn't know you'd gotten here already."

"Yeah, just about twenty minutes ago—"

I stop when I notice the older woman stepping out of the room behind Jack, shooting me a sweet smile as she meets my gaze. She pats Jack on the back and whispers into his ear.

"That's a good idea, Audrey," he says. "We'll do that." He turns back to me and Glenda. "Let's go down to the convenience store, get a slushie."

"A slushie? Like a *slushie* slushie?"

"What? Vincent Rubio's too good for a slushie?"

"No," I say, "it's just—you look a little tired—"

Jack punches the joystick on his power chair and it lurches forward, nearly knocking me over as he scoots past. "Come on, I'll pay. I'm sure you and Noreen need some time to catch up. Nostalgia always goes down better with a slushie."

His good mood seems forced, but it has been a while since I've tossed back a good slushie. Raptors are particularly susceptible to Icee Brain Freeze due to our large sinus cavities, so sometimes they're a little tough going down. But a free dessert is a free dessert, and so off we go, back down the elevator and into the limousine.

It's me, Glenda, Jack, Hagstrom, and Noreen, and despite the innumerable lines of conversation possible here, there's a whole lot of silence going on. Jack could certainly get the ball rolling if he chooses to, but he's slumped back in his seat, so loose he's nearly sinking into the leather itself.

"Jack," I say, "you sure you're feeling all right?"

He nods and gives the thumbs-up, but even that small effort takes something out of him. I wonder if this is the disease, the SMA, starting to progress further. Perhaps that's what we're all thinking; perhaps that's why we're all so quiet.

"Jack's going to be fine," Noreen says softly. It sounds like she's convincing herself. "He's just fine." She hugs her brother close, and he gives her a peck on the forehead. It's nice to see how far they've come since the noogies and tattletales.

Once we get to the 7-Eleven, Hagstrom checks out the store and gives the all-clear before he lets Jack wheel himself inside. "Can't be too careful," he says, holding the door open as Jack, Noreen, and Glenda pass through. He lets it close as I approach, the door hitting me as I try to walk by. Very mature. I can only hope Noreen caught a glimpse.

Only the cherry vanilla machine is working, so we order up five and fill up the cups. As I fill mine to the top, Jack wheels over to me and puts his arm around my waist. It feels even heavier than before, as if he's unable to support its weight.

"I want you to know," he says, "that I'm real happy you showed up. It means a lot to me."

"Me, too, Jack," I say, meaning every word for once. "I'm glad we found each other again."

"And I know it means a lot to my sister."

"Yeah, well . . ." Noreen and Hagstrom are off near the beef jerky aisle, giggling over something, making damned fools of themselves if you ask me. "She seems pretty happy otherwise."

Jack nods. "She is. Look, I know you and Nelly don't get along, but trust me, Vincent, he's good for her. You and him are extremely similar."

"I highly doubt that."

"Which is exactly what he said." Jack grins and slaps me on the rump, a sports-themed gesture I never quite understood. "Come on, these things are gonna melt in about thirty seconds if we don't get them back to the house."

We head outside; the limousine isn't waiting for us. "I hate when he does this," Hagstrom snarls. "Everybody wait here." He trots off to find the chauffeur, leaving me, Glenda, Jack, and Noreen sipping our slushies in the 7-Eleven parking lot. It's quiet, but not strained. Just a bunch of friends, hanging out, ingesting massive quantities of processed sugar and ice.

But the silence allows me to hear another noise over the dull hum of traffic, a low rumbling gradually separating from the din and becoming its own sound. A growl, but not animal. Mechanical, definitely. A car, old and worn, the muffler dead or dying.

It tears around the corner a moment later, a beat-up Lexus with tinted windows and, I'd bet, bloodstains on the ceiling. The passenger-side window is rolled down slightly, and in that instant of recognition, I catch a glimpse of a thin metal tube poking out into the open air.

The gun is exploding. Light is flashing. Bullets are flying.

Glenda's already hugging the pavement, and I'm down on the ground half a second later, throwing myself atop Noreen and Glenda both, covering their heads with my body, amazed that anyone in this day and age would resort to a drive-by shooting, especially someone of the reptilian persuasion. The rifle, the handgun, the arrow—these aren't our weapons. The monkeys need tools to fight. We use our claws, our teeth, our tails, our wits. This is cowardice.

Fortunately, it's futile cowardice. Rubber burns into the pavement as the car shrieks down the street, carrying its criminal cargo with it. It's not coming back anytime soon.

"Get the hell off me, Rubio," grunts Glenda, stumbling to her feet as I step back and help Noreen to hers. "I can take care of myself, you know."

Noreen's scream spins me around. Jack is halfway out of his wheelchair—his legs somehow supporting his body for this short moment, trembling but stable, and my first thought is, *That's amazing, he's walking,* followed shortly afterwards by, *Wow, those are a lot of bullet wounds.*

He collapses to the ground.

A thin trickle of blood trails out by his cheek, and within seconds it's a thick river, pooling beneath his body. Noreen runs past me, lunges at Jack, spinning him around, flipping him over, the holes in his neck and head large, ragged, bloody. I'm staggering back, head reeling, and Noreen is screaming and crying as Hagstrom tears around the corner and the 7-Eleven clerk races out of his store, his own shotgun at the ready, but there's nothing anyone can do about it: now even the lure of a hundred bottles of Infusion and a thousand late-night parties along Miami Beach won't bring him back.

Jack's mouth is opening, closing, forming soundless syllables as his fingers twitch, his chest heaving with his final breaths. I wonder, if I lean down to hear his last words—will he forgive me? For not moving quickly enough, for not recognizing the sound of the battered Tallarico Lexus. For hurting his sister, his entire family. For not having the courage to stand up for either one of us when we'd pledged unending fealty.

But Jack's chest falls and doesn't rise again. There's no time left for any of that.

11

"Nice work, Rubio! Score one for the home team!"

Eddie Tallarico dances through the living room of his crumbling mansion, a bundle of rosemary clutched in his fat fist. He's decked out in flannel paisley pajamas, the thick material clinging to his rubbery folds, undulating with each grotesque movement. It takes all of my strength, all of my willpower, not to deck the son of a bitch.

"Evening, Eddie."

"Evening, hell! It's sunshine in the morning, Rubio. Didn't ya hear the news? Jack Dugan is no more." He turns his little dance into a cha-cha. "No more, no more, Jack Dugan is no more."

"Right. Yeah, I heard that."

"Heard that, hell. Hell! I got my sources, Rubio. I know what happened. Coverin' up the dames so that fucker would be left unprotected."

He leaps onto a sofa and, in the best impression of a three-hundred-pound Fred Astaire I've ever seen, flips it over, walking down the cushions as he approaches me. "I had my eye on you," he says, "and I was wary. I'll say that much—I was wary."

"No doubt." The other men in the room are chatting among themselves, but have started to notice my presence, and a buzz is building.

"That's one of the reasons I sent you out on that racetrack job. To gauge you. To see what you're capable of."

I'm trying to keep it light, easy. I want to show him exactly what I'm capable of, but this isn't the time or place. That will come. "I kinda figured," I tell him, warming to the part.

"Kinda figured. Hell. You're a bright one, I can see that. I had all you L.A. types measured the same, you know? Every one of ya, outta the fruit cup—that's how I figured it. My brother . . . hell, my brother was one of the good guys till he moved out west, and now I gotta contend with his movie connections, and his actor friends. Like I need that in my life.

"But you . . . you got a good streak in you, Rubio. Sherm and Chaz tell me you did a real number down at the track."

I can feel it now, that hard nugget riding in my stomach. Something tight forming down there, a solid core of hatred, small but growing. "Doing my best, sir."

"Well, you got that taken care of, and then you paid off double. Keeping it together when the shit came down, playing it cool. You're in over there, baby—in and good, and that's just gonna come in handy when it all comes to a head."

I decide to play it a little harder. "You want me to make a move?" I ask.

Eddie just breaks out into a big grin and hugs me close. I can smell the tar, my nose pressed next to his scent gland, the molasses dragging me under. It's a heavy smell, a heady smell, and next to the stink of pepperoni and fried cheese, it nearly knocks me out cold.

"Lookit you," he drawls, and it's frightening to see this behemoth in such a good mood. "Already working your way into the plans. I love this guy!"

This seems to be some sort of cue for the other soldiers in Tallarico's family to approach and tell me that they, too, love me and my zany antics. I accept the hugs and the kisses and the pats on the back and return them in kind, and somewhere in the middle of it all—halfway between a bear hug from Sherman and an earnestly drunken conversation with Eddie's mafia accountant about the state of the union—I realize that in just one short week, I have worked my way into the inner circles of not one, but two of the deadliest dinosaur mafia families in the country. Where's my you've-got-no-direction high school guidance counselor now, huh?

Cheers fill the living room, toasts are made, and more congratulations are heaped upon yours truly as Tallarico hits the music and the party gears back up to full speed. An entire basil plant is shoved into my hand, and it takes me a second before I realize what I'm holding. I drop the entire thing to the ground, the pot falling to one side, dirt spilling out across the carpet where it's trampled into the fibers a moment later by a rampant, unstoppable conga line.

"Pssst! Vinnie! Can I speak with you a sec?" It's Chaz, ten feet away.

I saunter over to the corner, keeping my game face on. Chaz is jittery, clearly not enjoying the festivities as much as the rest of them. "Good to see ya," I say casually.

"Hey," he says. "Hey."

"Hey," I respond. "Are we talking? 'Cause there's a party back there . . ."

"Yeah, yeah," says Chaz. "Listen, after the racetrack job, I was supposed to talk you into going over to Dugan's, making yourself comfortable. Just to play an inside part, in case things got hinky."

"And . . . ?"

"Hell, *you* were there," he says, glancing around the room to make sure no one else can hear our conversation. "The stables,

Stu, that fucking Pepe, it was a mess. Guy screamed so loud we had to take off his fake feet and shove 'em down his throat. And then you were outta there before I remembered, so . . . I mean, it worked out real nice you being with Dugan like you were supposed to, but I didn't tell Eddie that I fucked up. And I was hoping . . ."

"You were hoping I wouldn't tell him, either."

Chaz's face flushes with relief. "Right. Right."

All I could do, back outside the 7-Eleven, standing there over Jack's prone body, helpless, nauseous, was think over and over again: *It was a gun.* A simple stupid gun that finally did him in, the ultimate mammalian weapon as executioner. And it made sense. Because while we've got our dissolution packets and our claws to the throat, our spiked tails or a razor-sharp bite from our fangs, it's nothing when compared to the crack of a rifle and the punch of a bullet. When it comes to taking out a rival gang leader, it's all about raw killing power, and the humans cornered that market a long time ago.

Now the Tallaricos would learn about it from a different angle.

"You know, Chaz," I say, pulling him close, buddylike, "I think we've got some deals ahead of us. I think we can work this out."

"That's great," he says, exhaling hard, as if he'd been holding his breath since this afternoon. His words speed up even more than usual, the rapid-fire speech harsh against my eardrums. "Super, just super. It's the kind of thing I was hoping for—"

I hold up a hand—big ole stop sign, and he drops the clamor. "You wanna check out a good scene?" I ask.

"Like what?"

"Like some primo herb. All gratis."

"We got that right here—"

"And the ladies," I add. "Oh, some fine women. I know a place we can go . . . All types. Hell, they even got a room—" I lower my voice a notch to give it that proper air of sleaze. "They got a room in back with mammals."

"Humans?"

"All tied up for you," I tell him. "Ready for a little meet-and-greet."

This is too much for Chaz; he's nearly become warmblooded just at the thought of it. "Come on," I tell him, heading through the hallway, away from the main room. "Let's keep this between you and me."

He eagerly follows me out of the compound, where Eddie has set up a round-the-clock guard service behind the main gates. Four cars wait in the driveway, a steel barrier against anyone who might want to come crashing through. We step into the Lexus and Chaz waves at the guards, who part their cars, open the gates, and wave us past. Within minutes we're off the island and heading toward the beach.

"How come I don't know about this place?" Chaz asks as we drive along the causeway.

"Don't know," I tell him. "I heard about it from Dugan's crew, so maybe it's a Hadrosaur joint."

He nods, as if this makes all the sense in the world. "Yeah. Yeah, that's probably it. But it's safe and all?"

"Oh, don't you worry. It's safe."

I hadn't planned on this next part; it's not my job. But there's a certain amount of curiosity that needs to be satisfied, and I've always been one dead cat, anyway. "How'd you know where to go?" I ask him.

"When?"

"With the Dugan hit. You have a tracer on me?"

Chaz laughs, shakes his head. "Nah, Vinnie. We got a guy on the inside."

"In Dugan's family?"

He nods and gives another chuckle. "Same as how we knew he was down at that club. Got the phone call from our source, found out where Dugan was going, that was the end of that. If it wasn't for the inside man, though . . . Hell, we got lucky."

An involuntary shudder passes through me as my spirits drop another notch. I'd suspected a betrayal from within—how else would Tallarico get the information about what went down inside the club?—but hearing it confirmed sends a small round of depression through my body. It's not like they're my men, but I'm sad for Jack, for Noreen, even a little bit sad for Hagstrom and the Dugan family in general. I'd hoped to find loyalty, if not honor, among thieves. Now I know otherwise.

"Which one of 'em is it?" I ask. "Just so I know who's who next time I go in."

But the little guy just winks my question away, and as soon as I catch that satisfied grin, I know there's no chance I'll get the information out of him.

Then again, I don't have to. That's someone else's job.

Three hundred feet before the causeway exit, I see the black limousine parked on the far side of the road, hidden beneath the darkness and the shadow of a palm tree.

"Something wrong with the car?" Chaz asks.

I decide not to answer him. I don't have to be coy or cute or smarmy anymore. That kernel of coal in my chest is keeping me silent.

"Vincent, what's up, man?"

Again, nothing. Every second I stay mute is another second I grow colder, and I find that ice is the only way to numb the pain right now.

"Why are we pulling over?" There's a note of desperation in his voice now, and it thrills me to hear it. "Vincent? Hey, Vinnie—"

I hit the brakes and slam the car into park. Chaz is glancing around him, frantically looking around the car, into the darkness, a cat thrown into a box, unsure of where it is or how it got there—

The passenger door opens. It's Hagstrom. "Get out," he tells Chaz.

The mop-top Raptor looks at me beseechingly. "Vinnie . . . what's going on?"

Hagstrom doesn't wait to tell him again. He reaches in and yanks Chaz out by an arm, pulling him to the ground below. I watch out the windshield as BB and two others muscle the little guy up and into the limousine, slamming the door behind them.

"Go on back," Hagstrom tells me. "Make sure you're seen."

I know the routine; I came up with it myself. I give a nod to Hagstrom and pull the car back onto the causeway, driving around for ten minutes or so before heading back to Star Island and Tallarico's compound.

I make sure to find Eddie as soon as I get in. "You partying it up, Vinnie?" he asks me, already half in the bag.

"Sure, Eddie," I say, convivial as ever. "Chaz just had me drive him out to some club on the beach. Hope that was okay."

"Chaz is a big boy," Eddie replies. "He can do what he wants. But you're no fucking chauffeur around here. Next time, find Raoul, let him do it. You're my guy, Vincent. You got that? You're my guy."

"I'm your guy," I repeat, and allow Eddie to give me a sloppy kiss on the cheek before he dances off into the living room and rejoins the festivities.

I make a show of partying it up with the other Tallarico family members, telling and retelling the stories of the hit on Jack Dugan, each time accentuating my role in the assassination. It's a tale that grows smoother with each telling, because with every iteration, another layer of coal wraps itself around my heart, making it that much easier to deal with both the past and the unpleasant, inevitable string of events yet to come.

12

F unerals. I go to way too many of these damn things.

Jack Dugan's body lies in an oak coffin, the wood burnished to a high shine. Seems a little silly to me; it's just going to get dirty in about thirty minutes anyway. But it's all about appearances at funerals, especially open caskets: makeup is applied, hair is combed, fingernails are manicured. Even the most slovenly of shlubs—that guy who doesn't bathe for weeks on end, or the woman who lets her hair grow into a rat's nest of snags and brambles—gets to say *hasta la vista* to life in style.

They're keeping Jack in guise, though, and it hurts a little to know that he'll be bound up in his straps and clamps and fake human skin for eternity. Not that I expect him to notice. Noreen told me that the funeral director was concerned about the size and number of the bullet wounds, claiming that trying to cosmetically alter his normal dino appearance would be next to impossible. So they just grabbed one of Jack's replacement guises from his bedroom closet and fastened it around his body. For that minor service alone, they charged two thousand dollars. Clearly, the reason you can't take it with you is because the funeral directors can.

"He looks good," Glenda whispers to me as we pass by the casket. She's right, too—his face is serene, his cheeks high and bright. "Almost like he's still alive."

But he most certainly is not. I was there. I saw it all.

Jack was dead two seconds after he hit the ground. That's what the doctors said, at least, and since I don't relish the thought of my friend suffering, bleeding out in the parking lot of a 7-Eleven while we futilely scampered around his dying body, I prefer to accept the report at face value and leave it at that.

Seconds after the gunshots and the chaos, we pulled Jack's body into the convenience store. With impressive speed and strength, Hagstrom ripped off his boss's guise, the tough polysuit giving way at the seams, and was pumping on Jack's chest with all his might, engaging in a furious bout of snout-to-snout resuscitation. But Jack was long gone by that point, frolicking in some mafia version of the Big Rock Candy Mountain where the cops take checks and all crime is neatly organized.

So it was while I was standing there, over my dead friend, fifteen years lost, five days found, forever lost once more, when I realized that it was time to come clean. Sort of.

It took me two hours to get around to it. Jack's body had already been processed by a medical examiner on the family payroll and delivered to the funeral home; the rest of us sat in the penthouse, shell-shocked, staring at one another with dumbfounded looks on our faces while Hagstrom quietly made sure that the cops in his pocket cleaned up the scene and didn't ask too many questions.

I was still caught up in the moment, replaying the scene in my mind. The car, the gun barrel, diving down, covering the two people in front of me, Glenda and Noreen—while leaving vulnerable the one I should have protected. Of course, if I'd jumped backwards instead of forwards, it might be me lying on a cold slab somewhere.

But the thing that's really getting me was the bit that came next: Had Jack actually managed to step out of his wheelchair before collapsing to the pavement? It certainly seemed like his legs were supporting him for a good second or two, and, if that's the case, does that mean he could always walk, or was it some last-breath spasm of super-strength? What would be the benefit in faking a serious illness like SMA? No one else seemed to mention it, and I didn't think this was the right time to bring it up.

While Noreen wept openly for her brother, Hagstrom and BB had already gotten down to business. They were discussing the possible culprits, but given the circumstances and the method of execution, only two possibilities came to mind.

"It was Tallarico or it was Rubin. One of the two, no doubt."

"Who's Rubin?" I asked, and Hagstrom was too caught up to tell me to shut my yap.

"Compy family," he says. "Ken Rubin. They're the only other ones I can think of would pull out fucking . . . guns . . ." His mouth puckers with distaste. "But he's got no reason to do it. We don't deal with them. They got their rackets, we got ours."

"So it's Tallarico," said BB. "That's all that's left."

"Tallarico," Hagstrom repeated. "Fucking Eddie Tallarico. And by now I'll bet he's got that compound locked down tight."

That's when I opened my mouth and blurted out, "I can get in there."

"What? Where?"

"Tallarico's place."

Now I had their attention. The two of them turned toward me like a couple of desperate insurance salesmen with a hot prospect on the line. "Come again?"

"Eddie Tallarico. I can get into his place. I can find out who did this."

BB wasn't going for it. He wore his disbelief like perfume, the acrid stink of his sweat washing over me. "And how do you plan on doing this?"

"I know his brother," I admitted, and here I knew I was treading along the edge of a very big pot of hot water. I had to pick my words carefully. "Frank. He's from L.A. It's a Raptor thing."

Hagstrom took a step forward. "And you think that will get you in? If they did this thing to Jack—if they're responsible—they'll be triple-checking everyone who comes in the joint. How're you gonna make it?"

"Leave that to me," I told him. "I'll take care of it."

"And then what?" asked BB, still unconvinced. "You find out who pulled the job and off him, right there and then?"

"Uh-uh. That's your domain. I just bring the guy to you."

They huddled together for a moment, whispering to each other and glancing over every so often in my direction. I busied myself with staring at the carpet. The meeting continued.

Noreen wiped away her tears and raised her voice: "Let him do it."

Hagstrom and BB didn't flinch; they kept right on with their conversation. Noreen stood, and this time her voice carried the weight of her brother; for a moment, I could almost smell him again. "I said let him do it."

I don't know if Hagstrom had heard that timbre from his fiancée before, but it either frightened or greatly excited him, because he involuntarily stepped back a foot.

"I don't think it's a good idea."

"He loved Jack," she said, and sat back down on the sofa. "Let him do it."

Strangely enough, the L-word was enough for Hagstrom. "Okay," he said, clapping his hands together and drawing me into his circle. "Let's hash this thing out."

Now, at the funeral, Hagstrom and BB are just behind me in the viewing line, waiting to pay their respects to their deceased boss and his family. I don't ask them what's become of Chaz; if they want to tell me, they will. I'm hoping they won't.

Off to one side, I notice Audrey, the older woman with whom

Jack spent so much time, speaking softly into a cell phone. As usual, she's smartly dressed, glasses perched perfectly on the edge of her nose, looking for all the world like that sweet little teacher everyone had in kindergarten, the kind they issue to every class-room before the school year begins.

Glenda and I move down the line, waiting for our audience with Pop and Noreen, who greet guests and accept condolences twenty feet away. Pop's mask sags off his face, the false skin wrin-kling even farther below his jowls. Makes him look ten years older, easy. Maybe that's the kind of thing that happens when you're too grief-stricken to apply the proper facial glue in the morning; maybe it's just the kind of thing that happens when you lose a son.

Noreen's wearing basic black, an austere number that never-theless hugs her hips and conforms nicely to her human shape. She's very Jackie O—grieving, but fashionable.

"So she's in charge now?" Glenda asks me as we move along.

I nod. "Thought it would be Hagstrom, but Noreen's pretty much running the show."

"Makes sense," says Glenda. "She's the one giving orders around the house."

Noreen had allowed Glenda to stay on in one of the suites in Jack's penthouse. Glenda might not be safe outside their protec-tion, Noreen reasoned, her being a Hadrosaur and, as of last night, a known crony of the Dugan crew. So it was all the free food and Infusion she could inhale, just so long as she kept quiet about it and didn't make too much of a fuss.

"Treating you nice, are they?"

"It ain't the Fountainebleau," Glenda sniffs, "but it ain't so bad."

"Hey, it's a hell of a lot cheaper than the Fountainebleau."

"Oh yeah, it's your basic Miami dream vacation," Glenda drawls. "The special mafia package—two weeks holed up in a high-rise apartment, all you can eat and drink. Very popular down here."

Pop barely notices as Glenda and I pay our respects. He's off in some other world, and I can't blame him. Part of me wants to come along for the ride.

As I approach Noreen, she reaches out with both hands to pull me close, and I hug her tightly. She's beyond tears; the last two days have been full of them, I am sure, and perhaps it's just chaste body-to-body contact that satisfies her now. She releases me, and I slowly pull away.

Glenda and Noreen go through a similar, if more impersonal, routine, and soon we're out of the line and released into the audience, where we find a seat and wait for the service to start.

"You ever find out what they did with Chaz?" Glenda asks me.

"Don't wanna know right now," I explain. "It's not my problem."

Glenda shrugs. "Still, you delivered him—"

"Not my problem," I repeat, barely believing the words myself. "I don't want to get involved."

"That's a good one," she laughs. "You're a funny guy, Rubio."

The service begins, and of course it's full of all the usual crap I've heard before. How the deceased was a pillar of the community, how he was beloved by his friends, how he wanted to make the world a better place, and so forth. And maybe it's all true. To hear his men tell it, Jack did give a sizable amount to charity, and clearly he valued his friends and family above all else, so it's not like the minister's lying to us. But just once I want to go to a funeral where they lay it on the line and accept the death for what it is: the end to a flawed life. When I finally go, I want no flowers and no flowery words. I just want someone to stand over my body and announce: *Vincent Rubio is dead, and he hopes you all enjoy the free dessert*—and then toss me into whatever hole is deemed big enough to fit my carcass.

But Jack has left no such instructions, and so we listen to some poems, a few tunes performed on the harp, and a stumbling speech by Hagstrom, who, though Jack's closest confidant, isn't exactly a Dr. King in the public-speaking department.

Halfway through the service, a low murmur splits the crowd, and Glenda pokes me in the side. "Now *that* takes a major set of balls," she whispers.

Eddie Tallarico has entered the room. He moves like a drunken rhino, ambling slowly but quietly through the pews, his hips brushing the wooden benches, flanked by Sherman on one side and an unfamiliar Tallarico family member on the other. A long, black coat is draped across his spherical frame; this despite the near-record heat thrown off by the sun on this hot August afternoon.

"That cuts it," I say. "The guy's insane. Coming here after what he did."

Glenda suppresses a laugh. "They'll tear him apart."

"No, not here they won't. And he's gotta have twenty guys waiting for him outside. This is just a show."

The service continues, doesn't miss a beat, but no one's paying attention to the minister anymore. Tallarico is a magnet for attention, fifty pairs of eyes boring into his head. At one point, he motions to Sherman, who reaches into a bag and produces a slushie, just like the one Jack was drinking when it all came down. Tallarico takes a long drag on the straw, the *sluuuurp* momentarily drowning out the eulogy. The room fills with an electric charge, the intertwined scents of ten tons of furious reptile clogging the air.

As soon as it's all over and the officiant bids us all to go in peace, Hagstrom and BB are out of their seats and surrounding Tallarico, ten other soldiers in tow. I duck out of sight, hiding behind Glenda's flowing dress; it's better that I'm not seen.

Tallarico pays no attention to the masses on either side. He speaks directly to Hagstrom, as if they're the only two in the room. "Of course, my condolences. Now that that's settled, perhaps we should speak about business."

I'm fully convinced that Hagstrom's about to answer in a manner that will sell at least ten more coffins for the funeral home, but before he can get a claw in, Noreen steps in front of her fiancé and into Eddie Tallarico's face.

"If you want to talk, you talk to me."

Tallarico's cheeks ripple as his lips pull back into a grimace. "You?"

Hagstrom pauses momentarily, then backs up a step, allowing Noreen to take her rightful place at the front of the Dugan family.

"That's right," she says. "And if we're going to talk—and I promise you, Eddie, one of these days, we'll talk—it's going to be on my terms."

Noreen stares Eddie down, and for a moment, the two of them are focused so intently on each other that I half expect them to fall into a deep, tender kiss. Eddie drops his gaze first, waving his people out of the room as he heads for the door. "You know where to find me," he says. "And, again, my condolences." With that, he disappears through the funeral home's double doors and into the bright Miami day.

They're all in a tizzy a moment after he leaves, roaring and growling about the nerve, about the disrespect, about how they're going to rip him a new one. Most of it is idle talk, routine bravado performed by seasoned thespians—Olivier had nothing on these guys when it comes to high emotion.

Those in command appear calm. Noreen and Hagstrom are already huddled up as BB fields a call on his cell. I stand and approach the trio, but Noreen raises a finger, and I stay my ground.

She's radiant, even amid the somber business of death, and it's not so much her physical attributes that get me as the air of confidence Noreen is exuding. As if she stepped not only into Jack's position, but also into his mind, instantly absorbing the command and presence that was once his alone.

And that breeze of mangoes, still so strong after all these years, has a new strain to it. Maybe I just never noticed it before, but I'd been intimate enough with Noreen to know every inch of her body and every nuance of her smell, and I'm convinced that this change is recent. A bit of lemongrass glides its way in and around her scent, just a pinch of flavoring, but enough to remind me that Jack will always be here, in one form or another.

BB flips his cell phone closed and approaches Noreen, whispers in her ear. She looks shocked for a moment, her nose tightening as if she's trying to quell an itch, and then covers it. She whispers back, BB nods, and Noreen wags a finger in my direction.

"Are we going outside?" I ask.

"No," says Noreen. "No interment. Jack didn't even want a funeral service, but I couldn't let him go without a few words."

"We're taking a drive," Hagstrom says, standing and smoothing out his pants. "You wanna come along?"

I look to Noreen, who nods. "Guess I do," I say. "Lemme get Glenda—"

BB steps in my way. "We'll get someone to take her back to the apartment."

There's something about the way they're treating me that reminds me—quite unpleasantly—of the way I spoke to Chaz the other night. As if getting in this car might not be optimal for my health. But I've thrown myself headlong into any number of nasty situations when intuition screamed at me to run like hell, and come out clean every time. Unless you count the broken legs. And the stitches. And the two subpoenas.

"Sounds great," I chirp. "Which way to the car?"

Chaz's severed head lies in the mud, undeniably separate from the rest of his body. I've never seen him out of guise before, so at first glance, I'm not sure who it is. Just another dinosaur noggin, snout aimed to the sky, no neck or torso to speak of. Small, deep slices along the flesh, each one precise, straight, professional. But I can still get a whiff, however slight, of human sweat, and that cinches it for me.

"That's Chaz," I say. "Half of him."

"Good guess," says Hagstrom. "But the test ain't over yet."

We're standing in the middle of a muddy mangrove swamp, our pants and shoes covered in a thick Florida muck. We drove for a good hour from the funeral home, heading west along a wide suburban street. The houses soon gave way to thrift stores and auto body shops, then abruptly shifted into retail chain outlets. All of a sudden, the road widened to four lanes of traffic, and we were surrounded on all sides by condominiums and development complexes, boxed in by Chili's and Outback Steakhouses and every mass-produced emporium I could think to name.

"This is where we're going?" I asked, wedged into the car between Hagstrom and BB, Noreen up front, driving.

"This is Pembroke Pines," Noreen called back.

"So what's here?"

"Everything. Nothing. Pipe down."

We continued our westerly path and soon popped through the corridor of suburbia and into a more rural environment. Here the houses and stores soon petered out, replaced by thin, winding mangrove trees and a strong smell of compost. Noreen parked in what looked to be an abandoned rec area, and we all trundled out of the car, setting off on foot, deeper into the muck. Three separate times on our walk out to this deserted section of the Everglades, I heard a sucking sound and looked down to find that my right shoe had been completely pulled off my foot by the fudgelike mud. The least they could have done was tell me to wear sneakers.

Noreen, Hagstrom, and BB stand over Chaz's decapitated head like football players waiting for a huddle. I'm not sure if I'm supposed to get in there and draw up the next play or stand back and wait for my number to be called.

"Where's his body?" I ask.

"Does it matter?"

"Not really," I say. "It's not like he's complaining about it."

Another moment of silence. Should I be saying something? "So what'd you get outta him?" I ask, figuring it to be as good a place as any to start.

"Quite a lot," says Nelly.

"Really."

"You'd be surprised," he continues, "what a little persuasion can do. Jack was always squeamish about this sort of thing. But I think he would have understood, given the circumstances."

I look back down to Chaz's head, at the small cuts along his snout. Torture, no doubt, which explains the precise nature of the lines. A claw, perhaps; more likely something inanimate, like a scalpel or hunting knife. Which makes the ragged tear below the chin that much more confusing. If they were going to use tools on the rest of him, why be so rough with the decapitation process? It almost looks as if the other section of his body were chewed away.

"So he talked," I say.

"And talked and talked and talked," replies BB, and he and Hagstrom share a little smile. "Gave us his mother's social security number, the names of girls he'd dated back in school . . . Yeah, I'd say he talked."

"That's great—"

"But it didn't take long to get at the most important piece of information," says Hagstrom, stepping through the mud, his feet squish-squish-squishing as he clomps over toward me.

"The mole."

"That's right," Hagstrom replies. "The name of the guy in our organization who's been telling secrets they shouldn't. The guy who worked for Tallarico to set Jackie up."

"Great," I say, suddenly anxious at the way BB and Hagstrom have carefully flanked me, more so at the way Noreen has remained in the middle, silent, refusing to meet my gaze. "So what'd he say?"

"The name he gave us," BB snarls, "was Vincent Rubio."

Suddenly I'm down in the mud, flat on my back, Hagstrom's knee on my chest, BB immobilizing my legs. I try to kick out, to get some purchase, but all I'm doing is kicking up a bucket of mud, probably upsetting eighteen different ecosystems in my attempt to get loose. Not that I care right now—I'd personally kill every last manatee if it meant I could work myself free.

"Lemme up," I grunt.

"Funny," says Hagstrom, "that's what the other Raptor shithead said."

Hagstrom doesn't even bother releasing his glove—he just lets his claws slide out of their sockets, the sharp edges slicing through the latex skin. He waves a single razor in front of my face, the tip barely brushing the edge of my false nose.

"First thing I'll do is cut off the guise, piece by piece," he says, his voice calm, even, as if he's reciting "The Road Not Taken"—

"And if I accidentally get a piece of your real flesh with it, well . . . whoops."

The more I struggle, the more I find myself sinking down into the muck. There's no use—they have all the leverage, and I have none. "Wait a second," I say, trying to keep my mind clear, my thoughts rational. "Wait, wait—you've got this backwards—"

"Ain't no backwards about it," BB sneers. But I'm not aiming this at him; I'm hoping Noreen can hear me, twenty feet away. If I've got a chance, it's going to come from her.

"Go through it," I said. "Please, before we—before you start in. Go through it, bit by bit."

Hagstrom sighs and glances at BB, who shakes his head emphatically. He wants to start in on the torture, and part of me can't blame him. The other part of me wants to slap that part silly.

But Hagstrom's got more brains than I gave him credit for.

"Okay," he says. "We got the guy out here, strapped him down, did our thing. BB pulled a few tricks outta his bag, and he gave you up."

"Gave me up *how*?" I insist.

"Said you were the one. Doubling back on us."

"Of course I am," I tell them, and Hagstrom's eyes blink in surprise.

"You are."

"That was the plan, wasn't it?"

I can feel a slight reduction in the tension on my arms and legs—they're starting to groove to my explanation—but I stay put. Gotta be in a helpless position if they're going to listen to the story.

"I went back there—to Tallarico's—and I wormed my way in. Let 'em know I was part of their group, a Raptor to the core. Told 'em I would double myself out, give them information. So of course Chaz is gonna tell you I'm the one who's playing both sides, 'cause I am. Only I'm doing it for you guys, not for them."

I may have pushed it too far; BB weighs down on my legs again, and I can feel the mud begin to seep in through the nearly microscopic seams in my guise. Hagstrom places his claw to my throat once again and looks to Noreen, five yards away, for instructions. "Give the word."

She's silent, her eyes closed. Breathing deeply. I take this moment to apologize to any and all religions I may have ridiculed over the years, just to cover my bases.

"Noreen?" Hagstrom says again. "I need an answer."

I watch her, standing immobile, dealing with whatever questions and doubts are popping up in her own mind, and I wonder: *Will our prior relationship influence her decision? Will the fact that I abandoned her at a bus station on her eighteenth birthday spell my eventual doom?*

"Let him up." Three words, so sweet.

Hagstrom and BB step off and back and let me struggle out of the mud on my own. My clothes are filthy, and this guise is going to need a good dry cleaning soon, but for the moment, I'm just happy my lungs are continuing to fill with air.

"Thank you," I say to Noreen. "For believing me."

"I don't believe you," she says, and suddenly I've got Hagstrom and BB on my case again. She waves them away. "But I believe that you're not the traitor. There's something you're not telling us, though."

I try to grin. Mud sticks in my teeth. "Girl's gotta have her secrets."

Hagstrom paces as he thinks. Why don't his shoes keep popping off like mine?

"Let me ask you this," he says. "Why now? Why does all this go down all of a sudden when you drop into town? Seems to me if they had someone in the Dugan family ratting us out, they'd have done this a long time ago."

It's a frighteningly good question. I seem to have a predilection for winding up at the center of any number of shit-storms, but I have a feeling this won't be the answer Nelly's looking for.

"Only thing I can think of," I say, "is that someone wanted it to look like I was involved. Like it all had to do with my appearance."

"Why?"

I don't have a good answer for this one, but the question goes to the top of my list.

"We're done here," says Noreen, as she bends down and wraps her fingers around Chaz's naked head, digging into the firm, stiffened flesh. "Do something with this." She tosses the head into Nelly's arms and turns around, clomping through the Everglades mud on her way back to the rec area. "We'll wait for you boys at the car. Vincent?"

I follow along at Noreen's heels, alternately hating myself for acting like a poodle and massively relieved that I'm still alive enough to do so. Once we're out of sight of Nelly and BB, I allow a little bit of comfort to bleed through.

"That was close," I say. "I thought they were about to—"

"They were," snaps Noreen, her jaw clenched. "And I should have let them."

"What? But we discussed—"

She stops, throwing up a wave of mud as her foot stomps into the ground. "Every part of my brain tells me you should be alligator meat right now. Not one little bit of this adds up, Vincent, and I want you to know that."

I nod. There's no way to let her into my mind, to show her how I feel about those days we were together, and, even more so, the days we were apart. But I can try. "Is this the time we talk about the bus station?"

"No," she says emphatically. "We never talk about the bus station."

"Noreen—"

"No," she repeats. "Unless you want me to tell those boys I've changed my mind."

"What bus station?"

Noreen smiles tightly. When we get to the car, she turns and opens the door for me, an almost chivalrous gesture, like she's just picked me up for a date at the malt shop. There's no doubt now about who has the power in our relationship.

"Vincent," she says, "I want you to know something. I'm trusting you because I think I know you well enough to do so. Because I know your scent almost as well as I know my own, and because I believe you would never purposely hurt Jack.

"You hurt me once, Vincent, probably worse than you'll ever know. I'm over it now, and I'm a stronger person for it, but that doesn't mean I can take a hit like that again. You used up your mulligan almost twenty years ago. If you betray me again—if you betray my family again, in any way—then the past won't matter any-more."

"I understand," I tell her, and boy, do I. Because it's not this new facet of Noreen's personality that keeps me on high alert, this cool calculation and eye for battle that she's inherited from her brother. What truly scares me is the most basic of elements: her femininity. There's nothing more dangerous in the world than an injured female. Hurt a woman once, she licks her wounds and limps off into the woods. Hurt a woman twice, and suddenly she feels cornered. Nowhere left to run, nowhere left to hide, and no choice but to lash out at her enemies and take them all down with her.

13

efore the bloodshed comes the rain.

South Florida, so I've been told, is due for a whopper of a hurricane. Sounds good to me; anything that gets this moisture out of the air and onto the ground can't be all bad.

Miami is a fertile breeding ground for that subspecies of news anchor known as meteorologists; when they get going, there's more hot air spewed in the television studios than there is in the weather patterns themselves. With their sharp jackets and sharper hair, they're ready to soothe or terrify at a moment's notice, tossing out latitudes and longitudes to anyone who doesn't know how to change the channel.

This one guy, Brian something-or-other, this Miami weatherman whose entire career revolves around his ability to come up with sixteen synonyms for the word *rain,* has 'em all beat. Because he's not only on the money with the weather this time around—he's on the money with *a lot* of weather.

"Hurricane Alison has reached category five status," he tells the viewing audience, among whose numbers I, unfortunately, count myself a member, "which means the winds are in excess of one hundred and fifteen miles an hour." He says this last bit as if the number 115 is entirely new to human consciousness, like it's some alien concept that we're never going to grasp, no matter how hard he tries to make us understand.

"Alison seems to be taking her time," he continues, completing the storm's metamorphosis from an inanimate collection of wind and rain to a complete human personality with feelings and critical decision-making capability. I almost expect him to breathlessly announce, "Alison has ordered pastrami on rye for lunch, but her situation is so volatile, she could change that to tuna salad at any moment."

Instead, he gives us more crucial information: "Twelve of the thirteen computer models have the hurricane striking Dade and Broward counties somewhere between eleven and eleven forty-five in the P.M., the eye coming ashore somewhere between Homestead and Hallandale."

"That's great," drawls Noreen as she hurries by the TV set, a cardboard box in her arms. "A hundred miles of possibility. Thanks for the warning, Brian."

Hurricane preparations at the Dugan penthouse are in full swing. Metal shutters are slowly rolled across the tall plate-glass windows; chaise lounges are dragged inside as we clear the patio of all furniture and debris. With hundred-mile-an-hour winds—excuse me, hundred-and-fifteen-mile-an-hour winds—it's not neighborly to leave potential six-foot projectiles out in the open. Everyone's making like turtles, sneaking back into the protection of the shell. Somewhere on the grounds, there's probably a team of Hadrosaurs figuring out how to encase the entire place in a gigantic condom.

Due to the proximity of the Intracoastal and the Atlantic Ocean, everyone east of US 1 has been ordered to evacuate their homes, and that includes all the nice folks residing in One Island Place, Noreen and Company included. The mafia, though well connected, doesn't get a pass on natural disasters.

"Where you want this box?" Glenda inquires as she staggers by, a heavy load dragging her shoulders down.

"Behind the bar," Noreen tells her. "Careful—"

"Yeah, yeah, sister, I got it."

Nerves are frayed all through the penthouse, and the constant drone from the radio and television doesn't help matters. You'd think these newscasters would have some sort of obligation to keep the peace, but their inflammatory predictions of the potential storm damage just make the natives more restless.

"What we're seeing here, Jane," one of the talking heads is saying, "is a storm of massive proportions—"

"Just massive, John—"

"Going back to Andrew, maybe even worse than that, back to Gloria—"

"Just massive, John."

I finish dragging the last of the patio furniture into the upstairs living room and decide to take a breather on one of the chairs. My muscles ache; my back is sore. My tail is stiff inside my guise, and if it weren't for the possibility of the condo guards coming up to check on our progress, I'd whip it out and go free and clear for a few minutes. It's a good thing I can make a living as a PI, because I definitely suck at moving furniture.

Noreen pulls a chair up next to mine, her movements slow but fluid. There's strength left in this gal yet, and I have no idea where she gets it from. I shoot her a weary smile, and she flashes one in return.

"How you holdin' up?" I ask.

"I'm up. Two hours left, looks like we'll get it all done. If it weren't for Glenda, we'd be in trouble. That girl knows how to hustle." She pours herself a small glass of Infusion and sucks it down. "Oh," she says, "I'm sorry, I forgot—"

"It's okay. It doesn't bother me anymore." Liar! After a hard day like today, there's nothing I'd usually want more than a tall plant and a hole to curl up in and chew. But that's advertising for you. YOU'RE WORKING FOR TWO RIVAL MOB FAMILIES, reads the billboard in my mind. YOUR OLDEST FRIEND WAS JUST ASSASSINATED. NO ONE TRUSTS YOU FURTHER THAN THEY CAN SPIT, AND NOW THE STORM OF THE CENTURY IS BEARING DOWN ON YOUR SCALY LITTLE ASS. BUT YOU JUST HAULED EIGHTEEN HUNDRED POUNDS OF FURNITURE, AND THOSE ENDORPHINS ARE KICKING IN. IT'S BASIL TIME!

"Where's Nelly?" I ask, just to get the conversation off herbs. "Kinda odd he's not here."

"His mom lives by herself on the other side of town," says Noreen. "We're all heading to the safe house in Lauderhill, but she didn't want to go all the way up there, so he took her over to a shelter."

So Nelson Hagstrom is a mama's boy. Who'd have guessed?

Outside, the sky is clear as ever, the sun shining bright on the blue ocean water, not even a trace of wind troubling the air. "Looks okay to me," I say.

"Calm before the storm. Every time." She shifts in her chair, and I get a whiff of the lemongrass riding her mango scent. Something's coming.

"Vincent," she begins, "I think you should spend the storm down south."

Down south. She means with Eddie Tallarico and his gang. "I'd rather stay with you," I say, "make sure you're okay."

Noreen smiles sweetly, but I know it's all business. "There's going to be a lot of confusion during the storm, and I need a pair of eyes down there. They think you're working for them. So much the better. If anything . . . hinky goes down, I need to know about it."

"So there's no chance of you and Eddie burying the hatchet? Before this thing gets . . . out of hand?"

Noreen turns away from me. "It's not that easy."

"That's what they always say."

"Maybe they're always right."

I hadn't considered that. "What is it?" I ask, turning my chair to face hers. "Is it the honor? That whole mafia thing?"

"No, no—"

"He killed your brother. I get that. I know that. I feel it, too. Not like you, but I feel it. And so you kill one of them, and then they're gonna find out and kill one of your guys, and—"

She kicks out at the seat of a chaise lounge, a sudden fire in her belly. "There's someone *in here*," she hisses. "He's got a guy in with us. Feeding him information. Telling him what we do, what we say. Do you know what that does? The betrayal? The paranoia?"

"It's tough—"

"I'm a prisoner in my own house. I can't trust anyone—"

"I know—"

"—because one of them . . ." She slows down here, regaining control, but the passion is still riding strong within her, flushing her false skin to a deep bronze. "One of them killed Jack, Vincent. And I know that next time, they'll be gunning for me."

She's right, of course. Noreen is the next logical hit on the Tallarico list, but short of wrapping her in plate mail, surrounding her with trained, rabid samurai, and prepping the house with antiterrorist devices, there's absolutely no way to guarantee her safety 100 percent.

Better not to bring that up.

"What is it?" I ask. "The two families, the bad blood . . . There's fourteen, fifteen different crews down here, what's so bad between the Hadrosaurs and Raptors?"

"It's Eddie," she says plainly.

"He's a fruitcake, I'll give you that much—"

"When his brother ran things, it was different. There was enough action for everyone, and nobody complained. There was a war . . . oh, hell, fifteen, twenty years before we even got down here, and it crippled the families. These are just stories I heard, mind you, but it happened. And afterwards, when the dust settled, they came together, all of them, and forged a new peace, and that's what Jack and I came into. When Francesco ran the Hadrosaurs and Frank Tallarico was in charge of the Raptors . . . It was good. It worked."

I prod her along. "And then Eddie took over."

"Eddie."

"So he's to blame for all this."

Noreen shrugs, looks away. "There's a lot of blame to go around."

A two-tone chime from the television set—it's 7:00 P.M. and the newest round of scare tactics is about to begin. True to form, the newscasters have donned their somber faces, eyes half-closed and cheeks hollow, as if they've just watched their children being eaten alive by monitor lizards. Then again, they've probably saved that footage for "film at eleven."

"Alison is bearing down on the coast," they practically scream, the glee in their voices belying their mellow, FCC-suitable demeanor, "and we're here to bring it all to you, live, as it breaks. Final evacuations are continuing for the following areas—"

Noreen clicks off the tube and tosses the remote across the room. "Go," she says. "Do what I need you to do."

I stand and stretch my arms, wishing like hell I could get into a bathroom and loosen up this tail. But I've got a long cab ride ahead of me, and the traffic heading away from the beach is gonna be a bitch, what with the Mother of All Storms—moniker courtesy Channel 7 News—about to toast the coast. "You think someone could call me a taxi?"

"Now? You'll never find one—everyone's home, putting up their shutters, hoarding their Oreo cookies. We'll loan you a car."

"I couldn't—"

"Don't be stupid," she says. "Take it."

"But—"

"Go."

There's no arguing with Noreen, and eventually I accept the use of a fine loaner—a 1998 Mercedes SL600, no less, the substantial German auto sweeping into the driveway outside the lobby in anticipation of my arrival. I slide into the rich leather seat, the contours of which just seem to caress my body.

"Oooh," I say to Noreen as I adjust the rearview mirror—electronically, no less. "I could get used to this."

"Don't get too used to it," she replies. "It was Jack's. Before . . . when he could walk."

She looks away, the hitch in her voice giving away her sadness. I adjust the lumbar support to cushion my crunched-up tail. "Oh," I say, sticking my head out of the window, "is there anything I'm supposed to do? Safety-wise?"

"Like what?"

"Back home, when there's an earthquake, you're supposed to huddle under a doorway, for the structural support. That kind of thing. Things to keep me from becoming less alive."

"If the roof comes off, run to the bathroom."

"If the roof comes off."

"Right. You run to the bathroom. Get in the tub."

"Why?"

She thinks it over for a moment. "I don't know. That's just what they teach you to do."

"Bathroom. Tub. Got it."

I wave good-bye to Noreen—that phrase running over and over through my head—*if the roof comes off, if the roof comes off*—imagining the process, the sounds of ripping shingles, creaking wood, the entire structure battered like the doll house of an angry preschooler—*if the roof comes off, if the roof comes off*—the screams and the terror and the eyes cast upwards as the sky suddenly bursts through, winds whipping down like giant fingers to stir up a whole heap of trouble and cut off lives before they've ever really gotten started—*if the roof comes off, if the roof comes off*—

And I gun the car engine—

Only realizing a split second later that I have just started the personal automobile of a known mafia kingpin—

And lived to tell the tale. The light hum of a precision engine rewards my turn of the key, and I ease down into the seat, exhaling softly.

Noreen must have noticed the anxiety etched into my face, because she just looks at me, laughs, and says, "Boom."

It takes me a while to get all of the adjustments right on the Mercedes; Jack was a lot bigger than I am and the mirrors and seat settings were all set to his specifications. Fortunately, the Tallaricos aren't into explosives; let's just hope they're not into cutting brake lines, either.

I eventually get the car's mojo working with my own, and pull the smooth wonder of German craftsmanship down the sloping driveway, heading for the gates—

Nearly slamming into a beige Buick sedan shooting out from the parking garage. I slam on the brakes, my hand instinctively batting the horn. The Buick shoots right on through, paying me little, if any, attention, and as it passes by, I get a glimpse of the passengers:

The gals from the talent pool. Five of them, at least, packed into the backseat of the car. And the driver is none other than Madame Audrey, her bob of gray hair barely popping over the steering wheel. I wonder how she can drive with her line of sight obscured like that, then realize that's probably why she nearly broadsided the first Mercedes I've ever driven.

I don't have any time to make side trips; if I don't start motoring down toward Tallarico's now, I'll never make it before the storm.

But I can't pass up an opportunity like this, a chance to learn a little more about Audrey and these ubiquitous girls. I drop behind the Buick, allowing a few cars to get between us as I follow them through the sluggish traffic leaving the beaches and across I-95, into the more central areas of the county. The homes are smaller here, the front lawns untended. Weeds choke off the surrounding foliage, and I get the impression that this is not the version of Florida they put on the brochures.

A faded sign on the side of the road reads WELCOME TO OPA-LOCKA. No wonder they let it get so run-down; it's hard to have pride in your town when you can't say the name with a straight face.

I follow the Buick down a series of short, evenly spaced streets, the homes adorned in a wide array of neon-glow colors. Back in L.A., you'd be roundly tossed from the neighborhood for even considering such a paint job; out here, it seems to be a badge of honor to throw a hundred bottles of Pepto Bismol on your stucco and call it a day.

Audrey manages to park the Buick in a small driveway, knocking over two lawn flamingoes as she goes; I hang back five houses and pull into an empty carport, hoping that the lengthening shadows will obscure the Mercedes.

The girls from the Dugan place tumble out and shuffle onto the small front porch. One knocks on the door, and a few seconds later, someone on the inside opens up, allowing the girls access. Audrey follows them inside.

A moment later, she emerges again, leading four girls back into the car. These gals are different ones, though; the guises are similar, but I can detect a change in their overall scent. The doors slam shut, and the Buick pulls out and disappears down the street.

Thirty seconds later, I'm creeping up the front walk, wondering if there's a window I can peer into, a hole through which I can peep—

The smell hits me first. Now, I'm an L.A. detective, and I take my fair share of cases that send me into the homelands of poverty and squalor. And while I know we've got some serious competition out here in the wilds of America, it's hard to beat the slums of Los Angeles when it comes to pure, unadulterated degradation. Crumbling ceilings, nonexistent plumbing, rats using major appliances as playground equipment, the works.

I had a case once that took me down to the Shacks, a four-block stretch of road near L.A.'s Little Tokyo, just a small section of a town where the American Dream has slammed on the brakes, smashed into a light pole, and been flattened by a meteor. Sheets of raw aluminum hastily nailed together form makeshift shelters, an encampment of the disenfranchised and disillusioned.

Humans, dinosaurs, and whatever wild creatures they've welcomed as pets pack into these makeshift cabins in the hopes of attaining some sort of protection from the elements. Three to a cot, head to toe, tail to claw, whatever it takes.

That's the first time I picked up on this odor. I'd hoped it would be the last. There's a stench that comes with sickness, a bitter alkaline that floats in the air, but that wasn't it. There's another that comes with decay, a sickly sweet burn that turns your stomach in and out and, at the same time, turns it on. But that wasn't it, either. It took me a second, back in the day, the same way it's taking me a moment now, to place this smell, but I know it's the very same one:

It's resignation.

The scent that says *I give up. I've had enough, and it's never getting any better.* And it's worse than the most fetid corpse, the moldiest bit of cheese. It's the smell of death—not of the body, but of the mind—and it's impossibly hard to accept.

As I pry open the front door and step inside, I realize the odor has coalesced into a mist, an awful gray pallor hanging over everything like a thick layer of dust. The living room—if that's what it is—sports a single sofa, circa 1969, the light-brown plaid stained with a thousand liquids better left unidentified. A twelve-inch television, black-and-white, one knob missing, is shot through with static, the picture flipping up and over every few seconds, but through it all I can make out Brian the weatherman, soothsaying his portents of doom.

Sounds—and smells—from the back room. I keep my head low and footsteps soft as I make my way down the hall. The girls are talking in some Asian language I've no hope of deciphering unless they suddenly break into dim-sum menu speak. I'm sure my presence will alarm them, so the best choice would be to stay down and silent.

"Hey gals," I say as I stroll inside. "How's it going?"

I expect them to shriek, or call for help, but they just give me a once-over and go back to their business of sitting and doing little to nothing. The room is trimmed with peeling wallpaper, ten small cots evenly spaced throughout. Another small door is set into the wall at the back of the room. Since no one's particularly interested in stopping me, I take a gander inside.

Four makeshift hospital beds have somehow been squeezed into this tiny space, and in each one is a half-guised Ornithomimus. Their torsos and faces remain human, while everything below the waist is relaxed and reptilian. The kicker is that the girls are all lying on their sides, their tails bandaged and freshly bloody.

"What happened?" I ask, moving to a girl whose scent I believe I recognize.

She looks up, and I see the telltale herb in her eyes. They've got the gals doped up. "Mr. Vincent?" she asks dreamily.

"Yeah, yeah, it's me. I know you, right? From the Dugans'?" She nods. "Are you okay? Are you hurt?"

She shakes her head, even though it's clear she's been through something serious. "They let us chew before and after," she sighs. "I don't mind it so bad."

A commotion from the main room behind me; I spin and get a look through the door. A stooped-over, elderly female, probably another Ornitho, is barking at the girls in her native tongue. She minces her way across the threadbare carpet, her short, hopping steps making me wonder if they bound her claws when she was a kid.

"You'd better go," says the girl, drawing me back to her. "She won't be happy you're here. We need our rest."

"I'll go, but first tell me what happened to your tail."

"They cut it," she says, as if tail-slicing is as natural as a manicure.

"Who?"

"The lady."

"The lady?" I repeat. "What lady? What's she look like?"

"The old lady on the boat." As the girl tries to sit up, a wave of pain registers in her face, twisting her features into a grimace. She reaches into a brown leather pouch sewn into the side of the bed and pulls out a wad of leaves. It's not even the good stuff—mostly stems and seeds—but she shoves the herbs into her mouth and chews. I resist the urge to plant a kiss on her and suck the stuff down my own throat. Seconds later, the pain subsides, and she relaxes again.

"It's not so bad," she says, reaching down and stroking the bandage where the remainder of her tail used to be. "It only hurts when it grows back."

"When what grows back?"

"My tail. It itches. Very badly."

Must be the herb talking. "Tails don't grow back," I tell her, ruining whatever fairy-tale dreams she might have of one day waving her scaled appendage again in the breeze. "Once they're gone, they're gone."

"Mine grows back. And the other girls'. This is my third time." She leans in then, and says, in a hopeful whisper, "Four more and I get to go home."

This doesn't make any sense. Dinos have our own special set of skills, but flesh and bone and nerve are flesh and bone and nerve, and once they're gone, that's the end of the game.

As I lean in to get a closer look at her tail, maybe figure out whatever bullshit parlor trick is being pulled on these poor unsuspecting girls, I'm whacked across the head with a broom.

"Get out!" shouts the crone in charge, who's managed to sneak her way into the room behind me. She takes another whack with her broom, the bristles ripping across my cheeks. Lady's old, but she sure knows how to choke up on a cleaning utensil.

"I was just asking a few questions—"

"Out!" she shrieks again, and this time she's shuffling toward the closet. From the way she's moving, I can tell she's got some weapon in there that's more effective than her current one, and though I could probably take out whatever firepower she's got, it would be unseemly to battle someone three times my age and of the fairer sex.

"I'm going, I'm going." I back out of the room as she pulls an old six-shooter from the closet. This is a gun that even Jesse James would have considered an antique, but I've no doubt that it has the capacity to shoot small hunks of lead far enough into my body to cause major discomfort. I turn heel and jog through the house, keeping an eye over my shoulder at Annie Oakley as I go.

My foot catches on the edge of the front porch, and I stumble out onto the front walk, rolling over into a pile of rocks and drying mud.

"Don't tell me he's got you doin' my job now. Fuck!"

I look up to find Sherman standing over me, hitting himself in the forehead with his palm and cursing at the top of his lungs. Staggering to my feet, I grab his arms and try to calm him down.

"Sherm, Sherm. Deep breaths. One, two. One, two."

Poor guy's crestfallen, his saggy cheeks hanging even lower. "I got a family to support, Rubio. If Eddie's tryin' to replace me—"

"Forget about it," I tell him. "I was up here on my own. Checkin' out the gals."

"Really?" he asks, wide-eyed as a five-year-old who wants so hard to believe that little Ruffles will indeed be frolicking with the other poochies up in doggie heaven.

"Really. You came down to . . . ?"

"Drop off the girls. Before the storm. Eddie don't want 'em hanging around at the hotel."

"What hotel?"

"Eddie boarded up the house. Says he wants us further inland, some hotel downtown." Sherman takes a look at his watch. "And we better hustle if we're gonna get this job done."

I don't like the sound of that. "What job?"

"Tell you on the way. Hop on in the car."

Despite my need to keep a low profile in Sherman's eyes, I can't leave Jack's Mercedes in the middle of Opa-Locka during a hurricane. Noreen probably wouldn't appreciate it if I returned the car without its wheels, engine, tranny, or stereo.

"Got a car," I say, nodding my head down the road.

Sherman gets one look at the Benz and his eyes go wide. "Damn," he says, "that's a fine ride, Rubio. Looks familiar."

"Oh yeah?"

"Yeah." We walk the quarter-block to the car, and Sherman clucks his tongue. Then—"Wait a sec," he says. "Ain't that Jack Dugan's car?"

I laugh it off. "Conned the broad into letting me drive it around. She's a pushover."

"Man, I haven't seen that car in years. Not since . . ." Sherm's expression suddenly turns from nostalgic to somber. "Don't tell me you drove it here."

"Yeah, course I did," I tell him. "What's up?"

Without another word, he drops to his knees and flips onto his back, shimmying beneath the car's undercarriage, wriggling like a worm who desperately needs to see a chiropractor. His puffy belly juts out from under the car, and as I squat by his thick legs, I can hear soft grunts as he works on the metal.

A moment later, he squirms out from beneath the auto, his hands grimy with oil and road filth. In his right fist he clutches a bundle of wires, below which dangles a metallic box about eight inches long.

"You started this car yourself?" he asks me, and I nod. Sherman shakes his head, laughs, and tosses the black box into some nearby bushes; as it falls, the top pops open and two small nuggets of plastique tumble to the ground, disappearing down a storm drain. "You are one lucky son of a bitch," he says, chuckling as he heads back to his own car. "It's a good thing the Tallarico family sucks at planting car bombs."

We drop the Mercedes down at the Omni Hotel, where the Tallarico clan will be holing up for the duration of Alison's wrath. Once I'm in that beaten-up Lexus sedan, Sherman tells me that Eddie has assigned him a special job, one he's itching to do.

"And I figure, you're the perfect guy to help me out with it."

"How's that?" I ask.

Sherman drops into silence for a moment, a small drop of liquid dripping from his right eye. It may actually be a tear.

"They got Chaz," he whimpers.

I tense up in the seat, then will my muscles to relax. He doesn't seem to have any idea that I was instrumental in said "getting" of Chaz.

"Who?"

"Those Hadrosaur fucks!" he spits. "Animals!"

I remember that BB and Hagstrom did away with Chaz's head and body.

"How do you know?"

"The sick bastards sent us his scent glands in the mail this morning."

"In the mail?"

"FedEx, actually. I opened it up and got a whiff of him right away. Two little glands, that was it, but I knew . . . I knew his scent like it was my own." Sherman's on the verge of letting go, and for some reason I find myself patting him on the back, trying to comfort him.

"So that's it?" I suggest. "That's the end of it? We took Jack, they took Chaz, all done."

"Oh no, that ain't even close. Eddie says it's time for the blood-letting."

I don't know if *the bloodletting* is some sort of official mob phrase, but I certainly don't like the sound of it. I need to get to a phone and tell Noreen what's going down.

"Man, I gotta rearrange my G-clamp. Find a gas station with a bathroom—"

"No time. We got the word that one of Dugan's big boys is all alone, and Eddie wants us to take him down." Sherman pulls the car onto I-95, heading north. Up toward Dugan territory. "Your job," he continues, "is to lure him out. He knows you; he'll trust you. Then we can go to work."

Again, I'm bait. And, again, I'm powerless to say no. "Who is it?" I ask.

"Hagstrom," clucks Sherman. "The little prick." He leans in and prepares to lay out the plan of attack. "Get ready to make the front pages, Vincent. This one's gonna have 'em talking all the way up to Tallahassee."

This feeling of dread in the pit of my stomach, this dark lump of pain down low near my bowels, might just be the stale ham sandwich I ate back at the condo. I'm hoping that's what it is, because whereas my digestive system isn't always on track, my intuition usually is, and it's telling me a lot of things I don't want to hear right now.

Other than the fact that I'm in a car heading up the South Florida coast with a history-making hurricane fifty miles offshore, on my way to interrogate, torture, and most likely kill my ex-girlfriend's fiancé, I'm running myself ragged trying to figure out who's informing for the Tallaricos. Someone's pulling off a double-agent bit better than I am, and it's partially frustration, partially professional envy, but it's hard to get it out of my mind.

"You know who this guy is?" I ask Sherm as we drive up US 1. The roads are mostly empty, eerily silent except for the occasional burst of wind or the roar of our own partially muffled engine. Windows all around town are covered in large sheets of plywood, homemade shutters that should keep out all but the most ardent gusts.

"Who?"

"The informer. Inside Dugan's crew."

Sherman shakes his head. "Wish I did. I'd shake his little rat hand—first things first—and then claw him in the belly till he dies."

There must be a communications error. "No, I'm talking about the guy who's giving Eddie all the information about the Dugan crew—"

"Right. I'd thank the little fuck, then kill him fast as I could spit."

"But he's helping us out."

"Yeah," says Sherm, "now he is. But a rat's a rat, and two faces don't change into one." He turns in the seat, eager to dispense his wisdom, learned from hard years on a hard crew. "You find yourself a rat, don't ever turn your back on him, 'cause no matter how close you think you are or how much you think you got on him, it don't matter. They got teeth and whiskers for a reason, and they'll bite you in the neck just as soon as they'll kiss you. Then you're on the floor bleeding out, and the rat's telling you to lie down and let the pain take you away."

The thing is, he's right. If there's one thing Ernie taught me, it's that folks don't change. We're static, solid. It's one of the things that helps in my profession—it's easy to locate someone if you know the kinds of things they like to do when no one else is watching. Gamblers gamble. Philanderers philander. Chewers chew.

We don't change. Period.

"This is the street," Sherman says, pulling the Lexus onto the curb and hopping out. "Stick close, and we'll play it like we said."

The homes in this section of North Miami look like the homes the people in Opa-Locka would buy if they won a very small lottery jackpot. A bit bigger, slightly better tended, and the colors are less likely to burn out your retinas. Down the road is the local hurricane shelter, a windowless three-story building that looks like it could take a direct hit from an atomic bomb and still come out with a few wings intact.

"They build these shelters pretty damned big," I say.

"It ain't usually a shelter. Rest of the time it's a high school."

Indeed, there's the sign outside the monstrosity: NORTH MIAMI BEACH SENIOR HIGH—HOME OF THE CHARGERS. "That's a school? How do they teach in something like that?"

"Dunno," says Sherman. "Probably not real well."

The home of the 1993 National Team Debate Champions— according to the trophy case by the front doors—is packed with flesh this evening, sweaty bodies boxed into the hallways and open areas of the school. Mostly humans, and their stink clogs every walkway and niche of the building, infusing the stairwells with a scent like feet gone to rot. And of course, they can never smell themselves; if they could, I am wholly sure their suicide rate would quadruple overnight.

"We gotta find a single ant in this colony," I say as we pick our way through the crowd. "Lemme stand still for a second, maybe I can sniff him out." It's mostly mammals in this joint; Hagstrom and his mom should stick out pretty sharp.

They do. Six minutes after the first whiff, I've traced them all the way up to a third-floor science lab. Here people are huddling beneath counters, fluffing their pillows and bedding down next to Bunsen burners and beakers, seemingly unconcerned with the amount of breakable glass around them. Then again, I guess if the wind is strong enough to break in the front doors, head back behind the auditorium, burst into the stairwell, and climb the three stories up into this chem lab, there are worse problems on hand than a little busted Pyrex.

"Two rooms down," I tell Sherman. "I can smell him from here. You go wait downstairs in the car."

"You sure you got it?" he asks.

"Positive. Go, downstairs. Trust me."

Sherman lingers for a moment, then disappears down the stairwell, leaving me to deal with Hagstrom on my own.

They're in a storage room, the shelves lined with sticky contact paper to keep everything in place. Eight of them in here, Hagstrom and his mother in back. Their smells are similar, and the guises have been constructed along proper family lines. As I enter, Hagstrom does a classic double take worthy of any of the original Three Stooges.

"Rubio? What happened to Noreen?"

For a moment, I'm touched that his first thoughts are of her, but there's no time for sentimentality. "Nothing, she's fine—"

"I thought you were down south." He utters this cardinal direction—*south*—as if it were one of the seven dirty words.

"I am. I was." I take a quick sniff around and make sure that Sherman's nowhere nearby. "That's why I'm here."

"I don't get it," he says.

I nod, then gesture over to the old lady at his right. "This must be your mother," I say, and the lady looks up, making no bones about giving me the once-over.

"This one of your little friends, Nelson?" she asks.

"Yeah, Ma—yeah. Vincent, this is my ma, vice versa."

"Does he want cookies?"

"I don't think so, Ma. Listen, you stay here. I'll be back in a bit." It's clear Hagstrom doesn't want to talk business in front of his sainted mother.

We step into the hallway, then drop back into another, slightly less crowded, room, keeping our tones hushed. "Okay, spill it. What are you doing here?"

"I'm supposed to kill you."

There's a claw at my side before I can get out another word; I can see the sharp talon sticking through Hagstrom's glove, his breath suddenly doubling in my ear. "Knock it off," I tell him, too tired to mince words. "If I was going to do it, you think I would tell you?"

A reduction in the tension at my side, but he doesn't retract. There are humans all around us, and he's taking great pains to keep his claws out of sight, but I don't doubt he'd drop me in a second if it came down to go time.

"Downstairs," I continue, "is a Lexus, and in it is Tallarico's right-hand guy. Sherman, the one who smells like cheese."

"The one who killed Jack."

"That's right. I'm supposed to get you in the car under false pretenses of going back to Noreen, and he'll be there to hold you under a gun and get you out to the pier."

"And then . . . that would be that?" Hagstrom asks.

"That would be that."

He nods and slowly slides his claw back in, understanding that my plans have changed.

"So what do we do? I bolt?"

"No good," I tell him. "If you bolt, then they blame me, and then I'm the one who ends up under the sea. No, we gotta turn this thing around."

Hagstrom looks around the science lab, at the huddled masses, at the fear on those faces, and I wonder if he, too, has gotten caught up in the storm's-a-brewin' hype. "How?"

"Two of us," I explain, "one of him. We get out to the beach and turn the tables. Maybe find out who's ratting out the Dugans."

Hagstrom nods; he's game. "I give you the high sign," he says, "and we take him."

I agree, but add on a rider: "Until then, we hate each other. You got that?"

"Oh yeah." He grins. "Think I can manage that . . ."

"You left out the part where you call me a dirty Raptor."

"Don't worry," says Hagstrom. "I thought it."

He pops back into the science lab to tell his mother that he'll be back in a little bit, to sit tight and eat her Oreos. She pats us both on the head and kneels on an air mattress, keeping her attention on the Channel 7 newscast.

We hustle down the stairs and out of the school grounds, and soon we're playing our parts to the hilt. And while my own dramatic skills might be worthy of a Golden Globe—or, in a pinch, a People's Choice Award—Hagstrom is chewing up the scenery left and right.

"Noreen wants to see me?" he practically yells as we cross the front lawn of NMB Senior High.

"Yeah, yeah, she does," I say, then mutter, "and keep it down, for chrissakes."

I dated an actress once who had a recurring role on a particularly bad television show, and the one thing I remember about our short relationship—it lasted for the duration of the show's summer hiatus, and not a day over—was how adrenaline, whether through fear, anger, or sexual excitement, threw her acting skills into overdrive. Any fight we had would then become the biggest blowout in

the history of the universe, and any makeup sex was wild and pas-
sionate enough to put all the lovers of the world to shame. Our
breakup, accomplished in a single, uncomfortable six-minute tele-
phone call, was disturbingly anticlimactic; she must not have
properly understood her character's motivation.

Hagstrom's got the same bug in him, and in the anxiety of the
situation, he's blowing things out of proportion. The Lexus waits
for us at the curb, and I pull the keys from my pocket and open the
passenger door. He just stands there.

"Go on," I say, trying to keep in character. "We're gonna be
late."

"Maybe I'll walk," he tells me. This was not in the script.

"Hagstrom, what's the matter with you? Get in the freaking car."

After a few more minutes of argument—none of which was
planned—he sits in the passenger seat, buckles himself in, and
we're off. A mile down the road, Sherman pops up in the backseat,
his pistol suddenly pressed against Hagstrom's head.

"Rubio, you lousy fink!" shouts Hagstrom. Idiot thinks he's Pa-
cino. If he so much as utters a single *hoo-ha!* I'll have to deck him.

But Sherman's dense enough to buy the corny acting, and he
gives me one of his little winks. "Take us down, Vincent," he says
confidently.

"Don't know where I'm going."

He deflates. "Oh. Right. Make a left."

Street by street, Sherman directs me out to Haulover Beach, a
small strip of sand and deserted boardwalks with a long wooden
pier jutting out into the Atlantic. A sign at the front of the parking
lot reads BEACH CLOSED. THANK YOU FOR VISITING!

"Screw it," Sherm says. "Go on in."

It's easy enough to maneuver the Lexus around the sign and
into the parking lot, where we hop out of the car, Hagstrom finally
keeping his cool. "Which way?" I ask Sherman, but what I'm waiting for is Hagstrom's signal.

"Out to the water," says Sherman, shifting the gun from Hagstrom's head to the small of his back. "The pier."

We slog our way out across the sand single-file, Hagstrom leading the way as Sherman directs him from behind. I bring up the rear, keeping on my toes, flexing my claws beneath my gloves with every step. Whenever Hagstrom gives me the sign, I'm ready to go to work.

But we take it easy on the way out to the pier; Hagstrom's waiting for the perfect moment, and I can't fault him for that. We reach the steps leading up to the wooden pier itself, but Sherman shakes his head as Hagstrom grabs onto the hand rail. "Uh-uh," he says. "Under there."

"Under?" Hagstrom asks, peering into the darkness beneath the pier. "Goddamn you Raptors—"

This gets Sherman going, and he shoves the gun deeper into Hagstrom's back. The Hadrosaur grudgingly takes another step forward, and we shuffle through the sand and into the heavy surf.

The thick wooden pylons that hold the pier aloft disappear into the sand, where they're probably anchored by fifty-ton cement blocks. All manner of graffiti can be found down here, tagging and artistry alike, but we don't have time to admire the handiwork of Miami's gang culture.

As soon as we're completely beneath the pier, I see Hagstrom's right hand begin to twitch; when he raises it above his shoulder, it's the signal to attack. It's on the move, going up, up, at his waist— I'm prepping my glove, my claws—higher—preloosening my G-clamp, ready to release my tail—higher, almost there—the saliva building in my mouth, teeth ready to chomp, to gnash, to tear—

"Look what the cat dragged in."

A voice, from the darkness, quickly separating itself. It's Jerry, another of Tallarico's many goons, his thick face roiling with hatred, a small-caliber pistol in his right hand. Next to him is another one of the faceless soldiers I've seen around the Tallarico compound over the last week, and he's no prettier. Neither is his gun.

Hagstrom shoots me a quick glance—*The hell is going on?*—and I risk one back—*I have no idea.*

Fortunately, Sherman seems just as confused, so we're not the only odd men out.

"Jerry, I got this one."

Jerry shrugs. "Eddie wanted I should come down, a little extra insurance."

Sherman seems pissed that the kill's being taken out of his control, but there's nothing he can do about it, and he knows it. "Fine," he says. "If that's the way Eddie wants to play it, so be it. Are we doing this thing or not?"

"Yeah," says Jerry, "we're doing it, all right." He reaches into the darkness and pulls out a duffel bag; from within, he extracts a long, thick length of rope and takes a look at his surroundings. "Which one you like?"

This is not going as planned. Now Hagstrom's got three guns trained on him, three bullets aimed at his flesh. The odds have dramatically switched in a few short seconds, and I mentally kick myself for not turning things around sooner.

But as they stand Hagstrom up against a wooden pylon—pressing his back against the wood, making sure that the water-soaked column will hold—I realize that despite my double-dealings, despite my slow metamorphosis into whatever creature of duplicity I'm becoming, I can't let it go down this way.

Three on two. I've had worse odds before and come out on top. Can't think of anytime recent, but I've never let my lack of a good memory stop me before.

If Hagstrom's not going to give me a high sign, I'll give him one. I step behind the trio of Raptors as they muscle their Hadrosaur quarry into place, rip the glove off my right hand, slide the index claw out three inches, and raise it into the air—

"You son of a bitch!" Hagstrom roars, throwing Sherman off his body and leaping through the air, arms extended toward my throat—

I fall backwards under his assault, stumbling, trying to maintain my balance, the soft sand underfoot grabbing at my legs, drawing them under—

I go down hard, landing on my side as Hagstrom falls on top of me, his hands reaching around and pulling at the back of my wig, drawing my face into his. Sherman, Jerry, and the soldier are running over to help me—

"Don't do it," Hagstrom whispers harshly into my ear. "We can't take them—"

"We *can*—"

"No!" he hisses. "Protect Noreen. Find out who talked—"

And just like that, they're pulling him away, and he's back to playing the savage beast, thrusting his claws out of their slots, flashing his arms in every direction. He gets in a few slices—a thin stream of blood spurting from Jerry's cheek, splashing against the sand—

"Get his fucking arms! His arms—"

The soldier rears back and kicks Hagstrom in the stomach, the strong blow knocking the wind out of him. He doubles over, and Sherman grabs his arms, quickly binding his hands with a length of rope. "You okay, Vinnie?" Sherman asks me.

"Yeah." I'm still a little stunned, not so much by Hagstrom's attack as by what he's sacrificing for his fiancée and her extended family. "Yeah, I'm okay."

We walk Hagstrom farther out beneath the pier—he's spewing venom all the way, really laying it on thick—"A curse on your tails, and on your sons' tails"—but if ever there's a time to overact, this would certainly be it. By the time we reach the far end of the pier, the water's up to our knees, and Sherman stops the procession by one of the wide wooden columns facing the open ocean. The storm clouds are visible even in the darkening night sky, hanging just off the coast, biding their time.

"This one'll do," Sherman says, and he throws Hagstrom up against the pylon. Jerry and the other soldier are instantly there with the rope, wrapping it around Hagstrom's body, lashing him down to the column, facing him out to the wide Atlantic.

Sherman calls me over. "His hands," he says. "Turn 'em in." And to Hagstrom he grunts, "Don't try nothing funny."

Hagstrom doesn't make me do the dirty job myself, and turns his fingers inwards, so that they're pointing toward his chest; Sherman does the same to his other hand, and the goons quickly bind them in that position. It's a mob trick, but I've seen it before: if Hagstrom tries to slide out his claws to slice the ropes, he'll impale himself on his own weapons long before working his body free.

We back up to take a look at our handiwork, and Hagstrom just stares out at the ocean, taking in breaths as deep as the constrictive ropes will allow. A few hours from now, when Alison eventually pounds her way to shore—thirty-foot swells, hundred-mile-an-hour winds, and all—Hagstrom will be there to greet her. I hope their relationship is over fast; she'll do him wrong, in the end.

"That's enough," Jerry says, testing the ropes with one hand. "It'll hold."

He backs off to allow Sherman a tug, as well, and he gives it a perfunctory yank, using it as an excuse to get in close to Hagstrom's face. "You have a real nice night, Hadro," he growls, patting Hagstrom on the head before slapping him across the face. "This one's for Chaz."

Then it's left to me, and I've got nothing to say. If I approach him, I might be able to slide out a claw, fray up one of those ropes, but the risk is too great, and I know Hagstrom wouldn't want it. Wouldn't allow it.

"Fuck him," I spit, feeling that knob of flesh in my chest grow harder, darker. "Let's get outta here."

We shuffle across the sand, three Raptors side by side, stepping out from beneath the pier, the sounds of the rising tide roaring in our ears. I don't look back. I don't think about it. There's nothing I can do, other than tell Noreen that the man she loves was killed for no reason other than revenge, and that the man she used to love stood idly by and didn't lift a claw to save him.

14

Mah-jongg.

That's what mobsters play: mah-jongg. At least, that's what the Tallarico mobsters play, and that's all that matters to me right now, because it's the Tallarico clan I'm holed up with for the duration of this damned hurricane.

"You're looking for a circle eight," Sherman whispers to me, keeping his voice low enough so the others won't make a big stink about how he's helping out the newcomer. They take their mah-jongg seriously here, and ignorance of the rules is not an excuse.

For the last eight hours, it's been all mah-jongg, all the time. Eighteen of Tallarico's closest associates, holed up in three separate suites at the Omni, four rotating games of mah-jongg keeping us busy—and, me at least, confused. There seem to be a thousand different tiles with a million different Chinese ideograms etched in them, and I honestly wonder if maybe there really are no rules and everyone just pretends to understand this damn game. That's what *I'm* doing.

The power cut out hours ago, so we're operating off candles and flashlights, squinting in the dark at our tiles. All contact with the outside world has been cut off—our portable radio died a while ago, and no one thought to bring extra nine-volts. Apart from the darkness and the isolation, I'm most affected by the loss of the air conditioner. If the truth be told, I don't even need my air *conditioned*, I just need it cold.

I can't get my mind off Hagstrom, though. I keep seeing him, lashed against that pylon as the hurricane waves pound the shore, gasping as he tries to keep his mouth clear of the rushing water, finally realizing the futility. On the drive back from the beach, there was no chance for privacy so that I could call Noreen or send someone down to the pier to free Hagstrom. Once we got back to the hotel, I tried to phone the apartment, but they'd all evacuated. I then tried Glenda's cell phone, but the call wouldn't go through. Soon enough, the winds picked up, and along with them the endless mah-jongg games.

"C'mon," Sherman grunts, "you playin' or not, Rubio?"

There are a few tiles in front of me with similar markings, so I toss them into the middle of the table and hope that the others can figure out what to do with them.

"Nice hand," says Jerry. He smells like wet talcum powder. "You hustlin' us with this beginner bullshit?"

I shrug, playing it cool. Jerry tosses in his own tiles; they mean even less to me than the ones I put together. Sherman claps me on the shoulder and leans into the table. "This guy," he says, "is one smooth, cocky son of a bitch. He cons the Dugan chick—"

"Lousy bitch," Jerry spits, and something hard twists in my stomach.

"—and she gives him the dead guy's car—and he starts it up! Sits down, turns the key, no worries. Ain't that right?"

"Fucking stupid, you ask me," Jerry says. "You wanna play with your life like that. Lucky we bite the big one on bombs. Ain't never put one in right yet."

I shrug. "Not really the way to do things anyway, is it?" I ask.

Jerry stops playing. Stops looking at his hand. That scent of talcum powder darkens a bit, as if someone has added moldy baking soda to the mixture. "What's that supposed to mean?"

"Nothing," I say. "'Cept that car bombs, the automatic weapons you used to take out Dugan . . . they're mammal weapons. Back in L.A., that's not how we do things."

Jerry reaches across the table, his hands digging into the soft felt top. He leans in, pulling himself across the tiles in a military crawl, drawing his face toward mine. "This ain't L.A.," he growls.

And just like that, I'm in a stare-off. Jerry's beady little eyes focused on mine, the washed-out green irises watering with the effort. This wasn't how I expected to spend my evenings in South Florida. I'd been hoping for delectables and debauchery, Latin beats and Caribbean treats, buxom Cuban women dancing suggestive salsas as they caressed my body and fed me foot-long *medianoches* on the outdoor patio of some hip South Beach hotspot. Instead, I've got incomprehensible tile games and the static blur from a busted AM radio.

A sonic boom disrupts the competition as the floor shakes beneath my butt, and I realize that Eddie Tallarico has just thrown himself onto the carpet next to me. "We all getting along?" he asks. His tone is somber, and I don't detect any herb riding his breath.

"New guy's questioning our methods," Jerry tells him. "Thinks we're pussies for using guns. I was about to tell him where to stick his California."

"Hey, hey," says Eddie, "maybe Vincent's got a point. We did it the natural way for a lotta years, and it got us pretty far—"

"Yeah, but—"

"*Hey!*" Eddie shouts, suddenly six times louder than before. He's up in a flash, at Jerry's side, his massive girth bearing down on the smaller Raptor. "You talking back to me?"

"Jesus, Eddie, no."

Tallarico, his stomach spilling out over his belt, scoops up a handful of mah-jongg tiles in his fist. He grabs on to Jerry's wig and yanks his head backwards, the sudden force dropping the underling's jaw. Eddie jams the tiles into Jerry's mouth, shoving as many of the small ceramic rectangles as he can past the fake teeth, way back to the dino's real molars. Jerry squirms, tries to scream, but it all comes out muffled, choked with saliva, along with the game pieces.

Eddie leans down and whispers hard in Jerry's ear. "Next time, they ain't goin' in your mouth."

Part of me wants to applaud; the other part of me wants to join in and shove a few more tiles down his gullet. I wonder where the third part of me went, the part that would be appalled at such brutal punishment for a minor transgression, the part that used to occupy a fair percentage of my brain.

"All clear!" shouts another Tallarico goon, stepping into the suite from another room. "A bunch of chicks next door got a radio, and they said the storm didn't hit."

I'm on my feet before anyone else. "What do you mean it didn't hit?"

"They said it went up north, way up the coast. Just blew around a lot of rain down this way."

As if on cue, the lights burst to life, and the hum of electricity returns to the hotel. The TV clicks on, and the same newscasters who were foretelling gloom and doom half a day ago are backtracking heavily in their attempt to explain the freak miss of Hurricane Alison.

". . . this low pressure system coming down from the north . . ."

". . . partially responsible for the shift back to the east, away from the coast . . ."

". . . still a very powerful system, moving up the coast, skirting the shore, but we've escaped the danger . . ."

I'm halfway out the door before Eddie grabs my arm. "Whoa, kid, what's the rush?"

"Stomach cramps." I double over, make it a good show. "You don't want me doin' this in your bathroom, trust me."

Eddie nods and releases his grip. "Get me a sandwich on your way back," he says. "Damn storm made me hungry."

Down the stairs, into the parking garage, hopping into Jack's Mercedes. If I concentrate, I can remember the way back to the Haulover pier. As I peel out, I dial Glenda's cell phone again. One ring, two rings, still no answer. The storm may have knocked over transmission towers. Her voicemail picks up, and I wait rather impatiently for the beep.

"Glen," I shout into my phone, "if you get this message, come down to the pier at Haulover Beach. Under it, to be precise. Don't ask, just drive."

Amazingly, my memory has held up well enough to get me onto US 1, and I find the turnoff for Haulover Beach. Soon I'm parking in the empty lot and running for the pier. The wind is still whipping hard and strong, and the waves would certainly make for good surfing, but the ocean doesn't look particularly dangerous. That is, unless you're tied to a post underneath it.

I slog my way through the sand and leap under the pier, sniffing deep as I go, hoping to get a whiff of Hagstrom's scent. "Nelly!" I call out, losing traction as the sand turns thick and wet beneath my feet. "Hagstrom, say something!"

A gurgle, a half-word, and then another gurgle. Something like *urrg-ubio-urgle,* but it's clearly Hagstrom's voice. The water is up to my waist, and as a wave washes in, it lifts me off my feet. I'm swimming now, dino-paddling my way through the sea, aiming for that far pylon. I can make out the ropes, still tied tight around the post. I redouble my efforts, swimming hard—

As the undertow pulls back, and the waves subside momentarily, I'm kneeling now, crawling forward, and as I stumble to my feet, I get my first glimpse of Hagstrom.

He's beaten, blood seeping from wounds on his head, the faux skin torn and the scales beneath twisted and bent. There must have been debris in the water charging at him; either that or the waves themselves packed enough of a wallop to make him look like he lost to Tyson in six rounds.

Nelly spits out a hunk of seaweed and continues his struggle against the ropes. "Wait, wait," I say, ripping off my right glove and shoving it in my pocket for safe keeping. "Relax. Relax."

"Easy . . . for you to say . . . Raptor."

Another wave washes over us, but this one is smaller, and I manage to grab hold of the ropes before it washes me farther ashore. Hagstrom is completely submerged, though, and I realize he's been holding his breath, off and on, timing it with the waves, for hours.

When the water pulls back, I make sure Hagstrom is breathing and quickly set to work on the ropes, using my claws to fray the outermost edges.

"Noreen," Hagstrom pants. "We have to . . . call her—"

"I've been trying, but no luck." I manage to get halfway through two of the main ropes, the edges frayed and loose. "Try it now. Push."

Hagstrom grimaces as his muscles contort against the ropes. The cords dig into his flesh, the skin beneath threatening to rip under the assault. "Come on," I say, trying to remember the mantras shouted by personal trainers and Little League coaches across the globe, "give it a hundred and ten percent."

Hagstrom cools me down with a single glare, takes a deep breath, and arches his back, puffing out his chest as the ropes tear free with a single snap. He falls forward into the next oncoming wave, and I grab him in my arms and make tracks for shore. The *Baywatch* babes are never around when you need them. Worse, they're never around when you don't need them, either.

Halfway to shore, Hagstrom squirms out of my grasp and stands up on his own. "I got it," he says. "I can walk."

Wet, exhausted, and paranoid, we bundle into the Mercedes. Hagstrom takes command of the steering wheel, while I work the phones. "Still no answer at the apartment," I announce.

"Dammit," he says. "How many times have I told Noreen to get a cell phone?"

"Noreen's not the kind of gal you can tell to do anything," I point out.

"You can say that again." He shakes his head. "Did you ever win an argument with her?"

"Not one I was proud of."

For a moment, we realize that we're talking about the same woman, on the same terms. That at different times we have had the same relationship with this lady. And, amazingly, we're not ready to rip each other's intestines out through our noses.

My cell rings, and I nearly drop it as I fumble the phone to my ear.

"Noreen?"

"Where are you?" It's Glenda. I can hear road noise behind her voice.

"Coming north. Where are *you*?"

"Going down to Haulover, like you said. What the hell's going on?"

"No time to explain," I say. "Is Noreen with you?"

A horn honks in the background, and Glenda, inches away from her cell phone mouthpiece, releases a barrage of curses sure to shame anyone within a ten-mile radius. She falls back into a more acceptable register: "Noreen's on the boat."

"Noreen's on the boat," I relay to Hagstrom. I remember that my cell phone's got a nifty speaker feature and, after a few moments of fiddling, punch it up so we're all conferenced in.

"She went on the yacht?" asks Hagstrom. "She hates that thing."

"I dunno," says Glenda. "That's what she said. Her and Audrey, they headed out half an hour ago, just after the storm passed."

Audrey. The little old lady, Jack's geriatric shadow. Always by his side, never saying a word, perpetually in his trust.

Audrey. Conveniently missing from the Dugan nightclub right before the dissolution-powder attack.

Audrey. Conveniently begging off from the slushie run on the night Jack was gunned down.

Audrey. She's got the inside knowledge and the means. And the fact that she's somehow connected to the girls of the "talent pool" means she's probably had contact with the Tallarico family, as well.

And now she's all alone with Noreen.

I snatch the phone and shout, "Glenda, you've got to get up to the marina. Stop that yacht from going out."

Hagstrom shoots me a confused look. "What's up?"

But Glenda knows my tone, knows enough to almost trust me. "You sure about this, Vinnie?"

"Sure enough. If I'm wrong, no harm done. Go, do whatever you have to, but don't let them get on that boat."

I hang up and sit back in the plush leather seat as Hagstrom speeds down the road, toward the marina and the yacht and Noreen, who has no idea that a set of old but deadly claws are aimed right at her back.

"Why would she do it?" Hagstrom is asking as we run from the parking lot into the Fort Lauderdale marina itself. "Audrey's been with Jack for years."

"And what does she do for him?"

"I don't know, really. None of us do. Helps out with little things."

"Yeah," I say. "Little things like getting him killed."

As we hit the piers, I can see Glenda at the far end of one dock, waving her arms to attract our attention. She glances around ner-

vously, her eyes darting back and forth like she's been caught steal-
ing cookies from the jar. There's a light smell of gunpowder drift-
ing through the air; some idiot must be shooting off caps nearby.

"You find her?" I ask.

Glenda bounces back and forth, light and easy on the balls of
her feet. "Yes and no."

"Give it to me."

"Yes, I found her, no, she's not here."

Hagstrom isn't in the mood to pussyfoot around. "Where is
she?"

"On the boat," Glenda says. "With Audrey." Glenda tugs at her
shorts, trying to yank them below her thighs. "I got here just as
they were pulling out. I tried waving. I mean, I had this whole excuse set up, this thing about the penthouse and flood damage,
whatever I could think of, but they were out of earshot by the time
I got here. I tried, I really tried, but . . ."

Audrey's out there with Noreen, right now, and she doesn't
have a clue what the old lady's thinking. I can almost feel her staring at the back of Noreen's neck, waiting for the right moment to
drug her or claw her or throw her overboard and let the sea do
away with the last vestiges of the Dugan family.

A fifty-footer takes the waves maybe half a mile away from the
shore, a gleaming white yacht bobbing up and down. "I'm sorry,
Vincent," says Glenda. "I thought I was going to make it—"

But I'm already scanning the marina, checking the docks for
what I need. And there it is, two piers down. I start running,
Glenda and Hagstrom surprised for a moment, but then right behind me, keeping pace.

"What the hell are you doing, Rubio?"

"What's it look like I'm doing?" I say as I leap into a racer—its
front end is long, wide, perfect for riding swells at eighty knots—
and quickly untie the line from the metal cleat on the dock. "I'm
borrowing a boat."

Hagstrom hops in next to me, and I've got it hot-wired and running thirty seconds later, the speedboat's powerful engine pummeling the water, eager to get moving. This is the kind of boat that needs to go fast; it actually hurts the engine to keep this baby idling. "You get back to the others," Hagstrom instructs Glenda. "I want them holed up at the shop in Dania."

"At the shop in Dania," she repeats. "Got it."

I shove the boat into gear—

And we slam into the dock. "Whoops," I say, throwing it into reverse and slowly backing away, the splintered wood of the dock cracking as we go. I spin the wheel, and we make a wide turn before I gun the throttle and push the racing boat into full-on forward. The sudden speed throws me back against the white leather seat, and instantly I've created three-foot swells in what was once a peaceful no-wake zone. But this is no time to pay attention to arbitrary maritime law. If I get ticketed, I'll pay the fine in fish.

The speedboat cuts easily through the light chop, the sharp hull breaking the waves, gliding over the water as if there were nothing holding it back. The front end rides a good five feet out of the water, the deep propellers in back doing all the heavy lifting, and the spray from the ocean mixes with the thick Miami air to give off a nice, fresh mist that coats my face and, temporarily, at least, cools me to a respectable temperature. This is the only way I could ever live in South Florida—7:30 in the morning at fifty knots.

Hagstrom has already spit out his bridge and released his claws in anticipation of a battle. "We go in fast," he says. "Noreen is priority number one."

I couldn't agree more. The yacht floats into view less than two hundred yards away, and I get a glimpse of the name painted on the side of the boat.

"*The Biggest Bill?*" I ask.

"It's a Hadrosaur joke."

There's no way to sneak up on them with the speedboat's engine blaring away like the final fifteen minutes of a Who concert, so I cut the power and hope that my momentum will bring us alongside.

I manage to edge the speedboat up to the side of the yacht, the hulls scraping against each other, the sound mostly hidden beneath the light hum of waves lapping against fiberglass. A skillful toss with the mooring line—okay, three fairly skillful tosses—and I secure the speedboat to the bigger vessel's deck.

The rail is a good ten feet above me, but, heck, we're a mile offshore, with no other boats around as far as the eye can see. Unless there's a satellite up in space peering down on us right now—and, chrissakes, there probably *is*—I figure it's safe enough to manipulate my guise just a bit. I loosen my pants, drawing them down around my ankles, like a seafarer who's lost his way to the head, and go to work on the G-clamp holding my tail in place. It takes a little manipulation of the snaps near my rump, but soon my human ass falls away—take that, Jenny Craig—and my tail is available for immediate delivery.

I leap, getting my full body and tail into the motion, and grab onto the lower railing. With a little help from Hagstrom, who's pushing from down below, I pull myself onto the deck, then give a hand as Nelly climbs aboard.

Noreen's mango scent is strong out here on the open sea, which means that she's probably still alive. Some scents linger after death, but they tend to go all gauzy, ephemeral. It doesn't take long after the blood stops rushing for the glands to shut down and halt production. The best dino forensic scientists can actually pinpoint time of death down to the minute, based on the remaining amounts of scent in a body, though they're not the kinds of folks you want to sit next to at a dinner party.

"Downstairs," says Hagstrom, leading the way down a small spiral staircase.

I underestimated the size of the yacht from back on land; it's at least an eighty-footer, maybe bigger, and the cabin space below is easily the size of my condo back in L.A. Better appointments, too: state-of-the-art appliances, plush carpeting, art on the walls. It's like a floating version of Jack's penthouse, down to the peach and purple decorations, the soft, interwoven color scheme.

Voices, farther in. We move through the main living and kitchen quarters, up to a small, closed door, probably leading to the private cabins. "You ready?" I whisper to Hagstrom.

He flashes his claws in and out of their slots, and I do the same. My tail is already free, but rather than waddle into the fight like a penguin, I take my pants off all the way and toss them to the floor of the galley. A quick spit of my dentures and my teeth are ready to chomp, the fresh air running through my open mouth, cooling off my gums. I reach for the doorknob—

And a scream pierces the air. High, shrill, pained. Feminine.

Hagstrom's first against the door, battering it down with a knock from his powerful shoulder as I slide in behind, ready to take out anyone who gets in my way.

I see the glint from the knife before anything else, and throw myself into Audrey's body even as I wonder why she'd use anything other than her natural claws. The old woman goes down easy, and despite the screams of protest from Noreen—screams of protest?—I'm able to grab Audrey's arms and pin them to the floor.

"What the hell are you doing?" Noreen is yelling, and as I look up, I see her sitting up off a small cot, her naked scales shining in the sunlight.

"Get out!" I shout back. "There's a speedboat moored to the deck. Take it and go!"

"What?"

"She's the one," Hagstrom says, stepping in front of his fiancée, claws and bills bared, protecting her in case Audrey should manage to squeeze out from under my grasp and make another move. "She's the traitor."

"She's not the traitor." Noreen sighs. "She's not even close. Vincent, get off of her."

I shake my head. "I don't think you're in the best mental state right now to make decisions—"

"Now."

I'm off in a flash. For what it's worth, Audrey doesn't try to lash out at me as she slowly climbs to her feet and brushes herself off. She reaches back down for her weapon—

"Uh-uh," I tell her. "Leave the knife there."

Noreen's slipped by Nelly and is at Audrey's side, helping her recover from my attack. "It's not a knife, you idiot," she says, bending down to pick up the item I clearly saw glinting in the light—

"It's a syringe. Audrey is my doctor."

It's good to see that Hagstrom is as stunned as I am; I'd hate to be the only one left without a partner at the big dance. "Your doctor?"

Noreen sits heavily on the edge of the bed, dropping her gaze as Audrey pats her knee softly. For the first time, I hear the older woman speak, her voice clear and strong. "I was Jack's doctor, too," she says. "For over ten years. I was the one who first diagnosed his SMA. We looked for a treatment together." She turns toward Noreen, who's begun to fidget with her own tail, the way she always used to whenever she got nervous or scared. I'm surprised that these emotions are still in her repertoire. "Do you want to tell them?"

"Tell us what?" asks Hagstrom.

When Noreen looks up, there are tears in her eyes, and the last thing I want to do is make them grow. But she starts in without any further urging. "Jack found a cure for his disease. For the spinal muscular atrophy. He and Audrey, they . . . they found a way to keep it at bay."

"It's not quite a cure," Audrey clarifies, "but it manages the symptoms."

"How?" I ask. "Jack said his nerve cells all died off, and the little bit I know about science is that nerve cells don't regenerate."

Audrey smiles the wide, satisfied grin of someone who's figured out how to beat the system. "Some do. Have you heard of the Sakai?"

I consult the sushi menu in my mind. "Sort of a fatty tuna?"

"The Sakai are a native tribe in the Thai jungles—all dinosaur, all Ornithomimus. Legend has it you can cut off the head of a Sakai warrior and it will grow back in seven days. Like most legends, it sounds ridiculous. But, like most legends, it has a grain of truth.

"The Sakai women can regenerate their tails."

"Like lizards," Noreen interjects. "More or less."

Audrey nods. "It's a slow process, and a painful one, but their cells duplicate, and at a surprising rate. I theorized that we could take some of these cells, introduce them into the diseased spinal column, and see if they could help regenerate the nerves needed for Jack to walk again. We were making great progress when he . . . died."

At least this confirms that I'm not completely insane—I *did* see Jack stand up from his wheelchair right before he fell to the ground. His legs were working, and Audrey's radical treatment must have been the reason.

"And the Sakai women?" Hagstrom asks. "Where do you get them from?"

Noreen shakes her head. She's amazed Hagstrom hasn't figured it out yet. "The talent-pool girls, Nelly. That's what it's all been about."

The lady on the boat, the young girl in the Opa-Locka house had said to me. *The old lady on the boat cuts our tails.* They've been using these girls for medical experiments.

"Jack's gone, though," I point out. "Great that you were his doctor and all, but what's that got to do with Noreen?"

She's crumpled on the floor, in tears, before I finish the sentence, and Nelly and I both rush to help her up. I defer to his status as fiancé at the last moment and stand back as he pulls her close, wrapping his arms and tail around her lithe body. A series of small pinpricks runs down the length of her spine, tiny droplets of blood a harsh red against the scales. Injection sites.

"I'm sorry," she sniffles into his chest. "I should have told you. I know I should have told you."

"SMA is hereditary," Audrey says softly, laying it out for us. "It often runs in families. Noreen felt the first symptoms over a year ago, and unless we continue treatment, she'll be in a wheelchair by winter."

Before I have a chance to comfort or soothe or take any of the socially appropriate measures, a thunderous boom shakes the boat, the world turns upside down, and we all go flying. The room tilts ninety degrees, and I get a split second of thought—*I didn't know that ceilings could spin like that*—before my head slams against the floor and the blackness invades.

15

"**G**et up! Come on, get up!"

Someone is slapping my face. Someone doesn't realize that it's not wise to slap my face. Someone is in for a rude awakening of his own.

I lash out, sitting upright, flailing my arms around, hoping to make contact, but as I try to move, my head gives off a warning flash of pain. It feels like the aftermath of a weeklong bender, only I can't remember the herb consumption that brought it on. Then again, if I actually was on a weeklong bender, I wouldn't have any memories to speak of.

"You hit your head." It's Hagstrom—I recognize the voice and the scent, both nearby. I try to open my eyes, then realize that they're already open. The darkness is all-encompassing; only a sliver of light peeks through the door at the far end of the room. For some reason, that direction seems like *up*.

"Hurts like hell—"

"Try again," he says. Then, perhaps to spur me on, perhaps just to let me in on an interesting tidbit of information: "We're sinking."

That gets me moving fast, blindingly painful head injury

notwithstanding. I stagger to my feet, water pooling around my ankles, rising to my knees, and I can hear the sound of rushing water,
like a huge faucet letting loose into a sink, the gurgle-gurgle of the
Atlantic Ocean invading the yacht's hull.

"Noreen's out cold," Hagstrom tells me. "Audrey's got her upstairs—"

"I'll help—come on—"

We climb our way up and out of the berth, dragging ourselves
along at a fifty-degree angle, using the fridge and the bolted-down
furniture for support. There's Noreen, slumped against Audrey's
chest, her meager frame weighing down the smaller, older
Hadrosaur.

I grab her around the arms as Hagstrom and Audrey take her
legs, and together we continue our trek, pushing hard against the
grade as we climb out from below and onto the deck of *The Biggest
Bill.*

Smoke pours from the starboard side—or is it port?—hell, from
the left side of the ship, a raging fire throwing flames into the air.
From my vantage point, I can only make out the top of the gash in
the ship's hull, but I can hear it taking on more water with every
passing second.

"Gas tanks?" I ask Hagstrom. "Is this thing going to blow anymore?"

But he shakes his head and points to the other end of the ship.
"Gas tanks are back that way. That fire there—that's what we call
a bomb."

So much for the legendary Tallarico ineptitude at demolitions;
looks like one of them finally figured out how to connect slot A to
tab B.

Another sudden lurch as the yacht descends another few feet
into the ocean. I can see pieces of *The Biggest Bill* fifteen, twenty
feet away, floating out to sea, alongside small scraps of what was
once the speedboat we came out on. Had I parked it around the

other side, it might have been in good enough condition to ride to safety; as it is, I'm hoping for a piece of driftwood large enough to hold on to.

"We're gonna have to swim for it," I tell Hagstrom, and he nods, grabbing Noreen's legs even tighter. "You can't wake her up?"

Nelly tries to slap her to consciousness, but she takes his abuse and lays there; if it weren't for the steady rise and fall of her chest, I'd be doubly worried. His next move is to try a Prince Charming, kissing her full on the lips, but I can't imagine he thought it would actually work—

Noreen sputters to life, spitting and coughing as the drops of water on her lips spray in a mist across the deck. She squints into the meager light—the sun not as strong as it was, some strange dark clouds covering it up—and up at Nelly and me standing above her. "What happened?"

"Bomb," I say. "Explosion. Sinking. Not a lotta time."

She gets the hint and totters to her feet, her sea legs wobbly but firm. There's a nasty lump just above her right eye, the distended skin twisting the scales into a knothole of bluish-green, and as she elevates her head, her eyes go googly, swimming in and out before she collapses back into my arms.

"Head wound," suggests Dr. Audrey.

"Ya think?"

I have no doubt that both Nelly and I could make it back to shore on the strength of our swimming ability. "Can you swim?" I ask Audrey, and she nods in the affirmative. Noreen is still out; we need something to lash her to, some way to keep her afloat while we push—

Ten feet off the bow—stern?—of the yacht, I see a familiar white-leather captain's chair, still attached to a ragged chunk of flooring from the speedboat. It bobs along the waves, up and down, back and forth, keeping above water just as everything else is sinking lower.

"That's the one," I say, handing Noreen off to Hagstrom and leaping into the ocean, hoping like hell on the way down that I don't bonk my head into a loose piece of driftwood. After everything I've survived so far, "I dove into a two-by-four" would be a crappy way to explain my death up at the Pearly Gates.

But my landing is clean, a 9.5 from the Russian judge, and I paddle over to the debris, wrapping my tail around the post connecting the captain's chair to the flooring. A few more strokes and I'm back at the ship, which is now three-fifths underwater and going fast.

Hagstrom's already on the ball, and after he lowers Noreen into my arms—I'm treading water as hard as I can, utilizing all the swimming skills those bizarre Progressives taught me back in Hawaii—he locates a length of rope and plunges into the ocean next to me.

"Around the chest," he instructs me, propping Noreen in the chair, keeping the whole platform as straight as he can. I'm tying her up as best I can, a difficult proposition while on land, nearly impossible while bobbing in the ocean.

Thirty seconds later, she's lashed to the chair, and Hagstrom, Audrey, and I are pushing hard, one hand keeping the makeshift bodyboard level, the other applying forward pressure as we kick out with all our strength, headed for the distant shore.

I can hear the final gurgle of the yacht going down behind us, the slurp as the ocean swallows up what remains of the once-beautiful vessel, and the whoosh of air that follows, blowing through our hair, nearly drying it out.

Only problem is, sinking ships don't make a whoosh of air.

But hurricanes do. I turn around, fully realizing that even Lot's wife would slap me silly for such a foolish move—

Something has swallowed the sky. Where once there were fluffy white clouds, now there is nothing but a swirling darkness, driving forward, gobbling up what little blue remains above. Now I know how tech companies feel when Microsoft comes knocking.

"Hurricane," I shout over to Nelly and Audrey, my voice weak against the growing roar of the storm.

"What?"

"Hurricane!" Holding on to Noreen's float with both hands, I duck my head beneath the water and give it everything I've got, caring less about direction and control than pure power. I can feel the waves at my back, pressing forward, as if they, too, are running away from Alison, breaking around my body because I'm too damned slow to get out of the way.

A slip of my fingers, and Noreen's float begins to pull away. I kick out hard again, grabbing on to the wood, just before another wave picks it up and yanks it from my grasp. Hagstrom and Audrey are barely holding on, their bodies buffeted by a sudden rush as the storm punches the FRAPPE button on the ocean surface, whipping the waves into a white, foamy froth.

A brilliant flash lights the darkening sky, followed almost instantly by an angry thunderclap. Great—I was just thinking we needed a few million volts of electricity to make this more interesting.

"That's weird," Nelly calls out. "Not a lot of lightning in hurricanes—"

"You're giving me a *weather* lesson now?"

Another wave crashes in from the right, the unexpected torrent of water flipping us up, higher, the left side dropping down, forcing the platform to its side—hanging on now, trying to remain upright—

Water is in my mouth, my nose, filling the space before my eyes. We've flipped. I can feel Noreen's body in front of me, still trussed to the captain's chair. She's upside down and underwater and doesn't have more than a few seconds before she's a goner.

I can't see a thing, but I can sure as heck still feel. The ropes in front of me are thick, but my claws are stronger, and a few quick saws is all it takes. Noreen floats free, and I grab her in my arms, hauling her up, out—

Gasping for air at the surface, checking Noreen's breathing. She's sputtering, coughing, barely conscious, but I can hear the rattle of air pumping in her chest. I've got her beneath the arms, lifeguard style, stroking backwards, still laboring to reach shore.

"Vincent!" Hagstrom is fifty feet away, paddling hard. "Where's Noreen?"

"I got her!" I call back. "She's okay! Where's the doctor?"

No answer as another wash of water blasts over my head, pushing me under, but I grab Noreen even tighter and haul us back to the surface once more. The rain has increased, the thunderstorm advancing on all sides, a sudden blitzkrieg of lightning crashing into the sea around us.

Hagstrom is suddenly by my side, helping me to keep Noreen's head clear of the water as we swim harder for the marina. The only good thing about this storm is that the waves are pushing us closer and closer to shore even as they threaten to gobble us up. If we can just stay afloat long enough—

Hagstrom's turned around, his kicks slowing as his body freezes up. "You gotta be kidding me . . ."

I don't even have time to see what he's scared of before a twenty-foot wave lifts me into the air, the wall of water pulling Noreen from my arms as I'm dragged three stories into the sky. I get a momentary glimpse of the marina—maybe a fifth of a mile away at this point, no more—before the wave drops me back down again, slamming me into the ocean surface like a wrestler pinning his opponent.

I don't take long powering myself back up to the surface; in my admittedly limited experience with floods and other water catastrophes, I've learned that it's best to get yourself up to oxygen as quickly as possible, because, contrary to popular belief, there aren't any singing crabs or redheaded mermaids to drag your ass to safety.

Noreen and Hagstrom are nowhere to be found. I try calling out, but the combination of the water in my lungs, the water in the air, and the water all around makes it impossible to get out more than a few decibels. Another peal of thunder rolls through the air, and I kick out yet again, hoping I'll make it to shore before my part of the ocean is drawn up into the eye of the hurricane, taking Vincent along with it for the final spin-cycle of his relatively short life.

A new blast of pain lashes out from my head—the right side, this time—and I grab hold of the long piece of driftwood that just conked my noggin. It's a good three feet across, eight feet long, and the blue letters on the side—*iggest Bil*—tells me that Jack, in the form of his decimated boat, has once again come to the rescue. I latch on and ride that thing like a hobby horse, flapping my tail back and forth like a propeller.

And, praised be Triton, it actually works. I manage to shift my weight around the rising waves, using my latent surfing skills to ride the storm right into the marina. The few boats still moored here are slamming against the pier, their owners either on vacation or not bright enough to dry-dock the things when the hurricane first appeared on the radar. The rain is thick enough to reduce visibility to no more than a hundred feet in any direction, the winds buffeting me in all directions as I leap off the driftwood and paddle hard for the last fifty yards.

I drag myself beneath the closest pier I can find and stumble onto shore, staying out of sight below the wooden deck. My pants and, most importantly, my G-clamp, were lost aboard *The Biggest Bill*, and I'm not entirely sure how I'm going to go about finding another set. Whatever bits of sun were left in the sky have completely disappeared, the wind whipping through the pylons, howling, as if the storm itself is laughing at me.

Audrey stumbles ashore a moment later and gives me a weak thumbs-up sign before collapsing in the sand. I take a quick look around—

A mild stroke of mango and cinnamon steals into my sinuses, and I peer through the rain, squinting into the storm. Through the drops, I can make out a silhouette dragging its way on shore, the movements rough and stiff.

It's Nelly, and draped across his arms is another body, a smaller body, wet blond hair dripping to the sand. I can make out a pair of arms, of legs, drooping down.

I'm running across the sand, farther into the storm, the rain slapping my face, the wind pushing me back, but in seconds I'm there, dropping to my knees as Nelly lays Noreen faceup on the ground.

She's not moving, her chest is flat, still. I lift her arm, and it falls back to the earth—dead weight.

"Vincent," Nelly says, but I push him away, push him down—

My lips contacting Noreen's, breathing into her, trying to force air into her lungs, hoping her snout is compressed correctly beneath the mask, that I'm blowing into her mouth or nose, anything that will get her breathing again.

Hagstrom is behind me, pulling me back. "Vincent," he says again, firmer, yet softer—but I can't listen—

I pound on her chest, pressing my hands together, forcing her lungs in and out, just like they do in the flicks—

Something's odd. Noreen's body doesn't resist; it just sinks lower, into the sand. And her lips, once upon a time soft and pliable and perfect to kiss, have no substance to them. It's as if her whole body were flat, missing its insides.

"Vincent," Hagstrom says one last time, "it's not Noreen anymore. It's not her, Vincent. She's gone."

But it has to be her. The hair, the face, the body—it's Noreen, just like I remember her—

Except it's just a guise. An empty sack, lifeless on the sand, six pounds of latex and two pounds of clamps, and nothing inside it except rainwater and sand.

"I lost her in the waves," Nelly sighs, and I can see that it's a different kind of saltwater streaming down his face now. "I lost her in the waves."

We sit by her empty shell of a guise, the two of us, side by side, cross-legged in the wet sand, ignoring the wind and the rain and the lightning, keeping vigil over the only remains we have, until another wave dashes on the beach and the undertow drags the final pieces of Noreen Dugan down into the depths of the Atlantic Ocean.

16

It wasn't a hurricane. Go figure. It was an unrelated weather system, a storm moving in behind Alison, discounted by the weathermen because of its relative weakness to its bigger sibling. Maybe it would have been better if it was Alison, backtracking, moving in on South Florida, because then there would have been too much damage for the rest of it to start up again. Then we would have had other things on our mind over this last seven days.

But it was just a storm, and the damage was minimal. A few downed power lines here, a few flooded living rooms there. Nothing to complain about, really; back in Malibu, throw in a fire or two on top of the flooding and you've got an average afternoon.

So rather than rebuilding and repairing, our minds were free to focus on those things that consumed us most, the three R's of any good mafia organization:

Revenge. Rage. Reason.

Revenge for BB, revenge for Jack, revenge, of course, for Noreen.

Rage at Tallarico, at the entire Velociraptor organization, at the way things had been handled.

Reason. As in a reason for all this carnage. The answer is there, somewhere, presently escaping us, but within our grasp. Someone inside the Dugan crew is leaking like a yacht with bombed-out starboard hull, and Nelly and I are going to find out who's responsible and plug up the hole.

I didn't go back to Tallarico's. I wanted Eddie in doubt as to my whereabouts. I needed him edgy, nervous, more liable to make a mistake. Maybe he'd think I was dead. Maybe he'd think I skipped town. It didn't matter; I simply couldn't go back there, not after what he did to Noreen.

Nelly, Glenda, and I made a pact not to tell the others about Noreen's death; Tallarico's mole was somewhere inside the organization, and the less they knew, the better. When we wanted to disseminate information, we would do it on our own terms. As far as anyone else knew, Noreen was in hiding at an undisclosed location.

Hagstrom sent Audrey packing. Without Jack and Noreen around—without their disease keeping her scientific studies alive—there was no point for her to be in jeopardy. "I wish you well with your research," he told her. "I really do. But you can't do it here, not anymore." He also released the talent-pool girls. Paid their safe passage out of America, back to Thailand. He couldn't guarantee that another one of the families wouldn't scoop them up again, but at least for now, they were free.

These moral niceties out of the way, it was time to get to work.

We didn't bother with the lower faces on the Tallarico totem pole; they wouldn't know a thing. So we started with some of the captains I knew from around the Star Island compound, the guys I'd first seen lounging around Eddie's living room watching bad sitcoms. They were easy enough to find at first; some, we just picked up off the street. Others we tracked down through a variety of sources—Nelly knows a lot of people in this town, and they all seem to owe him favors. When all else failed, we could casually drop Jack or Noreen's name, and that always seemed to do the trick.

The safe house used by the Dugan family was in a warehouse district just east of Aventura, surrounded by supermarket storage facilities and generic drug manufacturers. Between the crash of trucks and the clash of machinery, no one heard the screams.

When it came time to pick up Sherman, I petitioned to do the job myself. "I got history with this guy," I told Hagstrom. "He'll get in with me."

Nelly wasn't so sure. "This is the one that took out Jack, right? I don't think it's smart to go alone."

"Send me with two guys, then. If I can't do it, they can go in, but I wanna be at the warehouse."

He relented, and it came off smooth. Marcus and Andy, two soldiers under Nelly's command, accompanied me down to Calle Ocho, the Cuban section of town, where I found Sherman hunkered down in the back of a guise rental shop, one of these shady operations that offers black-market costumes to vacationing dinos who want a different body or face for their two weeks in the sun. Let's say you're a middle-aged, overweight accountant from Detroit who wants to impress some of the South Florida honeys. You can walk right in, flash a credit card, and in under an hour you're a dashing Nicaraguan with chest hair to spare. This differs from your standard black-market guise shop, like Manny's place up in New York, in two very specific ways:

One: there's no customizing allowed, and as such, mistakes can occur. The dude who wore your Nicaraguan *guapo* suit the week before might have run afoul of the local law enforcement, and you may end up getting snatched for his crime. On the other hand, he might have made a hit with the local lasses, so a false, but very flattering, reputation might precede you.

And two: it's all temporary. There's no rent-to-own policy, and the guises are retired after six months of use. If you want, you can always go down to one of the auctions they hold every year or so and pick up a used one on the cheap, but who knows where these things have been. After half a year of riding around on a hundred different dino bodies, the amalgam of scent residue alone is enough to make you crazy.

It wasn't hard to find Sherman, hanging out in the back room, noshing on a fat pickle and checking the racing papers.

"Eddie wants you," I said, walking in like I owned the joint.

Sherman nearly fell off his stool. "Rubio? Jesus, Vincent, where the fuck have you been?"

"I been out helping the family. And like I said, Eddie wants to see you." I was going to play it to the hilt; I had two guys outside to back me up if it went down bad. "I don't ask the guy questions, I just do what he wants. You coming or not?"

Sherman shook his head, cursed a little more, and threw his pickle back into the jar as he followed me outside and into a tinted-window Lexus we had rented and crapped up just for the occasion. He was so out of sorts that he didn't notice a thing until he was in the car and Marcus and Andy shot him up with a dose of some knockout drug and threw a sack over his head. Glenda was up front with Nelly, and they gave me the thumbs-up as we drove off.

At the warehouse, it was short and brutal. Nelly didn't mess around with the dissolution packets and the tail like Sherman and Chaz had done with Stewie at the racetrack. "That's a game," he told me, "a stupid little trick. You want to get information, you start off big."

They'd stripped Sherman down to his natural skin and tied him to a thick chair, his tail bound in heavy duct tape, his head pressed back against a post and cemented there with twelve-gauge aluminum wire. He was already awake, spitting epithets at us along with a fair amount of saliva.

"Hadrosaur fucks! He's gonna kill you all! When Eddie gets wind of this—"

Nelly whipped out a single claw, caught Sherman's forked tongue, and swiftly cut it off.

A river of pain poured from Sherman's throat, a garbled litany of unfocused vowels and screeches, and Nelly just stepped back, the pink wobbly muscle limp and inert in his still-clenched fist.

"How's he gonna talk now?" I asked. "I thought the whole point of this was to find out what he knows."

"He can still write, can't he?"

They waited until his screams died down, at which point, suddenly, miraculously, Sherman was most eager to help. Marcus held on to his arm while he guided a pen across a sheet of paper, answering any and all questions Nelly put to him.

And he knew a lot—business plans, murder plots, extortion schemes, all of Tallarico's dirty little secrets. Only problem was, he didn't know the one thing we most wanted him to know.

"Screw it," Hagstrom said after thirty minutes of senseless scribbling. "He's not in the loop."

I agreed. "But at least now we know where Hoffa is buried."

"Yeah, that and a quarter'll buy you a cup of coffee."

I decided not to tell him that Starbucks is charging upwards of three bucks these days. "Now what?"

"Now we cut him loose," said Hagstrom, and he gave Marcus the signal. I looked away.

Glenda didn't look, either; we both stared at the warehouse wall as Sherman's intense final gurgle filled the air. He had been dispatched to the great beyond, to an endless supply of nachos and pickles. Marcus and Andy would take care of the details, get rid of the body. Our job was to move up the list and snag the next Tallarico goon. Eventually, someone would have what we wanted.

But for every one of their guys that we picked off, they nabbed one of ours. Hagstrom was sure we had our soldiers well hidden, but somehow the Tallarico crew managed to find out where they were located. Most of the time, they killed them on the spot. Other times . . . Other times it wasn't so pretty.

Marcus went out on a scouting run one day and didn't come back. Six hours later they found him: dangling in the meat locker of a steak and burger joint, a restaurant where the customers can choose their prime cut from behind a Plexiglas window and watch it butchered before their very eyes. Some octogenarian with bad eyesight chose the healthy-looking slab of beef in the corner, and it wasn't until they pulled the hook over and slammed Marcus down on the table that the chef realized he wouldn't get any Porterhouse out of this beast.

We took out Jerry, the mah-jongg tile-eater, the next day. It wasn't so much retaliation as it was restoring a sense of order: he was next on the depth chart, right before the big man himself. We would have skipped right over good old Jer, but Tallarico'd pulled a Greta Garbo the day of the storm and none of our scouts could get a bead on him. In the meantime, we worked the underlings.

Jerry was holed up in a retirement home up near Dania Beach, a big mansion the locals called Tara, where he was fed, entertained, and surrounded by nurses twenty-four hours a day. The room he was in had last been used by Eddie Tallarico's dying aunt, and since her demise, they'd paid the home to keep it open for occasions just like this. It was a hard infiltration, because every visitor had to be announced, and by the time we could get to Jerry's room, there was no doubt he'd be gone with the wind.

But I knew Jerry's vices from our stint playing mah-jongg in the Omni for eight hours and suggested to Hagstrom that we stake out all the local delicatessens. Sure enough, he was spotted at the Rascal House getting corned-beef takeout, and we snatched him right off the street. A quick how-do-ya-do and he was in the car, in the warehouse, and spilling his guts. Hagstrom didn't even need to cut off his tongue.

That afternoon, they shipped Jerry's dismembered body back to the Tallarico compound inside a giant urn with two dead baby palm trees sticking out of the top. It cost the family $819, but when you want to deliver a message of doom, you've got to care enough to send the very best.

The next day, the cops were called to a local carnival, where the Ferris wheel had stopped working mid-spin. Upon further inspection, they found a body wedged inside the giant engine of the contraption, his arms and legs tied to the gears, his mouth stopped with pink insulation and duct tape. Their theory was that the victim had been alive all night, lashed down and awaiting the inevitable, and that the second the ride began its first revolution, his limbs were torn from his body one by one. Fortunately, there was a dino among the officers called to the scene. Unfortunately, the victim was Andy, and just like that, our two best enforcers were gone.

The next day, Glenda caught me as I was sucking down a breakfast of whatever protein I could scrounge together from the safe-house pantry. The regular beatings and torture sessions were beginning to wear on my body, and I felt worn, thin, like a tissue used one time too many.

She pulled a chair next to mine. "We've got to stop it, Vincent."

"You didn't know her."

"I did know her. Not like you did, or Nelly did, but I knew Noreen, and I agree, she was a good woman—"

"You didn't know her," I repeated, "and you didn't know Jack, so you can't talk."

Glenda kicked back from her seat, the chair clattering to the ground behind her.

"Then why the fuck am I here, huh? Because I'm helping your ass, like I always have. Who saved you when the McBride thing went down bad? Me. And who helped you figure out how to squirm out of those Council violations when you were high on enough herb to bring down a yak? Me. And I'm telling you, this isn't our battle anymore." Before I could protest, she continued. "Yeah, I know, you loved them both, I got that. I dig the whole thing. But look at yourself, Rubio. You've gotten wrapped up in a mob war. You're a PI, for chrissakes, not some big-time mafioso."

"That's not what this is about," I said, spooning more egg into my mouth.

"Of course it's not," said Glenda. "It's about finding something else to get addicted to. Only this time it's blood."

I was instantly up and out of my chair, arm flinging back, ready to strike, to slap that nonsense out of her head—

Glenda just stood there, waiting for the blow, and it sapped all my strength. My arm fell as it reached her, my blow ending up as nothing but a weak slap on her shoulder.

She shook her head. "You can't even see it," Glenda said sadly. "But I can. Let's get out now, while we've still got a semblance of ourselves left. We'll get on the next plane to L.A., go to a Dodger game, just chill and get our lives back."

I couldn't argue with her logic. I couldn't even argue with her emotion. But it isn't about arguments. It's about finishing something for those that are no longer around to finish it themselves. I sat back down at the table and snarfed down another egg. When I looked up again, my best friend in the world was gone, out of the safe house and, for all I knew, out of Miami. I didn't even hear her leave.

Which brings us to this afternoon, and a meeting in the small office Jack used to use when holed up here in the warehouse. Nelly sits behind Jack's burnished wood desk; I pace the room. Outside, the other members of the Dugan organization are getting restless; they're starting to wonder where Noreen is, and why she's not running the show. Defections are imminent unless something is done, and quickly.

"It's got to be Eddie," Nelly says. "If we're going to end this, we've got to end this with him."

"But he's AWOL," I point out. "And even if we knew where he was . . ."

"It doesn't mean we could smoke him out," Hagstrom finishes.

"What about his businesses?" I try.

"Checked out. Not there."

"The properties—"

"Checked out. Not there, either."

"Vacation homes, condos, favorite hotels. Maybe he went abroad—"

"No, no, and no," says Nelly. "He hasn't left the city—I can feel that much. Eddie Tallarico would want to stay where the action is, get in all the good kills for himself. But if he's too deep, we won't find him. And we've already gone through all his high-level men, everyone who knows him, where he'd go to cover up."

As Nelly hashes it out in his head, going over the obvious time and time again, I let my eyes wander around the room, at the furnishings that Jack had picked out with Noreen's able assistance. The deep, lustrous woods, the tasteful Early American finishings. Old World charm amid New World style. Very tasteful. Very Noreen.

Above the desk, a portrait, an honest-to-goodness oil painting of the Dugan family in happier times, maybe ten, fifteen years ago. Jack, Noreen, both Mom and Pop Dugan, arms around each other, the family together, happy, content. No disease, no animosity. Maybe they're all together again right now, posing for another one of these shots. Lord knows, there are enough Renaissance painters up in heaven, and it would probably get boring painting the same old cloud-and-angel scenes after a while. Get in a good portrait now and then, or a landscape with a horse—

Inspiration strikes. "We're not through," I say, the words coming out of my mouth moments before I even realize where I'm going with it. "There's one avenue left."

Nelly turns, interested. "How so?"

"We thought we'd gone through all the high-level Tallarico people—"

"We have—"

"Yeah, all the *current* high-level Tallarico people. I've got someone else in mind who might know where Eddie Tallarico is hiding, and here's the best part: if I'm right, we won't have to lay a single claw on him to get the answer."

"Jai alai is a Basque game," the lady at the ticket counter tells me in a bored monotone, "played in three American states—Florida, Connecticut, and Rhode Island—and numerous foreign countries. Bets can be placed downstairs, on level one, and a program guide is available . . ."

She drones on, and I wonder why they didn't install a tape recording; at least the clarity would be better. I pay my two dollars for standing-room admission and walk into Dania Jai Alai, one of the two major frontons—according to the robot out front, that's what they call these arenas—in the South Florida area.

I don't understand this game, and I don't want to. There's a court that's about a hundred feet long, no more than thirty feet wide, and a bunch of speedy little players with giant scoops strapped to their wrists are flinging a little ball against the far wall. They've got on knee pads and helmets, and since this doesn't seem like a contact sport, I'm assuming that ball is traveling at some pretty wicked speeds. All around me, gamblers clutch their tickets like security blankets, rooting for their player to spin or shoot or throw or do whatever the hell it is they do to win a point.

But I'm not looking for a jai alai player; I'm looking for a horse.

"Hey, Stewie," I say, sidling up to my favorite Thoroughbred as he sits in the VIP section down by the playing court.

This large but respectable-looking gentleman with a goatee and suede elbow patches on his jacket—a professor, no doubt at some tony New England college—barely looks my way. "I'm sorry, friend," he says, in a clipped Boston accent, "my name isn't . . . 'Stewie.'"

"Ya sure smell like Stewie," I say, getting a whiff of that whipped egg yolk scent. "Actually, you smell like Stewie trying to put on so much goddamned cologne that you don't smell like Stewie. Lord, how can you stand it?"

"Really," says the professor, "I don't know what you're talking about."

"Of course you don't." I stand, pat the guy on the back. "Sorry to waste your time."

"No problem," he says, turning back to the jai alai game. "Good evening."

"Evening." I walk a few steps down the aisle, then quickly turn and shout, *"And they're off!"*

Stewie flinches forward, a reaction trained into him by so many years at the track. He catches himself a millisecond before he leaps the row in front of him and settles back into the seat, glancing around to see if anyone else noticed.

I walk back, a big grin on my face. "How about I just call you Love My Money, huh?"

His composure is instantly shot. Hands shaking, legs trembling, his voice quivers as he pleads with me: "Not here. Please don't do it here."

"Hey, hey," I say, smoothing it out, trying to keep him level. He's easily twice my size, and I don't want him freaking out on me in the middle of the fronton. "Look at me. Look at me."

He gulps and takes a gander, but nothing's registering in those eyes. "It's me," I say. "The guy who saved your tail." I'm speaking Martian for all he cares, but then a light comes on in the attic.

"Yeah, yeah, that's it," I prod. "Think about it—you got it. The race, the stable—those goons using the dissolution powder on you—"

And suddenly he's in tears, sobbing openly into his hands. The other gamblers are, fortunately, caught up in a match between two jai alai players with too many consonants in their names, but if he really gets to blubbering, they'll notice. It's hard to ignore a 350-pound infant in your midst.

"It was terrible," he whines. "Terrible . . ."

"I know, I know, I was there. Listen, it's over now—"

"Those *monsters*—"

"You're safe now," I tell him. "They're gone, all of them."

This gets his attention, and his sniffles dry up enough for him to ask, "Gone?"

"Dead."

"All of them?"

"All but one," I say. "Come on, lemme buy you a hot dog."

He shrugs, wiping away the tears from his face, draining them off the goatee. "I kinda like nachos."

Not another one. "Great. Nachos it is."

We find the junk food on the second level and grab a table with a view so Stewie can watch the games he's betting on. His tail, he tells me, is all healed up; the dino docs down at Jackson Memorial took real good care of him. "You know," I say as we watch one of the players scramble up the far wall to get to a well-placed shot, "you were supposed to disappear."

Stewie looks down into his chips, ashamed to meet my gaze. "I know."

"It's for your own good."

"I know," he repeats.

"*Mine,* too. I told 'em you were dead, that I finished you off. And if you go showing up, it sorta casts doubt on my claim, doesn't it?"

Stewie nods, tugging on his jacket. "But I got myself this spiffy new guise, huh? I'm telling you, no one would recognize me."

"Uh-huh," I say. "Except for me, right?"

Stewie recognizes the flaw in his logic. "Right. Right. How'd you find me?"

"Nobody changes," I tell him. "I take one look at you, and I know you're the kinda guy who needs to gamble. Hell, that's probably why you stuck around South Florida and you don't even know it—just another little gamble, with your life, right?"

He's into the chips again, refusing to face reality. "I dunno about that—"

"You're gonna be a gambler wherever you go," I continue, "in on the action, one side or the other. Horse gambler or horse, it just took a little bit of searching to track you down."

He nods. "I hung out at the dog tracks for a while, but it wasn't that interesting. Besides, it's not like I'm ever gonna fit in a greyhound costume."

"No, most likely not." I don't tell him that before coming here, I'd already checked the dog tracks, the Indian casinos, even the illegal cockfights down in Hialeah. Better that I impress him with my Holmesian perspicacity, that I can find him again in a heartbeat.

"And I figured maybe jai alai," he continues. "I'm a big guy, I can get the mechanics of the game."

"Sure," I say, "sure. Now listen, Stewie, I think we might be able to help each other out."

"I'd like that," he says, stuffing half the nacho plate down his gullet. I check my wallet; not a lot of cash left in there. I'll have to get the info before the next course.

"Me, too. Now, you may have been reading the papers—"

"Racing papers?"

"I mean the *Herald*."

"Don't read the *Herald*," he says. "Any newspapers, really."

I go with the flow. "On television, then, you might have seen—"

"No TV. If there's something I wanna watch, I usually go down to the department store and pretend I'm buying a set. They let me stay as long as I want."

"I see." This is taking far too long; he's all done with his nachos and going for my share. "I'll make it easy: I need to know where to find Eddie Tallarico."

Stewie chortles, a big belly laugh that shakes the shoulder pads sewn into his jacket. "That's it?" he says, relieved.

"That's it."

"Damn, I thought you were gonna rat me out or something."

"No ratting," I promise. "You can hang out in South Florida for as long as you want, and the Tallaricos won't bother you again. I figure you were in tight with Frank Tallarico—"

"Damn tight—"

"Exactly. And you know the hideouts that the rest of these new shmucks don't know about."

He thinks about it for a second, and I can see the answer in those big blue eyes. He knows, all right. He knows it well. "Might be true," he says.

"'Course it is," I reply. "And all I need from you is a location."

He stuffs the rest of the nachos in his mouth and swallows them in a single, crunching bite. Perhaps it helps him come to his decision. "Hell, yeah," he says through cheese-flavored spittle, "I'll tell you where you can find the little bastard."

"You know what, Stewie?" I say, reaching for my wallet and extracting my last three dollars, the final bit of cash left over from Frank Tallarico's oh-so-generous advance. "Let's you and me go get ourselves another plate of nachos."

17

When I walk into The Dirty Dozen six hours later, I realize that the name of the store is something of a misnomer. Whereas everything in here is indeed dirty—filthy, in fact, in both the physical and Puritan sense of the word—there are certainly a lot more than a dozen items to choose from. In fact, this has got to be one of the larger clearinghouses of pornography, mammal and reptile, I've ever encountered. And I've had jobs up in Encino.

But this is the last possible place Eddie Tallarico could be, one of only four locations Stewie said Frank used to hole up in when the outside world got too hot. The first three were busts, no sign of Eddie anywhere. I saved this one for last, partly because I thought it was a long shot, partly because it's way up here on 167th Street, a good distance from the Tallarico compound, and partly because I was hoping to steer clear of porn stores this time around. Most of the good reptilian smut shops in L.A. tend to have an herb distributor on the premises, and I don't need the temptation right now. The urge to chew was strong after Noreen was swept away, so much so that I made Hagstrom hide the remaining bottles of Infusion, lock it all behind a set of double doors, in case the desire to get funky overcame rational thought.

But here I am, wandering down the aisles, still up top in the mammal section. The things these monkeys do to one another for kicks are incredible. The aisles reserved for straight sex are few and far between; most titles kink in one direction or another, and sometimes three at once. *Grannies Who Love She-Males, Midgets under the Whip, Me and My Love Sheep*—and these are just the coloring books.

The clerk is nothing but a kid, twenty-five at the most, kicking back on a high stool behind the counter—a sign up front proclaiming ALL AMATEUR WATERSPORTS 20% OFF!—and reading Camus. Probably working his way through college, figured this was an easy way to make a few bucks, get a chance to study, maybe make some new and interesting friends.

"Hey," I say, interrupting his reading. "You got anything else in here?"

"Like what?" he says, not taking his eyes off the page.

"I dunno," I reply. "Something . . . with scales."

He lowers the book, two brown eyes poking up above the jacket. "You a fucking sicko or something?"

"What? No, I'm just—"

And now he's all righteous, indignant. "This is a legal store, man—we don't carry kids, and we don't do animals. I should call the fucking cops on you."

I'm backing away now; this wasn't the best way to start. I realize that in my zeal I forgot to run a sniff test; just because they've got a dino section doesn't mean the owners didn't hire an ape or two to run the register.

There's a whiff of pine behind me, though, and I turn, relieved to find a hefty gent already in the process of calming down the college kid. "It's okay, Steven," he's saying, "I got it from here."

"That's right," Steven mumbles, going back to his book. "You better fucking take it from here, Harold, 'cause I had it up to here with these sickos . . ."

I'm led through the back, down an aisle reserved for latex and bondage games. "Gotta check before you do that," the dino clerk chastises me. "You freaked out my employee."

"Sorry 'bout that," I say, "but I'm in something of a hurry."

"You and the rest of the world," he drawls. "Right this way."

Hank leads me through the employee lounge and into the restroom, where we both crowd into a cramped stall. They're not too keen on their hygiene in here, either, but it might just be the proximity of Harold's natural odor.

"Flush," he says. "Three times."

Seems like a waste of water to me, but I give the handle three separate jiggles as Harold simultaneously presses up on the toilet-roll dispenser. There's a groan, a rickety creak, and the back wall of the stall pops open an inch. Harold reaches out and pushes on the tile, and the wall swings inward, displaying an even grungier, messier store beyond.

We climb over the toilet and into the aisle, and the first thing I see is a full-length guise hanging on the wall. Long legs, short brown hair, powerful flanks, a beautiful mane—it's a horse costume, just like Stewie's. Now I know where they got his suit for the races: he was running full-bore in a Dirty Dozen special.

Harold catches my stunned expression. "Takes all kinds," he says. "Now, what's up your alley?"

"I'm just here—"

"Wait, wait, lemme guess."

"You won't."

"I might. I been doing this ten years. Okay . . ." He sizes me up, as if a single glance at my costumed form could give him some idea on how I get my jollies. "You're a . . . *Tails and Mails* kinda fella."

"I don't even know what the hell that means."

"Tails and mails," he repeats, as if the first time he'd just garbled the words, as if there were no possible way such a phrase
hadn't entered my lexicon. "Dragons and knights—you're the
beast, she's the tamer. Chain mail, lances, that sort of thing. We've
got a whole section for it—"

I hold up a hand, preparing to grab him about the throat if need
be and choke this nonsense at the root. "Stop. Listen. I'm here for
one thing, and one thing only—"

"*Beat the Beast*—that's it—you're a *Beat the Beast* guy—"

"I need to see Eddie Tallarico."

That shuts him up. He takes a step back, as if the very words
themselves have knocked him off his feet. "I don't know who
you're talking about."

"Yes you do. Big guy, runs the Raptor mafia. Everyone knows
who he is."

"I don't."

"Yes, you do."

"I do?"

"Yes."

"Okay," he says. "Maybe I do."

"And he's here. You know how I know he's here?"

Harold swallows hard. "No."

Rule number six: If you're going to bluff, bluff hard. There's no
point in candy-assing your way around a lie.

"Because Eddie told me this is where he'd be."

Harold scratches his head. "He did, huh?"

Corollary to rule number six: When in doubt, bluff again. Better to go down in flames than risk running away from a sure thing.
"He did. Just the other day."

"He told you to come *here*?"

"Yeah," I say. "Funny how that communication thing works.
Eddie tells me, I tell you. And the next link in the chain . . . ?"

He thinks it over for a second. "I . . . tell Eddie?"

"Good boy. Run along."

Harold is sufficiently cowed to disappear into the towering aisles of smut, leaving me standing in the middle of this porn purveyor's paradise. I shuffle through the magazines, making sure not to take too many glances at any one page. I have a reputation to uphold, and it would be unseemly to engage in naughty activities while on the job.

The other patrons of The Dirty Dozen aren't quite so shy about their sexual habits. They hold the magazines up to the light to get a better angle, and question one another about the best interspecies videos they've rented here. It doesn't surprise me that their scents are strong, hyped up with hormones, streaming from their glands with intensity. And maybe if there were a female anywhere within a mile radius, they'd have a shot, but it's just us guys in here, same as it is in the monkey world.

A tap on my shoulder, and I turn to find a squat, hatchet-faced fellow waving a VHS tape in front of my face. I can't make out the title, but the green-and-yellow tail intertwined with a long set of spikes tells me it's some sort of interracial romp.

"I don't work here," I grunt.

"Just wondering if you've seen it," sniffs the guy. "If it's any good."

"Dunno. I'm sure you'll love it." I try to shuffle away, but he stays close.

"I tried to get into the story—you know, the description on the back cover—"

"Sure, whatever—"

"But it sounded kinda weird. Some Raptor from Los Angeles who comes out east but disappears for a while, everyone thinks he's dead, and then he pops up all of a sudden wanting to see old friends."

Now he's got my attention. "Doesn't sound very sexy," I say.

"It isn't. But the violence is delicious." I take a whiff—barely any scent off this dino, maybe a slight odor of Campbell's Chicken Noodle. The ugly little guy grins, as if he knows what I'm doing and finds it somewhat humorous. He crooks a finger at me. "Yeah, now I got your attention," he says. "Back this way."

I follow him across the video-rental section of the store and through a curtain with a sign reading PEEP SHOW $.50—CLOSED FOR RENOVATIONS. I wonder what kind of renovations one would do on a peep show. Clean the windows, perhaps, but I'd hope that was a daily chore as opposed to a monthly one. Maybe they're making it easier to feed the quarter machines with one hand.

There's a short hallway, the walls painted black, and a squat door at the far end. "In there," he says. I'm not one to argue. I pull open the flimsy door and stoop down low, stepping inside as the door slams shut behind me.

Darkness. I can feel the walls around me, smooth, circular. Like I'm standing on the floor of an upright cylinder, maybe twenty feet in diameter, at most. I reach out, hoping to find the center of this circle, and hit a metal pole, extending from the ceiling to the floor, the surface cool to the touch.

A hundred-watt naked bulb above my head snaps to life, and I shield my eyes from the sudden glare. But I adjust in less than a second and find myself staring at seven mirror images of yours truly, displayed at all different angles. I think my left side is the best, but it's open to debate.

But they're not actually mirrors—I can see that now. They're rectangular panes of glass, only the area behind them is still dark, while my room is spectacularly bright, and it's the contrast that allows me to see my reflection.

I'm in the peep show. I *am* the peep show.

A burst of static fills the room, and I flinch slightly at the invasion of noise. "Center of the circle, please," comes a deep, synthesized, Great-and-Powerful-Oz-type voice, and I do as instructed. After a long silence, during which time I shift back and forth from foot to foot, wondering when the visual inspection will be over, the light over my head clicks off again, and a slight whirr fills the air. A new source of light appears to my left, and I turn just in time to see a divider sliding up and out of the way, revealing a small room beyond.

Eddie sits in the peep booth, but rather than manhandling himself, he's got his fist clenched around a very nasty-looking handgun. I'm not certain about the caliber of that thing, but I can tell it's a seriously big bore.

"Vinnie," he cackles, his voice cracking as it rises higher. "Is that you?"

"It's me, boss," I say, turning to face him.

"Turn around," he instructs.

I pirouette, letting him get a good look at my whole costume. At the very least, I hope I get a tip out of this.

"The window," he instructs. "The back of your neck."

He wants to sniff me; so be it. Ten small holes, set in a circular pattern, have been drilled into each Plexiglas window, allowing the patrons to get a sniff of their fantasy girl. But Eddie just wants to make sure I am who I say I am. At least, I hope that's all he wants.

So I press my neck against the glass, and hear Eddie snorting away.

A relieved sigh from the booth. "You're my man, Vinnie."

"I know it, sir," I reply, turning back around, stepping into the center of the stage.

"You're my man."

The handgun, I notice, is not the only weapon Eddie's got in that little booth. There's a rifle on the floor by his feet, and clips of ammunition wrapped around his waist. Probably hiding a grenade or two in his belt; at this point, I make no assumptions and assume the worst.

"What's goin' on here, Eddie?" I ask, keeping my tone as calm and nonconfrontational as possible. Back in the day, Dan Patterson worked a few jumper calls, and he told me the only way to keep folks from doing harm to themselves or others was to start up a patter and never stop. "Never thought I'd be seeing you from this angle."

He cackles again, the laugh of an insane seagull, and bangs the handgun against the Plexiglas. "They're all gone, Vinnie. All of them."

"All of who?"

"My people," he cries, banging the gun barrel into the window over and over again. I wonder if the safety is on. More to the point, I wonder if this divider is bulletproof and up to code. I'd hate to die because someone at the Plexiglas factory was late coming back from lunch and decided to forgo the inspection on lot twelve. "Sherman—gone. JT—gone. Jerry—gone."

"I'm sorry about that, Eddie, I really am."

"All of 'em, gone."

"What about the one outside?" I ask. "The little guy, smells like soup?"

Eddie shakes his head. "Alvin ain't part of the family. He's Frank's wife's sister's boyfriend, that's all."

"I see."

"You know how those fucks sent me Jerry, Vinnie?"

Of course I do. I helped with the arrangement. "Not really—"

"In a pot! In a fucking *pot*, Vinnie. All cut up with two palm trees poking outta his body. That ain't right for nobody."

"I agree." This time around, I'm not lying. It wasn't fun.

He begins pacing, rapidly bouncing back and forth inside the five-foot booth, slamming from wall to wall like a pinball spinning out of control. Waving the handgun over his head, unconcerned with the direction of the barrel. "And they're gunning for me next," he cries. "I can feel it."

"Maybe you're just being paranoid, Eddie—"

"You're damn right I'm paranoid!" he screams, slamming into

the glass once again. The window bends beneath his weight, the pressure warping his features, twisting his snarl into a bizarre grin, and I wonder what it takes to snap one of these things.

But he backs off, slumping to the floor of the booth, his sudden energy spent. "Christ, Vinnie," he moans. "How'd it get to this, huh?"

I take this as a cue to bring everything down a notch, and I approach the glass slowly. Cautiously, I sit down, cross-legged, on the floor across from Eddie's booth. "Things fall apart," I tell him, citing Ernie's logic. I don't know if he'd approve.

"Got that right."

"We just gotta stand up straight and put it all back together."

He thinks it over for a second, nodding slowly. When he looks back up at me, his eyes are a bright yellow; his contacts must have popped out sometime during his manic phase. The irises are shot through with tiny bolts of crimson.

A buzzer interrupts our conversation and the metal divider suddenly descends in front of the Plexiglas, separating Eddie and me once more. Time's up.

"Mother*fucker!*" I hear him yell, and then, softer, "Hold on, Vinnie, I gotta get some more quarters."

So I sit alone in the peep show, waiting for Eddie to return. There's no guarantee that some other dino looking for his jollies won't come in here, press his face against the glass, drop his drawers, and plop down some change of his own, but he'll be in for a very different kind of show if he does.

A knock at the door, and suddenly Eddie is inside, his pockets turned inside out. "No change left," he says sheepishly, stepping into the circle, hugging me close. "No fucking change left, Vinnie."

There's no way to respond, so I accept the hug and step back. Eddie surveys me from his new vantage point. "You look . . . different, Vin."

"Same old me," I point out.

"Yeah, yeah, same old you. But there's something . . . Maybe you toughened up a bit, huh? Maybe we put some iron in those bones of yours."

"Maybe that's it," I say. "Listen—"

"Where'd you drop off to?" he asks, suddenly all business, and I realize that he's still holding the gun in his right hand, finger curled over the trigger guard. "I know you're friends with those Dugan apefuckers."

"Friends? I wouldn't go that far—"

"Oh yeah," he says. "Frank told me all about it. Said you and Jack went way back."

Frank? How the hell did Frank know about my relationship with Jack Dugan? As far as Frank Tallarico was concerned, I was hired to follow Nelly Hagstrom during an L.A. business deal. Did he have prior knowledge of my relationship with Jack? And, if so, why?

But Eddie's not giving me time to think it over. "So, lemme ask you again. Where'd you run off to?"

"Nowhere, Eddie—"

"Nowhere is right. All of a sudden, the shit comes down, Vincent's nowhere to be found." Now he's heating up again, circling me like a bull trying to figure out what to do with this pesky matador in front of him. The reflections from the peep-show windows give me seven more images of Eddie, pacing the room, spiraling in on me.

"Wait a sec, Eddie—"

"It makes me *nervous* to see one of my guys—my main man— disappear on me like that. Makes me nervous thinking about what he's doing—"

"Gimme a second," I say, "and I'll tell you—"

"Nervous as all hell, and I'll tell you, Vincent, I get itchy when I get nervous." He's got that hand cannon at waist level now, keeping the damned thing aimed more or less at my chest. I'd expected him to have a weapon; I didn't expect it to be so large. Then again, a bullet is a bullet—big or small, it tends to put holes where holes shouldn't be.

I drop a hand, reaching for my right pants pocket. "I got something here—"

"Watch that hand, Rubio—" Raising the gun higher.

"Something that might explain where I've been," I continue, keeping it cool, keeping it even, taking one breath after another as I reach into the pocket—

Eddie takes a swift step forward, pressing the barrel of the gun into my forehead, the cool metal ring firm against the latex flesh. "Goddammit, I'll pull this trigger—"

"Eddie—"

"Get your hand out now—"

"Eddie—"

His finger tightens on the trigger—I can see the trembling of his knuckles, the twitching muscle beneath. But I hold it steady; it's the only way to play it now. Eddie wants to believe, wants to know I'm on his side. I'm all he's got, and if he wants to see what's going down, he'll let me live.

"There," I say, pulling out the photograph and dropping it to the floor. "That's what I been doing these days. That's what I've been doing for you."

His finger still on the trigger, the gun still pressed into my head, Eddie glances down at the floor, at the photo flipped faceup, the beautiful bright Kodak moment. The blood is particularly red.

"Is that . . . Hagstrom?" he asks, half-suspicious, half-awed.

"It is," I say, reaching up and slowly pushing down on Eddie's right arm. He doesn't even realize I'm diverting the gun to the floor—he's more caught up in the picture now than any potential threat I represent.

Eddie lifts the photograph by a corner and holds it up to the light. It's a clear shot of Nelly Hagstrom tied to a chair in some faceless location, his body covered in blood, bruises, welts. One pathetic eye peers up at the camera as if to say *Stop, please stop.*

"This is from you?" he asks.

"A present," I grin. "For the boss man."

Eddie takes another look, running his fingers over Nelly's tortured body. "You do good work."

"Thanks," I say. "But it's not finished yet."

This gets renewed attention, some of Eddie's mania flaring up again. "What's that?"

"He's still there. I left him alive for you."

"For me?" he asks, a wide-eyed tyke who can't believe it when the ten-speed he wanted is there under the tree on Christmas morning.

"For you," I say. "'Cause I'm your man."

Eddie shows me the back way out of The Dirty Dozen, and we take to the streets. Inside Jack's Mercedes, Eddie crouches in the backseat, ducked down low, the pistol tucked into the waistband of his pants.

The drive to the warehouse is short, five minutes at the most, Eddie pestering me with questions the whole time: "How'd you get him? Is he talking? Can he still see?" and me trying to answer them on the fly as best I can while at the same time trying to make connections in my mind. Frank, Eddie, Jack, Noreen, Audrey—the matrix of relationships and betrayals finally begins to emerge.

We park outside the big building and Eddie hops out of the car, hand hovering over the butt of his gun. "He inside?" Eddie asks.

"Right in there," I say, and lead the way.

It's dark in the warehouse, but a strategically placed light illuminates the centerpiece: Nelly Hagstrom, trussed and beaten. Drying pools of blood surround the chair, and Nelly doesn't move as we enter; his head hangs low, his body limp.

"Christ Almighty." Eddie laughs, his paranoia gone, his sense of power rising. He steps into the building and I close the door behind us, quietly locking it up tight.

Tallarico doesn't care; he approaches Nelly confidently, casually, as if he's got all the time in the world. Kneeling down, he gets a good look at Hagstrom's face, his body, the blood caked onto the skin. "You did a number on him, kid," he says, turning back to face me. "You sure he's alive?"

"Oh, yeah," I say. "I'm real sure of it."

Eddie turns back around, that grin still etched in his face—to find Pop Dugan, whipping an iron bar at his head.

Tallarico flinches backward, hands coming up to protect his face, the bar catching him halfway up his forearm, and I hear a sharp crack—something broke. But this is no time to play amateur osteopath; Eddie's screaming, going for his gun even as Nelly, not injured in the least, leaps out of the chair—

I reach back and whip out my own rod, a telescoping iron beam that whistles through the air and smacks hard into the side of Eddie's head. He crumples to the floor instantly, the gun clattering to the ground next to his inert body.

"That was a little hard," Hagstrom says, dropping to one knee to check Eddie's pulse.

"He had a gun—"

"Don't sweat it. He's alive." Hagstrom clears away the fake blood we applied to his face and body, wiping it onto his already messy shirt.

"He better be," says Pop Dugan, dropping the rod to his side. "I want a crack at him, too."

Pop wasn't part of the plan; we'd agreed to keep him in the dark about the more unsavory elements of our plan. I look to Hagstrom, who shrugs. "I had to tell him," Nelly says. "He had a right to know."

Pop's cheeks pull back, and I can see him fighting off the tears. Both of his children killed in one week—there's no gauging the depth of his sorrow and loneliness. If he needs to help in order to get over his grief, then I won't be the one to stand in his way. Especially when he's so damned good with an iron rod. I give him a quick hug, and he clings tightly before letting me go.

Hagstrom steps behind us. "You ready to do this?"

"Not a bit."

"Good. Then let's hustle."

Nelly grabs Eddie's hands, and I get the guy's feet, and though we've done this before, it's clear from the first heave that he's at least three times Noreen's weight. We stumble out to the car, checking around to make sure there's no one else in sight, then dump Tallarico into the trunk, hog-tying him just in case he comes around during the forty-minute drive to the next location. When I whack folks in the head, they usually stay whacked, but I'm giving nothing up to chance. I haven't come this far just to screw up now. There will be ample time for mistakes if I ever manage to make it back home in one piece.

18

"Best thing about the Everglades," Hagstrom is saying to me as we tie the final knots around Eddie's feet and check the tension in the line, "is that it's big. Real big. Folks think about Florida, they either go right to Disneyworld, or they come all the way down to Miami, but no one thinks about the Everglades. Millions of acres of swampland, none of it inhabited, none of it patrolled—not heavily, at least. So it's good for . . . sensitive issues, like this one."

"Fuck you!" Eddie screams, his voice carrying far into the wilderness and dying out somewhere among the mangroves. "Fuck all of you! Rubio, when I get my hands on you—"

Nelly gives the rope another tug and Eddie, hung upside down by his tail, yelps in pain. "That's right," says Hagstrom, "keep it up, big guy."

Eddie's a good twenty feet away, dangling over a marshy expanse of water, hovering five feet above the surface. I wonder if the blood is rushing to his head yet. I wonder if he even notices. His face is flushed with anger, and if he's already got high blood pressure, I have a feeling he'll pop like a balloon any moment now. Hopefully we'll get what we want before then.

The rope tied to his tail is also wrapped around his feet for extra stability, then looped over a strong tree branch fifteen feet up. Nelly, Pop, and I stand on a wooden platform crudely built into the muddy shore. Nothing here is truly water or truly land; it's all a murky mixture, but Nelly knows where to step and where to avoid. He's been here before.

". . . and your children," Eddie is shouting again. "And your children's children."

"No kids to speak of," Hagstrom says.

"Me neither," I add. "And you already took care of that for Pop here. Sorry, Eddie. It's just the four of us. Well, for now, anyway."

A nearby splash echoes through the stillness of the swamp, and Hagstrom peers through the trees. "Might be him," he mutters. "Not sure."

"Want me to throw a chicken?" I ask.

"Sure," he says. "We got a bunch."

I reach into a Styrofoam cooler by my side, packed to the brim with defrosted raw chickens, and grab one by the leg. It's cold, slimy, and probably infested with a zillion germs, but I don't think the denizens of this deep will mind. "Any particular location?" I ask.

"Take your pick," says Nelly. "Just throw it far."

I toss the chicken high into the air, and we watch it sail in a wide arc across the swamp, heading for a splashdown ten feet away from Eddie's writhing figure. Before the airborne poultry actually strikes the surface, a massive wave of water bursts up as a gargantuan alligator leaps out of the bog and snatches it whole in his mouth like an oversized mutt catching a Frisbee. Only, Rover never swallowed his toys whole.

"Jesus Christ!" Eddie yelps, trying to twist his body away from the gator, flopping around like a fish on the line. But the rope holds steady, dangling him precariously over the water, just out of reach of the gator's last bite.

"We call him Snappy," Hagstrom calls out to Eddie. "I know it's not the most creative name in the world, but we were pressed for time."

I say, "I think he's kinda cute."

Pop Dugan nods. "It's the teeth."

"Yeah, definitely the teeth. He's very photogenic."

Eddie starts in with the screaming again, his high-pitched yowls more likely to attract the lowland creatures than repel them, but I'm not going to get in the way of any man's mating calls.

"Now, Eddie," I say, my grip tight on the rope holding Tallarico in place. "We can do this the easy way, the hard way, or the fun way."

"You backstabber—you lousy apefucker—"

I shake my head. "Flattery will get you nowhere. Now, the easy way is for you to tell us who your source is inside our organization."

"Bite me."

"No, that's Snappy's job," says Hagstrom. "And that, my friend, would be the hard way. The fun way is to spin you back and forth and let you hang there and starve to death, but of course it's only fun for us."

Eddie's clammed up. He's knocked off the curses and the screams and just hangs there, upside down, quiet as a ten-point buck on the first day of hunting season. Now that he's out of guise, I can see that my original prediction was correct: he's one chubby dude. It's rare to see a paunch on a Velociraptor, but he's packed on the weight over the years, and it explains the need for his custom guise. Hanging there as he is, the flab sags down, nearly covering up his smallish chest.

"He ain't going for it," Hagstrom says.

"No," I say, keeping to the vernacular, "he ain't."

"Throw another chicken."

I do my best Nolan Ryan with this one, winding up and really letting it go, placing the bird only five feet to the left of Eddie's dangling form. This time Snappy isn't so quick on the draw—he waits until it actually splashes down before he surfaces, his four-foot jaw clamping open and shut as he chews the appetizer-sized portion.

Eddie starts screaming again.

"That's getting old, Eddie," I sigh. "You wanna scream something *useful,* maybe we can do business." There's nothing from Tallarico but more caterwauling, though, so I turn back to Hagstrom. "Another chicken?"

"We don't want Snappy to lose his appetite."

"Hell, we're a long way from that. This is just popcorn before the movie."

Hagstrom nods and takes a step backwards, grasping the rope between his hands, bracing it with his right foot. He gives me a little nod, and I let go of my end; this part is a one-person job.

Pop Dugan takes the reins. "We're gonna play a little game, Eddie. You like games?"

All that comes out of his mouth is a soft mewling, a little hiccough.

"Good enough," Pop continues. "This one is called Lower the Asshole into the Lake with the Big Freaking Alligator."

"That's a little wordy," I point out.

"But it's easy to play. See, Nelly, Vincent, and I are going to ask you questions, and if we don't like the answers, we drop you another foot. Maybe Vincent throws a chicken in the water. Maybe he throws a rock, and Snappy gets real pissed off. Sound like fun?"

The roar that erupts from Eddie's mouth is primal, animal, and I take an instinctive step backwards. It's pure dino, that roar, a terrifying screech that's probably sent every bird for miles flocking home to Mommy. But it saps Eddie of all his remaining strength, and even the braggadocio and bluster are now gone.

"Super," I say. "Let's get started. Question one: Who made the bomb that blew up Jack Dugan's yacht?"

No response. Eddie just glares at us, refusing to play along.

"Now, technically," Nelly says, "he's not giving us an incorrect answer."

"True. But he's not giving us a correct answer, either." I think it over for less than a second. "Drop him."

Nelly loosens the rope and Eddie instantly plummets, his shriek simultaneous with the drop. Hagstrom catches him a split second later, but he's already a good foot lower than he was, eyes wide, efforts to escape redoubled.

"Let's try that again," I say.

Hagstrom grabs a chicken—"And for incentive . . ."—and tosses it into the swamp. It lands hard on an island of muck and begins to sink into the soft earth. But there's no Snappy.

A triumphant look on Eddie's face is erased a second later, when the maw of the gator pops from the water and swallows the chicken, the mud island, and the roots from a nearby mangrove tree in a single, catastrophic chomp.

"It was Sherman!" he cries, arching his body away from the surface of the water, trying to do the very first sit-up of his life.

I nod to Hagstrom, and he pulls back on the rope an inch or two. Not enough to get Eddie out of hot water, but enough to impress him that we're playing by the rules.

"Good," I say. "Then let's move on. How did Sherman know Noreen and Audrey would be on the boat?"

Another moment of silence, and Nelly sighs. I start humming the theme to *Jaws*. "*Dum*-dumm. *Dum*-dumm . . ."

"You realize that's about a shark, right?" asks Hagstrom.

"Couldn't remember the theme to *Alligator*."

"Fair enough," says Nelly, loosening his hold on the rope. "Should I drop him again?"

"No!" Eddie interrupts. "No, I—I don't know how he knew."

"You don't know? I find that unlikely."

"I mean—he knew because of the guy we've got in your crew. The source. We'd dropped off a package, this thing Sherman had made, a timer and remote and all that—and said if he got the chance, he should plant it."

"So you're saying Sherman made it, but the source planted the bomb?"

Eddie nods as best he can; all his blood is probably concentrated in his head right now, and I hope the bastard's got a pounding migraine.

"And all the others," Pop says, "Jack and Noreen and the rest . . . You got their whereabouts and movements from this guy, too? This rat gave it all up?"

Another nod from Eddie, and I can see Nelly's anger begin to take over his motions. His hands slipping from the rope, wanting to dunk Tallarico into the swamp here and now.

"You got that thing tight?" I ask.

"Tight enough," he growls, keeping his eyes locked on Eddie's. "For the moment."

"Fine," I say, clapping my hands together. "So, now the big question: Who's the source?"

Eddie doesn't hesitate. "I don't know."

"Drop him," I say, and Nelly is happy to comply. The rope slithers out of his hands, whooshing against the tree bark up above as Eddie's three-hundred-pound body plunges toward the bog and the gator below.

Nelly's timing is perfect: he waits until Eddie's head is nearly dunked beneath the water, then quickly applies tension to the rope, stopping him just shy of a certainly fatal splash.

The Raptor's breath is coming fast now; he's beyond screams. He's also beyond proper sentence structure. "Don't know," he babbles. "Know! Don't—I don't—who I don't—know who—"

I haul another chicken out of the cooler and tuck it under my chin like a shot-putter ready to approach the line. "Calm down, Eddie, or we end this right now."

"I don't know!" he screams again, offering us his first grammatical utterance in a while. "We leave messages, that's all, I swear it!"

"Messages?"

"Voicemail. It's a central line. I call in with my information, and I get information back. That's it."

"How do you pay?" I ask.

"Drop point," says Eddie, his eyes bouncing across the water, looking for any sign of Snappy's return. "We drop the money off at this abandoned dock out here in the Glades. Someone comes and picks it up. Frank set the whole thing up."

"Frank, as in your brother, Frank?" I ask.

"Yeah, yeah, it was all Frank's doing. He's the one that did it."

So the elder Tallarico has definitely had more of a hand in this than I'd ever imagined. Maybe he didn't want me down in Miami to tail Hagstrom after all; maybe he wanted me here to facilitate some bigger scheme.

Hagstrom yanks on the rope, drawing Eddie away from the water's surface, and the Raptor's face floods with relief. "Tell me something, Eddie. When's the next payment to this rat?"

"Tomorrow night," he says. "I can cut it off if you want, fellas— make sure the money isn't dropped off—"

"No, no," I interrupt. "We want the payment to go down. Only you're going to leave a voicemail, and make a few changes."

"I am?"

"You are."

"I think—"

"Don't think," Hagstrom says. "Just do." He whips out his cellular phone, a small flip model, and holds it aloft. "You're going to call, and you're going to leave a message telling the source that you want to meet. That you want to thank him for a job well done, in person, give him a bonus for a job well done."

"Nelly," Eddie says, addressing Hagstrom by his first name for a change, "we can work something out, you and me. We could run this town—"

"I already do. Listen up, you megalomaniacal fuck, because I'm only saying this once. You will call, and you will leave this message, and if you do it right, Vincent and I will let you go free. You'll leave town, leave the state—the fucking country, if you know what's good for you. But you'll live, and I give you my word on that.

"But if you do anything hinky—if you make a sound, a single word I don't like, one single thing to screw this deal—I'll drop you into this water faster than a newscaster can say 'His corpse was mauled by gators.' Are we clear?"

Eddie nods, but Nelly wants a verbal agreement. "*Are we clear?*" he asks again.

"Yes," says Tallarico softly. He's broken down, a shell of his former self.

Nelly rears back and tosses his phone through the air; Eddie reaches out to catch it, and the Nokia bounces off Eddie's fingers and into the water below, disappearing into the Everglades.

We stand there, the four of us—well, three standing, one hanging—and stare down at the bog, at the place where the phone vanished.

"Well . . ." I say.

"Well," repeats Hagstrom. "That's a tickler."

I'm about to move on to Plan B when I remember that I've got a cell of my own. It's not as fancy as Nelly's, but it gets decent service, even out here in the boonies.

"Try this one more time," I say, "and if you don't catch this one, I can promise you, you're going in after it." He gives me the number to dial and I punch it in. After a second or two, there's a long beep, and I know the recording process has begun.

I flip the cell to Eddie, a loping, awkward pass, but Eddie twists his body to the left and makes the catch of a lifetime, especially considering his wrists are still bound together.

"Go," I mouth to him, and he starts in.

"Hey," he says, keeping his tone even, Nelly's hand firm on the rope but ready to release at any moment, "it's Eddie T. Just wanted to say I'm real happy with the work you done, and I wanna meet up for the next money exchange. Maybe have some coffee, that sorta thing. So same place as before, same time. Maybe you and me, we can do some more business together."

Nelly's giving him the high sign, and Eddie wraps it up with a curt "See ya there."

"My phone?" I ask, and he hurls it back to land, the kind of lame-duck throw that presidents toss out on the first day of the baseball season. I retrieve it from the mud, wipe it down, and put it back in my pants pocket.

"So, that's it, right?" asks Eddie, a tremor of optimism in his voice. "I'm all done, you cut me down, we go our separate ways?"

Nelly gives me a glance, but this isn't my decision. "Family business," I tell him. "It's your call."

Eddie suddenly realizes that something's up, that Hagstrom's promise to let him go might not have been completely on the level. "Jesus," he says, his timbre rising to his usual screech, "you can't do this—"

"Why not?" asks Nelly.

"You promised—you swore—you gave your word—"

"What I said was that *Vincent and I* were gonna let you go. I never said anything about Pop here."

Eddie's flopping madly now; I can see the claws on his hands flashing in and out, powered by adrenaline, futilely scratching at the air. "No—no—"

"Pop," says Nelly, "this one's all yours."

Pop Dugan shuffles toward the rope and slowly slides out a single black claw. It's scratched, dull, but sharp enough to do the job.

He expertly slices through half of the rope holding Eddie in place. "This is for Jack," he says.

At that, Eddie loses it completely, the syllables streaming from his mouth no more comprehensible than conversational Martian, a single stream of petrified babble—

"And this," he says, positioning his claw against the already frayed strands, "is for Noreen."

Eddie isn't halfway in the water before Snappy is there, somehow bigger than before, his entire jaw clamped around Tallarico's torso, the teeth digging into his fleshy midsection. He screams once, twice, beating his fists against the alligator's snout, trying to dig his claws into some sensitive part of the beast, but there's no fighting it. The gator flips over three times in succession, full rolls that knock Eddie senseless, and within seconds the murky-brown swamp is a little redder than it used to be. Snappy's bulbous eyes remain above the surface for just a moment, locking on ours as if to say *Our business is concluded here,* before disappearing under the water, taking the last of the Miami Tallarico family with him.

There's no sleep for me tonight. Instead, I lay awake in the cot at the safe house, staring at the popcorn ceiling. I can almost feel the Dugan clan around me—not helping, not hindering, just looking on, waiting to see what I'm going to do next. Sometimes I get the feeling that Ernie's there, too, judging me, waiting for each action so he can comment, so he can say *Good job, kid,* or *Whoa, you pooched that one good.*

The next day is all about preparations. Nelly makes arrangements to rent an airboat to take us through the Glades, out to the abandoned dock for the money drop. I make a phone call to Sutherland to find out what I already know—that Frank Tallarico's phone records show he's been calling the same voicemail number as Eddie, setting things up from three thousand miles away.

And then it's just a question of muscle. Nelly and I don't want to take a chance with this guy; he might be bigger than us, stronger than us, and we're already aware that he knows how to set explosives. We want numbers on our side.

"I've got two guys," Nelly tells me. "A couple of soldiers, and they're clean."

"Good," I say. "More the merrier."

"They'll be packing heat."

"Guns?"

Nelly nods. "We should, too."

The very thought leaves a bad taste in my mouth. I haven't touched a gun since the Progressives mess back in Hawaii, and even then I wasn't thrilled about it. It's the smell more than anything—that tangy, metallic scent, sharp and painful. "Down to their level," I say. "That's monkey work."

"I know it is, but we know the Tallaricos aren't shy about putting a bullet through the air."

"Still—"

Hagstrom holds up a hand and approaches me, pulling back the thick mop of hair attached to his head. There, in the middle of his forehead, is the puckered scar; he seems to be calling attention to it.

"You see this?" he asks, and I nod. "This is what happens when you let your guard down when it comes to ape weapons."

"They . . . shot you?"

"A mammal crew," he explains, dropping the hair back into place. "When we first got down here, started coming up. A small war, nothing big, but I was on their list. Coming out of a club I owned, they tried to take me out from a distance, and I had no way to defend myself at a hundred feet. One shot, that's all it takes— the bullet went straight through—guise, scales, right at my brain."

"You lived."

"Thick skull." He laughs, knocking at his noggin. "The bullet's still there, halfway in the bone. The scales healed right over it, and I had the guise sewn to match."

"Doctors can't get it out?" I ask.

"They can. But the bullet—the scar—it's a reminder, every day. I can't take chances when it comes to adversaries who fight like the mammals. Claws don't cut it long-range. Guns do."

He's right, and I know he's right. But despite the overwhelming sense of his argument, I can't get past my innate distaste for the things. "You three pack the heat," I suggest. "I'll go without."

"You sure on this?"

"I'm sure."

Hagstrom puts his hand on my shoulder, and I put mine on his. Ten days ago, this would have meant an all-out battle, and most likely ended with either Jack or Noreen telling us to cut it out and shake hands. Now, we just stare at each other, and understand that whatever's going on inside our heads, we're probably thinking the same thing.

We cruise over the water at a gentle ten knots, keeping our speed low even as our profile grows higher. There's just no good way to sneak up on anyone in an airboat; these things are the mechanical poster children for noise pollution, but they get the job done. With all of the below-the-surface roots clogging up the Everglades tributaries, any normal propeller boat would get bogged down within seconds of leaving the dock. So these airboats, equipped with giant fans strapped to the back like some third-grader's science fair project, are the only way to go.

Nelly is to the left of me, steering the boat through the canals, the mangrove trees thick on either side of us. I don't know how he navigates his way through this swamp, but I get the idea that it's a popular mafia hangout for both sides, and always a good place to dispose of an annoying corpse or two. None of the newspapers made mention of Eddie Tallarico's disappearance, which means they haven't found any remains of his body yet. If Snappy was hungry enough, they never will.

I don't even know the names of the two soldiers Nelly brought along, and I don't want to. This isn't about revenge anymore, and it's not about honor or family pride. This is about finishing a job, even though it's not the one I was paid to do. I've still technically got two days left on my contract with Frank Tallarico, and though I intend to honor them—I'm following Hagstrom, aren't I?—other priorities have moved ahead on my list.

Eight forty-five. We're early, and that suits us fine. We want a glimpse of the mole before he gets a glimpse of us. It's all about information at this stage of the game, and though I have a feeling things are going to go very quickly once it all comes down, I don't want to be the one scratching his head in the corner.

So we wait. Nelly guides the airboat into the reeds and we shut the lights, covering up with a few leaves to give us the proper camouflage-in-'Nam look. The abandoned dock is just across the way, a light South Florida fog settling in, obscuring all but the largest objects.

"Here we go," I whisper to Nelly.

"Yep."

"You know," I tell him, "I thought it was you for a while."

"I know," he replies. "And I thought it was you."

We sit there in silence, knowing exactly why we each changed our minds. One of us has to bring it up; it might as well be me. "You miss her today?"

"Even more than yesterday," he says.

"Me too."

The air is still, the sounds of the Everglades soft and wild. A heron calling out its final cry of the evening, a gator sliding into the water to sleep off a kill. Nice place, if you can stand the stink.

It's a quiet spot, Nelly told me before we left. A spot where no one will bother us. I can't imagine that there are many spots out here in the Everglades where someone *would* be around to bother us, but this isn't my neck of the woods, and even the most seemingly uninhabited locations can stink with unseen denizens. But if Nelly says this place is clean, then it's clean.

We cut through a thicket of tall reeds, the long stems bowing down before us as the airboat slides into a small circular area surrounded by high mangroves. It's a little oasis of pure water in the middle of all this vegetation. Nelly gives his soldier the cut-off signal and he shuts down the fan, the big propeller blades slowing to a halt.

Glenda hasn't said a word.

"Here we are," I say, indicating that she can speak once again.

She nods. "Here we are."

I don't know if this is something Nelly wanted to do, but I think he understands, given the change of circumstances, that it's something I need to take care of instead. He backs off, stepping to the side to allow me better access to Glenda.

"Anything you want to tell me?" I ask.

Glenda grins, that wide joker of a face I know so well. "Guess this means I don't get the fifty grand, huh?"

"No." I laugh, allowing myself a real chuckle for the first time in days. "No, that's not happening."

"And Eddie?"

"Eddie's gone," I tell her. "He's not coming back."

She nods again. "Good. I hated that ugly bastard."

"But you worked for him."

Glenda takes a seat on the floor of the airboat, and I lower myself to the ground across from her. If we're going to be casual, we might as well be comfortable, too. "I worked for Frank," she corrects me. "Eddie was a side note. I didn't exactly have a choice about that."

Nelly steps into the conversation. "You were paid by Frank Tallarico?"

"Originally, yeah." She's not holding anything back. There's no point in secrets anymore, and Glenda knows it. Always a smart girl, making the smart move. Almost always. "Last few weeks, I picked up some money here at the docks, from Eddie's crew."

It doesn't take me long to put it together. "A few months back, when we talked, you told me you were in debt, pretty bad."

"To a loanshark," she admits. "Boss of the Raptor family up there."

My chest feels heavy, hard. "You coulda called me, Glen."

"You had your own shit to deal with. Thought I could handle it, you know? Make a little here, pay off a little there. But it got tough, and I had to go to a shark, and . . ."

"And Frank Tallarico bought your debt."

She nods. "Almost a hundred grand, without the vig. Told me I could work it off, and all I had to do was go down to Miami with a buddy of mine."

A birdcall breaks the stillness of the night, and we all jump a little. The breeze is light, but warm, and I find myself wondering what it would feel like to strip off all my clothes and dive into the water, to swim away from all this and never stop until I hit land, somewhere in the Caribbean, where the sky is clear and your best friends are as true blue as the water.

I remember back to the night Jack was killed, when Glenda was conveniently on the ground even before the bullets started flying.

I remember her face when we drove up to the marina, how her false skin was flushed, her eyes darting around like she'd nearly been caught doing something wrong. How something in the air smelled faintly of gunpowder.

I remember how she was in on all the meetings with the guys, how she knew where each of them would be, and at what times. How she even recommended places to go, places to hide out, where they'd be safe from the Tallarico gang.

I remember more than I care to remember, and more than I'll

ever forget. And Glenda knows that I know, and doesn't offer a single excuse. I'll give her that, at least—she's not trying to delude anyone, least of all herself.

"You know what you've done," I tell her.

"I do." Glenda takes a breath and tries out the sentence she must have been saying to herself all this time. "I was just a hired gun. It's not my business."

"It's not," I tell her. "And it wasn't mine, either. But you knew I was getting on that boat. You could have stopped me."

She's ashamed, it's clear, and that's usually the first step in admitting guilt. "I didn't know what to do. By the time I realized you were getting on the boat, it was too late."

"There's a time when you've got to make a mark in the sand and stand on either side of it," I explain.

Glenda's laugh is morose, almost wistful, twisting the side of her mouth. "You're sounding more like Ernie every day, Rubio."

"Thanks." She means it as a compliment, and I know it. But it makes me think of my old partner, and the way he would have handled this. The way he would have asked questions from the very beginning. The way he would never have gotten himself roped into this whole mess in the first place. "When you showed up at my place in L.A. and said I'd invited you to town—we'd never had that conversation, Glen?"

"Nah," she admits. "Figured it'd make it seem more natural I was just showin' up like that, pretend you'd forgotten it, what with the basil blackouts and all."

"Good ruse," I tell her. "Good play."

Nelly takes a step forward and places a hand on my shoulder. I don't need to look at a watch to know that the time schedule we set up is already off base. We have to finish this quickly, one way or the other.

I hop up and help Glenda to her feet. We stand there, a foot apart from each other, with nothing more to say. There are a million words we could exchange, lengthy speeches to each other in which we could philosophize about what we've done, about what we've become, but in the end, it would all be sound and fury.

"So now what?" she asks.

I can feel them—Jack, Noreen, everyone—pushing me forward, urging me to make a decision, to wrap this up, to bring some closure. They're not giving any suggestions as to the direction, but they want it finished so they can go about the process of disappearing into the void.

The first time we met, Glenda was standing by a hot dog cart, joking around with the vendor, telling him one dirty joke after the other, making him double over in laughter.

". . . wait a second, you heard me wrong," she was saying, winding up some raunchy punch line, "I didn't say I wanted a twelve-inch *pianist!*"

I was coming down off stakeout duty, one of my first gigs away from Ernie, and was in a foul mood. All I wanted was a bite of lunch and a quiet place to rest my head. But here was this loud, foulmouthed New Yorker, of all things, come along to ruin both plans at once.

"Hey," I said, after waiting five minutes for the vendor to recognize my existence, "some of us are waiting to eat over here."

That's when Glenda turned around, placed her hot dog in my hand, said, "Eat, bubbie, eat, God forbid you should starve," and then brought me into the rest of the conversation, spinning my head for an hour and a half with jokes so raw they made me blush straight through my guise.

When I think of Glenda, years from now, I won't think of her as this staid, sober creature standing in the middle of an airboat, blindly accepting whatever fate I choose to mete out. I won't think of her as a Hadrosaur who arranged for the deaths of countless other dinos. I won't think of her as the gal who betrayed me.

I'll think of her as the one who lifted me up when I was low, and who hauled my ass into action when self-pity had drowned all my will to go on. She'll always be that crude, annoying, and wonderful gal down by the hot dog stand.

"I'm sorry," I say, and Nelly takes my cue, moving his soldiers to either side of her, their presence solid, commanding. Glenda starts to shake a little; her hand trembles as she wipes away a single tear.

"This is how it's gotta be?"

"Yeah," I say. "Yeah, it is."

"I could skip town. Live in Europe for a while."

Nelly shakes his head. This is personal for me—for Jack, for Noreen, for my own well-being—but for Nelly it's business, too, and his livelihood depends on our getting it right this evening.

"I'm sorry, Glen," I repeat. "You can't imagine . . ."

The soldiers reach into their pockets and pull out matching pistols, direct the barrels toward Glenda's forehead; the sight of these human weapons sends a chill through me, and before they can step forward and finish the job, I put out a hand.

"Wait," I say, Glenda nearly collapsing with relief. "Not like that."

Nelly cocks his head, but I take a step forward. My chest feels heavy. Is it the air again? Is it the humidity? "Step back," I order.

Nelly nods, and the soldiers move away as I step behind Glenda, dragging my left arm around her chest, hugging her close, feeling her body next to mine. I move in behind her, my front pressed to her back, and we stay there for a moment, my face buried in her hair.

This is the hardest thing I've ever had to do, and I tell her as much.

"Then don't do it," she says.

I extend my middle claw, the sharpest, cleanest one of the bunch, and whisper, "I have to."

Glenda closes her eyes as I draw my claw across the soft nape of her neck, a soft coo escaping from her lips as she stiffens in my grasp—

I stop. My body feels lighter, my chest loose. As if that hard nugget of coal that's been wrapping itself around my heart for the last two weeks is beginning to break apart. I try to reach inward, to feel that comfortable ice, that rage and steel I felt when I held Noreen's limp polysuit on the Fort Lauderdale beach, but it's not there. Slowly, I may be coming back to myself.

"Take us back," I tell Nelly.

For a moment, I think he's smiling. "Are you sure? It's your call."

"I'm sure. Take us back to shore."

Hagstrom fires up the airboat and maneuvers the craft back toward dry land. Glenda doesn't say a word on the ride back, but doesn't try to squirm out of my grasp, either.

As we approach the dock, the wood planks poking out like a runway into the swamp water, I whisper in Glenda's ear. "Run. Get off the boat and run away and don't quit running, because I can't stop them once they're out of my sight."

Glenda nods and squeezes my hand in hers. We travel the last twenty feet in a tight clench, wondering if this is the last time we'll ever be this close with our hearts still beating. As soon as we reach the dock, she's off the airboat and speeding into the night, disappearing beneath the canopy of mangroves and palms.

Once she's gone, Nelly sits on the edge of the airboat, dangling his feet in the water below. I plop down next to him, the remaining strength draining out of my legs.

"You're not one of us, Vincent," he says softly. "You never were."

"I know it."

"I think it's time for you to go home."

"Yeah. I think so, too." I look out into the Everglades, at the still, peaceful water with all that danger hiding just beneath the surface. "Somebody's gotta feed the cat."

20

rank Tallarico is in the solarium, sitting in his rattan chair. A nearby servant—a talent-pool girl, it seems, petite and Asian and otherwise nondescript—waves a large Polynesian fan back and forth, moving the warm air of late summer across his body in this otherwise stifling room.

"Forgive the heat," he says, welcoming me back into his abode. "Our air went out a day ago and they haven't fixed it yet."

I toss a bag of Florida oranges on the table in front of him, and he nods in appreciation.

"A lovely gift," he says. "As you know, I'm a man who appreciates fine citrus. I trust you had a pleasant time in Miami?"

There's no reason to beat around the bush; I didn't come here for chatter.

"I know what you've done."

"Well," says Frank, "that's quite a way to start a conversation. Would you like an herb?"

He snaps his fingers, and another servant arrives with a familiar platter. I shake my head, and Frank snaps his fingers again, as if he'd just remembered something crucial.

"Oh, that's right. You're the one who can't hold it down, aren't you?"

"It was a setup all along," I say, realizing that for a split second, I really *didn't* want that herb. That it just wasn't all that important to me in the grand scheme of things. A moment later, the desire returns, but that single second of nonchalance is something to build on. "The whole plan from the beginning was to bring me in."

Frank Tallarico shrugs. "You're boring me, Rubio. Did you come here to tell me stories?"

"Just the one. About how you were upset that the Dugans were using your talent-pool girls for their own ends."

"It was disgusting," he spits. "He told me all about it. Cutting off their tails, using them as guinea pigs. Even tried to convince me we could market some kind of drug outta these gals, use it to get cripples back on their feet. The things I deal with . . ."

I don't want to get into a discussion of morals; I'm deathly afraid that Frank and I will come out on the same side. I don't condone what Jack and Noreen did, but then I've never been without the use of my limbs, never been up against the wall like that.

"So you decide to foster a gang war over it?"

Tallarico scratches his nose; I'm no more than a housefly to him.

"Those girls took six, seven weeks to get back on their feet. That's a lot of scratch in banged-up help. Dugan wanted 'em all for himself, for his little science project. Wanted to buy me out. No way was that gonna happen."

There's an ethics lesson for you.

"What better way to gid rid of the Dugans and your annoying brother in one fell swoop? Get Eddie all riled up and let him start killing. Both sides get decimated, then you walk right in and fill the vacuum.

"Only, you need a catalyst, something to play from both ends. A little research, and you turn up a private eye who knew Jackie

Dugan back when he was just Jack. And he's a Velociraptor—all the better to egg on the racial angle. Better still, he has a corruptible friend, a Hadrosaur, who owes one of your business associates in New York a lot of money."

Frank laughs, shrugging it off. "Took me a while, too," he boasts. "I went through three different scenarios before you came along."

"And my situation was too perfect to pass up."

"Perfect, I dunno. But it fit. It fit real nice." Frank leans back in his chair and stretches; the talent-pool girl increases the velocity of her fanning. "So that's it? That's what you came here to tell me— that you figured out my big evil scheme? That you're some kind of fucking genius?"

I reach down and pull out the velvet bag I came in here with, the same one that was given to me the first time I left Tallarico's mansion. His guards make a move toward me, but Frank waves them off, and I toss the bag into his lap.

"Twenty thousand dollars," I tell him. "Count it if you want, it's all there."

He doesn't make a move for the money. "But you did your job," he says. "You did it beautifully, and you didn't even know it till now."

I take a step forward, edging in on that rattan chair. "I don't want to work for you. I don't want to have ever worked for you. I'm giving you back this money because I never took it. I went down to Miami for a vacation, and whatever happened down there happened because I wanted it to."

"That's what you're going with?" he asks.

"That's what I'm going with," I reply, now only a foot away.

Tallarico shrugs. "Whatever helps you sleep at night, Rubio. Me, I'm content. I've got what I want, and the resources to back it up. South Florida is ripe for the picking, and I can run it all from three thousand miles away. The Dugans are gone, and Hagstrom doesn't have the manpower or the smarts to outplay me." He leans forward and smiles broadly; the same grin that made Eddie's face look too big makes Frank's look too small.

I lean in and grab the sides of the chair, pressing my fingers into the rattan strands themselves.

"Don't be so sure of that," I growl, and suddenly Tallarico's men are on me, pulling me away, wrestling me toward the door.

"You have a good afternoon now, Mr. Rubio," Frank says, grabbing an orange from the bag I brought him as his goons hustle me toward the exit, through the mansion's hallways, and back out to the front lawn.

I straighten up my jacket, brush off the wrinkles, and start the walk back to my car when I hear Frank's voice behind me. I turn to see his head sticking out of the solarium window, his body still lounging in the seat.

"One more thing," he calls out. "I'm curious—where'd you get the money to pay me back?"

I shoot my cuffs and adjust my watch—a new Rolex, actually, a recent gift. It shines in the afternoon sun, the light glinting off Frank's shiny head.

"I did a favor for a friend," I call back, then get in my Lincoln and drive off the property, content in the knowledge that I just delivered my very last package for the mob:

Florida oranges, filled with dissolution powder.

As I make my way out of the vast Tallarico compound, I believe I can hear a bird warbling a song loud and clear across the manicured grounds. It's that, or the screams of Frank Tallarico as swarms of bacteria begin to feast upon his lips and throat.

Either way, it sounds like freedom.

Acknowledgments

Presumably you're reading this after finishing the entirety of *Hot and Sweaty Rex*. If that's not the case, please understand that you're risking the element of surprise, as a few of my acknowledgments refer to events in the narrative. I'll give all of you end-skippers a chance to duck out now and return to your place in the book. Go on, shoo.

For those who remain:

A special note of thanks goes to Zeke Lerner and his parents, Kim and Garrett. The Lerners have always been close friends, fervent supporters of my work and I look forward to our weekly Saturday morning brunches, even all the way out at the Agoura Deli.

Zeke is an amazing little three-year-old who both adds and speaks Spanish better than I do. He also has spinal muscular atrophy, a surprisingly common disease (1 in 6,000), about which the general public knows little, if anything. Just as in the book, in which Jack and Noreen Dugan are afflicted by an adult-onset dino version of the disease, SMA affects the voluntary muscles used for walking, crawling, and, in severe cases, swallowing. Unlike the events in the book, there is currently no cure, though progress is being made every day. To learn more about SMA, please visit www.fsma.org.

Thanks to the fantastic copyeditor Ed Cohen. If you think the writing flows, thank Ed. If you think it sucks eggs, then I guess we can blame Ed, too. I've never met the man in person, but he keeps me honest and isn't afraid to suggest a line change when he thinks I've written myself into ugliness. In fact, he's probably scrutinizing this page right now. . . .

Thanks, as usual, to my wonderful literary agent Barbara Zitwer, and film agent Brian Lipson, who know who to push and how hard, and to Jon Karp, my brilliant editor and steadfast Rex fan.

No book would be complete without mentioning my wife, Sabrina, and my daughter, Bailey. Sabrina is the stabilizing force in my life that keeps me off the heavy medication; if everyone had a partner like her, there'd be many fewer folks on lithium.

At just three years old, Bailey is already way more creative than I'll ever be, and unafraid to show it. She tells me bedtime stories just as often as I tell her one, and most of the time she trumps me on character and plot. Thank God her syntax is still a little bit off or I'd be out of a job.

Finally, thanks to all my fans who e-mail me with kudos, criticism, and general comments. Writing is such a solitary endeavor that it's easy to forget that there are people out there reading what I put on paper. Anyone who wants to visit my website at www.ericgarcia.com or e-mail me at eric@ericgarcia.com will find that, though it sometimes takes me a bit to respond, I'm always happy to answer questions and chat, occasionally ad nauseum. Consider yourself warned.